HIDDEN JUSTICE

A SPY MAKERS GUILD NOVEL

DIANA MUÑOZ STEWART

HIDDEN JUSTICE

DIANA MUÑOZ STEWART

Hidden Justice, copyright 2023, Diana Muñoz Stewart

Published by Kiss and Tell Books

Cover by Elizabeth Mackey

Interior Design by www.formatting4U.com

All rights reserved. Thank you for respecting the hard work of this author. No part of this book may be reproduced in any form or by any electronic or mechanical means, including information storage and retrieval systems—except in the case of brief quotations embodied in critical articles or reviews—without permission in writing from the author. This book is a work of fiction. The characters, events, and places portrayed in this book are products of the author's imagination and are either fictitious or are used fictitiously. Any similarity to real persons, living or dead, is purely coincidental and not intended by the author.

❀ Created with Vellum

For my husband

BOOKS BY DIANA MUÑOZ STEWART

HIDDEN JUSTICE (Spy Makers Guild Book 1)

RECKLESS GRACE (Spy Makers Guild Book 2)

DARING HONOR (Spy Makers Guild Book 3)

FIGHTING FATE (Spy Makers Guild Prequel Novella)

BROKEN PROMISES (Bad Legacy BK1)

FATAL PROMISES (Bad Legacy BK2)

HARD PROMISES (Bad Legacy Bk3 Nov/25)

IT'S ALL IN THE HIPS

THANK YOU FOR BREAKING MY HEART (June/25)

AMOR ACTUALLY (Holiday Anthology)

1

JUSTICE

Apparently, camo doesn't make me invisible to thorns. Pulling free of another grabby claw in the brush-choked woods, I squat by the tree line and pull down my night vision goggles. A green-tinged version of the so-called *massage parlor*—a battered, white-shingled two-story—whirs into focus. The bleak-home-turned-bleaker-business sits on the poorest edge of a rural Pennsylvania town.

Rural as hell. Perfect for bad guys. No local police force. People here rely on Staties. That is, if they decide it's even worth their time to call the state police.

A press of a button on the side of my NVGs sets up automatic photos. I hear the click as I scan the gravel-and-stone backyard, the rust-coated propane tank propped on wooden legs like a mini-submarine dry-docked after fifty years at sea, and the unlit outline of a steel back door.

Dingy, dirty, and depressing.

Given the choice, any decent person would steer clear. Guess that makes me indecent. I want inside. Call it a childhood dream, making good on a vow. Call it redemption, making it up to Hope. Call it revenge, making them pay for Hope's death.

Patience, Justice. Reconnaissance always comes first.

Grrr. Just what I need, Momma's oft-heard mantra popping up like a jack-in-the-box to wave a scolding, white-gloved finger at me.

Got it, Momma. I'm doing recon. That woman would double-check NASA's calculations. And she has the degrees to do it.

I zoom in on the back door as my breath wafts across my glasses like a green fog. No exterior handle. We'll have to pop it.

I scan up. My auto-shutter snaps photos of barred and blackened windows.

I scan over to a rickety fire escape leading to a metal-gated door secured with thick, elephant-proof chains.

These guys aren't taking any chances. Probably because they have no security cameras. See no evil or, at least, record no evil.

I unclench my grinding jaw. Not long now. After two years of planning, the mission as dear to me as my own heartbeat—breaking up the human trafficking ring this home is part of—is only a few weeks away.

My earpiece clicks, and my brother's voice whispers into my ear. "Justice, youse... uh, you in position yet?"

Tony. He works so hard to weed out his South Philly. I like his accent. But being adopted into my big, diverse family has shown me people can have some weird issues.

"Aw, Tone, can't spot me? Is it my expert camouflage or that stealth gene you're missing?"

Truth? Even though I know he's close, I can't spot him either.

Tony snorts. The sound tightropes between amused and annoyed. "Yeah, you know as much about being a Choctaw as I do about being a chihuahua."

A sharp and unexpected knife of pain slices my heart. I

rejected that part of myself, my heritage, after my father's abandonment of me and my sister. I try not to think about the loss or acknowledge it out loud. "It's in my blood. Only thing in your blood, paisano, is cement shoes and boosting cars."

Laughter feathers through my headphones. "Just get the pic—"

Bam! The back door crashes open and a dark-haired teen, maybe fifteen, sprints out.

I watch her run, all gangly arms and desperate action. She's wearing a too-loose bustier and a thong as inconsequential as her chest.

Another bang of the door and a man breaks out after her. He hauls back with a belt thick enough to double as a swing.

Fuck. "Tony."

"No. Think larger mission here. Not one girl. All of 'em."

The heavy slap of leather across flesh ricochets like a gunshot.

Soundless, the girl keeps running, toward the woods, toward me.

Tony's voice, tight and fierce, "Stay put, Justice."

Adrenaline floods my body. The scene slows down, giving me time to absorb every detail. The girl's wide and frantic eyes. The man reaching for her, so close to grabbing her.

I can't just sit here—ass-on-haunches—and do nothing, as ineffective as government raids that take months to organize and end with not one conviction of a principle. Not one.

This is what The Guild does. It doesn't stand back. It stops the shit that other people let happen. It's what I should do. It's what Hope *did* for me.

Every nerve in my body begs me to act. But I keep absolutely still. Movement attracts attention. Stillness goes unnoticed.

The man grabs the teen by the hair and yanks her back.

Tony says, "It sucks. I know. Think larger mission here."

I should. I know I should, even as I stand and raise my weapon. Because I'm a good shot—the best—I also know I won't miss.

There's a sharp snap, like a broken twig, as the bullet fires from the suppressed Sig. The man's head flings back. He surrenders his ass to the gravel.

The girl skitters away like a gangly crab. Her eyes swing left and right before she darts for cover behind the propane tank.

Tony exhales, hot and frustrated. "Not for nothin', J, you don't listen to shit."

Yeah, I know that, too. I'm filled with knowledge.

I flip up my NVGs, strip off my face mask, and charge across the backyard. I want to get the kid, want to tell her it's okay, but, first, I check inside the doorway for movement.

All quiet.

Time's not on my side, so I make my way over to her. She's crouched between the propane tank and the house. She's all deep-set eyes and jutting bones. Like a terrified skeleton.

"Glock. Figures," Tony says from behind me, and I realize he's already checked Dead Guy for weapons.

I glance over and see him slip the weapon into the back of his belt. I turn to the teen and maintain eye contact as I reach forward. "It's okay. It's okay. I'm on your side."

Her copper-brown eyes track my gloved hand like it comes equipped with teeth and venom. For a moment, I'm sure she won't take it, but she does.

Brave kid. I pull her out. I've shouldered heavier backpacks. Shrugging off my jacket, I help put it on her. Gesturing at the dead man, then at the building, I mouth, *How many more men inside?*

The teen holds up an arm. Two fingers, rabbit ears, poke up from the long sleeve.

I nod. Two more men inside.

Trying for nonchalance, I shrug at Tony. "No choice."

His dark eyebrows join tightly together under his black knit hat. A muscle in his jaw ticks. He shakes his head and starts for the open back door. As he passes me, he bumps my shoulder and hisses, "Call it in."

Yeah, he has a right to be angry, but I elbow him in the ribs just the same.

He *oomphs*, but keeps walking.

When I'm sure he's far enough away, I put my hand on the teen's shoulder. Even through my jacket and gloves, I'm reminded of the delicate span of a bird's wing.

Feelings can be deceptive. No delicate bird broke out from her cage tonight, and I'll be damned if I leave her out here unarmed.

Shielding her from Tony's view, I hold out the G19. Tony's going to rip me a new one later. But this decision and the fact that I so expertly pickpocketed him are the least of our issues. I've jeopardized the mission. "Can you use this?"

The girl hesitates. Then, with a face as starved and empty as a runway model's, she takes the gun, caps her fingers across the top, and racks the slide.

Guess so. I point toward the woods. With a nod, she dashes in that direction. Grinding my teeth, almost like I'm biting the bullet, I press the button on my earpiece.

Gracie answers on the first ring. "You're kidding me, right, Justice?"

Why are my siblings always giving me such shit? "Get a van to Site 6."

I hang up and head inside before she can respond.

Creepy as hell in here. No lie. A dangling, red lightbulb bleeds along a narrow stairway and slim corridor. Everything from ceiling to doors to stairwell seems too small in this old house.

Taking up way too much space on the steps, Tony gives me a what-took-you-so-long stare.

I shrug, and his annoyed hand motions up. I nod, going the other way down the hall and check two rooms before sighting around the last doorway. Not that I need eyes to know someone is in here. It reeks of BO and whiskey.

What was probably once a living room has been turned into an office. A television sits atop a file cabinet tuned to Netflix, there's a desk, and, directly left of the desk, a saggy plaid couch. A man in boxers, his potbelly protruding from his dirty t-shirt, is passed out on the couch.

Eyes watering from his stench, I reach for a zip tie and step into the room. My booted foot toes into an unseen bottle of Jim Beam, sending it churning across the hardwood. Whiskey leaks everywhere in the absolute worst game of spin-the-bottle ever.

The guy who looked dead to the world jumps up, then blinks in my direction. His eyes go wide, and he lurches for me, arms outstretched like Frankenstein's monster. This might be the biggest guy I've ever seen. Also, the slowest.

I slip around him, reach up, and slam my gun into his head. One, two, three times.

He drops to his knees and shakes his head. Still conscious?

There's a tug of meaty fingers against my ankle and, in a split second, I'm horizontal. My elbow slams against the desk. My head smashes against the floor.

When I blink back to the world, Drunky is on me like a pro wrestler, pinning my neck with one beefy limb. Where's my fucking gun?

I can't breathe. His bulk crushes my left arm between us. I swing out with my aching right. Anticipating the move—obviously I'm not the first person he's held down—he grabs and forces my arm to the ground.

Panic edges over reason as my gaze bucks around the room. I can't draw breath. Heart frantic in my chest, electric currents zinging through my veins, I'm pinned. Like that night. My recurring nightmare. I need help. I need to...

No. Hell no. I'm not that little kid anymore. I'm *not* helpless.

Calming myself, I realize that my hand—squeezed between Drunky and me—is in the perfect spot. Trembling, I locate and squeeze one sweaty ball. Hard.

He grunts, presses harder against my neck. Hearing cartilage creak in my neck, I put a shark-like grip to his jewels. The damage might be permanent, but he's too drunk and determined to understand this.

It's basically which one of us can tolerate what the other is doing for the longest. But I'm not drunk. I feel everything.

Black spots cloud my vision. My lungs scream for air. I'm going to pass out.

Convulsing, I kick out blindly until I viciously connect with his ankle.

His body jerks, slips left.

Gathering every bit of energy, I thrust up my hip, swing my foot flat, and push.

He topples to the side.

Snakebite fast, I belly-crawl away. Where the fuck is my— I grab my gun and roll.

Drunky marches toward me. With no ability to shout, I point my gun in warning.

Bam! The guy crashes back and down, blood seeping through his dingy white T-shirt

What the hell? I didn't shoot.

Rolling to my knees, I turn to the doorway, gun aimed. All hollowed eyes and jutting bones, the teen lowers her Glock.

Holy Shit. The kid killed the guy.

Wheezing through a throat still aching tight, I lower my own gun and get to my feet. My legs shake under me.

Ignoring the twist of *things-are-so-fucked-up* nausea, I pick up my night vision goggles and stagger over to the teen. I shake my head and whisper-rasp, "Didn't have to."

Tiger-fierce, red-brown eyes scan over to the body. She

shrugs and, with a soft Spanish accent, spits out, "Pero, I wanted to."

Damn. It's weird, seeing that kind of anger in someone else. Like looking in the mirror. I understand it, but still...

A pounding upstairs reminds me where I'm supposed to be and who I'm supposed to be helping: Tony.

I pull the girl into the hall and push her into another room. "Wait here. Right here."

Leaving her, I swoop down the corridor and up the narrow stairs. Sighting around the corner, I check the upstairs hall. There's a partially dressed man hog-tied in the hallway.

Tony steps from one of the corridor's multiple doorways. "Did I hear a problem?"

The gunshot. Yikes. "Not anymore."

"Seriously, J?" He shakes his head. "Stop killing people."

I glare at him. I want to tell him this one isn't on me, but isn't it? I gave the kid the Glock. Definitely not the time to explain. "You weren't there. Guy had a hundred fifty pounds on me."

Literally.

Tony points at the knocked-out guy, hands bound behind his back and tied to his feet. "Dude's no featherweight either. It's called training."

Yeah, well, I didn't have time to train the kid. I don't say that. I *won't* say that. This one goes with me to the grave. "Where are they?"

He reaches past me and pushes a door open, nodding toward the occupants. "Salvadoran."

Inside the room, the young teens and girls who've been stolen, tricked, or coerced from their lives and countries huddle together in a dark corner. The windows are painted black. There's one dresser and a full-size bed. Probably the same setup as every room up here. My stomach twists at the thought. No individuality. No humanity. An assembly line.

Repressing my anger, I give instructions in Spanish. "Mantén la calma. Nadie te hará daño. Te estamos rescatando. Serás atendido. No serás lastimado. Mantén la calma. Síganos."

I repeat it in English. "Stay calm. No one will harm you. We are rescuing you. You will be cared for. You will not be harmed. Stay calm. Follow us."

The group begins to panic. Cry out. Someone throws a shoe at me.

Ouch. Great. Not my day. I step back to Tony. "You got this?"

A smirk on his face, he lowers his gun. "You're just not a people pleaser, J."

No kidding. I care—care more than I can say. But when it comes to getting that across to people... well, it's not my strong suit.

~

AT THE PICKUP location designated as Site 6, we load the freed slaves into the white panel van. The teen I gave the gun to, the one who reminds me of me, refuses to get inside. This time, I got it. I pull her aside and put a hand on the shoulder still wearing my coat. "What's your name?"

Cringing, she looks down and away. "Los hombres called me Cookie."

Cookie? That's not a name. It's a dessert.

"But what's your name? What do *you* call yourself?"

She shakes her head. Her lips tighten into a thin line.

Okay. Well, if Sesame Street taught me anything it's that C is for Cookie. "Can I call you Cee?"

"No me importa."

She doesn't care. I find that hard to believe. "Get in the van, Cee. People there will take care of you. You're free."

She shakes her head. "I want to go where you go. I want

to..." She hesitates as if looking for the words. "I want to be what you are."

In The Guild, this is the moment we all wait for. The moment that never happens. And now that it has, I wish it hadn't. Kid has no idea what she's asking for, what will be required of her, but rules are rules. If they ask and show any kind of real promise, they get to try.

"Get in the van. A woman with red hair will be at your destination. Her name is Gracie. Tell her what you told me."

"And she will let me do what you do?"

"She'll give you a"—I almost say *shot*—"chance."

Cee's fiery brown eyes, prematurely set to suspicious, appraise me. With a nod, she decides to trust me, climbs into the van, and drags the door shut.

I hit the door twice and the van pulls away, trailing a cloud of exhaust.

When the taillights fade away, I slip into the driver's seat of the black rental, next to the elephant in the room. Tony. Every inch of his five-foot-eleven frame looks ready to pound me to a soft, mushy pulp.

Instead, he rips off his hat and gloves, then runs agitated fingers through jet-black, wavy hair. It's damp with sweat, causing it to stand on end.

Starting the car, I tighten my hands around the steering wheel. He's got a lot to say; I can feel it. Time to pop this cork. "Stop pouting."

Tony hits the dash hard—and then again. "You *gotta* get over this cowgirl, *Kill Bill* bullshit. Why not send up a signal flare telling the Brothers Grim we're after them?"

The wheel spins through my fingers as I turn the corner, flick on the headlights, and accelerate onto the highway.

"Tone, if I'd known when I first saw you"—a twelve-year-old runaway scrounging for scraps—"what a pain in the ass you'd become, I never would've begged Momma to adopt you."

The first boy adopted into a large family of adopted girls.

He flings himself back against the seat and lets out a long breath. "We don't bust into a place like some eighties' Schwarzenegger movie. You think this won't get back to the brothers? Raise their suspicions?"

True. I fucked up. The Spy Makers Guild is designed for subtlety. Mostly, it's the velvet hammer—negotiations, forums, and charities that support women. Sometimes, it's the chainsaw of assassination, deceit, and violence. That's where I come in. "Sorry, Tone."

He makes a sound of dismissal, before stripping off his jacket and bulletproof vest. The navy-blue tattoo on his right arm, half of the family motto, *One for all*, screams at me. That tattoo says all anyone needs to know about how seriously Tony takes his responsibility to our family.

The first half of that plagiarized motto—let a bunch of kids choose your motto and that's what you get—is tattooed over his heart. That *All for one* tells more about me. That's why I do this. For one person. For Hope. That's why, despite what he thinks, I rescued Cee and jeopardized the mission. Because one person matters to me.

2

SANDESH

Dust and debris lace the hot, oppressive Syrian air. The explosive remnants cling to my body almost as thickly as the village mud to my combat boots.

Eyes watering and ears ringing from the barrel bomb, I hold steady, cradling the child in my arms as delicately as possible.

Not delicately enough. She lets out small, injured sound, and I try harder to keep her peeling and damaged skin from rubbing against my Special Forces uniform.

Barrel bomb chemicals inflict burns reminiscent of napalm.

"Heads up, Sandman," one of my rangers says, pointing toward the sky.

"Thanks," I murmur. I think. Everything sounds muffled to my ears, even the whir of the approaching Black Hawk.

The helo passes overhead, sending dust spinning into the air. The girl in my arms writhes, her eyes spring open.

"It's okay, dear one," I whisper. Though... it's really not. My chest is tight with a fist of anger.

The Syrian government attacked its own citizens, injuring bodies, hoping to also injure minds. It'll probably work. Violence usually does.

It was only a coincidence—at least I hope it was—that my Rangers and I were in the area. On the record, we're not here. Our mission is supposed to be outside of Syria, supporting the Free Syrian Army with training and weapons. But someone higher up wanted a better take on Assad's chemical profile.

Guess we found out.

The helo lands and pushes the smell of chemicals deep into my nostrils. Damn it. At least nineteen girls are injured. Many shuffle around like zombies as someone with a hose frantically tries to clean them off. I bend over the child, shielding her as best I can as we near her ride out of here.

Fuck mission parameters. We need to do something.

The girl in my arms stirs, and I look down. She says something, and I bend to catch her words.

"Please, Poppa," she says in Arabic. "Don't be angry."

I look into her face, expecting to see confusion and delirium.

Her dark eyes stare directly at me. *Into* me. Trembling, her raw hand rises to my chest, rests upon my heart. "There is more."

A ringing starts in my ears, my hearing coming back.

An awed gasp *whooshes* from her mouth and her hand drops. I've seen people die, seen how the body suddenly looked less real, less full. But this is different. It's as if I can feel the soul sink from the body, feel the tendrils of spirit wrap around my heart and whisper, "Poppa. Don't be angry. There is more."

The ringing gets worse, more persistent.

Hacking, sweating, I sit up and, in the dark of my unlit bedroom, grab blindly for my cell, accepting the call before I even have a chance to check caller ID. "Yeah?"

"Sandesh Julian Ross, head of the IPT?" This guy has gravel in his voice, like he had too much tequila last night. And every night of his life.

"That's me." What time is it? Wiping sweat from my brow, I

check the clock on my nightstand. WTF. Five a.m.? "Who's calling?"

"My name is Leland Day. I work for Parish Industries, specifically Mukta Parish. We've been told your charity, the IPT, works along the Jordan-Syrian border."

A business call at five a.m.? I'm almost too pissed to speak, but the guy did save me from that dream, and a Parish Industries representative isn't someone to hang up on. I blink the sleep from my eyes and mind. "No. I mean... sort of."

I've given the speech so often to media and at luncheons the words come by rote. "The International Peace Team aligns with organizations around the world, but, yes, we've aligned with Salma's Gems in the Middle East."

"I know. I read about you online. *WAPO* called you a complex combination of righteous anger, surfer-boy looks, and gritty naïveté."

That belittling article surely won't help me secure the funding IPT so desperately needs.

Sitting up, feeling a bit more human, I flick on a lamp. My neat, orderly, and essentials-only room—bed, nightstand, and lamp—snap into focus. You can take the soldier out of the military... "Why are you calling?"

To harass me about my pretty-boy media image?

"I'm calling to set up an appointment between you and Mukta Parish. She's starting an initiative to expand global philanthropy. You've no doubt heard of Parish Industries and the Mantua Academy for Girls?"

Of course, who hasn't? Mukta Parish—hell, the entire Parish clan—is mega-wealthy. A global powerhouse, they also run an exclusive boarding school for wealthy families. The elite campus that's home to Mukta Parish's It's a Small World clan. She's adopted troubled girls from all over the world.

"This isn't camp, Leland. We're run and staffed by former soldiers for a reason."

He clears his throat. Doesn't help. "I understand. In truth, we'd mostly be a financial support system and completely at your disposal."

It takes me a minute to process this. This guy calls me at five a.m. to offer me exactly what the IPT wants and needs: funding, a tie to a big name, and complete autonomy. Call me a cynic, but I'm not buying it. "What, exactly, would I have to do to warrant this kind of support?"

"We'd like to discuss that. Are you available to come to our Center City office?"

"Sure. When?"

"Is this morning at seven doable?"

I'd be there in thirty minutes if it meant what he's offering, but I'm not ready to play the eager beaver. I stand, move toward the shower. "Make it nine."

3

JUSTICE

My thick-soled boots squeak with each determined stride down the gleaming marble floors of the academy's main building. Right now, I know the thing that sucks most about a family business—the family part.

Our family business is both complex and a cover. To most of the word, the Mantua Academy is an elite school on a one-hundred-and-sixty-acre pristine campus in Bucks County, PA. It's filled with historic architecture and stone and spire buildings. It's also a front for our family's more clandestine operations. What it's not is a mumbo-jumbo, feel-good, mantra-loving freak-fest. Which is exactly what I'm going to tell her.

Having worked up a good head of steam, I reach the threshold of my sister's office... door? My eyes roll so far back in my head, I can see my ancestors. Great. Bridget followed through on her promise to have her door removed.

Trying to hold onto calm—not easy when she's making trouble in my cover job which I can't stand as it is—I rap on the wood frame.

She'd doesn't move. My pale-skinned sister sits cross-legged on her mesh Ergohuman office chair, eyes closed. Her silky black strands, a testament to her Asian ancestry, stabbed with a silver comb, droops lopsidedly like a hairy modern art sculpture.

Despite my annoyance, I smile. This is so perfectly Bridget it almost deserves its own word, like *freaktacular* or *weirdiful*.

I knock louder. "Bridge?"

Brown eyes, as serene as a gentle woodland, flutter open and lock onto me. Bridget is the kind of person who rarely blinks. It's like she's paying deep attention, always making me feel seen. Not in a good way. In a below the skin, all my broken secrets, my fear of suffocating, and dislike of the color blue way.

I fidget.

Shiva, *uhm*, Bridget quirks an eyebrow. "What can I do for you, Justice?"

"I need to talk to you about the yoga class. Is it true you have the girls chanting in Sanskrit?"

"Yes." She furrows her brow. "I'm not sure why you ask. Is there a problem? I submitted the yoga for approval through the director's office."

Strolling into her office, I plop into a purple chair, kicking one leg up over an armrest. "You got approval for yoga, She-pak Chopra, not to have the girls chanting in Sanskrit. This isn't good PR. And that's bad for me. Means I have to do work."

Work I'm not good at.

Thoughtfully, Bridget rests her hands on the desk. "I see. I will limit my teaching to poses and centering music."

Gotta love her. "Dammit, Bridge, you're so easy. Why can't I have more sisters like you?"

"Perhaps because you are as abrasive as a starving boar," a Spanish-accented voice says from the hall.

I know that voice.

I turn and see the beauty herself. Sheared head, lips

painted bright red, skin as satiny smooth and dark as a starless sky, and cocked against the doorway, the generous curve of boys-can't-help-but-wonder hips.

Dada, six-foot-two in spiked heels.

"This is the problem with having no doors," I say. Standing and crossing the room, I give my returning sister a hug. "You're home early? Aren't you supposed to be digging up dirt in Mexico with your Brothers Grim informant?"

Dada's forehead creases. She bites her full lower lip before peering down the hall. She needn't bother. The school staff, a.k.a. no-idea-a-secret-society-of-vigilantes-exists-under-their-feet staff, aren't in yet. Satisfied, she says, "Judging by your calm, I take it you haven't checked your secure email recently."

∽

I'M SO pissed that I practically bark at security at Momma's office building when they make me walk the ring of metal detectors before I'm able to head upstairs to the headquarters of the Parish empire in Philadelphia.

Head full of steam, I march down corridors lined with sharp corners, glass walls, attractive twenty-, thirty-, forty-, and fifty-somethings in power suits.

I'm too pissed to respond to the repeated nods and hellos. After Dada clued me in, I read Momma's morning email—which sent me scrambling for my Jeep keys. She's *not* doing this to me. I won't let her put my mission on hold.

I don't care if the Brothers Grim are on alert after my screwup with Tony last week. Who cares that the bad guys moved their meeting up by six weeks? Or that they've moved their meeting location to Jordan—one of the few places on the entire fucking globe where The Guild has no established cover? This is our best chance to take down a global trafficking ring. We find a way.

Yikes, having worked myself up, now I can't breathe. I loosen the scarf around my neck and hope the bruises don't look too bad now.

As I near Momma's office, her executive assistant—straitlaced Lorena of the cotton button-downs and starched pantsuits—blocks my path to the closed mahogany doors.

She crosses her arms. "She's busy."

Huh. A human barricade.

Good thing I've been trained for such an event.

I run straight at her.

She squeaks but holds her ground.

Good, because that's what I wanted.

Veering left, I lift my booted foot, plant the arch against the edge of Lorena's desk, toe into a leap, and vault over her.

She ducks and cries out.

Instant classic. I land with a thud.

"Thanks, Lorena," I say, pulling open the office door.

She's still sputtering vague threats as I close the door with a *click.*

For a confused moment, I stand within the inner sanctum, a huge corner office with buttoned leather couches, two flat-screen TVs, a hulking Thor of a desk, and a well-stocked kitchen. The satisfied grin slips from my face.

Momma isn't alone.

The man she's with drives the air from my lungs. Built for a hot night of unforgettable sex, he has wild blond hair like a sandstorm, eyes the color of the ocean after a lazy day in the sun, and beach-bronzed skin.

Come *on,* give a lady a warning. I'm used to finding stodgy business-type people in Momma's office. Like a deer caught in beautiful blinding blue headlights, I stare at the man.

"Here's Justice," says Leland, Momma's oldest friend and most trusted adviser. Man cannot be put off his game. He moves toward me, silver hair gleaming under the canopy of recessed lights, his gray-checkered Armani suit draped over him as if upon the shoulders of dignity itself. He extends his hand cordially, so very pleased I've made it.

Because I'm used to faking it—kind of been raised that way—I take Leland's smooth hand. He presses down firmly and tugs me farther into the room.

"Sandesh, I'd like you to meet Justice Parish." Only the stern grip of Leland's hand reveals how annoyed he is. "She does PR for the Mantua Academy and will be working on the Greenville Initiative. She's familiar with all aspects of our newest philanthropy venture."

Dude is good. Calm. Graceful. And full of shit. *Greenville?* What is that project about? Giving away money, judging by what Leland said.

Behind Leland, Momma's brown eyes show as little as the rose-colored niqab that covers her hair and face and scars.

I give Leland a rictus grin meant to be a smile that'll probably be the scariest thing he sees all day. I'm usually more successful at hiding my feelings, trained in it and all. But this high-pressure situation—Jack-be-nimbling Lorena, barging into a business meeting, and finding this perfect hot stranger—has me off my game.

Still, I recover quickly. "Actually, my role in all philanthropic projects is still advisory. I wouldn't want to mislead, uhm, Sandesh, right?"

His skin tone definitely matches the golden-brown hue of the Bengali desert he's named after. A delicious and surprising name for a delicious and surprising man.

Blue Eyes walks forward, hand outstretched. "Yes, it's Sandesh. I'm head of the International Peace Team. We're partnering with Greenville in Jordan."

His fingers slide along my palm with a brush of heat that sends my skin tingling. It's not his hot, firm grip, or his intense good looks, or his confident gaze, but a combination of all of that, along with his smile, that has me floundering in all the feelings before processing exactly what he just said.

"Jordan?"

4

SANDESH

Focus on the question, Sandesh, and not the brazen gaze of the hot woman standing before you.

I can't. This woman demands my attention.

Funny, since a moment ago, after the administrative assistant's loud objection, the *thud* of something I couldn't puzzle out, and another heavier *thud* before the door opened, I'd gone from corner-office mode to time-to-take-someone-down mode.

And then she'd burst into the room.

First thought: I hope I *do* have to take her down because that body underneath me would make my day. Second thought was: Sucked to be wearing a damn monkey suit because this is a woman of action. The third thought as she's introduced and her eyes sweep my body: There are no thoughts.

Her mischievous dark gaze and the fan and flutter of those thick eyelashes have swallowed every decent thought from my mind and replaced them with open admiration.

Indigenous, she has the cheekbones of an American goddess, sleek black hair, pert breasts under a cream silk blouse, long legs, and a boldness that has me paying careful attention.

"Jordan?" she asks again. "Sandesh, you've aroused my interest." She pauses, and I feel the word *aroused* tug at my insides. "Tell me more about your organization. IPT?"

Dear God. If her eyes are direct and aware, her voice is the promise of sex and the slipping of silk sheets against hot skin. My entire body catches fire.

Her eyes slide over me in a lazy, feline way. Her smile kicks up at the edges.

With effort I drag my thoughts back to IPT, the whole reason I'm here. The cause I've devoted my life to for nearly a decade.

Giving her a smile I pray isn't laced with lechery, I answer her. "The IPT is run and staffed entirely by former soldiers. It's designed to aid victims of war and disaster globally. We're focused on creating self-sustaining businesses. Giving options to people in difficult regions other than starve, flee, or fight. Die or be subjugated."

Her pretty smile fades, then turns downward. "But why soldiers?"

"Soldiers are skilled and adaptable. They're used to discomfort. Used to keeping calm and navigating through difficult situations. Used to assessing problems, implementing strategies in challenging places. Not having to habituate civilians saves us time and money, but I also wanted to give those soldiers having a problem going from warrior to Walmart a way to recover the compassion they may have shut down to get the job done."

Those fine gemstone eyes—onyx black and hot as pitch—widen with curiosity. Or doubt.

"A soldier is highly-trained for action and fighting, right? Aren't you afraid your volunteers will get bored and create more problems than they solve?"

That puts the fire out. *Thanks.*

Unable to help the surge of annoyance, I clear my throat. Her point is too close to one I've heard again and again—soldiers need aggression to keep them interested. It annoys the hell out of me. "No, I'm not. Are you?"

"I guess I am. It seems unrealistic to expect soldiers trained for war and action to be satisfied handing out water bottles."

"Unrealistic?" My voice rises before I can help myself. Seriously? She acts as if she has first-hand knowledge of the situation. I run a hand under my collar, massage my neck. "Soldiers are humans, capable of a range of emotions, including self-control and compassion. Is it so hard to believe they aren't mindless militants?" *Or mindless fucks.* That last part I have the good sense not to say.

"Mindless, no? Trained for—"

Mukta Parish laughs, cutting Justice off, and taking the conversation down a degree. She moves closer, her astute brown eyes framed by her rose niqab, her powder-pink business suit showing off a determined-shouldered, Hillary Clintonesque form. She claps her hands, heavy bracelets jangling. "Justice, I hope you'll be more supportive of Sandesh's charity when you're doing PR for him in Jordan."

Justice's eyes widen, as if this is the first she's heard of it. I wonder if it is, because I only heard the suggestion moments before she came inside.

"Of course," Justice says, giving me a coy smile that makes my mouth go dry. "I'm simply playing devil's advocate, so I know how best to defend the charity. When do we leave for Jordan?"

Now, she wants to go to Jordan after putting down the people working on my entire mission? Nope. I have enough issues with organizing things, I don't need to add her to the list.

Mukta steps forward. "We were just discussing your role when you arrived, and the fact that Sandesh wouldn't need to worry about transporting weapons for his own security. He could use one of our private jets and, of course, take off from our private airport."

Oh, that's right, these people are scary rich and have the ability to make my job a whole lot easier. Plus, the IPT is in dire need of capital.

Leland—he of the five a.m. phone calls and scratchy voice-grabs Justice by the forearm. "That's our cue, Justice. Let's leave them to the details."

Her eyebrows rise and those dark eyes twinkle. If mischief had a color, it would be the color of Justice Parish's eyes, fathomless black and able to swallow thoughts.

"Sure," she says, all knowing smile. "Let's leave them to the details."

She's cocky as hell, and I'm certain that comes from being rich as hell. I'm not a fan of rich as hell and cocky as hell, no matter how beautiful the package.

Leland guides Justice out of the room. Silently, I watch her walk out with growing concern. This woman is supposed to do PR for me in the Middle East, a place not known for its love of Western women. That job requires tac and, subtlety, and I'm beginning to worry those dare-me-to dark eyes are going to get me killed.

5

JUSTICE

Morning sunlight blasts through the conference room's forty-foot floor-to-ceiling windows, glimmering across the glass table, the steel and leather swivel chairs, and crystal chandelier. And me without my sunglasses or any idea what I'm doing in here.

Damn Leland. He marched me in here, refusing to answer any of my questions, ordered me to take a seat, and exited discreetly. Man does everything discreetly. Pretty sure he's even a stealth pooper.

I stand when the conference room door swings open and Momma enters, a billow of veils, a jingle of jewelry, and a whiff of Une Rose perfume. That heady Turkish rose layered over earthy mountain soil that so represents Momma brings me comfort.

I kiss her lightly on her silk-covered cheek. She sits in the chair opposite me, then crosses her legs. "I'm sure you've realized that I have provided a cover for your Jordan trip."

For a woman who hides her face, Momma can be incredibly direct. She can also be exactly the opposite. She's tricky that way.

"Yeah. I noticed the hot humanitarian in your office. Kind of big to miss."

"And I can imagine you are wondering why I'd send your team an email stating there would be a delay when I am providing the cover. A cover that will put you in Jordan within the week."

The week? "Yeah. Why?"

Momma fiddles with the numerous bracelets on her wrist, twisting them against her brown-skin before releasing them. She lets out a breath so heavy it seems expelled from the nethermost regions of her soul. The rose niqab moves with her breath. "I need to tell you something. Something painful."

My heart begins to fence with my ribs. Momma doesn't do drama. She's telling me to prepare.

I steel myself, nod to let her know I'm ready.

"I believe we have a traitor among us."

How do you prepare for a punch to the gut? My hand flies to my churning stomach. "Us? The Guild, us?" The stunned words emerge with barely any sound. I shiver as my blood plummets below cold, past chilled, and down to arctic. "No. You're jumping at shadows."

As erect as the Eiffel Tower and as self-assured, Momma says, "No, I'm not. I've managed to keep this organization a secret for forty years, and my instinct tells me the fact that the Brothers Grim changed the location of their meeting to a place where we have few resources is not mere coincidence."

"It's someone in Internal Security then? Someone hired to help with organization, strategy, or contacts. Not family."

Momma's gaze softens as it lands on Leland, who stands beyond these glass walls with Sandesh by the reception desk, looking over some papers.

As head of The Guild's tactical security and Momma's oldest friend, Leland knows more about Momma and her secrets than any person alive. But I've often wondered if there's more to them than that. They're so close. But intimate? I can't imagine it. Not Momma. Never that.

She turns back to me. "Leland has cleared Internal. Though there was little need. The information on your mission was given to a limited few."

A limited few? Besides Leland and a few in Internal, the only other people who know about the mission are...

No. My stomach rolls over so far and fast, I have to swallow to control my rising nausea. "You suspect someone in my unit?"

Even saying it feels like a betrayal.

In numbers, the Parish family could give the Kennedys a run for their money. Except all twenty-eight of my siblings are adopted. I'm loyal to them all. But my unit, the four I've trained with, played with, fought with, attended classes with at the Mantua Academy, are the ones I'm closest with—Tony, Dada, Gracie, and Bridget.

"Why would you think that?" It isn't true. Can't be. I escaped people like that. People like my maternal grandmother. Every member of my unit knows how much this mission means to me. And, like me, they've sacrificed and trained for years to make it happen.

"When dealing with the most injured of society, the group dynamic won't always supersede the instinct for self-preservation."

That's bullshit. "Why? Not for money. We have plenty."

"I don't rule out money. Not everyone is comfortable working within The Guild, being paid by Parish Industries."

She's talking about Gracie. "Not Gracie. No way. She makes plenty of money at her club, which is also a great cover for her."

Momma looks beyond me, outside at the city as the sun's light blushes against her niqab. "I can think of many other reasons. Money and therapy and purpose can't always root out stigma, shame, or the lingering need for self-harm. Those latent feelings could've been transferred to The Guild or me.

Instead of introspection, one of my children might have latched onto deflection or resentment."

"You rescued us." None of this make sense. "Besides, they all know... They all know..." I can't say it, can't speak the words, about how much this means to me, but Momma knows. This is my chance to make it up to Hope. For letting her die.

For letting Hope die in my place.

"Don't take it personally. Many of my children have tragic pasts. A broken mind is a mind in turmoil. You can't excise all those demons. Take for example, your brother—"

"Tony? Never."

"He is angry, Justice. He accused The Guild of reverse sexism. He believes we don't value him or his opinion."

"He said that? When do I not listen to him?"

Momma tilts her head toward me, a gesture that reminds me that I'd ignored his advice during our recon.

I don't reply, because that was different. "What about the others? You can't think Bridget would? She's practically a saint."

Momma's patient brown eyes stay locked on me. I can almost see her survey the texture of the words before she speaks. Momma is careful like that. "Being a Buddhist doesn't make you a saint. If anything, her recent foray into pacifism might lead her to try to thwart our more aggressive goals."

Impossible. Bridget didn't even put up a fight when I asked her to stop chanting during yoga. "And Gracie? She runs the underground rail—"

"She's still angry about John—"

"Dada's doing recon—"

"No one from your unit can be ruled out."

No one? What the hell? "So... what? I have to replan this entire mission in a few days and keep it secret from my four closest siblings?"

"I have all the information you need. The false identities the Brothers are using. Where they are staying. The layout of their hotel suite and a tentative plan waiting your approval. Including a PR convention in Houston your siblings will think you're attending."

Ice needles prickle under my skin. She isn't kidding.

"You're wrong. My unit wouldn't betray me. Us. The Guild. Isn't it more likely that my fuc—uh, mess-up last week alerted the Brothers? Made them cautious?"

Momma shifts forward, meets my gaze for a long moment. "Perhaps. But are you willing to stake your life and the freedom of thousands of women on that?"

If it means betting on my siblings, I kind of am. But, no, I won't do that. I can pull this off myself. It's too important to risk. I have to stop anyone else from being hurt. And the Brothers Grim need to pay for Hope. And for Cee. And many others.

Exhaling every bit of unease and sadness and determination, I voice my final objection. "I feel bad about using Sandesh."

"He needs money. We need a cover. It's win-win."

Sure, except for the part where Momma usurps his peace-loving purpose by secretly bending it to support her covert group of global vigilantes. Dammit.

"Send me the details."

6

SANDESH

Inside the elevator, I press the lobby button and watch as the doors begin to slide closed. I'm replaying the opportunity of today when a sultry voice calls, "Hold the elevator."

That sexy voice is unmistakable. I jump forward and slam the HOLD button.

Justice slides inside and her presence electrifies the air.

My heart, obviously deciding I need more blood flow, kicks into high gear.

God, she smells good. Her perfume is something soft and feminine, like a bath filled with milk and lavender.

It's happening again. I'm losing my ability to think straight. I remind myself that she's the last thing I need, and that conversation in her mother's office told me exactly what she thinks of me and my life's work.

I tense, waiting for her to continue the jousting, but... she doesn't. She retreats to a corner of the elevator and her eyes brush over me as if distracted. No, not distracted. Sad. "Are you okay?"

She startles, comes back from wherever she'd been in her

thoughts. The sadness falls away—or is willed away—as she seems to register exactly who is in the elevator with her. She winks. "Better than okay. Care to find out? The Ritz isn't too far."

Her dark, glossy eyes skim over me like she's starving and I'm the meal, and damn if it doesn't shoot me full of hormones. But that open invitation to fuck hits my every nerve, and not in a good way. Not all in a bad way either, but I'm ignoring that part—the part of my body swelling with heat. I want her, but what she said about IPT, the use of former soldiers, her snide derision for my charity, is beyond professionally insulting. It's personal.

Can't help but be annoyed, because it's so easy for her. Rich, beautiful, cocky, and self-righteous. She practically accused me, and all men, of having no more feelings than fight or fuck. And, now, to drive home the point, she invites me to the nearest hotel. "Justice, I think we should work on the business aspects of this interaction. There are a lot of details we need to work out first."

Her eyebrows rise.

Smooth, Sandesh. It sounds like I'm only putting things on hold until after Jordan. That's what happens with lack of blood flow to the brain.

The elevator dings again and the doors slide open. I'm not proud of the fact that I'm grateful to the woman who enters, toting a thick briefcase. Seeing a way out, I step past her and off the elevator.

Confused and maybe amused, Justice says, "We're not on the ground floor."

No kidding. But I can't be in that confined space, smelling the invitation on her skin, when I know damn well that I won't sleep with her.

Not just because her mother is my biggest investor, but because I've seen people who give up all control to anger or lust or the emotion du jour, and I'm not going to be one of them. Not again.

The elevator doors began to close. Boldly—which I'm beginning to understand is her calling card—Justice steps forward, stands between the doors, and holds them open. "Are you sure you want to *get off* here?"

The double entendre in "get off" makes my cock jump. I want her like gasoline wants fire, but degrading myself for sex isn't part of my programming anymore.

As if she has no effect on me and my body isn't screaming for me to jump back on that elevator, I incline my head. "I'm sure we'll see each other soon."

She smiles a grin so seductively promising I nearly *do* bolt back onto the elevator, but she steps back and lets the door close with a teasingly whispered, "Probably on the plane."

7

JUSTICE

My backpack bounces against me as, suitcase in hand, I cut across the Mantua Academy's parking lot. I'm late. Thankfully, the family airport isn't far.

Opening the door on my Jeep, I mentally calculate how long it will take me to get past security and to the airport.

My cell buzzes as I toss backpack and suitcase into the front seat of my black Rubicon. Gracie. She finally got around to answering my text about Cee coming into the family.

I don't know, Justice. This kid is kind of scary.

Climbing inside, I shut my door with a heavy slam—which is the only way you can shut the door of a Jeep What is Gracie talking about? You'd think the person in charge of computer operations, the person who found and safely placed victims would be less judgmental.

She's had a rough road, Gracie. Process her.

I watch the dots blinking... Until she answers with: *She'll never pass a psych eval.*

I snort and tap away. *That makes two of us. Do your job. I'll touch base when I get back from my convention.* AKA secretly going to kill the Brothers Grim.

K.

A one letter answer? She's pissed.

I drop the phone into my cupholder, then turn on the car. My cell rings again. I lift my eyes to heaven. *Really, God? I'm one of the good guys.*

I answer by clicking the button on my wheel. "Yep."

"Ms. Parish." A male voice pipes through my car speakers. "This is Guadalupe from external security. We need you at Southie."

"No can do. I'm late."

"Your father's here."

Shit. Shit. Shit. "Don't call him that."

I hang up and a moment later drive through the school's main gate and down the long winding road that leads to Southie—the parking lot where people who don't have campus clearance wait to get approval or for someone inside the school to come out. Usually, teen boys waiting on teen girls.

After parking my car, I nod to Guadalupe, then walk past the flagpole whose metal clip *clang, clang*s against it.

I see him right away. Cooper Ramsey. A drug-addicted narcissist with a poor work history. Hard to believe he's related to me.

He is. Proved by a paternity test two years ago. Not that I needed a test to see myself in his eyes, the hue of his skin, the pin-straight black hair. He was once a handsome, proud man. A man my mom hadn't been able to resist. Or maybe she hadn't been able to resist what he offered her, a life with him, far from her own demented mother, my grandmother.

I walk over to him. "Cooper."

His dull eyes blink and his sleepy mouth rolls into a smile. "Hey, kiddo."

Kiddo? I push up my sunglasses and run my eyes down his worn gray pants splattered with paint.

He shifts, not just his eyes, but his whole body and even his smile. Shifty.

I know the easiest way to get rid of my father: ask him to be direct. "Are you ever going to tell me who gave you the money to come here?"

He distributes his weight from side to side, rocking like a child, and shakes his head. The line of his mouth tightens. Genuine fear blankets his eyes.

It's always the same.

Two years ago, Cooper had been living in California. Out of the blue, he'd boarded a plane for Pennsylvania. He landed, gotten into a cab, and came straight here. The day before he'd boarded that plane, he'd had fourteen dollars in his bank account. I know, because I checked. I also know he had no credits card and no credit. Someone gave him cash and told him to come here.

Momma swears it wasn't her. I've investigated the hell out of it, but still haven't turned up anything.

I wave Cooper off. "Go home, Coop. I have no idea why you keep coming here."

He flinches as if my tone is as solid as a missile, and I repress the feeling of sympathy. He doesn't deserve it. He left me, left Hope, with my grandmother, that madwoman, so he could do drugs to drown out the pain of Mom's death. Even now, his brown eyes carry that tell-tale misty gleam. Yep. Drugs are still his refuge.

Blinking, he pulls a medallion from around his neck and holds it out to me.

No way am I touching that thing. I shake my head adamantly.

Confusion gathers in the earthy skin of his broad brow. "Your birthday's coming up."

"What?" The hair on my neck stands on end. "My birthday isn't for weeks."

He frowns. His slacker shoulders droop further. He opens the medallion. A locket? "I wanted you to have it."

He keeps holding it at me, and I swallow a chunk of irritation. Curious, I take it. The metal is warm against my palm as I stare at two small, faded photos. One of my mom at twenty-five or so, right before she'd died. God, she was so beautiful. A blue-eyed, blonde-haired woman who looked nothing like me but everything like... Hope.

The other photo is of Hope and me, arms over each other's shoulders. I repress the sound of grief. It's been so long. I have no other photos. I hunch over the locket and a lump forms in my throat. Tears threaten.

"Happy birthday, Justice. Love you."

That snaps me upright and into the past. I'm a child clinging to Cooper's legs, begging him, "Please take us. Please. Daddy! Don't leave us here. Please!"

He shook me off the way you shake off dust.

My heart stiffens in my chest. I'll keep the locket. He owes me that much. More. But he gets nothing in return. None of the absolution he is seeking by coming here.

Before I turn and walk away forever, I look him in the eyes and say, "Stop coming here."

8

SANDESH

Gut clenched in worry, I shift into high gear. The emergency SOS text wasn't specific. It could mean anything, but ten minutes after receiving it, I'm winding down the driveway leading onto the Mason Center grounds. The pristine grass and aged oaks that line the drive remind me of a cemetery.

I shudder. So much of Mom has already been lost. It seems impossible to believe that only five years ago, at fifty-eight, she'd developed Early-Onset Alzheimer's. It's so damn unfair. She worked hard her entire life, never took a sick day, and rarely complained. And this is her reward.

Pulling up to the main building, I park in our family's designated spot. My father paid extra for this space, and though I hadn't wanted to take his guilt gift, I did it for Mom. It's come in handy more than once.

I turn off my truck, then race up the care center's front steps with anxiety kickstarting my heart. The security guard buzzes me through with a nod. Damn. No checking my ID? It must be bad.

I'm running down the hall when I hear her voice, shrill and bitter, and nothing like Mom.

"You bitch! You bitch!"

A simultaneous ache of loss, anger, and fear swamps me as I round the corner and see her.

It doesn't look like her. Like the woman who wistfully named me after a traditional dessert her nani—grandmother—would make for her. The woman who once soothed my cuts, took me to football practice, and told me I had a lovely singing voice when I can't carry a tune. The woman who buried her artistic dreams at the insistence of an overbearing husband who wanted all her attention.

I can't see that woman in the woman who trembles with rage before the open door to her suite. Her thin blue shift shows a frail and wiry form. Her hands shake as she brandishes a worn teddy bear like a weapon. Usually, she holds that bear as if it's a child, singing and caring for it

Two nurses, along with the twenty-four-hour personal caregiver, stand near her, trying to calm her down. They speak in soothing tones, trying to break through the fog of delusion by playing into the delusion. Today, as with most freak-outs, Mom plays dual roles on the drama loop. Both the tormentor and the tormented.

The screeching bitch comments are a memory of my father. Not a violent man, just a cunning manipulator and an aggressive, demeaning prick. A deadly combination that made him an excellent businessman but a horrible husband.

If he'd always been loud and angry, she would've dismissed him, but Dad would alternate between faint praise, openly criticizing, and carefully constructed manipulations meant to destroy her confidence. After they'd divorced, when she'd begun to accurately assess what he'd done to her, she'd gotten sick.

I'd hated Dad for that, would probably still hate him right

now, but it's hard to hate someone when you understand them. And after my service, I came face-to-face with the same angry tendencies in myself.

Hands out, I near Mom. I enter her delusion. Not calling her *Mom*, which would confuse her. Her bear is a baby. "Lina, that's a fine baby you have there."

The nurse clears his throat, almost apologetically. "We already tried that."

I ignore him. It's not the words; sometimes, it's the tone. Conversational. Friendly. "He reminds me of your son. What is his name again?"

Mom stops. Her eyebrows raise and she jolts, as if she physically slammed from some other place back into her body, into awareness. She looks down, cries out in alarm, and clutches her bear to her chest.

She's back. I know it the moment she begins to shake. Her blue eyes clear then mist with tears. "Is it okay? Is it okay?"

My heart breaks into a thousand sharp and cutting pieces. "It's okay, dear. It's always okay between us."

Her face twitches as tremors—aftershocks of awareness—pinch the muscles beneath her too-pale skin. I understand. I've imagined what it must be like for her so many times. To be trapped beneath the cold memory of her illness only to have the clouds part and reflect a completely different reality. It must hurt.

I reach for her. When she doesn't pull away, I wrap an arm around her delicate shoulders and draw her to my side, under one arm. Like a tiny bird in need of great care, she leans into me.

I look at one of the nurses. "Please get her something to drink. Apple juice."

He nods and takes off. The attendant, the one personally paid to sit with Mom, asks in a low voice, "Would you like me to contact her private physician, Mr. Ross?"

"Yes. And I believe the first visitor coming in my absence, my buddy Victor, will be stopping in tonight. Make sure the guards know."

"Oh yeah. I already have."

Good. That's something. I hate that I have to leave when she's had such a bad episode, but the Parish family insisted on the timeline and the opportunity is too big to pass up.

9

JUSTICE

Except for the flat-screen TV showing world news, the only lights in the family's private jet are blue. They mark the galley, a few outlets, and the walkway along the cabin floor.

But I don't need more light to know the sounds and sights of a nightmare.

Sandesh's body twitches and jerks in the prone seat directly across from me. Should I wake him? I'd want to be woken. How many nights had I wished something would pull me out of that damn nightmare? Many. Knowing his history of service, I'm betting his nightmare is a rehash of past events, like mine so often are.

I shudder. To someone who has the same terrifying dream over and over again, the word *nightmare* doesn't cover it. It's torture. Personal and intimate torture.

That decides it.

I switch seats so I'm beside him and then, very gently, place my hand over the one fisting his blanket.

He sits up, jerks his arm away, gasping for breath, then switches on a reading light.

Three deep breaths pass between his full lips before he glances over at me. He smells of sweat and fear.

I lean forward, careful not to touch him now that he's awake. That would be a violation. I know what it feels like to be that exposed, to have something that you don't even like to admit to yourself, laid out for others to see. It's part of how I healed as a child, talking about my shit, but it didn't come easy. Or overnight. "Are you okay?"

Not answering, he rubs a hand across his face.

"Do you want to talk about it? The nightmare?"

He drops his hand, clears his throat. "No."

That stern word erects a wall between us. A do-not-cross, guard-dog-on-duty, enter-at-your-own-risk wall. I get it. I don't need him to tell me, but I do want to connect with him. I've fucked everything up between us. First, by casually challenging his business, second, by allowing Momma to use his business, and, third, by propositioning him in the elevator. It was a desperate attempt to make my own sadness over my siblings disappear. It was also a jerk move.

Now, there's a cold distance between us. For the life of me, I can't figure out why it matters to me, but it does.

He pushes aside the blanket on his lap and I'm sure he's going to get up, but he only adjusts the vent so cool air flows out.

Okay. I'm doing this.

Working a kink from my neck, I speak without looking in his direction. "I have this bad dream all the time."

He lets out an annoyed breath, as if he can't deal with me trying to compare my bad dream with his nightmare.

It pisses me off. I'm sure he sees me as the media does, a rich Parish Princess—trotting all over the globe and taking more credit than I should for doing what's right. I should let him keep thinking that. It'll make what's going to happen in Jordan easier, but I can't ignore his pain.

His trembling and, as much as he's trying to rein it in, it shows his distress. This is a good man. A man who started a charity to help people and vets all over the world. A man who is suffering.

"In my nightmare, I'm a child. A man is holding me down." I swallow through the ball of fear rising in my throat. "He's so heavy, it hurts. He has his hand over my mouth to keep me from screaming. I'm so little that he's cut off my nose as well as my mouth. It's a dream, but I can't breathe, and I can't wake up."

The explosive power of my words suddenly feels grotesque, rash, and stupid, like a punch to my gut. I slide my hand over my stomach to press down my revulsion.

Beside me, Sandesh goes still. Deadly still. "Justice, did someone hurt you? Did something like that happen to you?"

"No." God, no. Not me. I don't want him to think that. "It was Hope. My biological sister. She died saving me from that. Our demented maternal grandmother let some very sick men make kiddie porn in her basement. My father gave us to her for drug money.

"Thanks to the actions, or I guess *in*actions, of my addict father, Hope died. I saw it happen." I twist my hands in my lap, guilt rising, even though I know and believe it wasn't my fault. "I couldn't stop it."

He looks away.

I watch the tick in his jaw, as if he's fighting for control. Fuck. What was I thinking? I'd just tossed my pain out there like a live grenade and it'd exploded, tearing through the peaceful sound of the jet slicing through the sky and the air brushing the plane's hull. I should've let things be.

Sometimes, I forget how other people live, grew up. No one in my family *doesn't* have an awful childhood story. We call it our origin story, like superheroes, because we all know that we are the lucky ones. We are the rescued. The empowered.

"How do you wake from the nightmare?"

I'm surprised by the question. It goes right to the heart of the problem of that dream and doesn't shy from it. I appreciate that kind of bold. It's the kind of bold that's also a kindness.

"It's always the same. I fight and struggle and thrash. Bite. Which is me, how I live my life. It doesn't work. The thing that works... I'm not a religious person. At all. But when I give in and pray, something in that prayer lifts me, wakes me up, but the waking is the worst part. Because I know exactly how she must've felt. And I know that..." I take a deep, cleansing breath before I can manage, "My prayers didn't work for Hope."

Silence. I turn to him, stare directly into his eyes. It's an invitation to talk, a way of saying, *You can trust me. You can share your pain with me. I will respect it.*

For a long moment, he stares into my eyes, then looks away. "Thanks, Justice. For sharing and for waking me. I'm going to leave it there. Okay?"

When he looks back, he reaches to put his hand over mine, but stops. His hand hovers, waiting for me to reject him for not sharing his story.

I'm not built that way. I've shared too much with my siblings. I know how hard it is to break through the pain of our past, and I know how much a touch can do to ease that pain.

I flip over my hand.

He drops his hand into mine and we thread our fingers together.

It should be a sweet gesture, a comfort in the dark, and, in some ways, it is. My body sighs with relief, but also the heat of him...

My libido perks up. My body warms from head to toe. My mind begins providing images of our lips colliding, of him dragging me into his seat, into his lap. My mental images become us tearing our clothes off, our mouths and tongues searching. I groan. Out. Loud.

"Justice." Not a question, an affirmation. One word, but that tone... The invitation is there.

Kiss me. Taste me. Have sex with me.

I pull my hand away, lean back, and close my eyes. I can't allow myself to speak or look at him, because I want so desperately to engage in some hot, steamy sex right now.

But I have to face facts: fucking him will complicate my mission. I intend on leaving his side nearly the moment we land, and I can't do that if we get hot and heavy now.

I know his type. He'd feel a greater need to reach out, ask how I'm doing, worrying that he might've crossed a line. All of that wouldn't only endanger the mission, him, and his work. I want to screw Sandesh, not him or his charity.

I can feel him watching me, waiting for me. Gritting my teeth, I shake my head and let the images of his hot body play through my overactive mind, driving me toward a fitful night of hot dreams.

10

SANDESH

The smiling Jordanian customs official looks around the luxury aircraft, and I try not to think about the weapons I stowed in baggage or the weapon in the bag by my feet. My hands are sweating as he offers Justice and I kind words of welcome.

We pass him our documents and without questions he stamps them. A moment later, without any kind of search, he exits with a cheerful wish for a pleasant stay.

Relief loosens the knot in my shoulders. The last thing I need associated with my charity is a weapons charge. But it seems Mukta Parish is good as her word. I had doubts about the ease with which she said I could bring weapons into the country. I took a chance.

Most aid workers need some kind of protection in an active war zone, usually hired guards or, like I typically do, weapons purchased in country.

Shaking off the stress of the last few moments, I stow my passport and multi-entrance visa inside my backpack. Justice takes it all in stride, as if it's all her due. Another way we are so different. Except, last night she proved she isn't the Parish

Princess I'd thought her to be. She's kind, willing to sacrifice herself—her private self—to offer comfort to someone else.

After checking my email on my cell, I reply to a nonurgent update from Mom's care center, stow my laptop, then stretch the travel from my limbs.

Across the cabin, Justice's midnight-dark eyes skim my body.

I smile at her.

With an annoyed shake of her head, she returns to checking her emails or text or whatever has her interest on her cell.

Instant agitation marches like muddy boots down my spine. She's been distant since waking this morning. I'm hoping she doesn't regret sharing her nightmare so freely with me last night, especially after I *didn't* share. That would suck, because she gave without expectation last night, and that... that was beyond decent. Still, even if I don't know what her issue is with me, it feels like a problem, a problem that's about to get worse.

Ready to face the demon, I walk over to where she's enamored with her phone. I sit beside her. "We need to go over some rules."

Her brows and eyes go up, and she's kind of beautiful and fierce and a million miles above me.

She lowers her phone and puts it into her backpack. "*Rules?*"

Shit, I've handled military knives with a less sharp edge than the one she put on that word. I definitely could've chosen a better one. "Let's call them guidelines—and not even *my* guidelines. They're more like the country's guidelines."

"Such as?"

"Jordan is normally safe, but these aren't normal times. Amman is flooded with refugees. Not all are innocent, so don't leave the hotel without me. When we're working at Za'atari, keep a low profile, let me know where you are, and don't wander around without me."

I wait for her to argue, wait for her to tell me to shove my rules up my ass because, for a fraction of a second, that's exactly what her face tells me she's thinking. Honestly, I wouldn't blame her one bit because I suddenly *feel* like an ass.

She grins a little and all that annoyance falls away. "The Grand Hyatt in Amman is now like a Taliban hut in Afghanistan?"

Her smile, so coy and knowing, lights a fire under me. Now, I feel like explaining myself, justifying my speech. "There are a lot of people here, not just Jordanians, and not just people playing by the rules. This area is in flux, so if I'm eighty klicks away in Za'atari or even working with Salma within Amman, you're pretty much on your own. I'm only suggesting that you have some situational awareness."

She lets out a breath forced enough to knock over a tombstone. It's so exaggerated that I almost laugh, but she speaks first.

"You're right. In fact, I was thinking that after our initial inspection of the camp, I'd leave you to work with Salma. I don't want to get in the way."

Okay, that makes no sense. She's here, according to her mother, to get a feel for what IPT does so she can get a handle on PR. How can she do that at the hotel? Is she's hiding the fact that she's mad about something? I would normally press, but I can't wander into her emotional jungle right now. She'll have to cope.

I stand up and hold out a hand. "Great. You ready?"

Suddenly, something in her face shifts, softens. Her gaze travels up body and then she pins me with eyes made for midnight pleas and hot sighs. It's all I can do to stop myself from dropping to my knees, kissing her lips, finding her desire, and pulling free every soft and needy sound.

I flinch when she takes my hand and a surge of electric lust shoots up my arm. She steps closer and rises onto her toes. The space between us grows hot enough to give Death Valley a run for its money. My breath sounds as loud as an engine, which makes sense since my engine is roaring.

She grabs my waist, pulls my body flush against hers, and wiggles.

I am instantly hard enough that I lose the ability to think or move.

A grin on her lips, she whispers, "I have rules too, but I always seem to break them."

She kisses me. Heat explodes, detonates, takes out any feeling but her tongue as it races along the seam of my lips.

Oh, hell. I open my mouth, push my own tongue against hers, and explore her wet warmth.

God, kissing her feels amazing. I reach down, cup her ass, help her along as she grinds herself against me. She moans so deeply it cuts off all other sound, even the pounding *yes! yes! yes!* of my heartbeat.

Lifting her, I begin to back her toward a seat, any seat.

She stops me with a hand to my chest and a shake of her head. "I'm sorry," she says. "I really shouldn't."

I gape at her, and it takes me a full three seconds before I'm able to coax my hands to drop her ass.

With her feet back on the floor, she shrugs in apology. "There's too much at stake. I mean, for you and your charity. So, let's keep this PG while we're here."

A sharp and annoyed slap of disappointment. What happened? She was... I can't figure this woman out, but I'm not going to give her the satisfaction of saying so.

I smile as if it doesn't matter. "That's fine with me."

Huge lie. Growing bigger by the minute.

11

JUSTICE

Our transportation from the hotel to Za'atari refugee camp is a dusty old pickup truck, driven by a teenage boy thin enough to make me want to make him a sandwich. And I don't cook. Next to him is his grandmother, Salma, a small woman with brown eyes that are both open and shrewd. She's Sandesh's contact here and runs the women and children's center in Za'atari called Salma's Gems.

The IPT works alongside her, letting Salma make the decisions on what that IPT support entails. After all, who would know better than someone living here, on the ground here, what needs to be done. Another thing, that draws me to this handsome man—he's savvy.

As we drive along the dry road toward Za'atari's front gate, Salma explains she's a doctor who started a medical center when the refugees arrived. Since then, she's expanded her mission with small-dollar donations. Momma, through Sandesh's IPT, is the first big donor. I'm glad the money will be put to good use and ashamed that it took this operation to focus our attention here.

I look out the window as the Za'atari refugee camp flies by on our right. It's so big, a city really. Layered with sand and trash and plastered with Arabic graffiti, it sprawls across the desert in a seemingly endless expansion, a firm reminder of what happens when power-hungry men rule the world.

The city-camp is sloppy yet beautiful in places. Well-tended yet ignored. Serene yet damning. Crude yet artistic. Metal trailers used to house people, homemade shacks, and rectangular buildings with sheeted windows press up against miles of fencing topped with barbwire.

The white-and-tan UN Refugee Agency tents, trailers, and buildings are dusted with sand, but there are also bright garments and splashes of colors everywhere—in the laundry drying on lines, in the hanging painted wooden signs, in the awnings of market trailers, and the elaborately colored women's veils.

Salma turns in her seat. Her brown eyes, vibrant against the dark hijab tucked around her face, lock onto me. She points in the distance. "When we first started here, there were no shops or business, no hospitals or schools. But, after so long here, we have all that now. In fact, the aid workers call our business district the Sham Élysées, a play on the Champs-Élysées, like the street in Paris. But most who live here call it, simply, Market Street."

Their Market Street is a big difference from the one in Philly. The trunks of electrical poles, brown, skeletal fingers draped in black wires, crisscross dirt and paved roads. Atop some of the trailer homes are satellite dishes.

Along with the wind coming through the windows is the sound of hammers on metal from repairs and the whir of saws from construction. Loud, but not the kind of loud I'd expected. "I thought it would be noisier."

Salma laughs. "You expected bombs? Gunshots and screams?"

Embarrassed, I shrug. "I guess I did."

"You will hear those things. And laughter. And prayer. And songs of joy and wails of grief. You will see streaks of aircraft across the blue sky and plumes of distant smoke. There are many good people here who are stuck in a very bad situation. People who, not too long ago, lived a much different life, much like the life most people live with family, home, and routine."

Feeling too much like a war tourist, I turn my attention back to the interior truck, which smells of figs. Makes sense, since I'm stuffed into the back seat with box of the fruit and Sandesh. I feel suffocated with the presence of him, so I shift in my seat with a swoosh from my cargo pants. And even though we're not touching—thanks, figs—Sandesh readjusts as well.

Good to see I'm not the only hyperaware one. Because, really, could there be any man more suited to wearing sunglasses? Doubtful. The desert isn't the only thing hot around here.

His outfit is not even trying, but is succeeding. Desert-sand sweatpants ride low on his lean hips, a dark-blue shirt tight against his chest, and sexy, almost-a-beard stubble. This is the reason that I kissed him on the plane. He is irresistible.

Okay, it wasn't only the heat of him on the plane that drove me to toss aside logic for lust. It was the sweetness of him. That whole rules thing and how he tried to backtrack when he could see my annoyance. Not that my annoyance lasted. I quickly realized, I'd warn me too, if I thought I did PR for a living, and badly at that. Besides, his warning gives me a reason to make an appearance and move on, since I need to be at the hotel where the Brothers Grim are meeting.

Thankfully, my self-preservation kicked in enough to override my libido. If Tony were here, he'd kick my ass for letting my emotions dictate my actions.

Oh, Tone, I wish you were here. Or Gracie. I need to talk to someone about how damn guilty I feel about involving Sandesh and the IPT. The man has enough to deal with.

A glance over shows me he's busy texting his IPT partner, a guy named Victor. There's been a flood in the Midwest of the United States and Victor is organizing volunteers and aid, already working with local centers to supply water and clothing.

Apparently, Victor—also ex-Special Forces—is some kind of strategic god. And good friends with Sandesh. When they'd spoken on the phone earlier, Victor's voice had come through the cell. In a bone-deep friendly tone, he'd called Sandesh *Sandman*, a nickname that suggests a history. I'd like to know about it, the nickname, their friendship, and the IPT. Really, I'd like to know everything connected to Sandesh. He interests me, and that's unusual for me. Also, right now, stupid.

The truck slows as a camp guard walks in front of our truck with a hand raised. My heart taps Morse code for *Get ready* against my chest as he makes his way to the truck.

There are a lot of ways things can go sideways in a situation like this, so I'm on high alert. Apparently, so is Sandesh, who puts his phone down and his attention on the action in front of us. The shift into soldier-mode is obvious. His whole body radiates menace. I like.

As Salma speaks with the guard, she slips him some money, and we're let through. I relax, even though it irks me to think of the many men who pay to enter illegally and look for girls they can "marry" and then discard. Or "marry" off into sexual slavery. There are a thousand ways to take advantage of women and children already victimized by circumstance.

That's why scum like Aamir and Walid are here, to take advantage.

And that's why *I'm* here. Because trying to save people as Salma does is one thing, but stopping the hands—at least one of the biggest—that keep snatching those people away is another.

I can't fail. I... *won't*.

Which means snapping some "PR photos" here, interviewing a couple of women, and making my excuses, because —as Momma would undoubtedly remind me—reconnaissance always comes first.

12

SANDESH

Inside the trailer that serves as part of Salma's training operation, I finally get a break from my cell phone and issues back home. Now, I can participate in what's happening here. Not that I'm needed with Justice around. She's put herself right into the middle of the everything, interacting with a dozen women being taught to sew and make bags for profit.

Despite the displacement and loss of what had been routine lives in Syria, these women are eager and attentive. Seated at a long, yellow laminate table, Justice asks questions about the simple patterns they're using while joking with them in Arabic.

She continues to surprise me. One minute, she's as tough as nails, putting down my business, and the next, she's tender and understanding, sharing secrets on the plane to help put me at ease.

Salma stands beside me. "It's crowded in here, but your recent funding has made it possible for us to take in many more women. I have already negotiated a larger place, one left by departing aid workers. There, women can sleep and work, receive therapy and care. The children can be watched over and attend local schools. The mothers can be taught a skill by us or attend higher education classes in camp."

It's amazing that she's already gotten so much done. "I'm so grateful to you, Salma, and thrilled that the money Justice and Mukta have provided will be put to such good use."

"You and Justice have made a difference that will allow these women and children a better future." Salma says, nodding at Justice before moving to help one of the women with a sewing machine.

Justice waves away Salma's praise, seemingly embarrassed by it. She focuses instead on the women she's helping.

I'm beginning to understand that Justice, the real Justice, cares a hell of a lot more than she wants people to know. It's touching and a little confusing, as confusing as that kiss on the plane that'd been so scorching hot I get hard thinking about it.

Strange that, just like she pulled away from me on the plane, she's also begun to distance herself from the reason we're here, telling me she plans on spending most of her time at the hotel, organizing PR.

If that's the case, why even come here? She could've organized PR in the States. Is she a war tourist, here to look around and gain some street cred? Is she here to pat me and Salma on the head while getting to what she thinks is the real job? Or is she the Parish Princess the media portrays, here to take credit while doing little?

None of that computes. Look at her; she's genuinely interested in the great designs a young woman with a missing arm is showing her.

"You have *got* to stop staring at me," Justice says.

Busted. My skin heats and a few of the English-speaking women laugh. I should look away, but, honestly, she's so beautiful I don't want to. "Can I borrow your camera?"

One of her eyebrows goes up before she shrugs, takes the camera from around her neck, then hands it to me.

I take it. "I mean, if I'm going to stare, I should at least do something a little useful."

She evaluates me with suspicion, but the woman showing her designs puts her arm around Justice's shoulders and the two of them smile.

Clicking photos, I'm struck by the hope of this moment. These women, who've lost so much, even of themselves, have a strength that humbles me, inspires me. They're ready to take their pain and create a new future. My bargain with Mukta Parish is already helping to change lives, so in the end, it doesn't really matter why Justice Parish came here.

13

JUSTICE

Sitting in a lounge area off to the side of the concierge desk, I realize the Four Seasons in Amman really plays up the whole desert theme. Desert-tan marble floors, walls, ceiling, chairs... Even the uniforms on some of the staff are tan. It makes me, dressed in a traditional black niqab and abaya, stick out like a sore thumb. Good thing only my blue eyes—thanks, contacts—show.

It also makes me a bit anonymous, which is what I'm going for. Most of the Jordanian women here wear only a hijab head scarf, nothing over their faces. And they have some serious style with jeans, heels, and fashionable clothes. I'm not interested in fashion. I'm interested in hiding the fact that I'm an undercover assassin, so this outfit works for me.

The concierge passes me with a curious gaze, and I return to the open book of Sufi poetry on my lap. He's probably wondering why I'm all by my lonesome, but he won't dare question a guest at this hotel. I checked in under a false name with all the supporting documentation thanks to The Guild.

Two people walk up to the check-in desk, and I do a quick scan. They're not my prey. Too bad. I only have two weeks to do recon, discover a pattern, and make my move. The Brothers Grim usually meet for at least a month every two years. They're being awfully cautious by shortening their time together in Jordan. Which makes Momma's worry about a traitor in the family seem that much less paranoid.

Distress beats like a winged bird against the cage of my chest. I massage the area with the tip of my fingers. Please, God, don't let it be one of my own, not one of mine. Please, not one of the four in my group.

It's hard doing this job alone, without any of my four closest siblings. I keep thinking about what tactics Tony would suggest or what insights Dada would have. Keep wanting to text Gracie for cyber backup or hear Bridget's soothing voice. But I can't fixate on it right now, because this patched-together, last-minute plan is anything but foolproof.

Sure, Momma was able to place a reliable connection at the hotel. A former rescue, who'll get me a key to the suite and ID, but that's where her help ends.

With the security around the hotel, not to mention around the Brothers, I definitely couldn't get a gun into the room. Poison, it is.

I'll go in dressed as staff for turndown service and hope their security won't feel the packet on me. The packet is substantial enough to take up my palm, so that's an issue. I'm working on a solution.

Holy shit. I spy with my little eye a soon-to-be-dead guy.

One of the brothers. Not Aamir, the slick one who dresses like a *GQ* model, but the younger, uglier one, Walid. Early forties, dark-black hair, sharp brown eyes, and a rope burn scar on his neck.

According to the dossier my family compiled on Dead Man Walking across the hotel lobby, the neck burn was left by his father who'd tried to kill him. Aamir had saved his brother, which, unsurprisingly, made Walid a fan for life. A super fan from what I hear.

Walid would do anything for his brother, including killing his own father. Which is how the two of them got free and moved to England—where they promptly became victims of another, more violent man. Who they also killed.

The brothers are survivors. Survivors who became convinced the only way out was to make other people victims. Kind of opposite of the way The Guild operates.

I can almost hear Bridget's voice telling me that the brothers didn't have The Guild to rescue them and maybe they'd made choices based on fear, desperation, and need. Sure, Bridge, they need to hurt and kill others, like Hope, so that they would feel safe and superior. What about now? Wealthy and vicious, they continue their abuse based on greed and entitlement and misogyny. And a system that gladly looks the other way.

Walid's two-man security detail trails him. Only two and one isn't in front? Sloppy. Someone's been spending too much time at his isolated ranch in Mexico, gotten comfortable and lazy. Explains the paunch around his middle.

The elevator opens and one of his guards finally takes the lead, stepping inside. Walid doesn't follow. In fact, he turns on his heel and—crap. Walid is heading this way. His guards stay at the elevator, holding it open. What the hell? Don't they know an assassin could be lurking nearby?

I nearly give myself a headache trying to surreptitiously watch Walid while still pretending to read. He passes so close, his expensive cologne hits my nostrils and makes me want to retch.

Fuckity fuck. I'm itching to stick a leg out and trip the bastard. Then stab him in the throat. He's so close I clearly hear his raspy voice and oh-so-coy British accent ask the concierge about area restaurants.

The concierge makes suggestions and Walid picks one, instructing the concierge to make a reservation for two tomorrow night.

The concierge doesn't miss a beat. He looks at his watch, as if seeing into the future. "Two for dinner at seven. Of course, sir."

Two? Interesting. To avoid a host of threats, the Brothers Grim risk these meetings every two years for each other. So, what are the chances they *aren't* going out together tomorrow? Near zero. That and the sloppy guards have me rubbing my palms with anticipation.

Luck of the Irish or luck of the draw; if there were a deity dedicated to saving women's lives, that deity just handed me an opening. I mean, it's destiny. Even Tony would understand me forsaking recon to jump all over this.

⁓

BACK AT THE AMMAN MARRIOT, I give a big "fuck you" to the fact that I had to sweat in an abaya all day at the Four Seasons by whisking down to the bar in a short silk dress that skims my upper thighs. Good thing Jordan's a lot less strict than other parts of the Middle East.

Smiling and pleasant, the bartender asks what I'd like. I want a stiff drink. Or something stiff to help me get out of my own head. Because I can have neither, I settle for espresso. I'll drink when I get home.

After today's events, the opportunity of it, I'm beginning to feel optimistic, like I can end this quickly and get back home to deal with my siblings. I need this to be over. The number of times I've imagined it—Walid dying... Aamir dying... A knife under the ribs, a sharp point puncturing hearts as the boom-boom rhythm slows... that would be best. Their eyes knowing death came from me.

I'm so fucking mad, so fucking eager to have them hurt, have the men who denied Hope breath be unable to breathe. *Take that, you fucks.*

"Justice, are you going to drink that?"

Surprised he's here, I blink up at Sandesh. This man could distract a statue. Seriously, is it fair that he's so damn handsome and nice? There should be a law. What's he pointing at?

Oh. I look down at my espresso. Turns out, I'd been mindlessly tapping the edge of the tiny cup with a finger, spilling dark liquid onto the white ceramic saucer.

I push the small plate toward him. "You're welcome to it. It's a little cool now."

Unlike you, who are hot as hell.

He takes the cup, sips, then sits beside me. "Are you okay? You look a little intense."

Sheesh, I *would* happen to be traveling with a man trained to pay attention—and not just regular attention, but military-detail attention. I can feel the laser of his observation as if it's a shiny red light pointed between my eyes. "I'm fine."

He snorts.

God, he's even hot when he's skeptical. I doubt he could get more skeptical. Hmmm, I could use a distraction. Now that I've moved up my plans, there's no reason to keep my distance. I'll be gone soon. No one the wiser, and he'll be left to his own devices. Maybe, he could use a distraction too.

It's a good thing none of my siblings are here, because they don't know when it's a perfectly good time to take a risk. Playing it safe has never been my strong suit.

I pump my eyebrows at him, swing my chair toward him, then breathe, "Let's dance."

14

SANDESH

The music at the bar is barely loud enough to hear, but Justice's sultry invitation to dance runs down my body like a hot finger. I can't help the desire that surges through me. Or the hungry gaze that travels the silky blue dress clinging to her ass and hips like a warm hand.

I remind myself that I need her family money. Remind myself of her insults. Of her hot-and-cold tendencies. Of the complications this would bring.

She says nothing. She doesn't have to. Sun-drenched legs, nipples pressed against silk that swoops low against her breasts, say it all.

And, ah, her lips. So full. So damn sure. Her grin announces the game is won and dinner is ready all in one long, lazy, predatory stretch.

Part of me throbs in response.

The rest of me is pretty damn annoyed.

I frown. *Enough.* She's the one who suggested we keep it PG; why is she playing games with me now?

Her eyes, soaked in velvet onyx and framed by midnight lashes, narrow at my frown. "Okay, I give. You eat me up with your stare and then you hesitate. What is it with you? Do you have something against strong women?"

I can't help the annoyed snort. Not liking strong women suggests I'm not confident or capable. I'm neither. "For someone so direct, you are seriously clueless."

"*I'm* clueless? Buddy, you have no idea of the opportunity for friction and fun you are passing up right now."

I laugh because she's quick and funny, not afraid to speak her mind, heat and energy, and the promise of friction and fun... Oh, hell. Rangers, lead the way.

I grab her hand and pull her onto the dance floor, desperate to feel all of her pressed up against me.

I'm a little surprised when she doesn't resist because, a moment ago, she'd taken my hesitation personally. I thought she'd make me pay for it, but when I look over my shoulder, she bequeaths me with a *that's-more-like-it* smile. Seriously, this woman is scorching hot.

"At this Moment" by Billy Vera and the Beaters plays through the speakers as I pull her to me.

She curves into me, drawing a sound from my throat that's as involuntary as breathing.

"That's one," she purrs into my ears.

My grateful hand slides along the silk fabric of her dress, down her back to her smooth, round, and hot-as-hell ass. And there I go. Zero to sixty. What did she just say?

"One?" I whisper, bending to place my cheek to hers.

She runs a tongue over my earlobe and the warm wet stroke sends tremors zinging low into my body.

"I'm counting." Her sultry voice meshes with a teasing tongue that vibrates through me. "Counting how many different ways I can get you to moan."

My brain freezes and I growl, a raw, desperate sound that even I recognize as raging intent.

She laughs. "Two."

Okay. Definitely time to divert the conversation. Complex math, anyone? Or a subject destined to slow down any hot moment. "Have you spoken to your mother about our progress here?"

She laughs again, as if she can see me trying to wrestle control from the moment. She moves her mouth against my neck and breathes hotly, "No. But I'd like to meet *your* mother. You've met mine. It's only fair. What's she like?"

Sexy and interested in me; hard to resist. "You'd like her. At least, who she used to be."

"Used to be?"

"She's been sick for a few years. Early-Onset Alzheimer's. She's at a care center. I have friends and family scheduled to sit and read with her every night I'm away."

"Oh. I'm sorry." She looks past me for a moment.

I get it. Not exactly a light topic for this moment. Probably turned her right off.

Her gaze returns to me, intense and searching. She bites sexily and purposefully on her lower lip. "You do realize I already want to sleep with you, right? You don't have to sweeten the pot with your unflinching kindness."

I laugh again because only this woman would think talking about my mom—meant to cool things off—is sexy.

"Sandesh, I'm serious."

She rolls her hips against me and heat explodes through my body. My eyes roll back in my head. So good. That. Feels. So. Good.

I bring my mouth to hers, desperate and searching.

The moment our lips connects there's an instant and overwhelming zing of electricity. Mindless of where we are, I taste her, tickle and tease her mouth open. Her wet response, the moan against my lips as her tongue plays back, erupts fire and longing down my body.

Dubdubdub, dubdubdub pulsates through me. Hard to tell

what throbs faster—my cock or my heart. Instinctively needing to get closer, I deepen the kiss.

She opens wider, accelerates the roll of her hips.

Yeah. Time to go. Time to get her off the dance floor and into my bed. Or her bed. Which room is closer?

My phone buzzes in my pocket. I jump. As close as she is, Justice definitely felt that buzz.

She stiffens in my arms and pulls her sweet mouth away. "Answer it."

I tighten my grip on her, run my nose along her cheek, inhale her lavender-warmed-by-the-sun scent. "Ignore it." Please. God. Ignore it.

"Your mission." Justice shakes her head. "I can't do that."

The dead-serious look in her eyes jolts me back to awareness. I instantly feel like an asshole. This is not me. I know my responsibilities.

Heat searing my face, I step back and answer. "Hello."

"Sandesh, please, I need your help. Can you come to Za'atari?" The tremor in Salma's voice douses the fire in my body. A tsunami would've had less impact.

"I'm on my way."

15

SANDESH

The crumbling walls of partially destroyed buildings and large piles of debris block out the desert landscape surrounding the abandoned Syrian village where Salma and I are parked.

We've been here since dawn broke. Now, as Salma sleeps, the pink glow of sunlight fades to the blue-black edges of night. The truck is getting chilly.

I've spent most of today mapping every inch of this place and developing an exit strategy. Even though the Free Syrian Army is known to me—when the war first started it had been made up of moderate rebels trying to overthrow the brutal dictator Bashar al-Assad—I'm still nervous about this mission. How is Salma sleeping? She has nerves of steel.

Coming into a war zone to facilitate the transfer of Syrian and Yazidi women freed by the FSA is a huge risk. But one I'm willing to take if it means helping these women. I have no idea what my backers at Parish Industries would think about me diverting their donations to take part in a rescue operation, but I can't start second-guessing my decisions now.

The distant rumble of an engine alerts me to what might be

trouble—or could by the FSA finally showing up. I reach to tap Salma, but she's already up and turning toward the approaching truck.

"It's them," she says, moving to open her door. "Speak Arabic. The women will be scared and in need of reassurance."

I reach across to stop her. "Please let me check them out first."

She accepts with an annoyed, "If you must."

I keep my gun down as I get out. Men hang off the slatted sides of the truck that quickly pulls to a stop. The driver jumps out. Every hair on my neck stands on end, but I relax when I see the veiled women huddled inside. It's like Salma said; these are the good guys.

Back when the war had first started and the resistance had been made up of moderate rebels, my team and I had trained men like these.

So much has happened since then, but, in many ways, nothing has changed. There's still war, still uncertainty, and still a brutal dictator willing to kill his own people to remain in power.

The driver, a man in his twenties with hard eyes and a scar above his beard, quickly approaches me. His fellow freedom fighters keep their rifles at the ready, a fact that should bring me relief but doesn't. The skin on my back itches. Something's wrong here.

Despite her agreement to let me talk to them, Salma gets out of the truck. Guess she's nervous after all.

Since my Arabic is passing, I wait for her to come over.

She warmly greets the driver, who seems to be the leader. Her warmth quickly turns to alarm.

I lose most of what's said in rapid Arabic but get the important parts. They're being chased, and we need to take the women before their pursuers catch up.

We break into action. The leader issues orders to his

soldiers, who jump off the sides, drop the truck tailgate, and start helping the women out.

I rush over and assist each woman into our pickup. I wish we'd had access to or time to get a covered van or truck. This isn't a great way for them to travel.

Realizing this, Salma gives the women—I count eight of them—instructions to get in and keep low.

I do a double take on seeing a very pregnant woman waddling toward me. I grab her hand and gently guide her toward the truck's cab. The moment I open the door, a series of pops and clangs strike the door. The pregnant woman cries out. I shift next to her, shielding her.

Gunfire erupts as the FSA begins returning fire. Lifting the pregnant woman into the cab, I feel wet warmth on my hand. Her blood saturates my palm. My throat grows tight. "Salma, she's injured!"

Moving at a pace I didn't know she could muster, Salma darts over and slides into the backseat next to the woman.

Everything starts happening fast and not fast enough.

I close the tailgate on our truck, warn the women to stay down, then bring my weapon about to reinforce the soldiers.

"Yadhhabi! Go!" the leader yells at me in both Arabic and English.

His direction shocks me from what I was doing. Almost on autopilot, I'd begun to engage the enemy. That's not my job here.

Sprinting to the driver's side, I jump into the cab and peel out, heading for the escape route I'd mapped earlier.

16

JUSTICE

In the sixteen hours since Sandesh rightfully ditched me at the bar, I've been keeping busy. Mostly by worrying. Going to the Brothers Grim's room without backup has me missing my team more than ever.

If I had access to Gracie's cyber skills, I could've had her tap into the hotel cameras and watched the brothers' movements. If Tony were here, he could've watched the restaurant. The best I could do was call the restaurant and confirm dinner for two. This is all so damn risky, but worth it for the payout. *It's almost done, Hope.*

The stiff smell of starch from my crisp white uniform blouse overpowers even the flowers I carry between my white-gloved hands. The fact that Walid ordered flowers for his turndown service somehow comforts my nerves. I hold the bouquet of Jordanian black irises—which I'm pretty sure are dyed, considering the rarity of them—like a shield.

Though this floor has a limited number of exclusive suites, even if I hadn't had the room number, I could've identified it by the two brooding bodyguards stationed outside. I keep a smile plastered to my face, grateful for the prosthetics that make my nose and chin larger, and the honey-brown contacts that cover the scorn in my black eyes.

I blink down my rage and put myself into an appropriate frame of mind. Just maid service here to shut the curtains and turn down the beds.

The *whoosh, whoosh* of blood in my ears reminds me to take a few steadying breaths.

The guards appear bigger and more interested as I draw near. Both are armed. Obviously, getting guns into the hotel is easier for some than others.

I recognize these guys. They work for Walid, so says the intel Dada's contact supplied. The smaller guard is Dmitri. He'd been hired by Walid a few months ago after an issue with his security. The other one is... I can't remember his damn name.

Nameless speaks to me in Spanish-accented English. "Give me the flowers and hold out your arms."

I nod, hand him the flowers, then hold up my arms. Dmitri scans the flowers with a wand, then hands the same wand to Nameless, who runs it over my body.

"Where are the chocolates?" Dmitri asks in a thick Russian accent.

I point to the pocket of my black vest and the obvious candy bump. He frowns at me. "Why aren't you talking?"

Tilting my head, I open my braces-covered teeth and point into my mouth, displaying a badly damaged tongue.

"Disgusting," Dmitri says. "Shut it."

They exchange a look of unease. As well they should; that bit of F/X hurts like hell. The steel wires holding down my actual tongue pinch my gums at the metal braces attached to my teeth. Still, it doesn't hurt as badly as the obvious American accent on my Arabic.

Practicing every calming method I've ever been trained in, I remain still as Nameless goes from using the wand to patting me down, smoothing his hands along my hijab, black vest, pants, and up the V of my crotch. In some countries, and probably this one, this pat-down would be enough to consider us married.

When Nameless is done, Dmitri hands me the flowers and waves me toward the door. "Go. And don't forget ice water by the bed and chocolates on the pillow. Those are Boss's favorite."

Dammit. If I'd known he'd eat the chocolates, I could've poisoned them beforehand. Would've, should've, could've...

Reaching for the door handle, I use the key card our contact provided.

"Keep an eye on her, Dmitri," Nameless says, and Dmitri, grumbling, walks in behind me.

Shit. That's going to make things difficult.

"Be quick," Dmitri warns me, pointing to his left.

I set to work even as he scrutinizes my movements across the two-bedroom suite's central room and living area. It's opulent even by Parish standards, with thick velvet drapes that extended floor-to-ceiling, a large chandelier, velvet couches, a dining table, and a full bar.

Momma's contact gave me exact instructions for turn-down service, which I follow without fail. I replace yesterday's flowers with today's, close the drapes, find the engraved silver lighter behind the bar, and light the candles along the dining table. I go back to the kitchen, fill a pitcher with ice water, grab a glass and a square, marble coaster, then walk into the bedroom.

Apparently satisfied I'm following routine, Dmitri doesn't follow me, but does tell me to, "Leave the door open."

Shit. I need precious minutes without this guy's eyes on me. And this isn't the type of work that can be rushed without dire consequences. My pulse kicks like a mule against my ears.

As I turn down the bed, I spot a pair of brown loafers on the floor—an opening that nearly has me sighing out loud.

I shake my head, as if lamenting men and their barbarous ways, then walk the shoes into the closet.

Inside, I quickly reach under the nape of my hijab and pull out the slim packet containing the poison. Hidden from Dmitri, I fiddle with my braces and remove a sharp metal wire. The packet, an ultra-dense thermoplastic, requires something sharp.

Even with my hands double-covered, traditional white gloves overtop protective rubber gloves, I begin to shake.

Palming it, I slip out of the closet and into the bathroom. Logically, I'm aware the poison needs to be ingested. Emotionally? I hold my breath and squeeze a small drop onto an electric toothbrush. It seeps quickly into the bristles.

Now comes the hard part. I palm the wire and the packet and walk into the living area. Dmitri sits at the bar, texting on his phone. Jaw grinding against metal, heart pounding, stomach turning, I cross the room as quietly as I've ever been in my life. If I can get in and out of Aamir's bedroom without Dmitri challenging me again that would make my life and escape a lot easier.

Sweat has started to gather in my glove as I silently turn the handle and step into the anteroom. Aw, Walid gave his brother the nicer room. How sweet.

Fucker.

Traversing the outer room in a few steps, I swing open the bedroom door and freeze.

The bathroom door in this bedroom swings open and in a puff of steam Aamir, followed by a girl with long, damp blonde hair, steps out.

Hope?

No. Not Hope. Hope is dead. And the man who killed her stands here naked, leading a teenage girl, also naked. Her eyes stay down as she covers herself with her hands.

Unconcerned with my presence, Aamir smiles at me—

smiles as if shame and evil don't really exist. He struts across the room and tells the girl, still hesitating by the bathroom doorway, to get into the bed.

My stomach can't decide if it will spew vomit or fire.

Aamir passes close enough to the open door that I can see the water droplets on his eyebrows. He finally seems to take note of me or, at least, my reaction. In British-accented Arabic he says, "It's okay. We're married."

Fire, it is.

17

JUSTICE

Standing in Aamir's bedroom, witness again to a crime that brings me back to that basement and those precious minutes when Hope died, I am frozen with anger.

Two things happen at once. Dmitri enters the anteroom behind me and shouts at me, "Not in there!"

Aamir spreads his arms wide, as if to ask my frozen stance if I like what I see. It's not only his oh-so-slick smile, his can't-be-stopped surety, his nothing-you-can-do-about-it cockiness seeping from his pores that propels me forward; it's my own outrage and pain.

I'm moving with training and power and instinct, faster and more deadly than a cobra. Adjusting the sharp metal in my palm, I step forward and slam it up and through Aamir's ribs. It slides in like butter. He jerks taller, as if he just woke the fuck up. Piss runs down his legs.

Not enough. Not nearly enough. I smash the pod into his mouth, and even though he spits it out, I know it doesn't matter. That much concentrated poison causes an instant reaction. Foam spills from his lips. He lurches backward, tumbling on his heels, flailing backward until he falls.

Screaming, the girl jumps out of the way.

Aamir's head slams with a thick sodden *clap* against the marble tile at bathroom's edge.

One second, maybe two, before I have my gloves rolled off and am turning to the presence I sense charging at my back.

I snap a well-placed roundhouse against Dmitri's neck. He staggers right.

A silenced round misses me.

Before he gets off another shot, I punt his balls back to his ancestors.

Face red, he tucks tail and drops to his knees.

I grab his gun, thankful for the silencer, and smash it against his skull, hard enough to crack sanity. Of which he obviously has none. His eyes roll back and his body gives out.

The girl screams.

Fuck.

I remove my prosthetic tongue with a jerk that rips at my gums, sending warm, metallic blood flooding into my mouth. In Arabic, I beg the kid to stop screaming.

No go.

All bony knees, elbows, and long, blonde hair slick against a skeletal back, she runs screaming into the main living area. I follow, gun raised.

The suite door opens, and Nameless strolls casually inside. Little girls screaming? Just another day at the office.

He registers me with my gun in hand, chasing the girl, and he reaches for his weapon.

Too late. I shoot him in the head. *Crack*. He drops like a puppet whose strings have been cut.

A split-second later, the phone in the dead guard's pocket begins to play Ritchie Valens's "La Bamba."

That's inappropriate enough to halt me in my tracks before

I race into Walid's room, breathing hard. I spot the girl and approach slowly with my hands raised. My Arabic sucks, so simple works best. "Women are fighting back. I am here to rescue you. I need you to get dressed. Fast."

The girl's attitude changes instantly. Her blue eyes fill with tears. "I'm Amal," she says, surprising me by speaking English. "I'm the one who prayed for you to come."

As I rush Amal back to the other room and get her clothes, my throat grows so tight with grief, I can't speak. She prayed for me to come? I want more than anything to answer her prayers. I have to get us out of here.

When she's dressed, I take her hand in mine. She's shaking so hard it feels like she's tugging my arm. I squeeze her hand tightly, trying to reassure her, and we move as one out of the room, past the dead men, and down the hallway.

Amal is as determined as she is scared, and that makes two of us. But her quick response and obvious comprehension of my plan tells me all I need to know. Childhood is something only unused children get to enjoy.

At the end of the corridor, the elevator opens and two hotel security guards step out. They have weapons drawn. They look at us and then toward the room we came from.

As planned, Amal begins to cry. In Arabic she shouts, "The men are all dead! All dead!" As she sobs, I bend to comfort her.

"Wait here," one of the guards instructs us as they move together down the hall. I hunch closer to Amal, trying to appear weak, small, a nonthreat. The elevator dings. My mouth goes dry. My heart preps for takeoff.

The elevator doors open. Still tucked over Amal, I angle my head to see the men from the corner of my eye.

Oh, shit. Walid followed by two guards gets out of the elevator. They spot hotel security and begin to follow them down the hall.

For whatever reason, they don't register me or Amal. Or, if

they do, some part of their primitive brain tells them we're harmless—the opposite lesson Amal has learned.

She begins to tremble so hard against me, I fear she will fly apart. Her eyes dart to the elevator, dart to our escape route with the doors about to close.

Even though Walid passes close enough that I could shoot him, I don't even think about taking that risk. I need to get Amal out of here. Her panic is palatable.

"Run." Amal pushes away from me, pointing toward the closing elevator. "The elevator."

Her fear-shrill voice pierces the hall. Walid gaze falls on Amal in an instant that seems to last a thousand years. His eyebrows raise. A few feet ahead of where he's stopped, pondering her, two guards I recognize from surveillance photos of Aamir's compound turn and stop, too. This isn't good.

These are Aamir's guards, not the disorganized guards I just faced that belong to Walid. Obviously, even the brothers recognized the lower quality of Walid's men. So says the fact that Aamir gave the better-quality guards to his brother who was going out, not himself who'd stayed behind. Aamir always looking out for his little brother. Aamir always the smarter one.

Aamir who is fucking with me even in death.

Heart in my throat, I bolt forward, yanking Amal's arm, half dragging her to the closing elevator.

The guards prove their worth, reacting before Walid's eyebrows even drop. One drives Walid to the ground, covering him with his own body. The other swings his gun toward me and shoots as I dive with Amal into the elevator. The doors slide shut as another shot rings out and heat rips into my side.

Rolling to my feet, I begin to press multiple floors under the one I plan to get off on. I help Amal up. When the elevator stops, I breathe deeply. "Calm," I tell her. She nods but looks pale and terrified. We exit quickly and move down the hall to the stairway.

Inside the stairwell, we race up, the sounds of our footsteps echoing. Two floors up, I use my keycard to get us onto the floor and move quickly down the hall.

I'm struggling to remember my training. A bad sign. Training should just kick in—like coughing when you swallow water incorrectly. But that isn't happening. Might have something to do with being shot. The ache in my side feels like gasoline and fire. My heart pounds like a jackhammer. The weight of my gun remains steady and comforting even as the fragile feel of Amal's small hand urges me to keep going.

We make it to the room I booked, and I'm glad I spent an entire day arranging this. Leaving my hotel down the street, changing at a restaurant, then coming here in disguise with false ID and credit cards... All worth it.

Time isn't on our side. No doubt Security is already looking for us, scanning the cameras.

Without me saying anything, Amal follows me into the bathroom. The lights flick on when we enter. I catch sight of myself in the mirror, blood splattered across my F/X distorted face. How desperate must Amal have been to be to come with me?

Peeling off the nose and chin prosthetics, I grab a hand towel and begin to clean off, instructing Amal to do the same. She is frozen, staring at my face. Crap. I explain as quickly as I can that it was a disguise.

Nodding, she begins to shakily clean up. As she does, I grab another towel to staunch the wound on my side. I don't have time to do more.

My body's shaking under the surge of adrenaline. Yanking the last piece of metal from my mouth, I race to my suitcase. Inside are three airtight packages and clothes. Nothing that can be tied to me. Except the locket Cooper gave me, which I kiss and quickly put on. Using scissors from my bag, I pierce each of the three packages. A noxious chemical smell fills the room as the sponges expand fully.

Two of the sponges in one hand, I go to the bathroom, place them on the side of the tub, and strip. Everything that's bloody or damning gets tossed into the tub and the packets go on top. I wash my hands again, and make sure Amal is clean.

Back in the room, I see the last sponge has expanded to the proper size. I take this big-bellied, big-breasted foam and tie it to my front. Over this, I slip my abaya, before adding my niqab and blue contacts.

Amal watches the transformation of me into a pregnant woman with eyes growing larger by the minute. She probably would've been less stunned to see a car turn into a Transformer.

Making quick work of it, I grab scissors from my bag, and cut a large enough strip from the sheet. I hold it out to Amal. "Can you make this into a niqab?"

She nods, taking the material, and does a fairly good job of it. I tuck some ragged edges under. Not perfect. Not with her blue dress. But it'll have to do.

Wiping down any surface we've touched, including my suitcase, I go back to the bathroom toss in the last bit of evidence, stroke the wheel on my lighter, and light the two highly flammable packets.

Whoosh. They catch fire. I blink away the orange light on my retinas. A chemical smell fills the room along with a lot of smoke. The material will burn to ash quickly, so it won't be a danger to the guests, but it will destroy the evidence and create enough smoke to set off the fire alarm.

I strap the gun to my forearm under the wide sleeve of my abaya and grab Amal's hand.

"When the alarm goes off," I say, "we head out, down the stairs, and don't stop until we get outside. Not for anyone."

The fire alarm blares.

18

SANDESH

Beneath the streetlamp-lit patch of dirt outside Salma's Gems, I clean bloody strips of cloth from the truck cab and toss them into a steel barrel of trash. My mood is as dark as the night sky.

Since Salma's grandson has already taken the rescued women to the new, larger facility, my duties tonight are cleanup. I take longer than necessary, scrubbing everything down, including my hands, because I know what waits for me inside that medical tent.

With a purposeful mental shove, I walk back inside and inhale the sharp odor of blood and death. A dull light hangs down from the wooden support rafter over a gurney. Salma is cleaning the exam table of blood. I comfort myself with the fact that the pregnant woman survived, even as I reprimand myself for the fact that her son did not.

I avoid looking where the small body lies atop a metal cart as I ask, "Do you need me to take him somewhere?"

Salma looks up from rinsing her rag in water gone pink with blood. "No, it is being handled, but thank you." She pauses and takes me in for a full breath. "You saved many lives tonight, but this does not comfort you."

It does not. "I should've kept my eyes on the fight, the action, because if I had, I'd have seen the danger coming."

"Sandesh, you have dealt with conflict for so long, you can't even find peace within your own mind. You made the right decision. Believe that."

Her brown eyes glisten with knowing intelligence, but I can't let go of the responsibility for how things turned out. "After she was shot, I wanted to fight so badly I almost told you to take the truck and leave."

Her eyebrows go up. "That would've been a problem as I don't drive."

I smile. That somehow makes me feel better. "How do you do it, Salma? Work here, witness what happens, knowing you can only save the moment for someone, leaving them alive in a violent and unfair world to save all the succeeding moments for themselves?"

"What would I do differently? I heal. That is my mission. To soothe the ache that too much anger and too many ideas of God's justice has done to our delicate minds."

Delicate minds? That seems an oversimplification. Or is it? Is it as simple as not allowing certain beliefs to take root, make patterns in the brain that cause kneejerk reactions? I wipe at my face. God, the whole room smells of blood.

Salma stops from cleaning and meets my gaze. "Tonight, you came face-to-face with where two sides of yourself meet—the soldier and the humanitarian. You naturally had a reaction coming to the crossroads of your identities. Stay and fight as a soldier or run and help without violence as a humanitarian. For me and those other women, you made the right choice."

What she says makes so much sense that I find myself becoming choked up. She's right. I made the choice to change, because I believed there were other ways I could help, other ways that didn't involve a gun.

A swish of the tent flap has me turning for the opening. Another pregnant woman in niqab and black abaya, holding her side, staggers inside, supported by a teenager, maybe thirteen, who looks at me with eyes much too old for a child.

For a moment, I'm frozen.

Until the girl whispers, "Help."

I rush forward, catching the pregnant woman as she falls. I lift her easily and carry her to a gurney still stained with another woman's blood.

Salma moves quickly to the woman's side. "Are you in labor?"

"No," the girl says, gripping the side of the gurney. "She's hurt. Her side. She speaks English."

The woman proves this immediately by saying, "We're being followed. Please hide the girl. Her name is Amal."

That voice hits me like an open hand, a sharp sting across the face. "Justice?"

Salma breaks into action, reacting with a speed that indicates she's been here before. She directs the girl to hide in a steel cabinet.

Amal darts into the cabinet and shuts the door with a metal clang as I stand there with my mouth open.

Justice with her face hidden, wearing blue contacts, injured, and with a daughter. No. Not her daughter. That's panic trying out logic. "What's happening?"

"I think I'm being followed," she says, with a confused tone. "I don't understand. They were here when we got here."

What is she talking about? How is she injured? Who's after her and how do I rip their head off?

Fisting my hands, I tie down the dog of war that wants to break whoever hurt her. I need to use my brain, not panic or anger. "Who would want to hurt a public relations specialist? Why do you appear pregnant?"

Before she can answer, the tent flap is tossed open and two armed men bully there way inside.

"Who is that on the table?" one asks in Arabic.

I slip forward, preparing to disarm him and take down the second.

"Get out!" Salma answers in Arabic. She waves her bloodied hands at them. "Can't you see that she has lost her baby?"

The men hesitate, taking in the lifeless baby cradled inside the metal infant scale.

Figuring out quickly what she's doing, I take over, pushing at them physically, "Outside, outside. She's lost much blood and might die."

On the table, Justice begins to moan. There's a moment of resistance from the men I'm trying to push out, but they finally give way, turning on their heels and leaving. I follow them out, making sure they're going.

They're not. They stop a short way away, fish out a cell, and make a call.

They'll be back.

By the time I return, Salma has pulled Justice's abaya up, revealing a foam belly. She pushes it aside and locates the wound. "There is a piece of metal in your flesh. Not deep."

"Not a bullet?" Justice whispers disbelievingly.

Salma shakes her head. "No. I am going to pull out the metal. Do you understand?"

"Yes. Quickly. Please."

My heart in my throat—why would she think she'd been shot?—I slip on hospital gloves. "Salma, what do you need?"

"Watch the door." She doesn't glance up as she begins to work. "The men. How long?"

"Not long."

I move to obey her, even though I'm filled with doubt and anger. And regret. I left my gun outside in the truck and don't dare retrieve it.

"Wait. Take this," Justice says, removing a gun she had hidden up her sleeve and holding it out to me.

I step back, take her weapon with the hard, stinging acceptance that she is no public relations specialist.

Salma cuts off the foam belly and begins to tear at Justice's dress. Justice puts her hand on top of Salma's. "I need this dress."

She tucks the abaya up as high as it can go, exposing delicate pale skin, black panties saturated with blood, and a deep gash, a quarter-inch wide, below her hip. A slice of metal fills the wound.

Salma cleans the blood from the wound only to have it refill as she picks up a pair of forceps and bends close to it. "A tiger stalking, no sound, brave one."

Justice nods, and even when Salma begins to dig into her skin, plucking at the edge of the shrapnel—once, twice, three times—she remains impassive. Her face is blank with concentration. She's putting herself somewhere else, like someone accustomed to dealing with pain.

I open the tent flap again, check the men. They aren't there. That's good—I hope.

I turn back to the room. It's nearly silent. The only sound from Justice is slow, deep breathing. She's some type of operative. She has training.

Salma digs in again, grasps the metal, twists, and pulls it out.

Justice lets out a sharp breath. Tears roll down her cheeks. "Is it over?"

"You need stitches."

Salma grabs alcohol and cleans the wound with quick, almost brutal actions.

This time, Justice does cry out, a whimper that has her tossing her head back and closing her eyes.

With steady, learned fingers, Salma stitches her up quickly.

Justice inhales and exhales with each pinch and pull of needle and thread. She does not cry out.

Whatever she is, this woman is highly trained.

When it's done, Justice swings her legs over the side. "Thank you, Salma. Please take care of Amal."

I hear men talking outside and glance out the door. They're back and talking rapidly into a cell.

When I look back, Salma is crouching next to Alma. "I will hide the girl with a family I know here. Take her." She motions toward Justice, who already has her legs under her. What kind of training has this woman had?

"No." Justice supports her own weight. "I've risked you all enough. I can get out from here. But take care of Amal. She has a family she wishes to return to. I can arrange—"

Salma waves away the words. "I will arrange it. This is what I do. But you cannot go alone."

"Sure, she can." I hear the words laced with my own building anger. I've been an idiot. "This is no woman accidentally hurt. She's an operative. Her backup is probably on its way. I'll stay and help you deal with the men she's brought here."

Moving across the room, I pull up the tent side and hold it open for Justice. Steps labored, she moves toward me. For a second, I want nothing more than to hoist her up and carry her to the nearest safe place.

No. I've been enough of a sucker, and it's like Salma said earlier: I made my choice. I'm not here to fight. Justice isn't helpless and she isn't what she appears.

As she bends to clear the side of the tent, I lean into her. "I'm going to find out who you're working for, and I'm going to have your ass."

Glancing up at me, she smiles, wicked and full. "Flirting at a time like this, Ranger?"

With a wink, she ducks under the tent side and walks confidently into the night.

19

JUSTICE

Cursing myself for putting Salma and Sandesh in danger, I move behind trailers with breath loud enough to make people worry death itself stalks these streets. I feel like death, like shit. That look Sandesh gave me... As if he knew what I was. What I'd done tonight.

It hurt almost as much as my damn side does. It's like someone holds a red-hot poker to my side. Not shot but pierced by metal. The gunshot must've torn off metal, which ricocheted into my hip. Not my luckiest night.

The thread pinching my skin together stings like barbed wire. If that was the worst of what I had to deal with right now, I'd be good. This situation is well and truly fucked. Hopefully, the worst of it falls on me, follows me. I wouldn't have come here if I'd thought for one minute there was any chance I could've been followed.

How did Walid's men follow me from the hotel? They couldn't have. But I'd spotted them just before Amal and I entered the tent. It makes no sense—unless Walid had already had men in the area and tracked me somehow.

For any other person on the planet, that would seem impossible. For me? There's always a way to know where I am. Just like there's always a way to know where any of my family members are. GPS. Every family member has one implanted.

Usually that information is only monitored for missions by Leland, his security team, and Momma. For this mission, only Leland and Momma have access. But it wouldn't have been hard for someone in my family to figure out how to gain access to that information. Especially since they have similar tech implanted in themselves.

My heart now aches as much as my side. Someone in my family betrayed me and nearly got me killed. And, if Momma is right, it wasn't just any old somebody—it was one of my most trusted, most loved siblings who could be, right this moment, feeding my whereabouts to people who are trying to kill me. Or take me back to Walid, so that he can kill me. Slowly.

Does the traitor care? Who would hate me that much? What have I missed? Who have I misjudged? Gracie, Tony, Dada, or Bridget?

Stop thinking about it. I need to focus. Let go of the failure. One of the two brothers is dead. That means something. Too bad the other is well and truly pissed, smart enough not to touch anything in the room after seeing what happened to Aamir, and even now might have access to the GPS that will tell him exactly where to find me.

I pick up my pace, each step rocking me with pain as I put distance between me, Salma, Amal, and Sandesh.

A mental diagram of the camp swims through my brain, and I automatically turn toward a hidden exit. Momma's right again, recon really is essential.

I need *out* of this camp. Once out of here, I can get out of this country. Someplace where I can make another plan because Walid isn't going to give up and go away. Hell, no. He gets me or I get him before he finds my family and the school.

Somewhere behind me, I hear the footsteps running, the shouts, and know deep in my bones they're coming for me.

I run, sprinting down the block. Burying the pain, I weave down roads until I'm so sick with stinging sensations I'm dizzy.

Crouching, gasping, my hand against an old truck for support, I bend and release the contents of my stomach.

"This way," I hear someone say in Arabic.

They know every move I'm making. Time's up. Taking a chance, I try the door of the truck. It opens. I slide inside and silently click the truck door closed. Judging by the holes in the floorboard, this truck isn't going to start, but I take a chance and try to hotwire it.

No go.

I check my ammo. Well, technically, Dmitri's ammo. Half a clip.

What the hell? I'm going to die. I'm going to die in a truck that smells like goats. I'm going to die in a truck that smells like goats after failing my most important mission. After failing Hope.

Who turned on me? Gracie, Tony, Dada, or Bridget? I can't die without knowing—which means I'm *not* going to die today.

A shot is fired into the truck. A warning shot, because Walid's men know he does not want me dead. He wants me in pain. There was only one person in this world he loved, and, tonight, I killed that person.

I know the brothers' tragic story. Two boys, orphaned on the streets of India—granted, they'd made themselves orphans —then, afterward, trafficked to a man in England. They'd killed him, too, and taken over his business. Despite having experienced the pain of being abused and trafficked, they chose to do that to others.

I get that, unlike me, no one plucked them from their path and introduced them to a different way. They'd made their choices from a place of desperation. Later, they'd made their choices from a place of wealth. And paranoia. And cold indifference. The only way to stop the cycle is to stop them. One down. One to go. I can't die here.

Someone calls out to me in English, "Come now. You are endangering the people here. Come out. We will take you some place to talk."

Oh. They just want to talk. Silly of me to think otherwise.

Tucking myself onto the floor, I call back, "How's Aamir? I hope I didn't break his heart."

They begin to fire at the truck.

20

SANDESH

Salma prepares Amal for what happens next as I check out front again. A few locals, but the men who'd busted in here haven't come back.

After Salma has dressed the girl in different clothes, she walks over to me. "You must go after Justice."

"No. Justice has people. I guarantee she's already with them. You need me."

"No, I don't. These men will let me be. They will not harm a Jordanian woman—a doctor and devoted Muslim with ties to this community. One of my sons is on his way here. He works for the government." She holds up her cell. "Those men will not want that trouble. They want Justice."

She pushes my chest, trying to shove me out the door. Pathetic and so damn frustrating.

"No, it's like you said earlier. I am here for this. I changed my life to be here for you, for this cause, for people who want to make things better."

Salma lets out a frustrated sigh. "You are a good man, but stupid. Her cause and ours are the same. Do you not see the girl?"

I look at the girl, now dressed in clean clothes. Her eyes pin me with disappointment and fear. Justice saved this child. "But—"

Salma holds up her keys. "When the leaves fall, you will see further. Take the advice of someone who has lived longer. Destiny isn't always the path we've chosen for ourselves. It is the one that most clearly matches the values we aspire to protect."

The crack of distant gunfire punctuates her meaning. Salma thrusts her keys at me. "Go."

Keys in hand, I run out into the shot-riddled night.

∽

DRIVING SLOWLY down streets with the windows open and the lights off, I listen. I can't allow myself to think of Justice as anything but a target that needs to be acquired. How far could she have gotten?

After the gunshots, no one walks the dirt roads in this area. The moon and some lights in the camp allow me to see clearly enough as I swing Salma's old pickup around a corner.

Shouldn't have let Justice go. Shouldn't have made my decision to let her go based on anger and hurt. I'd been so furious. She lied to me. Mukta lied too. No way her mother doesn't know what her daughter is doing here.

It's the only thing that makes sense. It explains the early phone call, squeezing Justice into my mission, and yet... If Justice has people, why isn't anyone coming for her?

Gunshots. There. I turn, drive down the road and park. Slipping out of the truck, I crouch, then run to the end of the trailer. I site around the corner.

Bam. Bam. I duck down, even though the gunfire hadn't been directed at me. It'd been directed at the rusty truck sitting twenty feet to my right. No doubt Justice is in that truck.

What was it Salma had said about destiny? I couldn't have gotten closer to where Justice hides if I'd been airlifted in. She's not firing back. Either to conserve ammo or because she's out of it. Either way, we have limited time before the bad guys close in or the authorities show up.

Belly-crawling, I dig my elbows into gritty soil until I'm beside the truck.

The crunch of tires on sand and the flash of headlights has me dropping flat. Another truck rolls into the street. Reinforcements or the authorities? Or some gang here to clear their territory?

A man with a spotlight hangs from the passenger window, sweeping the area.

The authorities.

The light hits the men crouched on the other side of the street. The guard calls for them to show themselves. The men reply with something I don't catch.

Gun still in hand, one of the camp police gets out of the truck and waves to the men—a little too friendly for my liking.

I begin to inch forward, then stop as the truck door opens and Justice drops out of the cab, nearly on top of me. She points her weapon. I raise my hands. "It's me. Sandesh."

She lowers her gun.

Wordlessly, I get up and lead her around the corner, then point out our ride. We jump in on either side of Salma's waiting vehicle.

Heart pounding, I rotate in my seat and back up at full speed, lights still out.

A spotlight hits us. I don't look. Don't need to. I know the authorities are following us.

"Don't stop," Justice says.

No kidding. The boundaries between who works for the government and who works for themselves are murky at best.

At the crossroad, I spin the wheel hard, sending up dust, before throwing the truck into drive. We lurch forward.

Bam! The back window erupts into shards. Tear gas hisses into the cab. "Throw—

My sentence isn't even out of my mouth, before she reaches down and tosses the tear gas out the window. She's fast, but not fast enough to prevent the reaction. Even with the windows open, we both start to hack. Wiping at my dripping nose, I swing down a side street. It's impossible to hide here. The whole thing is a grid.

Turning in her seat, she raises her gun.

"Careful. Civilians," I say, the warning in my voice obvious.

"I got this." She fires through the broken back window. Once. Twice. There's a shattering sound, and the spotlight winks out.

Nice shot. I take another turn. This is a shitty place to try to escape. Penned in like a damn prisoner on all sides, where people could pop out anywhere.

Sinuses burning, I tear down the road, straining to make out any movement from behind or ahead. Everything has gone remarkably quiet.

"Fucking contacts." Eyes tearing, Justice bends over and pulls out her contact lenses, then spits into her hands and tries to clear her eyes. "We can't go out the main gate."

"Agreed." A little respect or a *Thank you* would be nice. "Where'd you get inside?"

"Not far from here. I can show you. One sec." She slides to her open window and checks the area. "Slow down." She coughs into her hands. "They're not following."

I pull over. A glance behind us tells me she's right. Confused, I look to her. Her face is half-lit from a streetlamp and half in shadow. "Why aren't they chasing us?"

"Probably because we aren't making it easy. That shot... Things are getting messy. People will talk. Ask questions. And, like you said, people here could be hurt. Better to wait, then try to ambush us."

"Ambush how?"

She holds up her wrist. "I'm pretty sure they're tracking me. There's a device under my skin."

With a shuddering deep breath, I fill my aching lungs, trying to process her words while she picks up a penknife lying in a cup holder. She flicks it open and puts the knife to her wrist.

What the hell? I grab her hand. "Hold on. Let's think about this for a minute."

"Think about it? What's there to think about?"

I let go of her wrist, wiping the tears and snot from my face. Beautiful. "Let's not be rash. I need information. Where'd you get the tracker? How do the people chasing you have access to its technology?"

She stiffens. "I was born with it. Like an electronic birthmark."

"Okay, well, not telling me gets you nothing since I'm not an idiot and can put two and two together. You have the tracker because it's part of your job. These guys following you shouldn't know about it, and they sure as shit shouldn't be able to track you. Which means someone on your team is tracking you and reporting the information to whoever is chasing you."

She flinches, looking shaken for the first time since I met her. She places the knife against her skin again. "That's why I'm taking it out."

"For Christ's sake, wait. If you take it out and we escape, we lose a valuable opportunity. You go back home none the wiser or safer. It's better for us to handle this here."

"Us?"

"By setting up a reverse ambush—there's a perfect place not too far—we can stop them from following. Hell, we might even get lucky and get some intel."

As if all her muscles have failed her, her hand opens and the knife drops back into the cup holder, embedding itself in plastic. For a moment, she stares at me and then her open hand rises and clasps something under her abaya. "You're offering to help me?"

"Of course."

She whispers, "But why? I lied to you. Used you."

The galaxies in her eyes hold me as surely as the universe holds the sky. I've surprised her. And, honestly, myself, too, but even after all that's happened, I understand something in my bones. "Yes, but you also rescued Amal, and no matter what else any of this is, that wasn't self-serving."

Her hand fists her abaya. "I'm sorry I dragged you into this."

It's a small comfort, but I'll take it. I pull out the knife and close it, meeting her gaze again. "This is a short-term pass. After we get these guys, we go somewhere quiet, and you answer every question I have." I brush a finger along her wrist. "Including how you got this."

She snatches her hand away.

"You're going to fight me on this? Really?" Chick has teeth. I'm her only lifeline here. "I could walk away, and you *might*, judging by your skills, make it all the way home to safety."

She leans back, satisfaction and wariness on her face.

"Once there, you'll spend every waking minute wondering who betrayed you and if these men followed you back."

Her eyes widen—which is to say they swallow me whole—and then her rich, dark lashes lower. "An ambush sounds like a great idea. I'll show you the way out."

21

JUSTICE

Even in the dim light of the truck cab, I can see Sandesh's hands strangling the steering wheel. Yeah, the road is bumpy, but not that bumpy. He grumbles something and hits the steering wheel. Not sure I want to know what he's thinking.

I guess now that we're relatively safe and driving toward our ambush location, he's coming to terms with the facts of this night.

He's got reasons to be upset, so I'll just have to wait for my moment. I lean back and watch as the truck's headlights cut through the night like cones of yellow glass. The road's deserted. Not much call for traffic into Syria from Jordan these days, especially this late.

Except for the wind whining through the old weather strip and Sandesh's grumbling, this night has turned as solemn as a tomb.

I'm sure Sandesh expects an explanation. And the thing is, I *want* to explain things. Unusual for many reasons. First, I was brought up in a secret society of vigilantes—not an open-book kind of group. Second, I don't do relationships.

Biting back the urge to explain—and biting the inside of my cheek—I realize something has to break this thick silence. Well, if Sandesh is anything like Tony, I know how to get him to talk. "Stop pouting."

For a moment, he doesn't react. Then he glances at me with fury etched on that too-handsome face. "*Pouting*? No, Justice, you don't get to put this on me. I want an explanation. What are you doing here? Who were those men? Why were they after you?"

"I can't answer those questions."

With a sharp turn of the wheel, Sandesh swings the car to the side of the road.

I slide along the seat, my stitched side shooting off hot protestations.

Sandesh throws the car into PARK. Plumes of gray dust mushroom over the headlights.

Turning in his seat, his blue eyes stab me with ice and steel and accusation. "Actually, you have no choice—says the only guy willing to help you. I need to know what I'm up against."

Whoa. He's playing a dangerous game of chicken. If we're going to implement our plan, we need to keep moving.

I shift and roll my shoulders as if it's all the same to me. Silence, along with the vast cold of the desert night, quickly seep into the truck and my bones. We lock eyes for long moments that stretch into impossibly longer ones. I fist my hands in my lap. Tension rides my neck. Crap. Judging by Sandesh's chilly stare, he's not going to break first. I shiver, then give in for the sake of winning the larger battle. "Drive. I'll tell you what I can."

With the unhappiest winner's smile I've ever seen, he turns in his seat, shifts into drive, then peals onto the road, kicking up sand. The tires eat up ground with a steady chomping sound.

His patience snaps quickly. "Let's hear it, Justice."

Oh hell. "I do what Salma does. Sort of."

"Sort of?"

Damn, sharing the truth hurts. My chest feels like someone has taken a scalpel and cut strips called loyalty from my heart. I've never told this much to anyone before. It's about the hardest thing ever—though not quite as bad as facing the fact that one of my siblings has betrayed me. That makes this telling not only easier, but necessary.

"Salma helps the women and girls being lured or sold or tricked into sex slavery. I go after the men who are doing the luring, tricking, and selling."

In this instance, anyway. The Guild is just as likely to go after men who stone women, burn them with acid, beat them, gang-rape them, and commit femicide with impunity. Wherever society lets bad things happen to women, The Guild is there. No need to tell him that.

Sandesh breaths out a sound that's part curse. "But she saves girls. You aren't saving these men."

"No. I'm saving many girls and women by *killing* the men."

Shaking his head, he taps the steering wheel.

I'm not sure if that's disgust or curiosity on his face. Or maybe something more complicated.

"Your mother obviously knows. Is this what she does? Is this why she covers her face?"

"No." Anger at the suggestion drives my teeth together. Momma doesn't hide her face out of fear. "She was a teenager, a pre-teen really, when she refused a man. He attacked her with acid because of it. That man picked the wrong girl."

That gets another glance in my direction. Now, I can read his expression easily. Curiosity.

"I read that she was adopted from Pakistan by two wealthy women and brought to America. It would seem the happy end to a sad beginning. But she wasn't satisfied—she wanted vengeance?"

So not going to answer that. Subject change. "The men

who chased us work for a sex-slaver called Walid. Earlier tonight—or I guess that was yesterday now—I killed his brother. If I had gotten them both, their business would've crumbled."

"An underling wouldn't simply take over?"

"No. That's actually how they got their business. Killed the boss. Not wanting to meet the same fate, they hoard power and are militant about it actually, changing out their second-in-command regularly. So, it really is 'get the head of the snake and the rest collapses'. I would've gotten away clean yesterday but for Amal. Obviously, I couldn't leave her."

For a moment, only the sound of the tires spinning against the road fills the cab.

"I'd wondered why your mother would fund my charity."

Okay, he's not easily distracted—like a dog with a bone. No matter how I try to steer him away from Momma, he keeps going back to her.

"A start-up with no reputation. Obviously, that's exactly what she needed. Give them money, use them, control them, and I played right into it. Idiot."

I hate that he's angry with himself. Hate that I used him. I don't want him to feel suckered.

In the side-view mirror, I see only darkness behind us. We've been through so much since we left PA and it's not over yet. He deserves answers. "Remember what I told you on the plane about Hope?"

A long pause. "Yeah."

"The man I killed tonight killed Hope."

The wheels process earth as Sandesh drives in silence. I can practically hear when he realizes what happened tonight is very personal. A lifetime of plotting, planning, and pain.

"You're seeking revenge."

"No. I'm seeking what's right." I want to call it justice but hate puns that use my name. "And maybe a bit of redemption for not being able to help her. Isn't that why you started a charity? To seek redemption for a military life?"

Sandesh scratches roughly at the back of his head. "Redemption? No. Redemption indicates I thought what I did in the military was wrong. I didn't. I don't. I started my charity for another reason. And I don't expect you to understand right now because you're in the thick of it, but the kind of anger you have, the kind of anger I had... It doesn't go away when you take off the uniform or put down the gun, and that's something you need to learn to live with. Something you need to learn to understand."

I lean back, rest my head against the seat, and stare at him. I'm so tired right now, but I want to learn more about him. "You've never struck me as too angry."

"Trust me, if we had met a few years ago, it would've been one hell of an explosion. When I first left Special Forces, I'd had an excess amount of anger and no skills to diffuse it."

He did? We're more alike than I could've guessed. "I know that excess. I use it."

"Sure. I get that. As a Ranger, I had a place to direct it, a need to direct it, but when I got out... It became wild. Everyday, normal encounters would escalate and I'd find a way to fight my way through. Even if it was some dude trying to bring twenty items through the ten-items-or-less aisle."

A *lot* alike. Tonight, my rage had been unleashed on the world, and it'd felt justified. "Sometimes, you have to fight. Especially when there's no one else to do the job."

He exhales slowly through his teeth, a whistle of wind. "I know there's a place where you can't give an inch to the enemy. I've stood on that line. I've defended that ground, refused that inch, with every ounce of strength and courage and determination I possess. But once I no longer had to do that, I ended up trying to fight myself, trying to fight my way out of anger."

This strikes me as a battle I might need to wage someday. *If*

I'm lucky. "*Can* you fight your way out of anger? *Is* there an end?"

He looks at me, as if reading the sincerity in my face. He shakes his head. "No. I got out of it the opposite way."

He stops talking, but I don't press. I know there's more, and I also know it's not an easy tell, so I wait.

Five minutes pass before he speaks again. "A few months after leaving the service, my friend—the guy who'd eventually help me start the IPT, Victor Fuentes—asked me to go to Louisiana and help in his childhood neighborhood. They'd been hit by a hurricane. From the moment I had boots on the ground, I felt useful. It was kind of amazing, seeing so many people with no idea what to do, but we were soldiers, we knew how to organize, keep calm, work in tough situations. I helped for weeks and realized only after I got home that I never once felt rage.

"That's when I realized that part of me—that boy who'd tried to save the life of a dying bird, who thought that being a hero didn't mean crossing lines, needed…"

He stops again, releases another long breath that I'm sure includes more of the anger from earlier. "Does it make sense to you if I said he needed air?"

"Yeah. It makes perfect sense." I close my eyes for a moment, drift, for a second, into nothingness, then come back. "But that's exactly what my anger needs. What my cause needs. What women need. What Hope was denied. Air. And, if not me, then who?"

He shakes his head. "That's your choice, but I'm done with that chapter. I'm done walking through each day with my hands balled in fists. I'm done questioning when the violence I did helped, when it hurt, when it made a difference, when it fucked things up—fucked me up—when it saved people, or let people down. I'm done. Or, rather, I'd *thought* I was."

The last he doesn't say accusingly, doesn't even glance my

way, but I feel remorse like an iron-hot brand against my chest. My war doesn't involve him. Not if it's not what he wants. Not if he's forced into it.

I so want to tell him I'll make it right and get him back to where he should be. But, right now, any promise would sound hollow. And, judging by what we're about to get into, it might, in fact, be hollow. All I can do is apologize, for what that's worth. "I'm so sorry, Sandesh."

He doesn't accept the apology or tell me it's okay, but something in him seems to soften. "Do you feel better now? Less angry?"

If he'd asked me that with an ounce of sarcasm in his voice, I wouldn't answer, but he didn't. He asked as if sincerely interested. Which makes me think about the answer, think about the fact that earlier, I finally destroyed the man who destroyed Hope.

A chill works its way up my spine. "No." I turn from him and rest my head against the frosty window. "I feel tired. I've never been this tired before."

My body is telling me to sleep. It pulls me toward the dark, so I give in, drifting closer.

Sandesh's voice covers me as I succumb. "It's the adrenaline backlash. Murder does that."

22

JUSTICE

The abandoned village in Syria is more ruins than town. Crumbling structures of stone so bombed-out, they seem to be dissolving into sand.

The truck rocks and jolts as Sandesh maneuvers it inside the remains of a deteriorated building with only three sides. My wound screams like a banshee. Holy hell, I thought it'd hurt last night.

Sandesh wisely parks with the truck's grill pointed out the opening. That'll make it easier to get out of Dodge should we need to.

I climb out of the cab and make my awkward way over rocks and around the building. Surveying the main street and the remaining buildings, I begin to plot how this operation should go down as the cold night air sends my teeth chattering. It's downright chilly out here.

Sandesh joins me. "I've been here before. Managed to go through most of this place, but for a few buildings down here."

I nod. "Let's get to work."

We walk together, making a quick sweep of the buildings. We split up, checking out different sides of the street, weapons drawn, and on high-alert. I make my way inside an official-looking building with little damage.

It's as empty as it looks. Except...

"Sandesh." He comes running, and I hadn't even shouted for him.

"What's up?" He's scanning for danger, so it takes him a moment. Once he spots the ordinance, a smile stretches across his face.

"Will this work?" I ask, already knowing the answer.

"Oh yeah," he says, and we begin forming a plan, using not only the ordinance, but the one building left fully standing, as well as a blockage of rubble that damns up the other end of the street.

It happens quickly, the meshing of our personalities in this joint cause. We work well together. Sandesh is smart and considered, easily offering modifications of my grand ideas for simplicity's sake. We don't have time for much else.

Once we have a firm grasp of things, we get to work implementing the details. Even though I wish like hell I hadn't dragged him into this, it's great to have someone on my team.

When we're done, sweating despite the cold, we head back to our hiding spot. I nearly twist an ankle on the rocks as I'm climbing over them to the truck. Yeah, I'm that tired.

"I'm taking first watch," he says, picking his NVGs off the seat of the cab as he makes his way over rubble to the front of the building.

"No, I should—"

Glancing over his shoulder, he cuts me off with a look that will brook no argument.

I shrug acceptance. Too tired to fight with him.

With a winning smile, he climbs up another mound of rocks and sits in the empty husk of a blown-out stone window.

I take him in. He's steady and practiced as he scans the darkness with night vision goggles. My heart warms more than it should looking at him. I have to get control, but I'm a ball of confusion—though not just about him.

Honestly, I'm not sure if I want Sandesh to see someone or to *not* see someone following us. If Walid's thugs show up, it means they've followed my GPS, which then means that someone in my family gave them my location.

As hard as I'll fight, as hard as I know Sandesh will fight, there's no way to fight off the pain of knowing one of my one siblings has betrayed me. And not just betrayed me; they want me dead. Being stabbed in the chest would hurt less.

Sandesh looks down at me. "Nothing so far. Check your bandages."

Even though I'd love to end this here tonight so that Sandesh can go back to his work, I'm relieved by his announcement. I follow his directions, checking the bandage on my wrist where Sandesh took out the tracker. He has some skill. My wrist doesn't hurt near as bad as my damn side. Not shot? Really?

My wrist is worth every bit of pain to know no matter what happens tonight, these men won't be able to follow us farther than this village.

Per our plan, we left the tracker in a building across the street. Even if they can't pinpoint exactly where I am—though the cell service here is surprisingly good—that building is the most obvious for someone to hide because it's the most intact.

"Justice?"

Damn. I feel the tendrils of his voice work through my body like a hook, latching on to me, pulling me toward him.

I look up.

Small rocks tumble down from the window as he lifts himself onto the balls of his feet. Rifle across his lap, he reaches down and brushes stones from under his fine ass. He nods toward me. "I just thought of something. You should take that off."

My eyes go wide. He grins, but I don't have the heart to flirt. I hate the waiting, the waiting and not knowing is the worst. I tug at my abaya. "I don't have anything else to wear."

"Check my weapons bag. I took it the other night when I went with Salma to Syria. It's in the back of the truck cab. There're extra clothes and a bulletproof vest."

The clothes will be too big, but I honestly don't care. "You wear the vest."

"No, you'll be the one out in the open. Put it on."

I don't bother to argue. His tone tells me it'd be useless. I hate that tone.

Wobbling back across the rocks and demolished concrete, ankles barking in these rubber-soled shoes, I open the door. The light stays out because we'd disabled it.

I pull out the bag, find the clothes, then lift off the abaya. My side yelps in protest and I suck in a breath.

Sandesh's head whips toward me.

"I'm fine," I toss back, happy—for some insane reason—that I stand here half naked.

He clears his throat, shifts, and I look up to see him turning away. Such a gentleman.

Shame. I put on the bulletproof vest—it chafes around my shoulders. Over that, I add the too-big shirt, rolling up the sleeves as tight as fists. The pants I roll to the ankles, folding them twice at the waist. Not good enough.

Having seen it a moment earlier, I take out the KA-BAR combat knife and use it to cut a series of holes in the rolled-up waist. Luckily, I don't stab myself by moonlight.

I complete my ensemble by tearing my head scarf into strips and threading it through the holes in my pants, tightening so they don't fall off while running. I then make sure my beggars-can't-be-choosers Glock 20—hello, future carpal tunnel—has a full clip.

It does.

I hear the movement on the road a split-second before Sandesh's warning.

"They're coming."

A sharp slice of pain pierces my heart. My throat tightens. I'd expected it. Of *course*, I'd expected it, so why does it hurt so badly? Why does it feel like one of my siblings just stabbed me in the back?

Lights from the approaching vehicle bounce between the gaps of stone. I duck down and move around the truck.

Sandesh slides from the window and holds up two fingers. Two cars? Shit. Not good.

Heart in my throat, I creep forward and crouch beside him. Balanced on a pile of debris, we watch the scene through broken gaps in the wall.

The cars slide to a stop, one behind the other. The first blocks the second from our sight line. That makes things difficult.

The four men in the first car exit and go toward the decoy building. The men in the second—impossible to tell how many —stay put. Cautious fuckers. And smart.

I inch toward Sandesh. He smells like action, as if his pheromones coat the air in an excited combination of sweat and intent.

I flick my head to the side.

He nods.

Game on.

Taking a breath, I slip away, out a side door, then around the building. Outside, I crouch-run, keeping to the path we'd cleared earlier. When I stop by the mountain of debris that's dammed the whole street, my focus is tight and my breath controlled. This barricade, erected at some point in this country's sad history, plays a huge part in our plans.

I give Walid's men plenty of time to get deep into the building. Hands as steady as steel, I take out Sandesh's cell. We've rigged my burner phone to the explosives we found. The good thing about being in a war zone: abandoned ordinance.

I tap in the number and wait for the boom. Nothing. Something's wrong.

Holding my breath, I put in the number again. Still nothing.

Okay. Backup plan.

Heat fills my limbs. My ears fill with pressure. My heart fills with dread. In a crouch, I race along the hidden side of the barricade. My footing teeters as I try to avoid debris, barely keeping my balance, as I cloak my actions in silence.

Once across the street, sweat rolls into my eyes. My heart refuses calm like a bull refusing a rider. The cars are diagonal to my position. From here, I can see the second car has tinted windows. No idea who's inside, but one guy stands outside the car, using night vision goggles to scan the building Sandesh hides behind.

Two other men watch the rigged building. There could be more in the tinted window vehicle. So, how many inside? The answer is not nearly fucking enough.

Snake-on-a-hot-road fast, I scurry through the five feet of open ground where the barrier ends and the building beings. My heart in my throat, my gun in my hand, I'm counting steps. One. Two. Three-four-five. Safely behind the building, I swipe the sweat from my eyes and make my way to where we threaded the fuse. I crouch so my back—and this *so* doesn't feel right—is to the men in the cars. I can't risk them seeing me light this thing.

Fingers shaking, her heart squawking and clucking like a chicken, I take out my lighter and jam my hand into the fire hole. It's deep enough to block any sparks, but I'm not taking a chance. My hand shakes as I put thumb to wheel and spin. An orange light bursts to life. I touch the flame to the sharp point of the fuse. It takes a breath-holding second for it to catch, hiss, and spit fire as the light races away.

Spinning, I race to the edge of the building. Shit. A guy is headed in this direction. I've got no time for subtlety. The fuse isn't that damn long. Fuck it. Things are going to explode.

I break cover, shoot the man who is close enough that I clearly hear his grunt of pain, and run like hell.

My eyes track poorly in the dark, but I keep firing until I make the relative safety of the barrier. Skidding down behind it, I lope forward, uncoordinated and uncertain, like a gangly puppet. Hotfooting it over the rocks, my ankles scream with each unexpected test of balance.

Gunshots glance off the top of the barrier. Tiny explosions of sand, grit, and powdered stone rain down, pelting me. I imagine the men walking closer, firing as they go.

This visual is solidified in my mind when I hear shots being fired from where Sandesh is stationed.

Fuck. When is that building going to bl—

Boom!

A plume of smoke and dust rise into the air with the concussive wave. I hit the ground, shield my head. There's an ominous moan, like from an ancient warrior who's taken one too many arrows, and then a *crash!*. Rumbles of stone against stone and a wave of heat pounces over the barrier, bringing a hot spray of gravel.

Despite my attempt at protection, dust and grit steamroll the air, coat my lashes, rush down my throat and into my esophagus. Hacking, I shake out my hair, crawl forward blinking dirt-caked eyes. My ears ring. My head spins.

Smoke and gray dust are so thick in the air, I can barely see. A grinding crash of steel and tires against stone has me looking up as rocks landslide down. Jumping back, I gape at the top of the constructed hill where headlights teeter. How the hell?

The car rocks at the top of the barrier, vacillating like a seesaw, front wheels beating against air. Two blurry shapes fling themselves out.

I run. Gunfire follows me, spitting up rocks and heat. I look back. One of the men disappears before my eyes. Well, part of his head explodes with a spray of bullets and the man pitches backward down the other side of the barrier.

Sandesh has some skills.

The other man charges down the barrier, knees bending, feet sliding. He's obviously trying to avoid his partner's fate and still get me.

Mistake.

I swing around, shoot, and he goes down.

Back behind the relative safety of the building, I race for the truck. "Let's go!" I call to Sandesh over the firefight.

Sandesh motions me to get into the truck before he launches a grenade—like a baseball—up and out of the window he'd been sitting in earlier.

He's down the pile of debris and into the cab before the explosion hits. We take off as a concussive boom rocks the air.

Driving like a maniac, bouncing us out and around the building, Sandesh gives me his assessment: "Five, likely six, left."

Clear of the building, we head the opposite direction from the barrier.

"Damn it. I thought I killed more than that."

He grunts, steers around a corner. "Don't lack for confidence, do you?"

Since there's no other clear way out, we break from the relative safety of the side street onto the main drag. We instantly take fire. Bullets *ding* into the steel hull.

He jams the gas.

I turn in my seat, pinning my spine to the dash, and my feet to the back of the seat. "Steady!" I shout, seeing an opportunity.

I shoot as a man runs from cover toward the second car, which stops to collect him.

Boom, boom, boom.

"Got one."

"As fast as we're going? More likely, he tripped."

He should have more trust in my abilities. I slide a bit as he dodges a chunk of concrete and then swings right as the second car catches us. The truck rocks. We're nearly upended.

The moment we're steady, I hook my arm around the headrest, hang out the window, and pull out a grenade.

"Justice, don't!"

Ignoring him, I lean far out, pluck the pin between my teeth, then toss it, wild-thing style.

Ba-boom!

The truck jerks forward. I crash back against my seat, watch as Sandesh glances through his rearview and spots the car, lit by orange flames.

Stunned, he looks over at me. "You hit them."

Shrugging, I lean back. "They weren't that far away."

23

JUSTICE

Hair still damp from my much-needed shower, cross-legged on the edge of the lumpy bed, dressed in panties and a t-shirt, I hold my recently acquired burner cell to my ear.

This Israeli hotel room is claustrophobic, heavy with the smell of overly used bleach. Not even enough room to pace, but better than dead.

And a lot better than where I slept last night. Thanks goes to Victor, Sandesh's partner, who, apparently, has more contacts than the CIA. He was able to get us over King Hussein Bridge, into the West Bank, and to this hotel. Though his contact refused to give us his name, he provided us with food, water, a bit of cash, and clothes.

Not that I'm about to tell Momma that. Bad enough that the sound of Sandesh in the pipe-rattling shower nearly drowns out her voice.

"Justice, I need to know what you've told this young man."

A lump rises into my throat. I don't lie to Momma. Well, not about important stuff. Here it goes. "He knows nothing about

The Guild." I swallow what feels like betrayal. Technically, he doesn't know about The Guild *specifically*.

Momma makes a stern *tsk*ing sound. "M-erasure is painless. Harmless. And in his case, we only need to alter his memory very slightly. Not removing actual events but shifting just those moments of heavy suspicion and distrust, where he suspected you and our operation. When he thinks of it, he will dismiss his suspicions and be reassured it was the price of doing business in the area. Nothing more."

Harmless? Really? Momma *would* see it that way. But just because you employ and train some of the greatest scientists in the world, women who could not only implant memories but also erase them, didn't mean you should use that power. Not on Sandesh anyway.

"Leave this to me. I've got him."

Momma makes another soft sound, letting me know she's not onboard with that plan.

Shit. I'll deal with that threat once I get home. "Did you take care of security at the school?"

"Of course. I increased it, but you need not worry. We already have the best security of any school in the world."

Momma. She doesn't mess around.

"Justice, we have some time. Walid will surely mourn his brother and lick his wounds. You've done well. Our informant tells me their operation has already ground to a halt in Za'atari."

That's something—a bit of relief—since the pleasure I'd thought I'd feel after killing the man who'd killed Hope hasn't materialized. And, in fact, the regret of destroying Salma's and Sandesh's good work and putting Salma's family in danger overrides most everything right now.

"Are Salma and Amal okay?"

"Yes. Victor, has taken care of them. He mobilized his

volunteers at a speed that I envy. They've replaced her truck, and seen them and Salma's family to safety."

Amazingly, Victor managed to locate and organize two former soldiers fighting with the Kurds. Even now, they're protecting Salma and the women she'd rescued in a secure location while they wait for the volunteers from the States to arrive in Jordan. Sandesh managed to get his buddy to help while keeping my secrets—which is why I'm not giving Momma anything on him. Plus, I owe him my life.

"How long until you arrange to get me out of here?"

"A few days. I'm working on covering up your abrupt departure."

"Am I a suspect?"

"No. You did good going to Za'atari. There is no one to connect Justice Parish with what happened at the hotel."

The running shower stops. "Okay. Thanks for all your help. Got to go. Love you."

"Love you, daughter."

Lying back on the bed, I tuck the phone under my pillow and listen. I can hear Sandesh moving in the bathroom, hear him grab a towel and dry off. There'd been only one towel, so he's using the one I used.

Strange, but I can't help smiling at the idea of him wiping himself down with a towel that has been against my body. I imagine him all sexy, wet, and naked, moving the towel across his chest, biceps, and abs. Lower.

I close my eyes and force myself to stop the mental ogling. The guilt over involving Sandesh in all of this, risking so much, so many, makes me want to deprive myself of every little pleasure. Even the ones only in my head.

Facing the surprisingly elaborate, wooden bathroom door, I curl up into a fetal position and remind myself Aamir is dead. *I did that.*

The door opens. Sandesh walks into the room, bringing the

smell of hotel soap and warm steam. He's wearing only boxers and has the abs and pecs of a man who needs no help getting laid. Damn.

Seeing me checking him out, a grin spreads across his handsome face. "'Shall I compare thee to a summer's day? Thou art more lovely.'"

Snort. He left out the "more temperate" part of that line.

"So, in addition to being smoking hot in boxers and providing expert cover fire, you also recite Shakespeare. Guess that's not something you learned in the military."

He strolls to the bed. His eyes jump along my body, the curve of my hip and up. He shakes his head, stops before sitting on the bed. "As a kid, my mom read poetry and Shakespeare to me."

"Was she okay when you called?"

"She's doing the same. Victor goes over nearly every night and reads Shakespeare to her

while she eats dinner. He says sometimes she likes it."

"Victor of the many contacts sounds like a good guy."

"He is. Most of the time. He's a bit of a flirt." That last seems almost like a warning. His eyes wander again down my body, then back up to my face. "He would like you."

"What about you? Do *you* still like me?"

The bed dips with his weight as he finally sits, close enough I can feel the moisture and heat on his skin, see the sky-blue of his eyes grow serious, detect a subtle tightening along his sharp, kissable jaw. This can't be good.

"You're a vigilante and you've started a war that risked my life, my charity, and the lives of many good and hardworking people."

Okay. We're going there.

I rise up, so we're eye level, because I don't like to be in a position of weakness, even when I feel guilty. Especially when I feel guilty. "No. Men started the war. I'm just defending my sisters."

"*Men*? Not me. I didn't start this war. You dragged me into it."

True enough. "But you're a good man; why not fight bad ones?"

Anger flashes across his face and his lips thin. "Because I've tried that way. Tried it until I didn't recognize myself, and that's not my job anymore. There has to be more than that, Justice. Helping in *that* way can't be my only choice."

Not just handsome, but right. It is his choice. Like it's my choice to fight. "I'm sorry."

Again, he doesn't accept the apology, but continues to stare at me.

I don't hide myself, don't hide my desire as my eyes chart the muscles in his forearms, the length of his fingers, the spread of his hand. Strong and gentle. I want to know more of him. I want to know *all* of him. "What made you decide to do this, to start a charity? Was it just that experience you had helping Victor? Or was there more?"

Unexpectedly, he starts to get up.

I stop him, putting a hand on his thigh. I swear I can feel my palm burning a brand into all his muscle and tension.

He looks at me for a long, long moment, then runs his thumb along my brow, across the edge of my eyes, and whispers, "Your eyes are endless."

He drops his hand, clears his throat. "Partly, my time with Victor. Partly, my mom getting Early-Onset Alzheimer's. It made me realize I wanted to create more good memories. I saw what the bad memories did to her. The terror of an abusive relationship she escaped too late, one that is now part of her waking nightmare, but it was also... my own nightmare."

"The one from the plane?" When he nods but doesn't

answer, I press. "You have to know that I'll listen without judgment. Trust that I'll keep your secrets like you've kept mine."

"It's not that I don't trust you. It's that... you have your own shit, Justice. You don't need to carry mine around, too."

What? That's why he didn't tell me on the plane? "So, what? I burdened you when I told you about Hope?"

His eyebrows raise as if he hadn't thought of it that way before. Heat flushes up his face.

I sigh. "Men. Sometimes they get such a bad deal. Don't share. Be tough. *Sheesh*. Tell me."

He takes another moment to chew on it before saying, "I was on a mission in Syria. We were training the FSA."

"FSA? Free Syrian Army? The good guys, right?"

"They weren't the good guys, but a whole lot better than the Syrian president, Assad. Trainees usually met us in Qatar, but we'd been sent into Syria. We were close by when Assad dropped a barrel bomb filled with chemicals on the local girls' school."

He scratches hard behind his ear, as if digging out a memory. "Someone had a hose out, trying to wash the girls. The kids were screaming. Frantic. A young girl came running at me. I mean *directly* at me. I didn't even think. I just picked her up. Her skin sloughed off in my hands."

My stomach turns over. "Oh God."

"Yeah. I didn't know what to do. Nearly vomited. One of my team had called for an extraction earlier. He alerted me to the helo. I started to walk toward the LZ. Thought I could get her to safety. I was so tense with anger I could feel it harden my veins. The kid was shaking like a leaf in my arms when she reached up to me. The bones... The little bones in her hand were visible." He rubs his eyes, but I don't miss the tears. "Before she died, she said, 'Poppa, don't be angry. There is more.'"

More. More than violence. More than pain.

He's reaching for the pot at the end of the rainbow. Maybe

not something that easy, but a way to feel something other than anger. And he deserves that. He deserves the other side of the coin. He's fought enough.

Something in my chest, a kind of hopeful ache, moves forward as if seeking him. "What did it mean to you when she said that? The *more* part?"

"It could've meant nothing to me, and in that moment of intense rage, it should've, but I knew exactly what she meant. She was telling me that as total and awful and fucked up as that moment was, it wasn't all there was to life. She was telling me to keep going. Reminding me my life wouldn't end that day. For me, there would be a lot more than the moment of violence that ended her life, even more than the violence I'd participated in. And she was telling me it was okay for me to have that more. So now, I'm trying to make my more be a way to help others, kids like her."

Aw, hell. There's so much I want to say, so much about my goals and reasoning, but I can't take this moment from him, twist it back to me. Instead, I rise to my knees. "I'm sorry, Sandesh. Sorry I dragged you into this. I'm going to make this right. I promise."

I run a hand along his clean-shaven jaw. It's smooth and still damp. I feel compelled, called by his skin. I kiss him there, suck away that moisture.

His breath catches with a gust of minty toothpaste.

Moving up, I kiss the side of his lips. He sits deadly still, but I can tell he wants me. So says the boner tenting his boxers. I kiss along and up his jawline until my tongue reaches that soft place below his ear. I lick.

"Justice." He sighs my name. A plea. A prayer. A promise.

I sweep my tongue inside his ear and breathe, "Sandesh."

He moans a sound so hot it burns away walls. Invitation is in that sigh, and I take it, wrapping an arm around his neck and tugging him forward as I lean back. He rolls on top of me, solid and hard. His eyes search mine for the answer my wet core is already giving him. I arch, letting him know with the rise of my body that I want this.

His body pressed so intimately against me I can feel the pulse in his cock. He closes his eyes. "Justice, let's share details. I had a whole workup before I left the States. I don't have any STIs, but I also don't have a condom. So...?"

His battle for control as I writhe under him might be the hottest thing I've ever seen. And that *shouldn't* seem like an opportunity, but it does. I grip his ass and make pleading sounds. The man of steel, my new nickname for him, shakes his head and tries to lift off. I put my arms around his waist and hold on tight. *You are not going anywhere.*

He moans. "One of us has to think here, and it's getting really difficult for me to think with you rocking under me."

That's kind of the point, but he's too cool for school. I put a palm against his face, wait for him to look at me.

He does. He stares at me like it would cause pain for him to look away.

"I'm tested regularly. All good. And the GPS isn't the only thing implanted. I'm on the pill. Long-term. But I don't want you to stop thinking. I want you to think. Be aware of this moment with me. Feel it with me. Don't let go of this day, this room, us. Stop talking. Be with me. Please."

I lift up and kiss him, drawing it out before I sweep my tongue into his mouth. I probe the slick, soft connection between us first gently, then with growing urgency until there is a fire raging between us.

He responds in kind, meeting me stroke for desperate stroke.

He feels so good, I want to shout with the pure, electric joy of him against me. Skin. I need...

Pulling at his boxers, I demand, "Off."

He blinks at me and rolls off, complying with a speed I now

match. It feels like an eternity that we're apart, but it's only seconds until we unite with a groan, hot skin against hot, smooth skin. Glorious. I'm wet and crazed with the need to have him inside me.

I reach for his cock. "Please."

I feel him smile against my mouth as he pushes said cock against my hand. I whimper.

He says, "I want to kiss you first."

What?

He kisses his way down, sucking at my breasts, stomach, then moving to my center.

I arch expectantly as he brings his lips down around my clit. I gasp at how incredibly good his soft tongue feels.

He begins to suck and lick and stroke me, and I am helpless. My head falls back and I moan loudly, repeatedly.

He's so good at this. His tongue dances along my edges, dips inside, until I lose my mind. I thread hands into his hair, press myself hard against his mouth. The sweet, unyielding pressures builds and builds. The orgasm is tantalizingly close, but I want...

I grab his broad shoulders, pull him. "I want to come around your cock."

He growls approval and need, shifting over me so his cock rests between my legs. He lowers his head, kisses along my cheek as he pushes inside.

I cry out, filled with him, so hot and thick, the most perfect feeling that I can't imagine anything better, until he thrusts.

Better. So... much... better.

He begins to thrust and retreat, deep then shallow, deep then shallow.

I rock my hips, keeping pace, making desperate sounds of want and need and please-don't-stop.

He responds by thrusting harder and faster.

I'm thanking him and moaning and pumping my hips to

meet the slam of him. My core grows tighter, tighter, impossibly tight around him then... I break. Tremors release and pound over and through me.

Waves of shuttering vibrations kept me moving, grinding and moaning against him. I'm distantly aware that he watches me, drinks in my curves, slick with sweat.

I slow my frantic hips. My body melts around him. My nerve endings celebrate with continuing shocks and tremors.

He kisses my lips, teases my mouth open as he put his hands under my ass, scoops me up, and slides his knees under me. I'm boneless as he drapes my legs, one and then the other, against his chest, my ankles up by his ears.

The elevated position gives him better access. And me less control. Not that I'm complaining.

"Justice," he whispers, "watching you come is the sexiest thing I've ever seen." Then he plunges thick and heavy inside me.

Air breaks from me in a startled grunt.

He moans a rough oath, a gritty promise followed by the single-minded declaration in the slap and slam of his body.

He thrusts deep and fast, but not mindlessly. He watches me so completely, so fixedly, that the action of his hips meets the sighs on my lips. His hard body responds to me, sliding against my pleasure points, teasing helpless cries and soft moans from me.

His own desire lines his brow, tightens his jaw, parts his lips.

When the second orgasm crests inside me, I can see the knowing in his eyes, feel it in the increased speed of his hips. *Oh. God. Talk about sexy.*

The sharp muscles of his stomach coil. The lines of his biceps stand out as he squeezes my ass and drives into me.

I rock with him, the pressure rolled up so tight, I can't take it. It's too much.

The electric, hot feel of him stretching me... the look on his face... the heat of him... Too... much.

I come again, the swell and roll wracking my body, sending me heaving back against the pillow, whimpering and calling out his name. It feels like dying, like nothing exists in the world but the trembling, hot push of his body into mine.

He responds to my cries with a hot groan before he loses himself. Thrusting without rhythm or control, he breaks, hot and heavy, inside of me. Slick heat pulses out from him. I can feel every bit of his release. With a final thrust and moan, something that sounds like willing surrender, he unwinds my legs, then collapses beside me.

Kissing my forehead, he draws me closer, nuzzles my ear. The sound of our heavy breaths fills the room for quiet, comfortable moments. And then he starts laughing.

Okay. Apparently, I'm amusing. Not insulting or anything. Not at all.

He says, "The way you move—all gyrations and fury. Damn. I can't get enough of it."

If it weren't for his tone, a hot whisper of satisfaction, I might find that a bit annoying. "And that amuses you?"

"I love how carried away you get."

Uh? What? Doesn't everyone? "You have had sex before, right?"

He chuckles again, moves his head down on the pillow so his mouth is closer to my ear. "I'm not saying it's a bad thing. It's a good thing. You're easy to read."

"I'm easy? Careful, charmer." I grin at him, enjoying this part. Who knew pillow talk could be fun?

He uses his thumb to brush a strand of hair from my cheek. "You tell me what you want with the double-pump action of your tits and hips. And those *yes-there* sighs and the way you beg. Oh God, the way you beg me not to stop. Like I have a fucking choice. Like seeing you moan and grind under me does anything but make me too crazy to do anything but lose myself fast and sloppy inside you."

Huh. I still don't get why he's so amused, but it doesn't seem like a bad thing. "So, you're saying you really like having sex with me. Like, it's the best sex ever. And you're helpless under the spell of my hot, heaving body."

It takes him a second before he speaks, but, finally, he does. "I'm saying..." He stops again, thinks, and I realize he's taking my joke way too seriously. "You asked me earlier if I still like you. I do. A lot. More than I have any other woman in a long, long time. Maybe ever."

My cold, cold heart melts. He's not allowed to be so sweet. It makes me feel so guilty. Because, as soon as my transportation is arranged, I'm going to ditch his sweet ass and get back home to run interference with Momma. For his own good, because Momma's words, *"M-erasure is painless,"* chills me through and through.

I won't let Momma take advantage of him anymore. No. He's sacrificed enough for my mission, a mission that's in no way his. He's a good man and should be free to do his good work. Which means keeping him away from Momma.

But, first, I'm going to fuck this deliciously sweet man until his eyes roll back into his head. Fuck him until he can do nothing but pass out. I'll leave him, yes, but I'll leave him satisfied—and sans passport, visa, and identification. Good luck getting out of Israel, buddy. No point telling him that. He definitely wouldn't understand.

I snuggle closer. "Get some sleep, charmer. In a little while, I'm going to wake you up so you can show me again just how deeply you like me."

He snorts.

I kiss the crook of his arm and inhaling the musk of him, decide there's nowhere else I'd rather be right now than pressed up against this man.

24

SANDESH

I roll onto my side and watch sunlight play across the lean curves of Justice's sleeping body. At some point, the stitches in her side bled through the bandage. The bloodstain is dry and dark now. There are other scars here and there, some savage, some delicate.

They tell a story of survival and sadness. Such an amazing person, complicated and interesting, caring and dedicated. I move closer to her, pressing my hard-on against her smooth leg.

Eyes still closed, she smiles.

I press closer and she giggles, turning so that her sleek, wet core is right against me. That's exactly what I wanted. "Oh, Sandy, did you want something?"

Sandy? I haven't heard that since grade school. Not a fan. "You. In every way imaginable. Back, front, over, and under me."

She laughs in a way I don't like. I know enough about Justice, learned through repeated exchanges, that she likes to joust. If last night was any indication, sometimes her jousting involves games of teasing. I do not want to be teased right now. I want to fuck.

Maybe she needs convincing. I run a hand along her breast and the tip perks up.

She hums an "*Oh*", then grabs my hand and pushes it aside.

Yep, Justice wants to play.

She bats her big, dark, magic and mystery eyes at me and begins to sing that song from *Grease*. Which is a boner-killer, nearly.

Honestly, how can anyone ever be stranded at a drive-in? Aren't there like a thousand people there with cars? "Stop that."

She sings faster, louder now wanting high school to be done.

The stanzas aren't even in the right order. "You're bringing up some really painful childhood memories."

She laughs and keeps singing.

Smiling myself at her joy, I cover her mouth.

In a flash, flames spring into her eyes. She knocks my hand away, rolls on top of me, and glares down. "Don't ever put your hand over my mouth."

Why did she just react as if I'd held a knife to her throat—oh, shit. Her history comes back to me with excruciating awareness. Boundary alert times a thousand. I'm such an idiot. "Sorry, Justice, I wasn't thinking."

Seated on top of me, she waits like a cat for a mouse to come out of its hole.

Feeling awful and regretful, I don't move. Well, *most* of me doesn't move. Part of me is swelling against her. I'm not sure what it says about my degenerative nature that I'm hoping we can get past this and have sex. Preferably soon.

That cat-like smile on her face and an equally mischievous glint in her eyes, she starts singing that song again. This time, there's an air of teasing.

I guess all is forgiven and we're back where we started: with her issuing a challenge to my manhood.

I'm game.

Driving my hips up fast and hard, I lift her into the air, shoot up into a seated position, then catch her carefully in my lap, so that we're face-to-face. On equal terms.

She curses and glares at me, and I begin to think I've misread the situation. It would really help my reasoning abilities if a pissed-off Justice wasn't the hottest thing I've ever seen, and if my cock understood when to stand down. Her wetness pressing against me is sending an entirely different message.

Trying to manage my feelings and hers, I put my hands on her shoulders. "Stop squirming, Justice. I want to talk."

Her left fingers snap out, jab me in the neck, and send me into a coughing fit. I'm struggling for air when she pushes me flat onto the bed, straddles my middle, and presses her knees onto my biceps, grabbing my wrists. Damn it, how did I misread her so completely?

There's a serious challenge on her face... alongside decades-old rage. What started out as playful wrestling has taken a turn that borders on a test. I have no idea what she wants right now.

She puts her face within inches of mine. "What are you going to do?"

Yep, this is very much a test of some kind, and I'm probably going to fail because every instinct in my body is screaming for me to use my strength to flip her over and take control. It's an intensely real moment to be caught in, where my cock and fists are equally hard, but instinctual reactions haven't had the ability to override my reasoning for many years.

Sucking in a breath, I calm the emotion and see her pain instead. I scared her, challenged her, and she feels vulnerable. Probably confused as well.

All of this pours into my consciousness as she continues to

play her game of control. I see it all as she rolls her ass across my hard-on—that's her way of egging me on—but there are other, more important signs.

Like the strength she puts into holding me down, her hands tightening around my wrists much harder than necessary, causing her forearms to tense so much I can see her veins.

For her, this has stopped being a game, and she needs me to prove I won't use strength against her, even if she's taunting me. She's asking if she can trust me.

If she were any other person, I'd probably buck her off, stand up, and leave.

But this is Justice and I desperately want to know her. And I want her to know me. Know that I would never purposefully cross any line she's uncomfortable with, not emotionally and not physically. I messed up a moment ago, misunderstanding what she needed from me, but now that I see it, I'm still game.

Gritting my teeth, I hold absolutely still as she rolls her ass across the tip of my cock. She's torturing me and we both know it because my breathing is loud enough to testify to my absolute agony.

For a long moment she stares at me with her dark eyes walking the edge between teasing and serious, wanting and fury.

She begins to hum that song again as the softest part of her body, the moist wetness, gyrates against me, and this might be the hardest thing I've ever done. Literally. I'm going to explode.

Humming louder, she increases the friction.

My body responds automatically, but I squelch any instinct to move. More than anything I want her to trust me so I wait for her to get it, wait for her to see there's nothing she can do to make me cross that line. Wait for her to understand that she is completely safe with me.

A well-worn Shakespeare phrase filters through my head as I watch the play of emotions across her face. *If you prick us, do we not bleed? If you tickle us, do we not laugh? If you poison us, do we not die? And if you wrong us, shall we not revenge?*

I have the good sense to keep that quiet.

This torturous, sweet friction has me feeling like I'm winning as much as losing.

When she eases up, she smiles as if we've reached some kind of understanding.

I see the shift, see the gratitude that I know she won't express verbally.

She lowers her face to mine and whispers, "I like you."

With those words, the tension in her hands relaxes and she kisses me long and deep, setting fire to my already thrumming body. Again, she whispers, "I really like you."

Her soft lips press mine, then slip to my chin, neck, and down to the hollow at the base of my neck. She strokes my biceps, chest, while rolling her hips simultaneously against my cock.

I fist the sheets to keep my hands to myself because I get that she needs to be in the driver's seat right now, and I really want to see where this ride takes us.

With a deep moan, she sucks on her pinky fingers, then trails her hot lips, kissing, down my abs until she gets to... oh, God...

She sucks my cock into her mouth, without using her hands, which are busy sending my senses reeling, as her pinky slowly circles and enters me from behind. So smooth and sweet and talented. She knows exactly what she's doing to me as her tongue moves against the head of my cock.

Her mouth grinds lower, adding pressure and releasing in a pace that's excruciatingly good. There is no control as I moan and buck into her mouth. She takes all of me, fingering me while stroking the base of my cock with her other hand. Sucking me off and gyrating the tip of her finger inside my ass.

I've had blowjobs before, had amazing blowjobs before, but I had no idea anything could feel so fucking good.

She sucks and rolls and pumps with a faster pace and I realize I have lost all control. I try to rein it in, try not to—

"Fuck. Yes. Justice. Fuck!" The orgasm slams into me as hard and uncontrollable as a summer storm. Exploding, I rock into her mouth as she sucks me down, her eyes dipping closed.

When the final shocks of pleasure recede, my body collapses back against the mattress, and she sits up and wipes her mouth with the back of her hand. I want to reach for her, grab her, hold her, but she's absorbed every bit of energy out of me.

I'm too satiated to stir when she flops on top of me, grinning like she's won the trophy, has the blue ribbon and the crown. And, damn, yes, I'll give her all of that. The smell of her, a combination of Justice and my musk has me closing my eyes in deepest satisfaction.

I kiss the top of her head, find my voice, barely, and promise her, "In two hours, I'm going to wake up and return the favor. Then I'm going to roll you over and fuck you until you scream my name."

She chuckles, low and sultry. "I'll set my clock."

25

JUSTICE

Two hours ends up being four, but in every other way, Sandesh proves as good as his word. Electric zings still ricochet inside me from the orgasm that made me scream his name.

Now, his strong hands grip my sides and flip me over. He pulls me over to the side of the bed, and I oblige with a happy little raise of my hips. Still not high enough, so he positions me on all fours and slaps me lightly across my ass.

Saucy. I look back at him and my heart fills with something both joyful and painful. It's more emotion than I'm used to and I need to move past it. Quickly.

"Ready when you are."

He grins and shoves himself inside me so fast that I gasp. There's nothing better than the feel of him entering and filling me. Except... He grasps my hips and drives into me again and again. Oh. Yes. That. Much better.

I moan with pleasure, so he knows exactly how very good this feels. He picks up the pace. The friction is so good, my body begins to hum with each slap of his body.

The heat and pressure build, a quick and coiled energy that

pulls at my core,. I'm almost gone when Sandesh reaches around and rubs his thumb against my clit. I cry out, rock frantically back into him, slamming against his every demanding thrust.

Losing his tempo, he curses hotly, then regains control, and keeps pace for me. His thumb moves wetly against me as the orgasm breaks, racking me from the inside out.

Sandesh lets out a grown that's part relief, part single-minded intent. His fingers dig into my hip bones. He pushes wild and hard, sending the tingles of my orgasm rippling through me.

His pace shatters. "Justice," he breathes.

My name on his lips surrounds me like a declaration, and the thick heat of his come fills me like a confirmation.

A moment later, he pulls out and I crawl up the bed, leaving a space he quickly fills. I press myself to his front, and he snakes his arms around me. The blessing of him, this moment, is not lost on me. Or him. We stare at each other. The space between us heats with our heavy breaths.

When our breathing slows, his eyes turn serious and caring. He says, "In all the things I've seen, places I've been, women I've known, you are so solely unique, so fully yourself that..." He trails off, traces my lips, nose, and cheek with his finger. "If I were a writer, I could use words to tell you. A sculptor, clay. An artist, paint." He runs his hand along my body and cups my ass. "But I'm a soldier, and all I have is my allegiance, so that's what I'll use."

He rests his forehead against mine. "Someone has betrayed you. You're in danger from them and Walid. I might not have started this war, but I'm in it now. With you. Where you go, I go."

I can now see in his gaze, the declaration his body gave me moments ago. Overwhelmed, I can't speak and don't try because he's looking at me as if seeing something wondrous. As if, somehow, I've killed him and saved him. He's looking at me with understanding, acceptance, and affection.

And, right now, he is everywhere for me. In the heat between my thighs. The moisture in my mouth. The beat of my heart. The pull of my thoughts. The scent on my body. Everywhere is Sandesh.

26

SANDESH

I know the reality of my situation the moment my eyes blink open to sunlight streaming through the hotel window: Justice is gone. She fucked me into a coma then left. I fling an arm over my eyes to block the sun. This is one messed-up situation, but I know if I were given another chance at it, I'd do it all again. Justice is absolutely worth it.

Plus, I know where she lives and I've been expecting this. Reaching over, I grab my cell and check my email for the flight confirmation. I've got a couple hours.

With a groan that's part satisfaction and part annoyance, I roll out of bed. My jeans are thrown on the floor and that isn't good.

Shit. Knowing before I know, I check the pockets, check my bag, and even though I already understand how useless it is, I check the nightstand.

Fuck!

I'm going to kill Justice. She took my ID, passport, and multi-entrance visa. What was she thinking? Does she think she can throw me off the trail of what she and her family are doing? Does she think a couple of days stranded here will keep me from asking questions or from stepping in to help her against Walid?

Feeling like an idiot, I spike my jeans onto the floor, then drop back onto the bed. I'm part of this now, in this war that Mukta and Justice brought to my door. More importantly, Mukta Parish owes me the truth. The whole truth, not merely the bullshit Justice shared with me, but all the things I'm beginning to suspect.

The Parish clan is notorious worldwide for their wealth, intelligence, drive, and involvement with social and global issues. They're everywhere online, working globally, lobbying for reforms, and even visiting world leaders.

Could those situations play a part in deeper, hidden activities? If I do enough research, will I find that Parish family travels mirror darker events in certain areas? Events aimed at taking out those who harm women or women's rights?

Too angry to think, I turn on my side and breathe deeply. The smell of Justice is in the sheets and pillows, a tantalizing whiff of her unique, spicy scent—distinctly female.

God, even now I want her. I'm into her deep, and I have no idea when it happened.

There's no exact moment I can pinpoint, but a dozen vivid images of her torture me.

Justice pushing boldly into her mother's office. Justice's hand opening to mine on the plane. Justice's eager responses as I thrust into her body, alongside my own overpowering need to get deeper, closer... and that final orgasm that felt like surrender, finding home, a purpose. And more.

All of these images bring warmth to my heart, which makes no damn sense because, at this very moment, I can't recall ever being this pissed off at anyone. Odd that this pillow smells so sweet when the woman herself is frustrating as hell.

Shoving the pillow away, I grab my phone and call Victor. If Justice thinks she can sneak out and leave me trapped in Israel so she can take on Walid by herself, she has another think coming.

27

JUSTICE

I barely slept on the twelve-hour-plus plane ride home. Too guilty. Sandesh had looked so perfect when I'd left him sleeping in Israel. All the more reason why I'm driving up the winding hill toward the Mantua Home with a plan.

Joy threads through my heart at seeing the mansion that sits atop the highest hill on campus. I swing around the stone fountain then park. Climbing out of the car, I stretch and instantly regret it—my side still aches. Not as badly, but bad enough.

Nerves start the moment I climb the front steps of my home. Coming home usually brings me only a sense of peace. Not because of the house's opulence, its thirty thousand square feet above ground, the hidden acres below ground, the mullion arched windows, or any of the historical stone etchings, but because of the people.

A thorn of pain grabs at my throat. Gracie. Dada. Tony. Bridget. One of them gave Walid the ability to track me. One of them almost got me killed. It hurts so deeply I almost don't want to go inside. But not facing things isn't my style. Besides, Sandesh needs me to stick up for him.

Above, pink lines streak the clouds as the departing sun winks away in the dusk. Exterior lights pop on along the stone stairs and the cobbled driveway. I start up the expansive entryway stairs, the bright perfume of the early flowering hawthorn filling the air. That smell—more than anything—reminds me of childhood. Of testing boundaries and getting into trouble with Gracie. How many times did Momma warn me, "Justice, there are some lines you cannot cross"?

I crossed them repeatedly, resigned to pay the price for my freedom. Now, my rash actions might mean Sandesh is punished. No way. I'll pay whatever price I need to pay. But I won't let anyone, including Momma, take his memories.

At the top of the stairs, I push the handcrafted, twenty-foot-tall double doors. They swing open with gentle ease. The grand foyer's beauty—fresh flowers, marble pedestal table, and the multilevel split staircase—reminds me that I'm one of the lucky ones. I survived. Thrived.

The comforting noise of my big family envelopes me as I shut the doors. Upstairs, two girls argue. Their harsh words echo down the wide hall and mix with the training session in the gym. Only my family would put a gym—not a library or a sitting room—off the entryway. The explosive grunts and forceful "hiyuhs!" reverberate through the open doors.

Striding past the gym, I glance inside and see Bridget training a group of teens. She waves me over. Her smile is genuine. I can't imagine her as a traitor.

Waving her off, I keep going. Bridget undoubtedly wants to grill me on the mission. By now, they must all know. With Walid still out there and a new mission looming, Momma had no choice but to come clean.

Well, partly.

They all know about my failure. Know I snuck out behind

their backs. Know how I relied on Sandesh when things got dicey. Know that we have to band together to form a new plan. What they *don't* know is what has me feeling, grimy, used, pissed off, and sad to my soul. They don't know I did all of that because I suspect we have a traitor among us.

Shoulders tensing, I stride down the long, ornately decorated corridor, past the sunken library.

"Justice?" Tony pops out of the arched library doorway and grabs me into a hug.

I almost don't hug him back.

He squeezes tighter—so tight my ribs almost crack.

I give in and hold him back. He smells like Tony, like celery juice and ginger.

Could he be the one who told Walid where to find me in Syria? My heart shrieks denial. Not Tony. Not him. I might not know much, but I know that.

He releases me. "Justice. I..." He breaks off. A large, disbelieving smile cracks his face nearly in half. Damn, the family orthodontist got so carried away with Tony's braces. He has the best smile I've ever seen. No need to tell him that. In fact, he needs to be taken down more, not built up.

"Nice smile, Tone." I push his shoulder. "You could actually double as a Muppet."

He opens and closes his mouth in exaggerated delight. Like a Muppet, Tony. Not easy to rattle. I'm smiling despite myself.

"Funny, J. Now tell me what the fuck happened out there? Forget shutting us out or lying to your unit—you don't do recon anymore? You pop into Jordan and attack the Brothers like you're taking down a massage parlor in the middle of nowhere?"

Sheesh. Even when not on the mission, he critiques me. I hate this. But until I know who the traitor is, until I know I won't risk him by telling him the truth, until I'm able to explain to him why I had to lie, I have to keep this truth to myself.

I go with the story Momma and I concocted when we spoke on the plane. "I was doing recon, but I saw an opportunity and took it."

Spreading his hands wide like someone describing the big fish that got away, he shakes his head. "You left that fucking sadistic, crazy-as-shit brother alive. He's got no control, not even of his own people."

"That's why I went for it." This part, at least, isn't a lie. "His people had terrible training. They practically sent me an invite."

"No, shit. I told you all..." Tony exhales and rubs at the back of his neck. "So's y'know we gotta go after that fucker, right?"

Gawd. The situation seems so much worse when summarized with curses, hand gestures, and South Philly. "Yeah. Well, at least he isn't the smart one. Any thoughts on how to get at him in Mexico?"

As if I've physically hit him, Tony jerks back. "You mean other than the detailed plan I laid out to Momma about getting the brothers separately? The plan I put in a heartfelt and detailed letter that I sent to her before you even left?" Tony glares. "Did Momma even tell you?"

Yikes. Tony's so sensitive about what he interprets as the family ignoring his opinions.

True, I haven't seen it, but that has a lot to do with other factors. Like the opportunity with Sandesh and his charity. All of which, I can't get into with him without exposing the truth. "It was my mission. I said all along we had to take them out together to keep one from alerting the other."

"Yeah. Well, that worked out great."

"I know, Tony. I was there. And so was Sandesh. Which is the problem. I have to talk to Momma about him." I run a hand through grimy hair and breathe through my agitation. "Sorry. I'll catch you later. Okay?"

Suspicion and hurt fill his eyes. "Sure, J. Later."

Without another word, I stride to the middle of the corridor and turn right at the elevators. Once out of his line of sight, I relax and lean against the wall. This lying to my siblings is going to kill me.

Knowing Momma will be in her office, I slam the UP arrow on the elevator. I'm not going up. There's a *ding* and the doors slide open. Inside, four round yellow buttons indicate three floors and one basement level. Not accurate. There are three more extensive floors deep below ground.

I lift my wrist above the number pad. Nothing happens. Oh. Right. That'll take getting used to. I lift my other wrist, the one with the chip I inserted on the plane. There's a beep of recognition. Yes. Welcome back to Elevator-X.

I say, "Subfloor 4B."

The smooth feminine automation responds, "Access is not operational. Two unauthorized personnel remain within unacceptable distance of the elevator. Please enter via another route."

Gah. She's probably talking about a cleaning person or chef lurking nearby. Sometimes, the security here is over the top. As if these already well-vetted people, who are probably up to their eyeballs in work, are going to be aware if the elevator doesn't arrive where it's supposed to. No. Hell no. I'm not going back out and through the garage. "Override."

"Wait for verification."

I tap my finger beside the pad as I wait for the system to check that the unauthorized personal aren't standing outside the elevator doors on any floor. *Come on. Come on.*

"Override accepted. You have been processed and cleared for Subfloor 4B. No cameras, cell phones, or unauthorized electronics permitted."

Bracing my feet wide, I wait for it. And even though the waist-high handholds are tempting, it's been a family challenge since childhood not to hold on.

"Proceeding."

The elevator plunges down.

My stomach slaps into my esophagus along with my heart. My teeth clench. Sheesh. No matter how many times I do this, the velocity of this drop twists my stomach.

When this elevator was first put into operation, it went at a normal pace. Or so I've been told. It was modified right before my arrival. Apparently, it really freaked people out knowing just how deep underground they were going.

After the sinking freefall, the elevator slides to a weighted stop. I lock my knees into place.

The automated voice intones, "Subfloor 4B. Welcome. You are being monitored. Entering unauthorized areas will result in immediate expulsion."

Shaking off the warning I've heard at least ten thousand times, I step out into a spotless, windowless hallway. Unauthorized areas are any of those accessed through the large, misted-gray, glass double doors to my left.

Not a problem. I go right. Nothing against Internal Security, but I learned a healthy respect for them growing up. They're kind of the cops of my adolescence, led by Leland. I respect their rules. *Now.* Going against them is a line I rarely cross. Well, not after that time with Gracie. I shudder to think about it. Teens think having a parent pull you out of a party is bad—ha. They have no idea. Being a teenager with an attitude and a deep, dark family secret was hell.

My senses make their normal adjustment to the new environment. It feels... off. Sound doesn't travel the same way. Maybe it's the muffled ear feeling. This deep underground, the loudest sounds are the rhythmic humming breaths of the ventilation system.

The air is dull and manufactured, I prefer the floor above this, 4A. Not just because the gym and gun range are there, but because it isn't so stiff. This is an authoritarian prick of a floor, strict and watchful.

With a bare knuckle tap on Momma's office door, I enter before getting a response. Once inside, I instantly feel better. Momma's office makes up for the lack of decorations on this level. It's kind of a testament to Momma's colorful soul and upbringing.

Thick, hand-woven rugs splashed with bright colors decorate the floor. Ornaments of every conceivable hue line the built-in bookcases. Lush, gold damask wallpaper, sub-Saharan artwork, elephant lamps, brightly painted masks, and a delicate, hand-carved desk of bleached wood complete the room.

Wearing a silver silk niqab, Momma works at her desk. Seated before her, in one of the two robin's-egg-blue chairs, Leland works on an iPad. Probably monitoring the many security cameras, though he usually does that from the command center in Internal. He probably jogged over here when he realized I was on my way down.

Momma raises her head. "Justice. Welcome home." Her eyes are bright and pleased to see me. It's a look that she has bestowed on me from the first moment we met. A look that won't deny her love for me.

But I can't get sucked into the comfort of her and the attention she so freely lavishes on family. "I need to talk to you."

As dapper as the silver suit he wears, Leland stands and puts the iPad down before walking around to sit on the corner of Momma's desk. Not sure why he doesn't just wear a T-shirt that says *Team Mukta*.

No need. These two are spookily coordinated. Seriously, her niqab almost matches his suit. Do they talk about these things or does it just happen?

Hyperaware under their gazes, I can even feel the fibers in my socks as I walk across the room. I kiss Momma on her silk-lined cheek and get a whiff of the flowery, earthy richness of her signature scent, Une Rose.

I nod slightly to Leland, and he points at the chair he'd been sitting in. "Please sit down."

Please? Okay. That's different.

I sit. The chair's still warm from Leland. Hot even. *Huh—* I'm in the hot seat. Shit. That isn't funny. What is it about these two that makes me feel like a goofy kid?

I inhale a deep breath then release it to keep from laughing. I need to keep control of this situation and its topics.

"I know you want details on the mission, but I need to talk to you about Sandesh."

Leland shakes his head. "First, you listen."

Okay... Again, different. Usually, after a botched mission, they want to question me for hours.

Showing her nerves, Momma tugs at the fabric draped across her shoulder. "Yes. We need to discuss your young man."

That's why I'm here to discuss Sandesh, but that "your young man" thing has my shoulder blades itching. This doesn't sound good.

I make eye contact with them before drawing a line. "Momma. Leland. I won't stand for you taking his memories. I won't."

"Calm down and listen," Leland says. "Sandesh is with Gracie."

"Gracie!" I jolt to my feet. Nightmare. "Where? When?"

Poor Sandesh. I have to rescue him.

"Sit down, Justice," Momma says. "And let us explain."

I sit and cross legs that feel dull and heavy. Gracie has my... What is Sandesh to me? *Great lay* sounds a bit cold. "Why Gracie? She could be behind all this."

"If she is," Leland says, "she won't like the fact that we're bringing a man into the organization. Your man. Especially when we made her give up hers."

So smart. So damn manipulative. They've put Sandesh in the line of fire with Gracie. And Tony. Neither will like some random guy—wait. *What*? "You're bringing Sandesh in?"

Momma shifts in her seat. "Yes. It is imperative for his safety and our security."

I'm still not sure if this is good or bad. It seems good. "What do you mean?"

"According to Dada's informant, the Brothers Grim, or I guess we can call him the Grim Brother now, believes that your *friend,* Sandesh, has a deeper connection to our mission than he actually does. In fact, he believes Sandesh to be the mastermind of his brother's death."

"Why the hell would he think that?"

"Apparently, he and Salma intercepted a shipment of women bound for Walid and the Americas the night before he helped you escape."

Looks like Sandesh held back a little side mission. Not that it surprises me. Well, now that I think about it, I'm not surprised. Salma *did* call him away the night before my mission. And all the blood in Salma's tent... That sad little infant body... I'd never asked.

"What's the plan?" I can already guess. "Use Sandesh to flush out the traitor, dangle him in front of Walid as bait, and then, after he's served his purpose, M-erase him?"

Momma sits up straighter. Offended? Good, because I'm not beating around the bush.

Leland puts a gentle hand on Momma's raised shoulder.

She relaxes. "Justice. I am allowing Sandesh his memories so that he is aware of the threat and can defend himself and his charity."

"How totally selfless of you."

The clap as Momma brings angry hands together makes me jump. "Would you have me throw away the opportunity to flush out whoever betrayed you? Betrayed us? That person might now grow angry and careless, but will fear revealing more information to Walid, knowing that, doing so, will bring them more easily under our scrutiny. At the same time, I am giving Sandesh a chance to prove himself. Perhaps we can continue this business relationship." Momma's silk-surrounded gaze bores directly into me. "Can you say you have dealt as fairly with him?"

That hits home. Of course, she's right. My mission—scratch that, my *direct actions*—jeopardized his charity. And even knowing this, I'd left him alone to pick up the pieces while I came here to take on Walid and Momma.

Heartsick. That's the only way to describe the feeling in my chest. Like my heart has a fever and chills, and is curled under the blanket of my chest, moaning in pain. *Oh, Sandy, I'm so very sorry.*

I school my features. "And you're going to trust him? You're going to allow him to know our secrets?"

Leland shrugs. "This wasn't our choice." His eyes accuse me.

There's a sudden rush of blood to my cheeks as a wave of cold dread settles into my stomach.

Leland's intense stare seems to weigh me—and not just me, but my thoughts and emotions. He smirks. "Besides, trust won't be an issue. First, because he has more to lose than us. Second, because you are going to stick to him like glue. And third, because he's being brought here to be tagged."

No way. "He's agreed to have a GPS implanted under his skin?"

Leland waves a hand dismissively. "We expect you'll handle that minor detail."

28

SANDESH

The petite redhead with the stiff and fiery grin, a stiff and fiery bun, and a glare so stiff and fiery it could smelt iron, leans over the desk separating us. "I'm not messing around here, big guy."

As if she needs to tell me that. Under her black business jacket, she has a Beretta Tomcat. A tiny little thing that easily hides its real potential for danger. Telling.

We've been in this windowless, colorless, almost airless ten-by-ten room for hours. Annoying as hell, considering Victor pulled some major strings to get me a seat on a VIP jet from Israel to D.C. and I'd planned on beating Justice back here. Almost made it until Red appeared at the private airport and had ordered me to get into a limo.

Knowing her to be Gracie, Justice's sister, I did. I'd thought she'd take me to Justice or Mukta. I didn't think she'd bring me here and interrogate me.

My neck hurts. My ass hurts. And I'm finally more pissed off at this situation then worried about Justice. Is this the way the Parish family treats business partners? They sit them at an

Amish-crafted wood table on a schoolmarm-straight wooden chair, while accusing fluorescent lights glare down at them?

"As I told you, I'm not answering any more of your questions until you tell me where Justice is." I'd also like to know where *I* am. Though I have a reasonable guess. After I'd agreed to being blindfolded and going with her—agreeing seemed a big deal to her—it'd taken us four hours to get here. The Mantua Academy is around three and a half hours from D.C.

Where else would they take me?

The only issue with this conclusion is that the limo had driven downhill at the end of our drive, like into an underground garage. After that, we'd ridden in an elevator that had felt more like a ride at an amusement park.

So, I'm deep underground, which is confirmed by the muffled feeling of being surrounded by earth. Could there be an area on campus way below ground? I have no clue, and I'm tired of going over this detail in my own mind. I sit back and stretch because Gracie and I are at an impasse.

She grins at me. "When was the first time you and Justice had sex?"

I snap back to attention. This is a turn in a new direction. We've spent the last few hours discussing Jordan, Salma's Gems, the IPT, and now she wants to get personal? Curiosity... or some weird suspicion? "That's not significant to this discussion."

"It is to me. And since you need our protection—"

I laugh. "If you didn't get the memo, I did just fine protecting myself and your sister. Unlike your supposed group of professionals."

Gracie's green eyes narrow and her pale skin reddens.

I've never been a fan of blushing, but frustrated and angry has me wanting to taunt her to see if I can provoke a deeper skin tone. "Where am I?"

"The Mantua Academy." She smiles after telling me what

she surely knows I already know. "When was the first time you and Justice had sex?"

Does she seriously think I'm going to answer that intrusive question? "None of your damn business."

"Fine, don't answer me. I guess you don't care if Salma and her family are in trouble?"

My fists clench under the table. "What are you saying?"

"Well, tough guy, you rescued a group of enslaved women and girls on the same night Walid's brother was killed. Walid followed the trail of those women, and it led to Salma and you. He's convinced you and she are his enemy."

I let that sink in. Not just the statement—how the hell did she have access to that information?—but the domino effect. Salma's organization—her safety, the safety of those they'd freed—the IPT's mission... all compromised. And the final domino is the big one.

I'm being bribed. *Stay in line, do what we say, keep our secrets, and we'll protect your friends and business.* These are mob-like practices, but I keep my face impassive, giving away nothing, not even my growing annoyance. "What do you want?"

Gracie jerks her head sideways, as if cracking her neck. Frustration? "What do I want? Or what does Momma want?"

"There's a difference?"

She rolls her eyes. "A big difference. Momma wants your help taking out Walid. She wants you brought into the family, into our inner circle. I have no idea how they can possibly think that you're worth it. When other men—good men—are... lost to us."

Brought into the family? That fact angers her. People make mistakes, reveal things when they're angry. *Good men lost to us?* "You don't have sex yourself; is that the reason you want to hear about your sister's sex life?"

Face heating a deeper shade of red, she takes a step back. "Justice spoke to you about me?"

Damn. My good guess struck bone. Too bad she looks anything but annoyed or suspicious; she looks hurt. I'd let up, feel some compassion, but I'm tired and sore.

Pushing back in my chair, which creaks under me, I snap my spine into better alignment. "Let's say I agree to keep your family's secrets and join them."

"You don't dictat—"

"You don't tell me what to do." In a flash of anger, I bring my hands up to emphasize my point.

Gracie flinches, then reaches under her jacket for her gun. I freeze.

It happens so fast, the threat of violence from this woman. My heart thuds in my chest as I freeze, waiting out the next moment with growing tension. Blinking, she draws her hand back out without the gun.

Not the trusting sort. Not at all.

I desperately want to ask her if she trusts anyone, if she thinks she's her sister's keeper, if she thinks I'd have put on that blindfold and come here if not for Justice. I don't because she's a loose cannon who's obviously hiding more than she says, and is a secretive, temperamental woman.

Although Justice was scarce on details, someone in this family has betrayed her. It could be this woman. I intend to find out. Whether it's her or someone else, I'm going to make sure they'll never be able to do it again.

And that means... "I'm in. For as long as it takes to find and take out Walid, but that's it. Justice and I have a personal relationship, and if you want to know more, ask her. Or you can steal into her room at night and read her diary."

Gracie laughs, then quickly schools her features. "A bad boy who likes to do humanitarian stuff. Is that your story?"

"And I'm sticking to it." Though the whole bad-boy thing is an insulting way to describe a grown man with specialized training and skills. Still, I've got better things to do than throw down over poor word choices.

Gracie walks around and sits on the edge of the table, close enough that I can smell her fruity-candy perfume.

We lock eyes and something shifts in her demeanor, softens.

She leans toward me, showing much more cleavage than seems accidental.

I push up from the chair and stand to create some distance between us.

She eases off the table and follows me.

I step back.

She takes two steps forward.

Justice has some messed-up family. If I didn't worry she'd bring out her gun, I'd put out my arm to keep her at a distance She takes another step forward, too close. She's practically pressed to my front.

"What are you doing?"

She grins. "Come on. I saw you checking out my backside when I picked you up at the airport."

I can't help but laugh. Backside? Maybe the most unsexy word in the English language. She's joking, right? "I want to speak to your mother. The sooner the better, and, like you, I look at a lot of people, even evaluate them. It's a reflex."

Tilting her head, she stares at me. "Guess Momma was right. You are a good man."

Seriously? "So, you're using your looks to try to manipulate me into revealing what a dog I am?"

She shrugs.

No. Not good enough. "First, my actions aren't that involuntary. I don't knee-jerk fuck women. Second, and this I really don't get, how can a group of women dedicated to female empowerment use their own sexuality to gain position? Isn't that what you're fighting against?"

Gracie slaps an angry hand to my chest. "If you're stupid enough to fall for those things, if you can't overcome your own programming, please don't think that I'm dumb enough not to use that to my advantage."

Damn, she's scary as hell.

GRACIE LEADS me inside the brightly decorated office of Mukta Parish. My heart jumps at the site of the dark-haired woman who last left me with a smile on my face. Justice.

She stands up, turns, and those eyes—a deep darkness that captures pinpricks of light and turns them to stars—open wide for me, welcome me, greet me like I carry something she'd been desperately waiting for, something she desperately needs.

Dammit. I wish I could be angry at her or, close down what I feel. But I can't forget that she'd told me her nightmare as a way to offer comfort, forget that she'd risked herself for Amal, forget the intent in her seamless nighttime eyes as she'd launched the grenade that saved us, or forget the lilt in her voice as she'd serenaded me with that damn song. And I won't ignore now the lost and broken parts of her that call to me, this woman who once threaded her hand through mine, her body around mine, and herself around my heart.

I give up trying to scowl at her. Anger won't take root right now, not when I'm so grateful to see her here and okay. I understand her too well and realize after my time with Gracie that Justice leaving me was her way of protecting me.

Not that I need protecting—and that's something she has to understand.

As I walk across the room with her singularly in my focus, I notice she looks shaken and worried. Two states I'm not used to seeing on her.

What happened?

I risk a glance at Leland and Mukta and find them exchanging a silent and telling look. I don't give a shit. If they want my cooperation, they'll have to put up with me being here for Justice. A woman I care for so deeply that looking at her without touching her causes a pain in my throat that blocks me from speaking.

She lowers her eyelashes. "You looked so peaceful sleeping. I didn't want to disturb you."

The corners of my mouth twitch, but I hold back the smile. Not because I want her to feel worse, but because I don't want to give any leverage to Mukta Parish. "I appreciate you leaving my passport at the airport. That was kind of you."

I'm so close now that we are inches apart. Warmth and a subtle odor of lavender radiate from her. There's true regret in her eyes when she dips her head and whispers, "You don't have to join my family. Or this mission."

Oh hell, bye-bye leverage. I wrap my arms around her and nearly groan with relief as I pull her close. "It's done, Justice, so let's not discuss it anymore because I'm in it with you."

She wraps her arms around my waist, burrows into me so close that I can feel the entirety of her—the spread of her hips, the bend in her shoulder, the length of her neck, the muscles in her arms, the tip of her nose, the lay of her forehead against my cheek. Everywhere she touches leaves an impression of her as sweet and powerful as her kisses, her sighs, her tears, curses, and laughter.

I dip my head and kiss her, expecting her to hold back with her family in the room, but she doesn't. She pushes her tongue into my mouth, tastes me as unconsciously and fully as if we were alone.

Sharp heat knifes through my heart and my body. I should walk away. Protect myself and my charity. But as Gracie put it, that's not in my programming.

We break apart, and I realize if we'd gone a moment longer, it would've gotten really awkward.

I rub my nose along her forehead and whisper, "Tagged and tailed."

She steps back. "You're okay with inserting the GPS?"

Okay is a stretch. In fact, when Gracie had brought it up, I hadn't intended to go anywhere near it, but seeing Justice when I walked in here reminded me *who* there is to lose. Hell, to keep Justice safe I'll upend my privacy, lend my strength, and temporarily redraw a line on covert-ops I'd never thought I'd cross.

I scan the office, taking in Mukta and Leland, the architects of my involvement with this situation. They lured me, endangering my charity and Salma's Gems, and I'm not letting them off the hook that easily.

"Of course, I'm going to need some things in return. For example, Mukta agreeing to fund IPT startups for the next ten years—twenty if something happens to me."

That request hits the room like a gong, with Mukta and Leland exchanging a long glance that conveys a message I can't decipher.

I wonder if they suspect the truth behind my request. I don't want any ties to Parish Industries or their covert operations, not for ten years—not even for two—but I want them to think I'm in it for the long haul. Another cog in their giant wheel of using peace operations to secretly kill and maim in the name of a higher cause—until I find out who's after Justice, take out Walid, and extricate me and the IPT from Parish Industries.

Leland nods slightly and Mukta says, "Consider it done."

"Great." I step past Justice and hold up my arm for the tracer. "If you don't mind."

"Of course," Leland says, reaching into an ivory box on the desk. He pulls out an instrument that looks like a weapon but for the surgical metal tip.

Mukta reaches into the same box and pulls out an alcohol swab. She rips open the package and hands it to me.

I wipe down my wrist as Leland gives me his spiel.

"This tracking device will give us an update on your location every fifteen minutes. As head of Internal Security, I'll also be able to see your exact location at any time."

Great, can't wait to be constantly watched.

"Of course, since you are agreeing to this surveillance, you will also have access to campus, this home, and certain areas on the lower level. Justice will show you around, but even when she's not here to tell you, you'll know areas you don't have access to because those doors won't open to you."

Leland places the cold tip of the instrument against my wrist and presses. There's a pop and a sharp stab of pain. Heat spreads along my skin. For one moment, the cylinder outline is visible under my skin, but I flex and release, then the chip disappears.

When I turn around, Justice is there. She brushes a finger back and forth across my wrists. "Ready to be initiated as a member of The Guild?"

I huff. "Sounds incredibly painful."

She laughs and stares at me, her eyes—those cool, sunless depths—invite me in. "Actually, it all started with your elevator ride. How did you feel going down, Sandesh? Want to go again?"

When I fully grasp the invite, a shocked laugh breaks from me, followed quickly by heat in my face and an instant surge of lust. I'd definitely like to go down on her. "I'm in. But how's tomorrow? I need to check in on my mother."

Cocking her head, she eyes me coyly. "Stop trying to seduce me."

29

JUSTICE

It's butt-crack a.m. and I'm standing in the hallway of Sandesh's Conshohocken apartment. I take out my cell.

He answers on the fourth ring, his voice fuzzy. "Justice? It's"—he pauses, probably checking his clock—"six a.m."

Oh, he sounds so vulnerable when he's sleep-deprived. Just the thing I can take advantage of. "Open up. I'm outside your apartment door."

"What? Security didn't call me."

Can't help the snort. He's seriously doubting my stealth skills? "And yet, I'm still here."

I hang up, smiling. A moment later, the covering over the peephole clicks open and then closed. The door swings open, his body positioned behind it. He's offering me unfettered access. Trusting.

I stroll inside his apartment, taking in every detail. This place speaks of him, with its open floor plan and natural wood floors, lovely big kitchen with a breakfast bar. There's a two-person, bar-height table by a sliding glass door that leads onto a balcony. A gray leather Chesterfield sofa with thick scroll arms and a high back are flanked by two equally deep upholstered chairs. And huge flat-screen TV stationed is on the wall over a fireplace with a green-marble mantel. I love it. Okay, he's a keeper.

Behind me the door clicks closed.

I turn.

Whoa. Disheveled hair. Shadow-lined jaw. That just-woken-up confusion in his bleary blue eyes. Fucking hot. And *hello.* At least one part of him is awake. "You sleep in the nude."

He moves like a panther, grabs me by the waist and drags me up against his hard-on. He kisses me—kisses me with skill and insistence. Kisses me as if the time we'd spent apart is years, not days. His need, his wordless hunger, take my breath away. His tongue sets me on fire.

I arch into him, inhaling sleep and man. Warm, velvety liquid saturates my panties. *Sooo* glad I broke into his building this morning.

His demanding lips work on mine. His stubble scratches. His hot hands travel up my body and he pulls out my hair tie, then tangle in the strands. He angles my head so he can deepen the kiss.

This man knows how to fucking kiss. Our tongues—wet and hot—our lips—soft and needy—reacquaint themselves. Our breathing grows loud and strong enough that we both know next steps are needed right now.

We break apart. His breaths are ragged. His hands grasp my hair tight enough to hurt and he demands, "Take your clothes off."

An excellent idea. Too bad I don't have enough air to say that; a visual aid will have to do.

I guide his hands from my hair, then step back, whisk off my shirt, undo my bra, and free my breasts.

He groans long and low.

Not gonna lie, I'm kind of loving the stark need on his face. I turn up the heat by unzipping my black jeans. I turn around, lower the pants to my ankles without bending my knees.

"Dear God."

What man doesn't appreciate a good thong? I let him appreciate it, taking my time unlacing my boots. I flick them off, wiggle out of my jeans, then make a show of losing the thong.

When I stand up, before I can turn around to see his reaction, he is there, pressing his hard body against my ass.

He runs a hand over my breasts, squeezes and fondles them. "Fuck, Justice. I need you."

"Thanks, Captain Obvious." I lean back into him. "The feeling is mutual."

Laughing lightly in my ear, he reaches down, strokes a finger through my folds, grunting in male satisfaction at my silky wetness. Two of his long fingers crook inside me, and I nearly come. I moan my pleasure. I am strung so tight, am so ready.

His fingers slide in and out, the palm of his hand rubbing against my clit, his ragged breath loud in my ears.

"Sandesh. That feels so good."

Encouraged, he pumps his finger faster, pressing his other hand flat against my stomach, pulling me tight against his hard-on. His arms around me, his hot breath in my ear, his hard-on pressed to my ass, he envelops me, big and warm and solid. It's more than enough.

My body tightens, the tension so good, then I break. Panting hard, I writhe and moan, arch my head back, dig my hands into his biceps as trembling, electric pulses ride over me, shatter me. "Oh. Sandesh. Sandesh."

He whispers, "Watching you come... Can't get enough."

The aftershocks tingle through me as his fingers slip out. Still losing my mind over him, I turn, seeking the hardness of him between my throbbing thighs.

We kiss, wild with need, crazed with excitement.

No time for niceties, I break from him. "Ride me hard."

He grins dazedly at me, then points around the room. "Lady's choice."

Oh, yes and yes. I know exactly where to go.

I hustle over to the end of the couch, draping myself over the tall scroll arm. Cushiony.

Putting my hands flat against the seat, I turn my head to see if he's followed.

He's still standing where I left him. So cute.

I raise an eyebrow at him. "How's this?"

For a moment, he doesn't answer. I watch his Adam's apple work in his throat. He swallows. "Prettiest sight I've seen in my entire life."

Crossing to me, he rubs a warm hand along the curve of my ass.

I am losing it again, and when he squeezes and spreads my cheeks, I cry out, and then louder when he thrusts into me.

The insistent pull-and-stretch is everything as he delves deeper and deeper. So deep, the tip of his cock seems to be hitting the end of my cervix. But I want fast. And he is slowly pulling out. Slowly torturing me.

"Sandesh," I reprimand, and he slams back into me, fast and rough.

I gasp, lose my bracing, and slip against the cushions, before I can regain my position.

He doesn't stop, driving hard, panting at the increase in friction.

My hands slip again. I re-brace, moaning approval at the increase in speed and friction.

My core trembles and tightens around his thick thrusts, and I watch him, the beauty of him, reflected in the glossy blackness of the TV screen.

His long, muscular frame with one palm pressed flat against the curve of my back... His head tipped down to watch where he enters me, a look of exquisite need on his handsome face... His perfect ass tight and hard as he pumps into me...

He thrusts so rapidly my clit rubs hotly against the couch. Still sensitive from his fingers, this causes an intense and uncontrollable reaction. "Oh God."

Caught between him and the couch, the friction so delicious it only takes a moment.

Bliss.

I cry out as electric pulses crash into me. The tremors obliterate awareness of everything but the overpowering, exquisite release.

When I come back, I'm panting and the muscles in my arms are tense. Aftershocks tingle along my core. I wiggle and squirm under Sandesh, press the tips of my toes against the floor, raising up, giving him greater access.

"Justice," he says, and there is no doubt that he means that as a warning. He won't last much longer.

I've already had two amazing orgasms, but the change in angle has my body tightening again, and the pressure of his cock strokes and pumps against my G-spot.

The thick width of him plunges with frantic abandon... the feel of him... So good. "Yes. Yes. Don't stop."

Greedy, sure. But it feels so damn good.

He grunts, "So fucking beautiful," then slaps himself into me again and again and again.

I'm so helpless, I whimper and moan beneath him as another wave of pleasure rises and rises then crashes through me.

Nearly on top of my shout, Sandesh comes with a drawn-out groan so scorching hot it singes my ears.

The rub and tug of my final orgasm slows with his pace.

Breathing like he'd run a four-minute mile, he slumps over me, kisses me on the back of the neck.

My body is so charged with energy, so tender to the touch, I jerk.

He smooths a knuckle across my cheek. "You okay?"

Is he kidding? "I love this couch."

He barks a surprised laugh, helps me up, then turns me to face him before kissing me long and hard.

Releasing me, he puts his hands on my shoulders, turns me toward what I assume is the bedroom, then smacks me on the ass. "Get going. I'm going to teach you what getting up at a decent hour means."

My ass tingling, I look back at him. "A little bossy now."

"Get into my bed, Justice."

I shrug. "Turns out, right now, I like bossy."

30

SANDESH

With the curtains drawn and the bedroom dimly lit, I find myself as satisfied as I've ever been. It's hard to imagine a more perfect morning. It's not every day a hot woman breaks into my apartment building, asks to be let inside, and orders me to ride her hard.

I'm getting hard just thinking about it. Then again, she isn't just *any* woman. She's one of a kind, and my heart is as tangled up with her as she is with my sheets.

Deep in the softness of my bed, Justice snuggles up to me, puts her lips to my ear, and continues whispering soft sounds of appreciation. Not that my ego needs it, but I like making her as happy as she makes me.

I close my eyes and drift off.

"What's the meaning behind Sandman?"

"Huh?" I pry open my eyes.

"I get your name, Sandesh, because you're as tasty as any dessert."

I snort. "My Pakistani great-grandmother made the treats for my mother, and she loved them so much, claiming she's never found anything as sweet before I was born."

She smiles. "Smart woman, but why Sandman? You said they called you that in the military."

She's so warm against me. Why won't she go to sleep? I yawn. "Are you a morning person?"

"Yeah. Didn't you notice that in Israel?"

"That room was so dark I lost track of night and day. We barely ate."

"True." She rubs a hand across my chest. "Answer the question. Why Sandman?"

There are some people you can't tell secrets to, some people you *shouldn't* tell secrets to, and some people you *ache* to tell secrets to. Justice's eyes are a velvet night sky that demands soft confessions. What am I to do? "Remember when I said in Israel that I liked you?"

She smiles. "I believe you said you liked me a lot. Maybe more than any woman ever."

I cup the back of her head, pull her close enough that our foreheads touch. "No *maybe*, Justice. I've never felt this way before about anyone."

We're so close our breaths mix. She kisses me softly. "Same."

Strong, grateful emotion rides through me, so I gather all that feeling and confess. "Sandman," I close my eyes, "because you can sleep easy if I'm on guard duty. I've got great hearing and won't fall asleep on my watch. If something's out there, I'll know about it way in advance."

She snorts lightly. "Funny, I thought it was because you liked to sleep. You seem really sleepy right now."

Oh. Man. "You're not going back to sleep, are you?"

"Nope. I have a traitor to catch. Kind of hard to sleep."

My eyes spring open. "Anything new?"

"I got news from Internal Security this morning. that there was no electronic trail or any evidence that someone in the family had asked for GPS information on me."

"Meaning?"

"In order to get GPS information, you have to go through three layers of security: password, the inserted chip, and facial recognition. There is no evidence that anyone in the family did that."

That's a lot of steps and not something that sounds easily bypassed by your average person, even if you were aware of the technology. "Didn't you mention that Gracie is into computers?"

"Yeah. She runs a cyber-crime unit for The Guild out of her club. The information she gets helps us rescue people and track down predators. She's really good at it."

I hear the note of sadness in her voice. "You think it's Gracie."

She takes a deep, steadying breath before whispering, "She's the only person with the ability to do something like that."

Oh, man. My heart is breaking for her. This is beyond tough, and I want her to know I have her back. "What's your plan?"

"I want to interview her this morning." She tugs at the blanket. "Any interest in tagging along?"

Like she has to ask. "You go, I go." She grins unabashedly at the words I told her in Israel. Brat. "Gracie's not a fan of mine, though. Or maybe that's the point? You think I'll throw her off?"

She metronomes her head from one side to the other. "More that you might spot things I'd miss. I'm too close to this. Same with the rest of my family. I'd like to tag team the whole bunch."

"What do you need me to do?"

"Gracie this morning. The rest of them... I'd like to do some light digging this afternoon. But if you could come by for dinner later, you could take a second crack at them."

It's as good a place as any to start. "Okay." I rub my eyes. "I'm up."

She grins at me. "Stay put. I'm going to make you coffee."

"You're going to make me *coffee*?"

"Baby, after three mind-blowing orgasms, I'm pretty eager to please. Coffee, no problem."

She rolls out of bed and walks out with a strut that has me licking my lips. Best morning ever.

31

JUSTICE

I pull into the parking lot behind Gracie's Club When? and hit the brakes. Maybe a little too quickly because Sandesh is yanked back by his seatbelt. The coffee in his hand sloshes onto his pants.

I grimace. "Whoops. And I took such care getting you clean during our shower."

A smile graces his handsome face as he places his cup in the cup holder, grabs a tissue, then dabs away the moisture. "I'd think you'd worry more about the suit you insisted I wear."

"Suggested, not insisted. And, trust me, if you're coming to the house later for dinner, you'll be glad. Momma does not mess around with that stuff."

"I'll keep that in mind. Anything I should know about Gracie? Any issues with you?"

Does she have any issues with me? My heart hurts. "Believe it or not, we used to be best friends growing up. We shared everything—our secrets, our first drink together, our first sneak out of the house. Not an easy thing when you have armed guards around your home."

"What happened?"

"When Gracie was sixteen, her bio mom showed up, sick. Dying, actually. She wanted Gracie to come live with her. Momma left it up to my sister, and, much to my shock, Gracie left. She started this club with her mom."

"That bothered you?"

"At the time, I didn't understand it. I wanted nothing to do with my bio dad, and my bio mom died long ago, so I might've been less than supportive."

"Less than supportive?"

"I was an asshole. A hurt teenager who didn't yet have the skills necessary to realize I was also jealous. After Gracie left, she became..." I chew on my next word before spitting it out. "Distant."

"Distant toward you? Or toward the whole family?"

"Both. We never became truly close again. We might've, except she quickly fell in love with a boy. I was shut out completely. That relationship ended badly two years later. She told him about our family."

"I take it that's a big no-no."

"The biggest. It's kind of like being a spy for the CIA—you can have a family, have a love life, have a regular cover job, but you sure as shit can't tell your spouse and kids what you're doing on the side. That decision needs to be approved by Momma and Leland and it's a rarity. For a good reason, because the problem with Gracie's ex wasn't my family. It was him. He was disgusted by what she'd told him. Especially since, by then, they'd had a baby. He threatened to reveal what he knew if she didn't let him take the kid and go. To keep the family secret, she let them both go."

Sandesh shakes his head. His mouth tightens. "That's awful. Poor Gracie. And now your mom is bringing me into the family when she must've wished for something like that for herself all those years ago. I take it she's still single?"

"Yep. Coming from a family of vigilantes limits the dating pool."

Sandesh snorts, then grows serious as his eyes skim the outside of the club. "Do you think she could've become so sour on the family that she'd try to sabotage your mission?"

"Don't know. Like I said, I'm too close to this. My gut answer is no, but that gut instinct extends to all my siblings."

Sandesh reaches across the car and squeezes my hand before he climbs out. I join him and we walk across the gravel lot to the back of the club. I like him at my side. It's nice not only for backup. Especially when all the people I used to trust are now suspect.

Though it's barely eleven, the club is already open for lunch. An eighties' Prince song pounds out into the lot. Sandesh digs a knuckle in his ears. "Prince seems a little dated."

Man has no musical taste. "When Gracie and her mom started the club, they argued over the music. As a compromise, they settled on changing it up. Now, Club When? changes musical eras every eight weeks or so. It's fun and turned out to be a genius marketing tactic. Enough that she began opening early for food."

"Ah. Explains the smell of French fries."

The music, which had sounded loud outside, hits us with a punch once inside the small, crate-stacked back corridor. I expertly avoid a food-carrying waitress and, biting into an onion ring, lead Sandesh to the upstairs offices.

He catches up with me. "How did you get that?"

"Classic distraction. It's a technique used by pickpockets worldwide and perfected by Momma when dealing with the media."

"Go on."

I like sharing this stuff with him. "Sometimes, a pickpocket will pinch a mark, bump into their arm, anything to get their attention away from the area of actual concern. Sometimes, they'll have an accomplice come up and distract the mark by asking for the time or holding a flyer out to them."

He frowns. "Okay. You didn't pinch anyone. And I get how I missed it, I was distracted coming from the light into a new place, but how did you distract her?"

I wink at him. "I didn't, handsome. You did."

He shakes his head as I give him the rest of the onion ring.

At the steel number pad by the security door leading upstairs, I wave my wrist. Nothing happens. Oh, right. I wave the other arm. There's a beep and a warning *beep, beep, beep*.

I point at Sandesh's wrist. "You have to do the same. It reads the number of people out here and won't open if everyone doesn't have clearance."

Still chewing and a lot less cheerful, he puts up his wrist. The pad stops beeping and clicks.

I pull the heavy-as-a-tomb door open, and we head up the stairs.

Behind me, Sandesh studies the closed door before catching up with me and asking, "Blast-proof?"

Dude does not miss a trick. "Yep."

At the top, all club sounds are muted. I stop at the beginning of a hallway lined with steel doors, much like the one we'd just entered through. The cameras over these doors swing in our direction.

"What's back there?" Sandesh asks.

Information systems, computers, and servers for the underground railroad and its operations, but I don't tell him that. He's in this enough; no reason to give him a point-by-point tutorial on family operations. "Gracie lives in an apartment at the end of the hall, but she's probably up in her office by now."

I head toward her office door. I knock, wait. Sandesh clears his throat. I can feel him watching me, like he wants to ask more about the club and Gracie.

I ignore him.

"Behind you, dork."

I spin around to find my sister standing there, lips cocked in a smile.

A smile echoed by Sandesh.

"You're all kinds of ninja, Gracie." I say, bending to throw my arms around the petite redhead. She smells like watermelon Jolly Ranchers. Girl is obsessed with those candies. Has been since she was a kid. How she still has such a bright and beautiful smile is beyond me. I squeeze her extra tight, trying to see if she tightens or tenses, feeling less like a sister and more like a traitor.

She does stiffen, but I have to admit it doesn't mean she's a traitor. Truth is, since losing John and Tyler, she shies away from hugs.

Gracie pushes away. "Why are you here?"

I've got my reason, my lie—which technically isn't a lie since I do care. "The kid. Cee. I'm here to check up on her."

Frowning, she glances at Sandesh. "And you? Why are you here?"

Sandesh has an equally tense look on his face. What happened between these two? He says, "I'm a prisoner of love. And your crazy-ass family."

Gracie raises an eyebrow at the word *love*. And, truth, it makes my heart skip like a kindergartener during recess.

I knock my shoulder into his arm. "He's the Scully to my Mulder."

"I think you have that backward," Sandesh says.

I don't. "I was going by personality. Not gender."

With an I'll-give-you-that-one frown, he steps back as Gracie moves to the door and opens it with a wave of her wrist on the small black pad. Sandesh and I follow her lead, waving our own wrists.

Gracie's office is modern, white, and meticulously clean. White bookcases line the wall behind a bleached white desk. In the corner stands a white grandfather clock with a round, white face. And in front of the desk are two modern, white Belgian linen chairs.

Type A, party of one.

Gracie's neatness makes me itchy. Loosen up already. I nearly laugh when Sandesh brushes at the coffee stain on his pants before sitting down, and Gracie eyes him like he's carrying the plague. Okay, so this is a party.

I sit next to Sandesh, crossing my legs ranch-hand-style—right foot on left knee. "What's the holdup with Cee? You haven't even given her a psych eval yet."

Sitting at her desk, posture straight as a board, she levels her all-business gaze at me. She isn't that much older than I am, but she has an ancient attitude. Kind of a contradiction—a club owner whose hairstyle, usually a tight little bun to go with her tight little body, makes her look deadly serious.

Gracie puts a finger on the trackpad and clicks something open. "Who shot the sex-slaver in the distribution center?"

Whoops. I drop my eyes, watch my toes curl and uncurl, bowing the cheetah-print fabric of my flats, before deciding she probably already knows the truth. "The kid did."

Sandesh's head spins toward me like a rock from a slingshot. Of course, I filled him in on the way over about how I initially screwed up the Brothers Grim mission, but I hadn't told him, or anyone really, *that* little detail.

Gracie sits back as if vindicated. "And you ask me what the holdup is?"

I can't help jumping into this. I, more than any of my siblings, knows how much the group can mean to those of us whose past included abuse at the hands of Walid and Aamir. "Big deal. She took matters into her own hands. Sounds perfect to me."

Gracie's eyes widen, furrowing her brow. "Sounds sadistic to me."

Sadistic? "She killed the guy to save my ass." Not that I needed her help at that point. *Shh...* Keeping that to myself. "Besides, who else could she depend on? How many times have we seen raids go down at these places and the slavers go free and the women end up punished? How many times have we seen the women who have been trafficked put in jail? What were her choices? And even you can't deny she's got real potential."

Gracie's perfectly manicured eyebrows crash together. "To be adopted as a sister?" She shakes her head. "No. She's rejected. She's way too old."

"She's fifteen."

"Possibly sixteen. We don't adopt that late. Besides, the unit she'd be adopted into is already at capacity."

"Fuck that. She saved my life."

"Yes. You should be grateful and more careful. But that doesn't mean I'm going to go through the trouble of giving her a psych eval, making sure no family is out there, and then washing her to make her look like a legit adoptee. No. She has too much history. Besides, I don't need a psych eval to tell she's messed up."

That pisses me off. Cee is my save. She's my hope. "Not all of us can be adopted from the cradle, Gracie. Some of us are used, abused, angry, and messed the fuck up."

Crossing her arms, exposing cleavage and a lacy red bra totally at odds with her bland, black silk, button-down, she barks, "Don't belittle me simply because I was adopted as an infant, Justice. You know what I've lost because of The Guild."

I know. I also know that she has to stop using the past as an angry excuse to justify everything she does. Not that I'd know anything about that. "This isn't about Cee's qualifications. It's about the fact that she's the same age as Tyler."

"Don't do that. Don't bring him up. Ever."

I exhale frustration so hot I'm surprised I don't see fire. How is it we can push each other's buttons minutes after sitting down? I do it like it's my job. But it's not. She can deal with her own stuff, because, yeah, I got my own shit to deal with, too. "Look, Gracie, she asked. You know how rare that is. They never ask. And she's determined. I saw it in her face. She's not going to forget about us. It's safer for The Guild to have her brought in."

"Not if I M-erase her."

I know, even as the rage overtakes me, that Gracie is beyond pressing my buttons; the suggestion is mean. I can't even bring myself to believe Momma would allow erasing the memory of a fifteen-year-old. Still, I take the bait. Using the one word, I know will hurt her most. "You bit—"

Bam! Gracie slams her hands on the desk. "Don't, Justice. I won't put up with that word being uttered in my office."

Caught in the middle of a sister squabble that includes a culture he can't hope to understand and things he should know nothing about, Sandesh looks over and mouths, *M-erase?*

Clenching the seat's arms, I do my best to control my voice. "Tell me what you have against her. Tell me why she can't be brought in."

Is it because you're a traitor and secretly hate the family and the sister who loves you?

Grabbing a watermelon Jolly Rancher from the bowl on her desk, Gracie unwraps it quietly, expertly. The grandfather clock *tick*, *tick*, *tick*s the seconds away. She puts the candy in her mouth. "I've never encountered a rage like hers before. Not since..."

Her eyes shift away from me. Her face reddens.

She doesn't want Cee here because she's like me? Okay. That fucking hurts.

I press harder, trying to get at any hateful feelings she has toward me. "Yeah. I'm angry. I've always been. I punched you in the face the first time we met."

A sad smile flits across her face. "Because I called you my sister. You told me your sister was dead then punched me." She licks a red tongue across her lips. "That was different."

"How? How is my childhood anger different from hers?"

As if pondering the question, she clicks the candy between her teeth, turns it over, sucks it back in. "Don't you have enough, Justice? Isn't getting first Tony and now Sandesh into The Guild enough? Now you want the kid indoctrinated, too?"

Indoctrinated? I drop my foot to the floor with a thud and sit forward, close enough to see how fast Gracie is breathing. "This isn't about Cee. This is about Momma, our home, The Guild. You think you know better. You think Cee can do better than us."

"Yeah. Fine." She throws up her hands. "It's about the way we were raised, and the way I was raised before my mom came. Being a Parish, having all that money, having your values and knowledge filtered through The Guild and the trauma of our sisters messes you up, but it's different for me. I was freed, so I see things differently."

I bite my lip. If I have to hear one more time about Gracie's miraculous transformation into worldly woman and how the rest of us were sheltered for too long, I'm going to lose it. We needed that time being cocooned in the family to heal. She was adopted as a baby, not as an injured child or teen. She doesn't understand.

I don't say that, but I do hit back. "You can't use your injury to injure others, Gracie. I'm sorry about John. I'm devastated about Tyler. I wish things had been different. But he left, he chose to get out, so stop blaming us."

Working the candy in her mouth, Gracie glares like only a redhead with green eyes can—all spit and fire. "God, Justice, you really are the baby of our unit. Grow up. John would never have done that."

The baby of our unit. She means the youngest, not the last one adopted into our group. That was Tony. I was fourth. Dada second. Bridget third.

Confused, I let the anger simmer, ready to heat it back up if needed. Beside me, Sandesh keeps quiet. Handsome and smart. This line of questioning is getting us somewhere. His silence will keep her talking.

I ask the obvious question. "What are you saying?"

She rubs at her eyes. If she had on a stitch of makeup, that would've smeared it. But Gracie has no interest in dressing up, face or body. Her biggest fashion accessory is the fit body she gets from her devotion to the Cambodian martial art of Muay Thai. And genetics. "Leland found out John knew about The Guild."

"Yeah. I remember the shouting. And?"

"And when he found out, he told me there were three choices. The first two involved killing or M-erasing John. The third was me giving up John and Tyler."

I grind my teeth. Again, she mentions M-erasure in front of Sandesh. It's no mistake. She wants him to ask, wants him to know exactly the type of dark shit my family can get up to.

I pause long enough to get control of my agitation and absorb exactly what she just told me. "Wait. Leland threatened John?"

"Yeah, he did. I made John leave to save him. I told John I chose The Guild over"—her voice wavers—"them. I told him I'd fight for full custody if he ever breathed a word of the family, so he left, staying silent and alive all this time."

The room goes unnaturally quiet. I ache for Gracie. I'm hardly able to believe that John didn't leave but was forced to leave so Gracie could save him from the family. It shouldn't surprise me, but, honestly, it does. She had to give Tyler up to save his father. It seems so unfair. I got Sandesh into the family and got to keep him. But Gracie...

Gracie licks her lips with an artificially red tongue. "You

asked me how your anger was different from Cee's? You were six. You wanted love and kindness, even if you couldn't admit it. Cee just wants to hurt people. The Guild is bad enough without adding people like that."

Faced with the pain my sister has had to carry, I suddenly can't breathe. I can't imagine the rage she's been holding against Momma and Leland.

A sinking feeling pulls at my stomach. A tremor of doubt convulses inside my heart. The traitor could be Gracie. It could.

32

SANDESH

After my messed-up morning as Justice's Scully, I arrive at the International Peace Team's headquarters in a suburb outside of Philly. Walking toward the entrance, I'm still rattled by the encounter with Gracie. If she hadn't been top of my list before, she would be now. She was asked to give up more than any person should have to for her family. I can't blame her for her attitude and anger—though I *can* blame her for finding any blame with Justice. Still, I get the feeling that she can't separate Justice from that time in their lives.

I pull open the front door and enter, unable to shake my suspicion of Gracie and my worry about that term, M-erasure. If Justice hadn't been so upset after the conversation, I would've asked about it, but, honestly, I don't need them to tell me the details. I got enough from context. Their family, or one of the many Parish companies, has developed a way to alter people's memories.

A chill runs down my body as I walk through the sunlit atrium. What exactly is the Parish family capable of? Do I even want to know?

I pull off my tie, hoping Justice appreciates what I'm going through for her. The dress uniform is one of the things I don't miss about being a Ranger. To my mind, ties are a way to make men uneasy, reminding them to choke back any spark of individuality.

I push the UP elevator button as my phone rings. I pull it from my pocket. Doesn't Leland know how to text? I answer. "Yeah."

"I see you are at the IPT."

I'm so not interested in weighty reminders that I'm being watched. How *I Know What You Did Last Summer*. "Yep. I'm at my place of employment, my business, because I'm not a prisoner to you. Bad enough I have to keep looking over my shoulder for Walid and his men."

"We thought you were spending the day with Justice. What are you doing there?"

This guy doesn't trust me and the feeling is mutual. "Actually, I was just headed upstairs to prepare my press statement on global covert Parish family activities. Can I get a statement from you?"

There's a pause, hard and solid enough to feel like a punch to the gut.

"Don't let this get messy, Sandesh. We care about Justice. We'd hope you do too."

Was that a threat to Justice? What Gracie had revealed earlier makes it a distinct possibility. These people are seriously messed-up.

With effort, I swallow the gonna-eat-you-up-and-spit-you-out rising in my throat. "Look, Leland, we both understand the situation. I'm on your side."

For now.

Another weighty pause. Like an orca circling a seal.

"Will you still make it to dinner tonight?"

"I've already got it penciled in on my company calendar as a meeting with the head of a secret society."

A sound shockingly like a laugh erupts from his mouth before he hangs up.

I look at my phone. Before this call, I was wavering on doing what I'm about to do, but Leland's threat to Justice, even as mild as it was, has my defend-and-conquer genes racing. So, now, I'm going to find out everything I can about the Parish family.

The elevator jerks to a stop, the doors open, and I step into a hallway lined with steel-framed, black-and-white photographs.

Victor is there. He whistles at me, taking in my suit. He's dressed casually, khaki slacks and a screen-printed T-shirt with a colorful logo of a woman twirling, arms outstretched. He has the sleeves up, showing his *Death Before Dishonor* tattoo, and his brown hair buzzed down to military attention.

Knowing what's coming as I push past him, but he still coos at me, "Oh, Sandy. If I were into discipline, I'd be all over you."

I shake my head. After ten years of friendship, I'm used to my bisexual friend who flirts like his agenda is to make everyone in the world shake off their uptight restrictions. "I appreciate the love, man. Especially since I pretty much abandoned you for two weeks."

"Forget it. How's things with Momma Warbucks?"

We walk down the hall and into our suite of offices. The receptionist greets me and I wave back.

"Actually, we're going to need to talk about that." I raise my eyebrows in a way that lets him know it's private before adding, "In my office."

The moment we enter my corner office, I realize the office isn't as I'd left it—clean.

Three gray-and-red-striped chairs have been pulled out around a table with two tablets and multiple files scattered across it. My U-shaped desk is also covered with files. Looks like the staff was here late last night, organizing volunteers. I have no idea why people gravitate to this office during a crisis, but it's good to know they do it even when I'm not here.

Victor puts a hand on my shoulder, drawing my attention from the mess. "Okay, big guy, that's a lot of brooding silence. Should I pull a fire alarm?"

I really hate to do this to Victor, who's already done so much for me. Sure, he has the contacts. Sure, he spent years undercover after leaving Special Forces. Sure, he'd do anything for me. All of that makes it harder, not easier, to ask. "I know you're the last person I should be asking, but I need a favor."

"Para ti..." He waves his hand instead of finishing that well-known *for you, anything* phrase. "My currency is favors, but please tell me this isn't about one of those Parish hermanas?"

I slip behind my desk, dropping my keys and cell atop a stack of files, before plopping into my leather swivel. "No, it's... I mean... yes. I guess it is."

Tugging up his pants, Victor sits on an edge of my desk. "Which one?"

For a moment, my mind goes blank. Which *one*? The only one who matters. Knowing I can't say that—and unsure what it means that I thought it—I stare through the thick glass windows and the Schuylkill Expressway traffic below.

"Dude, tell me it's not that mad scientist. That chemist chick has a patent on some sort of mind serum shit. She's selling it to the government."

"You're paranoid." Actually, he might not be. I never did ask Justice what M-erasure was, but it seems pretty obvious from the content of her argument. "No, it's Justice."

"Oh. The hot Native American chick. Papi likes."

Indignation flares in my chest. I turn from the window, hold up one finger. "Don't."

Whatever Victor sees in my face has his whole demeanor changing. The humor dies. He meets my eyes with a nod.

Warned. Backing off.

Good.

I don't want Justice compressed into anything—not into a race, not into a woman, not into a *hot* woman, not into anything that identifies her in a way that lets her be simplified. It's wrong, like calling the Pope a religious guy.

Victor smiles knowingly at me before picking up the bronze Wounded Warrior statue on my desk, turning it over. "What's the favor?"

"I know you have connections."

Victor grunts in amusement.

Yeah, that's like saying Bill Gates has money. "Can you see what you can dig up on Mukta Parish, the Mantua Academy, and four of the Parish family?"

I begin to write down the names of Justice's suspect siblings with Gracie at the top of the list. That woman has good reason to be angry, is secretive, and doesn't trust anyone. Seems like the traits of someone who can't be trusted.

Victor raises a hand to take the list, but I pull it back. "Can you make that five?" Though he isn't a sibling, Leland of the we're-watching-you phone calls goes on the list, too. I'm still annoyed by his threats.

Victor takes the paper and reads the names. "Easy enough, I know someone, former NSA. She owes me a favor or six."

Victor has contacts because Victor did top-secret, undercover work for years while in Special Forces. After that, before the IPT, he worked as a private contractor with a global security firm. "You ever miss it, man?"

He raises his head, shrugs. "Do I miss danger, near misses, starving my ass off in the middle of nowhere? Hell, yes. But that was a high. It's not satisfying to me the way this job is."

That, I get. "What have you heard from Salma?"

"With the big bucks you got us, we were able to settle them in Jordan."

"That's good to hear." Turns out Syrians don't give up easy. "I'm glad they're okay at the warehouse."

"Doing great. I'm not sure what else you have going on with Mukta Parish, but she's done right by us. She helped shut down and evacuate Salma's entire operation, then she rented a warehouse in Amman under the guise of a bakery. But how'd you get kicked out of Za'atari?"

Hearing this should make me feel better, but the weight of this entanglement settles heavy against my chest. We've been organizing for over a year, and though we have no problem with volunteers or organizations to partner with, funding has been a big issue. Until now... but this gift horse could screw everything else up.

I go with the half-truth, telling him about the mission Salma and I put together because he has to be aware of what's out there. I'm hoping *that* awareness is where his knowledge of this stops.

33

JUSTICE

Elevator X slides to a stop on 4A. Gym, firing range, and lots of secret society classrooms. Pretty much my favorite floor.

I step out into the processed-air-and-show-your-pores-bright corridor. Tinted glass runs along the hall as I walk toward the gym. Even though they're tinted, I can still make out one of my siblings and people from Internal at the firing range. Their shots are muffled by the thick glass walls.

After my morning with Gracie, I changed into workout clothes, black leggings and sleeveless tee—dark clothes to match my mood. And, also, to make it easier to move during my training session.

My cross-trainers squeak, echoing in the high-ceiling hallway, as I walk the floor. Feels good to be home. Would feel better if I weren't trying to figure out which of my siblings betrayed me.

Next up, Tony.

A sensor at these gym doors reads my upraised wrist, and, with a low *click*, they *whoosh* open.

My shoulders tighten. Odd. Being tracked hadn't bothered me before. Now, I feel exposed.

Still, my heart lightens when I step inside. The gym is fully-equipped, state-of-the-art, and huge. No lie. It easily accommodates treadmills, weight machines, trampolines, punching dummies, dojo, boxing ring, and, at the farthest end—*shudder*—the Devil's Gauntlet. The DG employs balance obstacles, a salmon ladder, cargo net, warp wall, spider climb, and impossible ledges and agility leaps. I hate that thing.

The grunts, slaps, clank of weights, and treadmill *thud*s echo along the huge space with its thirty-foot ceiling. I skirt the training mats until the speaker system announces my and Tony's sparring session.

Right on time.

Shirtless, shoeless, wearing only his well-worn white gi pants, Tony does a double backflip off the trampoline, landing in the sparing arena with an eager smile.

What a showoff. Normally, I'd be all about shutting him down and shutting him up, but not today. The best time to talk with Tony is while fighting him. He loosens up. So damn loose and talkative. It's like trying to hit a cross between Stretch Armstrong and Elmo.

I slip off my shoes. We meet in the center of the yellow mat, one of four colored mats where people spar. Usually, we run through pattern practice, a series of training skills, and then do a bit of free sparring. But, today, I think it's best to get right to the fun stuff.

Stretching out my arms—a distraction—I say, "Tony. How's my favorite sister?" and send a spin kick at his ribs.

Tony dodges the strike like water sliding across ice.

My toes skim his skin.

He dances back, lean, flexible, and a bundle of muscle. He rubs his rib, in the general vicinity of his *All for One* tattoo. "Old moves, J. Rib still pings from last time."

Huh? I'm getting predictable? I charge in, trying for a neck lock.

He blocks, gets control of my arm, traps it.

Fuck, that hurts.

I send an elbow at his head.

He dodges, but my strike does the job because he loosens his grip.

I break way, back off, shake out my arm.

Seeing my discomfort, Tony flashes his pearly straight teeth at me.

Ass. "I'm pretty sure I could get my entire fist into that mouth, Tony. *While* you're eating an apple."

He smiles wider. Under that great smile, he's all deadly charm and South Philly. "Did ya know female ducks got a hidden uterus?"

He's trying to distract me. Kind of his thing. Still... "Like a covert uterus?"

While I'm pondering this, he sends a front kick at me.

I grab his heel.

He twists, breaks away, and uses his other leg to sweep me to the ground.

I roll, bounce back up.

I'm breathing heavier now, starting to sweat. He's taking charge of this session when I'd hoped to dictate the moves and our discussion.

"Know how some animals go all-out, plumes and dancing and whatnot, to impress the females?"

I keep him at arm's length, watching the spread of his hands, the shift of his hip, and the slide of his feet against the cushioned mat. "Yeah, so?"

"Well, male ducks ain't goin' for that shit. They just up and rape the females. Fact, they do it all the time. So much so, the female's anatomy adapted. Not only are their duck vaginas ridged like a screw—going the opposite way of the male penis ridges—"

Ouch. "You're making that up." I block his right jab, strike out with my free hand.

He steps back instinctually, and I'm there.

Hooking his leg, I trip him onto the mat, then drop on top of him. We wrestle. And he's still fucking talking.

"God's honest," he says, nearly in my ear.

My grip slips from around his sweaty, shirtless torso. Probably why he wears no shirt.

Reaching back, I grab his leg instead, manage the lock, put pressure on it.

He taps out, and I let go.

Even though I bested him, he gets to his feet, smiling, dancing, and still talking. "Their vaginas are like a labyrinth with fake little offshoots for the sperm the female don't want."

A labyrinth?

We exchange a series of strikes and counterstrikes, with him moving closer each time.

He gets control of my neck, forces my head down.

I make a move toward his balls.

He jumps back and leaves go of me.

Wiping sweat from my face, I try to match his casual banter. "A species has developed, through the violence of their own kind, physical ways to prevent rapists from procreating with victims. Wasn't there a weird senator who claimed a human female's body did the same thing?"

"Yeah. *Dick.* Like women are raped as much as ducks and evolve that kind of shit."

"What? No, I meant—"

He hits me with a series of fast, hard, and angry strikes.

Too fast.

Unexpected and not even *close* to the playful way we'd been sparring.

I step back.

He keeps coming.

I put up my hands, expecting a hit.

He sweeps my legs out from under me.

My head bounces against the mat.

Cushioned or not, that shit hurts.

Breathing heavily, I stay down, stretch my legs out.

Tony comes over and offers me a hand.

Hmmmm. Accept his hand, or use it to retaliate? I'm angry. Why change the tone of our sparring?

Ah hell. I *know* to expect the unexpected.

I take his hand.

He pulls me to my feet. Once up, I slap his arm. "Charming story, Tone."

"It's easy with you, Justice. You bring out the charm in people."

That edge of anger in his voice confirms my early thoughts. "Some kind of lesson in that story?"

Grabbing some towels and floor spray from the cleaning station, he hands them to me because loser has to clean. "The lesson is, even the cold gaze of evolution knows when something is dead wrong and so do you, so stop using this guy and his charity; it's not right."

I figured that he'd heard about Sandesh. I also figured everyone in this loud, opinionated family would have something to say. Inviting new people into The Guild is a big deal, but I hadn't expected this objection. "Sandesh knows the score. And, for the record, using the IPT wasn't on me. It was Momma's decision."

He snorts. "Just because Momma decides it's okay, doesn't make it okay. She's shitting on The Guild's greatest strengths—independence, closed ranks, and family teams—and you're following along to gain a new cover? It's not right."

Unable to answer, to tell him what I can't fully admit to

myself—that I don't give a shit about the cover, that I want Sandesh to be part of my life and this family—I begin to clean the sweat-soaked mat.

He shifts on his feet as he talks. "And, just for the record, it's bad enough Momma fucked with this guy's company, but you're fucking with his heart. How long before he begins to see that you're always going to choose The Guild over him?"

My shoulder blades draw together and my neck tenses. *Tony.* This was supposed to be about me getting under *his* skin, not him getting under mine.

I wipe the mat angrily, grateful when his next session is announced. "Why do I have to choose? He knows what I'm about, knows why I do what I do, and he's okay with it."

He barks a sound that easily tips over from humor to sarcasm. "Sure. Mr. Peace, Love, and Charity is fine with you being an assassin."

Pain, as thick as a post, spears my heart. "He's in The Guild and the family. He's not going anywhere and neither am I, so get used to it."

"Fine. Go the way of Dada. Make that colossal mistake."

I spray his toes.

He jumps back.

"What does that mean?"

"It means Dada has spent more time mooning over her informant than doing the job, and it's costing The Guild and the family. Ask Jules."

Another set of toes with nails neat and trimmed and painted black appears next to Tony's.

Juliette, aka Jules.

I stand, take her in for a moment, confused and wary. "Don't you usually train with Dada?"

She shrugs and fists her hands at her sides. "She says she's sick, but I just saw her pigging out in the break room." She points at Tony. "Now I get to train with Monkey Man. Again."

Tony feigns hurt, putting a wounded hand to his chest. "Monkey Man's gonna kick your ass, Jules."

Break room? Dada has to know Tony already has his hands full with Jules's twin, Rome. Their birth names were Romeo and Juliette—God, some parents are so fucked up. Good thing they opted, like Bridget, to change their birth names at adoption. Sixteen now, they were adopted eight years ago. He's only the second male adopted into the Parish fold. Tony loves the kid.

A quick visual sweep and I spot Rome working the heavy bag. He's grown into a big kid. Muscular. And though he's Jules's twin, he shares little in common with her. She's blonde and golden-skinned, he's dark-haired and pale.

Needing to say something because Jules is looking at me like I've got the answers to this situation, I say, "I'll talk to her.'

Jules turns her head slightly, as if to avoid a bad smell.

Yeah, fine, that was lame, but what else can I say? It's not like Dada answers to me.

"Monkey Man has his next victim," Tony says. Letting his arms drag to his sides, he begins making monkey noises.

Jules looks worried and pissed. "Tell Dada she sucks."

Will do. One *you-suck-Dada*" coming up. Sub-headlined with, *What's this I hear about you and your Brothers Grim informant?*

Still a sweaty mess, I slip on my shoes and heel-toe my way down to the break room. What the hell is up with Dada? She abandoned training her little sister—which is bad enough—but getting close to her informant?

With a wave of my wrist, the door opens and a softly spoken computer warning issues from above, "Authorization for forty minutes in Lounge B. No weapons allowed. Please do not abuse this privilege. Thank you."

Security around here is too damn much. Like all the slackers—of which there are none—would be tempted to hang out in a boring break room watching CNN. Yep, nothing more fun than plastic seats pushed up against round, white-laminate tables.

The red spikes of Dada's size-nine Jimmy Choos are propped against said tables near a bottle of imported water when I enter. To my surprise, she is leaning back watching TV. Her indigo skirt has slid up, revealing her long, dark, beautiful legs.

Smells good in here, like freshly baked bread and marinated chicken. Before I sit down in a chair across from her, I see her reach for the remote. Her eyes flick nervously to the television screen bolted to the wall.

Before she turns it off, I take a look at the soccer player running across the screen, recognize him from prior mission briefings, and choke out, "Is that your informant, back when he played?"

"Yes. Why?" Turning off the TV, she slides her feet off the table and sits up straight. She's trying to act like it's no big deal, but she fingers the thick, woven-leather bracelet on her wrist. A nervous habit tied to her childhood.

Dada's story isn't too dissimilar from many of my siblings. You don't rescue children from great situations. You rescue them from shitty ones. Kidnapped as a child, she spent years as one man's prisoner. He lavished her with jewelry and presents, as if that could make up for his abuse. Momma rescued her at twelve. She'd been giving birth. The bracelet she wears is in memory of the child. The boy who died. The comfort she gets from that bracelet tells me everything I need to know about her unease.

I wave toward the now silent television. "This doesn't look like research. It looks like a crush. Like you've blurred the lines and fallen for your informant. A man who helps the slavers get around by providing them papers."

Dada's honey gold eyes widen, then narrow. "You know as

well as I that he became involved with them while trying to rescue a former student. You also know, he was the one to inform us of Walid's move to Jordan."

I scramble back through my memory for details on this guy. In Mexico, he goes by John, but that's not his name. It's Sean Bradford, former Welsh soccer player turned art teacher in El Salvador. And, yeah, he got involved with Walid to rescue a student taken from under his nose. So, he's not an awful guy, but that doesn't mean he couldn't switch sides if it meant saving his own skin.

I go on the offensive. "Why do you think the Brothers picked Jordan? A place where we have so few resources? Coincidence?"

"I have an informant, not access to their brain waves."

"If you had to guess?"

"If I had to guess, I'd say someone betrayed the mission and warned the Brothers Grim that it would be an ideal place to get away from an imminent threat and still proceed with their meeting."

Guess the cat is out of the bag and peeing all over the bed. This is the problem with trying to get information from trained spies: they're always one step ahead. "Could your informant have told the Brothers—"

"No. He gives me information. I don't give him information."

"But—"

"I am no novice. Believe me, I know how to manage an asset."

"Really?" I gesture at the television again. "Do you spend as much time managing this guy as you spend watching old videos of him?"

"If you are asking if I am sleeping with him, the answer is yes and it's quite enjoyable."

Whoa. What? If she's willing to admit that, admit the violation, she must be in it bad. Or guilty and trying to throw me off the track of something bigger. "What the *fuck*? You've risked The Guild. Your informant has obviously told Walid about—"

"Wrong. He hasn't any information to give Walid, and, you have no room to talk after you revealed secrets to Sandesh—"

"That's not the same—"

"Agreed, it's actually much worse. Sandesh gave nothing to this operation, whereas Sean has risked himself repeatedly by providing us with secret information about Walid's organization, like their weak security, sexual proclivities, numerous comings and goings, and the shift to Jordan. And, yet, he isn't being brought into the family and welcomed because he does not have a charity Momma can use as a cover."

My head spins with this tirade, but I can't get past what she's also revealed. "Speaking of covers, aren't you undercover as a nun in Mexico? How the hell do you two even manage—"

"Enough. Unless you have something related to the operation to ask, I'd prefer this questioning stop."

On the offense *and* the defense. She more than *cares* about Sean. She might even be in love with him. If so, what would she do to protect him? Warn Walid? Try to scare the family off the mission, so she can extract an asset? Risk me?

Best way to find out is to press her buttons. "I'm going to need Sean's help getting into Walid's Mexican compound. I'll need Walid's daily schedule, codes for the security system, number of guards for every shift, and a better layout for Walid's underground chamber."

"No." Massaging her temples, shakes her head slightly. "Walid is attempting to find the mole in his organization. Anything Sean does could draw suspicion. Let alone having him walking the compound, secreting out notes."

"All the more reason for him to help."

"Stop," Dada slaps her hands together, a Momma power

move. "You're talking about going on the offensive against organized crime at their home base when they are on high alert. It's a reckless suggestion."

Like we have a choice at this point? "Wrong. I know of many brutal retaliations carried out by The Guild with minimal prep. *And* more exposure."

"By our sisters in arms in poorer countries. In places where men can be scared from their abuse, but this isn't something done with a cudgel or by threatening to slice off someone's balls."

Sensing I have the upper hand for once, I don't relent. "I need *in* there, to end this, to end Walid. Momma's already given her approval."

Not true, but Dada doesn't need to know that.

Face pinched, eyes wide, she points a desperate finger at me. "Please, for once, think of others. You can't use your temper to shape the world to your desires."

"Actually, that's kind of our company motto."

Though it hurts to see her so distressed, I stand up and approach the exit doors, throwing back one last, "Talk to Sean and let me know what he says."

Out in the hall, I almost fall against the wall. After a moment, I push off the wall and push away guilt as I make my way upstairs. If we were normal sisters, maybe that conversation would've been different. Maybe, it would've been about her attraction to a man, my attraction to a man, the sharing of stories and winks and nods of understanding. Instead, of the sorry mess of accusation and jousting has my stomach turning and everything in me feeling... empty.

Shit. It's not like Sean is endangering himself for no reason. I do need that information. Still, I hate what I asked of him enough that I nearly run back down the hall and take it all back.

I don't. I wasn't kidding when I told Dada that I need this to end. If she's the traitor, this will force her to make a move. A move I'll be ready for.

34

JUSTICE

It's been a long day, as evidenced by the squirming line of four girls and one boy on the dojo floor before me and Bridget. If Cee is adopted and added to this unit, it'll be the biggest one ever.

My unit, the Spice Girls—so named by the class above us—wouldn't have survived another member. We had enough drama all on our own. But this class, Vampire Academy, they're... I guess the best word is unshakeable.

Even so, they're not paying attention to Bridget. Probably nervous about dinner. If you aren't on time, you skip dessert. And they still have to go upstairs, shower, and get dressed.

Bridget claps her hands, a sound that is all Momma. "The three moves Justice and I demonstrated are for quick defense, and only part of what you need. Remember what I said about keeping your eyes open, your spirit open, always noticing the world, even if it's uncomfortable. In fact, if it makes you uncomfortable, pay even more attention."

That's good advice—good advice that no one absorbs.

Bridget doesn't understand that not everyone has her limitless patience. Most eyes are on the door.

I give her a let-me-in-coach raise of my brows.

She sighs, giving me the go-ahead.

Yeehaw. "Sisters!"

All heads snap up. Rome's eyes, a tapered edged, amber brown—as if somewhere buried within his Slavic ancestry was a long-gone relative from China—narrow. Huh. Sensitive. With a too-high opinion of himself. Probably because of his good looks.

"All for one and one for all isn't just a motto. Trust us. If we hold you here longer than necessary, it's because this matters more than dessert."

They quiet, but across their faces plays a range of emotions: anger, embarrassment, and defiance. A difference in skin tone, eye color, height, weight, and yet, they all have the fire that marks them as part of this family.

Bridget takes over again, meeting each of their eyes before bowing at the waist. "Namaste."

With those words, five teens tear up and out.

Bridget frowns at their exit, but I smile. I remember being a teen in training and waiting impatiently while an older classmate went on and on about stuff that seemed irrelevant when compared to the fighting itself.

Bridget watches them go with that frown still on her face. She's usually a ray of positivity.

I try to ease her out of her mood. "We should get the Troublemakers to rename that unit." I incline my head toward the stampeding teens. At the landing, one of the girls uses the banister to slingshot herself up the next staircase. "They're more Fast and Furious than Vampire Academy."

"True." Her Bambi-brown eyes crinkle at the edges. "But we nailed the Troublemakers. Those three need meditation."

I pick up my towel and cell. "Or a bonfire of sage."

Bridget laughs, a forced sound that ends quickly as we exit into the foyer. Her gaze goes to the stairs. "Whoever started the idea of letting the older unit name the unit directly below them?"

Hmmm. "I'm not sure. Momma's been adopting lost girls since she was twenty-three, for over forty years, so she must've named the first unit, the Fantastic Five. Our unit's the third of seven, and we have the A-Team to thank for our awful name, Spice Girls."

Bridget shakes her head. "God, Tony hates that."

"You mean Sporty Spice? Yeah, he does. But I still think the youngest unit has it the worst. Really? The Lollipop Guild?"

Bridget frowns. "I'm not sure. Lost in Translation has always struck me as kind of a mean name."

"*Mean*? It's funny as hell. None of them spoke English or even the same language when they were adopted. Lighten up. It's all a normal part of having a big family. Teasing."

"I'm not sure. Things have gotten more contentious in these past years. More fights. More issues. What worked for the older groups isn't working for the younger ones."

More discontentment is what she's getting at, but I think it's the natural evolution of our family. Things started out smaller, more manageable. The Fantastic Five was the first group of adoptees. They'd honed their skills and developed the program. When Momma added another unit, things got complicated, but she'd managed the older groups by pitting them against each other. The A-Team had worked furiously to outdo the Fantastic Five and that had kept things productive. But then came our group, and we developed our own way of doing things.

The first boy in the family—Tony—and the first child to leave our home as a teen—Gracie—rejecting, for all intents and purposes, our way of life. And, of course, Bridget who always seeks to taper our more aggressive practices.

Bridget and I have stopped moving. As if we both know this conversation has grown serious, we stand together in the front hall. I tell her, "Problems are to be expected. It's a mansion full of kids. A mansion full of *damaged* kids, sorted into units based on age, not when they were adopted. So, someone adopted for six years could be in the same unit as someone who's been here for six months. That's why we have weird rules that evolved over decades. Which is *also* why supervised fighting is encouraged. As is speaking your mind."

"Speaking your mind?" She raises her eyebrows to make her point.

In the hall, the echo of Vampire Academy teens running around upstairs crashes down the steps. *Whoa.* Bulls at Pamplona up there.

"You think those kids are shrinking violets?"

Bridget glances up the steps as if she can see the offenders. "I'm not sure we're doing right by any of them. Are you?"

She can't be serious. "Hell, yes. We saved them. Taught them to fight. Taught them not to be victims. Where would they be without Momma and The Guild?"

Bridget's cheeks grow red. "I know. I agree with that. It's just... The violence. They're so young."

Young in age, maybe. "Each kid here has been through some serious shit. For them, self-defense isn't violence; it's empowerment."

She purses her lips, and, without saying a word, her chin drops toward the floor. She's pointing out that what goes on below ground *is* violent. Still...

"No one under ten is allowed below for training. No one under eighteen goes on missions. And before they do either, they're given a choice. We all have the choice. You did."

"Do they? Did I?"

What? My mind skips to the past. Bridget—her chosen, not given name—was adopted from Laos when she was ten. Eight months later, I came to the family. I was six. Still, she and I went below ground together four years later, when I was ten and she was fourteen. Granted, she'd been living in a toxic home, addicted to drugs by an addict mother who'd died, leaving Bridge ripe for exploitation, so she had a lot to deal with when she came here. But was her delay more than that? "I remember riding Elevator X with you, and you seemed as excited as I was."

We'd held hands and had fallen on our assess, laughing.

"Of course, I was trained to want it, like all of us. Going underground was exciting."

A buzzing reminder of Bridget's earlier words zips through my head: *If something makes you uncomfortable, pay more attention.*

Bridget's always been less enthusiastic about the family's more violent leanings, but that's never bothered me. In fact, I thought of it as a good thing. We could use her Lisa Simpson to balance out our aggression. But could she regret all of it? Could she be trying to expose our covert ops or make Momma feel threatened enough that covert ops are stopped?

"What would you have us do differently?"

Her lips thin and tighten, like the boom gate falling across a train track. For a moment, I'm sure the conversation is over, but her lips unclench. "We could shift our practices, take people's emotions and personalities into account. Units are made of people. They're not soldiers."

I'm on the defensive, I know it, but I still can't stop myself. "We have three therapists living on campus and working in Internal Security. They're chipped, know The Guild, and work exclusively for our family. We have care staff that have been here as long as Momma has been adopting. They're family, too."

"Yes, but children become what you teach them to become."

"So, we should teach them only good, happy thoughts." Realizing my voice is echoing and I'm on the verge of shouting, I bring it down. "That didn't keep them safe. What *we* do keeps them safe. The price is that they have to turn around and help others. You think that's bad?"

"No. That's not... I believe we should also teach them how to do a mental detox. The same way we teach them to avoid bad food, drink, substances, we can teach them how to step away from destructive, patterned thoughts. Thoughts create our worlds."

Oh. Boy. How come when people go all cosmic interface, they forget what's weird? "Bridge, we're a school. Meaning, our job is to teach kids *to* think. We can't go around teaching kids how *not* to think."

Her lips tighten again. A firm, disappointed line on a face that's usually bright and open. She fiddles with the black belt around her gi. "You know, sometimes you act like what I do makes me a pie-in-the-sky hippie, but you're wrong. Meditation allows me to see a macro view, not just of my own thoughts, but of the thoughts of people around me. It's incredibly enlightening. It's almost a superpower."

A cold knife of fear unsheathes itself and presses to my throat. That's a very creepy statement. "So, you're smarter than the rest of us?"

Could macro-viewpoint Bridget have plotted against the family to show them the error of their ways? Under all her kindness and equanimity could there beat a Machiavellian heart?

"Not smarter, just less attached to the thoughts that might keep your mind looping, keep you from seeing the bigger picture. You are very much a product of The Guild."

"Keep me from seeing the bigger picture? Like we should just hold hands with sex-slavers?"

"It's not like that." Bridget looks down, sighs lightly, then shakes her head. "It's like with your humanitarian—there are other ways to help."

"He's not *my* humanitarian."

"He's not?" She looks back up. "But he's okay with all of this? With what you do?"

"He's implanted, so yeah, I assume he's okay with it."

Bridget's eyes slide away. "You should definitely ask him before making that assumption. He wasn't raised in The Guild, so he actually *does* have a choice."

She turns and leaves me standing in the hallway with doubts about Sandesh, my upbringing, and my siblings.

35

SANDESH

My truck idles before the Mantua Home's front gates as armed guards check my credentials and the undercarriage of my truck. There is some serious campus security here. Can't help but wonder how people don't question just how serious it is. Not like every school has enough security to anticipate armed gunmen or bombs. Then again, maybe every school in America should.

Still, none of it matters when the threat is inside the building.

I pick up my ringing cell.

Justice says, "You ready for my family?"

My heart warms at the sound of her voice. "Ready and willing." Knowing we have end-to-end encryption, I ask, "What'd you find out today?"

"Dada's sleeping with her Brothers Grim informant." Maybe I should take back the *ready* part of my statement.

"That can't be good."

"Yeah. Betting money's on her or Bridget right now."

The guard approaches my window. "One sec, Justice."

I take the ID he hands me, along with a printed pass with a

barcode that he tells me needs to be displayed on the dash. "Will do," I say, as the other guard withdraws the mirrored pole she'd been using to check beneath my truck. They wave me inside.

Slowing over the speed bump, I stop at the stop sign. This is my first time entering here on my own and unblindfolded. The overcast and misty afternoon doesn't lessen the beauty. Of *course* it would be beautiful; a school this prestigious has a reputation to uphold.

"It's beautiful here," I tell Justice.

"It is." There's a smile in her voice. "Go left at the stop sign."

I do, starting my drive through a campus that stretches over rolling hills.

"What do you see?" she asks me.

There are brick school buildings, dorms, a library, and cafeteria hub, and winding among all of them, walkways lined with elegant streetlights. "A lot of girls of varying ages. They all look so young. Innocent."

Is it possible for Walid to find his way here? I grip the steering wheel and talk myself down from that thought. No. Mukta Parish has kept this school safe for forty years.

"Looks can be deceiving. Just look at my sisters."

"Speaking of... You're no longer thinking it's Gracie? Having to send away your son and the love of your life because he found out the family secret sounds like serious motivation."

"I don't know. Bridget said some weird things today. She thinks she's got some kind of super-brain that can tell what people are thinking. Or something like that. It was really weird."

"Strange." I wait for the teens passing through a crosswalk before I turn right on Parish Court, then head up the hill to the mansion. "What about your brother, Tony?"

"I got nothing from him today, but the day I arrived back from Jordan, he told me he'd given Momma a plan before the

BG mission to take out the Brothers separately. She never brought it up to the team, and he seemed really upset about it."

"Have you seen the plan? Could we use it to get Walid?"

She pauses as if that thought hadn't occurred to her. "I have no idea, but I'll reach out to Leland and ask to see it."

I crest the top of the hill and pull around the fountain, parking in one of the few open spaces. "I'm out front."

"Almost ready. Be down in a sec."

She ends the call and I get out of the truck, surveying the 1914 stone mansion that was here long before the school. I did some research today and learned that there had been a massive renovation thirty years ago, but, for the life of me, I can't tell the old from the new.

The mansion is three stories of finely crafted cornices, arches, and long, elegant windows that fit together seamlessly —proof positive that with enough money, you can hide anything, even a secret society of spies. As I near the front steps, a lean, sixtyish woman with military-straight posture, shiny silver hair, pale-blue eyes, paler-white skin, black suit, and a jagged scar across her nose approaches.

She holds out her hand. "Welcome, Mr. Ross. My name is Martha. I'm head of Home Security. I'm here to show you to the dining room."

Okay, another term to add to my growing Parish family lexicon. Head of Home Security. So, if I have it right, there's Home Security for the house, Internal Security for underground ops, and External Security for the grounds and the school. It's pretty damn secure.

Martha silently and briskly leads me through the maze-of-a-house to the doorway of a large banquet hall. We stand at the entrance.

Justice didn't steer me wrong with her comment about dressing for dinner. In many ways, going to dinner at the Parish residence is like going to a dance at an all-girls' school—lots of beautiful dresses and not a lot of guys. Girls of varying ages and one out-of-place teen boy slip past us like we're rocks in a stream.

Martha gestures toward a thick-legged wooden beast of a table that dominates the huge room. "Would you like me to show you to your seat or would you prefer to wait for Justice?"

"I'll wait."

With a nod, she moves away, and I stand there, hands in pockets, taking in the enormous dining hall. Above the goliath table are a series of beautiful, mismatched crystal chandeliers suspended from a fifty-foot vaulted ceiling. Thick, hand-carved chairs, crystal glasses, yellow roses, gold silverware, gold-edged plates and napkins. It is lavish. Multiple smaller side tables with seating for two or four or six flank the walls. Not sure if those seats are for staff or nannies.

I spot Mukta and Leland walking around the table, addressing children here and there, directing others to seats. They make their way around and finally take two seats at the head of the table.

Now that I know a little about how things work, thanks to Justice's tutelage, I can pick out the groups called units. Kids around the same age, within five years or so, automatically sit together.

A warm hand slips around my waist. I turn toward her and heat shoots through me. She wears an apple-red, juicy-as-sin, off-the-shoulder, like-a-second-skin dress. Damn, memory is so inadequate when it comes to this woman. I draw her closer to my side.

She rises up and whispers hotly into my ear, "Hungry?"

The message delivered within the waves of heat in her voice have nothing to do with food and everything to do with the feeding of my lips against her skin.

Yes. Starved. My eyes feast on the pert, juicy curves of her body, swallow. "Where do I sit?"

She winks with lashes so lush they seem made of silk and sleep. Looking into her eyes reminds me of the dark—of the dark covering bodies. Of the dark covering our intertwined bodies. And I am all about that.

Grabbing my hand, she pulls me after her. "Keep looking at me like that and we'll never make it through dinner."

36

JUSTICE

I try not to show my nerves as I tug Sandesh, in that yummy blue suit, through the dining hall. Knowing how overwhelming being introduced to our large family and unique culture can be, I explain seating as we go.

"We have five units here tonight. Mine." I point toward the head of the table near Momma and Leland, then whisper, "We'll sit up there. Concentrate on Bridget."

He nods. I jolt to a halt as a child races by, nearly squashing my toes. "That would be Bella. For now, she's one of three members of the Lollipop Guild."

"You think more will be added?"

"Oh, definitely. And unfortunately, the youngest unit always sits near Momma—gives the nannies or what we call care staff a break—so you'll get plenty of time to become acquainted with Bella."

We continue on. The Troublemakers' Guild, capital *T* for Trouble, catches my attention. They've already scored some vino. I stop and introduce them to Sandesh. They wave hello, almost like normal people, but, as we walk away, I spot them eyeing Sandesh's fine ass appreciatively. Well, they have good taste.

Mid-table, I introduced the teens of Vampire Academy and then the tweens of Lost in Translation.

"Lost in translation?"

"Not a one of them spoke English or even the same language when they were adopted."

"Sounds challenging."

I snort. "You have no idea. But they made it work."

We head to the head of the table, where Momma and Leland stand to welcome Sandesh.

Much to my surprise, he greets them coolly. Still some anger there, which makes me wonder if Bridget was right. Should I be asking him if he's okay with what the family does? What *I* do?

Sandesh grins as I pull out a chair for him, then he takes the seat. Tony and Bridget sit across from him and Bella's directly to his left. I sit on his other side.

The moment I do, he leans all his beautiful, blond self toward me. My heart approves by doing a *yeehaw!* high kick, followed by a *hot-damn* jig in my chest. This man.

"Is it rude of me to ask—"

I lean in closer, inhale. "I sure hope so."

He laughs and brushes the hair from my bare shoulder. It's an intimate gesture that has me instantly uncomfortable, though he seems unaware of it. Unaware of the fact that we are in a circle of two, and, for me, that never happens.

He waves at the large dining table with its usual mix of loud and louder, and finally gets around to asking his question. "How do you keep everyone straight?"

I smile, because, not twenty minutes ago, I called one of my siblings by the wrong name. "Sometimes, it can get confusing with my older siblings. Especially since many aren't living at home and have branched off into diverse careers in Parish

Global Industries. But, mostly, it's like keeping your extended family's names straight."

He doesn't look convinced. "Even my extended family doesn't include thirty people." He takes a sip of water from a gold-ringed, crystal goblet. "What about getting to know them all?"

"Yeah. That's harder than remembering names. Dinners help. We have huge family dinners regularly."

His eyes grow wide and disbelieving. "This isn't a huge dinner?"

Snort. He's so cute. "No. This is regular dinner. It's expected for each member of a unit, if in the area, to show up once a week to these dinners."

"Unit? You said that had to do with your age, not when you were adopted, right?"

I like that he's so interested in this and, apparently, so does Momma, who I can see paying attention to our conversation. "Yep. It's an age range."

He looks around the room. "Sounds like a lot of planning goes into it."

He's wondering how someone gets the golden ticket. I have no idea. "Momma plans everything." I wink at her, and she rolls her eyes. "Which is why she rarely adopts a child into a unit that already has five members." Actually, *never* is a more accurate description, but I'm laying out hope for Cee. "Kids in the same unit share a bathroom, share a floor, and share a tutor." Share covert training.

"Gracie's a year older than you, so she was in your unit? Who else?" He knows who else, but he's asking so we can engage with the people across the table. I get that without him telling me.

"There's Dada." I look around. Gracie never comes, but where's Dada? "Hey, Tone." He looks up from talking to Bridget. "Where's Dada?"

"Sick."

Again?

I'll delve into that later. I point at Tony to include him in my discussion with Sandesh. "Dada is the oldest in my class at thirty-six. Since she's not here, the next oldest is Tony at thirty-four. Say hi, old man."

Tony's eyes sweep over Sandesh. For a moment, I'm sure he's about to say something embarrassing. Like, *Dude, she's using you.* I transmit a warning to him through slit-serious eyes.

Tony smiles, nods at Sandesh. "Hey."

Sandesh acknowledges him with a return nod.

No humiliation yet. *Phew.* I wave at Bridget, who's next to Tony. "Bridget's the middle kid at thirty-three. And our local yogi." Who apparently has super mind powers.

Bridget waves back, but doesn't engage him. Neither does Tony. Unusual, since they are both friendly and big talkers normally.

I smile at Sandesh as if I haven't noticed. "But, of course, you already know the best."

He leans into me, brushes his hot lips against my ear.

Oh. Yes. That. Feels. Great.

"Is it Gracie?"

I cover my mouth and smother a giggle. Mortifying. I *don't* giggle.

He smiles, and the heat in his playful blue eyes is deadly serious. I can sense Tony and Bridget gaping at me. Good. Let them feel off-balance. Maybe it'll shake something loose.

"Are you in love, Justice?"

Holy shit! Bella just asked the most embarrassing question known to big sisters everywhere. As if she's cool now, the five-year-old Russian with big brown eyes and a long, evil grin jumps up and down in her seat.

Turns out, the younger kids' group name is dead-on. Like the Lollipop Guild from *The Wizard of Oz*, they should've been cute, but they're actually quite shocking. I'll have to make a point to get to know the evil monster better. She could come in handy.

"For a little while, anyways," Tony says. *Gawd.* Tony and all his South Philly. I knew it was too much to ask that he not embarrass me tonight.

For his part, Sandesh doesn't look the slightest bit concerned. In fact, he looks like he's enjoying himself as he gazes down at Bella and says, "Love takes time, Bella. But I hope Justice and I can spend as long as it takes." He winks at me. "And then some."

Aw, seriously, that might be the cutest answer ever. And my own damn heart tells me I don't need even one more minute. What's that about?

Before I can say anything, Sandesh dips down to Bella's level and stage-whispers, "How long do you think it's going to take me?"

And... that's it. The room, now laser-focused on us, erupts with speculation.

37

SANDESH

After dinner, Justice and I step outside into cool, rain-showered night air. Throughout dinner, this woman had teased me with her words, subtle gestures, and looks. Now, I'm so keyed into her that I'm transfixed as she buttons up her jacket, hiding the soft curves underneath. I swallow hard. I'm in it bad.

We descend the stone steps and walk down the driveway, past my truck and the row of cars parked there. I tuck my hands inside the pockets of my slacks, and she loops her arm through mine.

"You really enjoyed it? That dinner? Despite all the giggling and talking and squeeing?"

"Squeeing?" The cobbled driveway gives way to the paved drive, and we stepped onto a sidewalk. Justice's heels click against the concrete. Wrought-iron lampposts light the way, appearing as if they float in the foggy night.

"It's a sound girls make when they're very pleased."

Unaccountably, I found myself angling my walk, as if drawn to her body. Truth is, I've had worse targets. "I think I've heard you make that sound before, but it was louder and involved more sighs." I wink, and since I know exactly how to follow up sexual banter with action, unhook my arm from hers and put it around her waist.

She leans into me. "Sandesh, truth. If I didn't have to sneak you past my little sisters, I'd take you up to my room right now."

My heart and expectations perk up. "I'm not exactly sure how I'm supposed to answer that, but somehow doubt the fact 'I can scale the side of this house and into you room' is the appropriate response, so I'm going to settle for, 'I'm good with my truck.'"

Laughing, she snuggles closer. After long, easy moments of silence, she whispers, "Did you get any vibes?"

I let out a breath. I did. Tony gave off some weird ones, but I don't know enough about any of them to say anything yet. "I'm going to withhold judgment for now, but I'm open if you have anything else you'd like to add from your day's chats."

She lifts her head off my shoulder and her gaze goes the skies. "Guess it was too much to hope we'd be able to sort all of this out in one day."

"Whoever it is has to be a little afraid, afraid enough to hold back from any activity that might draw attention to them."

"Let's go this way. I want to show you something."

We go right, moving down lamppost-lit lanes with elaborately carved shrubs, flowers, and evenly spaced trees. The silence is both comfortable and sizzling with energy.

In the distance, a grotto lit by spotlights with a series of iron candleholders with white candles along the perimeter comes into view. We walk closer, stopping before the candles, and a small wood carved sign. I read it out loud. "Before us, you."

Inside the grotto are numerous statues of women. One with basket on her head, another bent as if to gather a harvest. There are soldiers, suffragettes, a scientist with a microscope, a doctor, and an indigenous woman on horseback. There's a woman carrying a child, with another clinging to her dress.

At the center of these statues is a lone figure on her knees with her arms thrown wide, her head thrown back, as if she's wailing to the heavens. None of the other statues face her and she seems so alone in her grief.

Justice grabs a long match from a lidded tin, lights it from one candle, then transfers the flame to another candle.

"What is this place?"

She blows out the match and passes the burnt stick through a slot in a small silver box. "The Grotto of Shoulders. I light a candle for my sister, Hope, whenever I pass it."

"Grotto of Shoulders?"

She gestures at the statues. "A symbolic representation of the women whose shoulders we've stood upon. Women who were strong so others could benefit. They weren't always acknowledged or even recorded in history. We light candles to mark them and to let them know we carry on their light. Can I light one for someone you know?"

My throat grows tight because I saw her this afternoon, but she hadn't been there, not mentally anyway. "My mother."

Taking another long match from the tin, she lights the candle. When she's done, I hold out my arms, and Justice walks into my embrace. I wrap her tightly, securely. "I'm so sorry, Justice. I wish I could spare you even the memory of that pain, that basement, your sister's death."

"The memory is my strength. I need it."

"No." God, no. "That's what we tell ourselves, but it's not the memory of pain we need; it's the good stuff, like me and you."

With a bit more force than I expect, she grabs the front of my shirt and fists it in her hands, then leans her forehead against my chest.

Uncertain, I brush back her dark hair for long minutes. "Are you okay?"

She looks up at me, her gaze worried and serious. "Something Tony said to me has been bothering me. I don't want you to think I'm using you or your charity. Or that you don't have a choice here."

"What?"

"You said you were looking for more. But I have my more. Because, more than anything, I want to set people free. I want to tell them—*show* them—that they are more than their worst moments, more than the abuse or disregard that scarred them, more than where they've been or started from. *We* are more. So, if you can't deal with that, can't accept that part of me and my life, maybe we should stick to just physical stuff. Just sex. Okay?"

Nope, it's much too late for that. "Where is this coming from?"

She scrunches up her face and latches onto my shirt again. "If not me, who? Who will rescue the unseen, the neglected, the desperate and broken that so many vilify or ignore rather than protect?"

"Justice? I—"

She releases my shirt, pushes against my chest. "I'm not quitting The Guild. Ever. You have to know that. If you're thinking to wait this out, wait until this mission is over, and make your escape from The Guild, realize that you're also making your escape from me. Got it?"

I had thought that before this night, before seeing her with her siblings. But, even if I had had the passing thought, there's no way I could only be physical with her. If it's her and The Guild or no her, I know my answer. "Look, Justice, I get it. I think better than I did before coming to dinner. This place, your family, those kids are more than whatever covert activities your family conducts. A lot more. I would never ask you to give that up for me. It would be like asking you to give up part of yourself."

We're both breathing heavily now. I realize this has turned into something much more serious than either of us might've wanted, but I'm not backing away from what she is really asking me. I cup her face with my hand. "Don't worry about my commitment. I made my choice when I told you, 'You go, I go'. I made my choice when I came here tonight. I make that choice every time I look at you. Touch you."

Her breath hitches and the worry in her eyes eases.

Gently, almost reverently, she turns her face and kisses the palm of my hand. "I bet you're like some kind of grotto gigolo, making a move on the women as they swoon over the candlelight."

I laugh. "That's it exactly. Ready to drop your panties yet?"

Of course, I remember a second too late that I'm dealing with Justice Parish and sexual banter is more like a rowdy pole dance than a slow striptease.

"Maybe I was unclear earlier. Basically, you can take me behind that tree and have me right now." She pumps her eyebrows, and I'm seriously growing to love that gesture.

Easing closer, she lifts onto her toes and angles her head for a kiss before whispering, "I'm serious."

God help me.

38

JUSTICE

Sighing with desperate relief as Sandesh's mouth drops to mine, I slide my tongue inside his hot, eager mouth. His skillful tongue greets and welcomes me. Our playful exploration quickly rages into hot, frantic kisses.

Grasping my waist, he pulls me decisively against his hard-on. The tight ache of need speeds up my heart and flushes my skin. I wiggle against him. He moans, and I get that this is going to happen here.

Wait. I pull away, kiss my way to his ear. "Cameras are on the walk. We need to go into the trees."

Our mouths collide again. He lifts me up, cupping my ass with large, kneading hands, and carries me behind the trees.

Like a horny adolescent, all I can think about is the cover of darkness and his expert hands under my jacket. I pull at his clothes, urge him deeper into the woods.

Finally, hidden by trees and darkness, he thrusts me against a tree. His body is hot and hard against me.

The taste of his mouth, the tingle of his tongue, have my entire body screaming for him. More. Closer. *Skin.* I need his skin.

My trembling, frantic hands explore under his shirt, finding skin and muscles and warmth. I stroke and rub the sharp lines on his abs while he undoes the buttons on my jacket.

I slip out of it.

He reaches behind me, unzips, then pulls down the strap of my dress. Releasing a breast, he expertly teases the taut, sensitive nipple with his nimble fingers. *Oh.* That feels so good.

Nearly as good as the feel of his throbbing, hard cock against my core. I roll my hips, satisfied when his breath hitches and he moans a deep and wild sound. A deep and wild *promise* that would've buckled my legs if the press of his body didn't pin me so firmly against the tree.

I'm so hot and wet and ready I can't stand it.

Breaking the kiss, I arch against him, reach for him. "Now."

Smiling against my cheek, he rubs and excites my other nipple. I toss my head against the rough bark. Beg. "Please."

"Not yet." Releasing me so that I'm forced to drop back onto my feet, he drags down my dress then thong, letting them fall to my ankles, before helping me step free. I'm naked in the moonlight, and it feels raw and cold and fucking fantastic.

He teases the curls of hair as his fingers dip between my saturated thighs.

He groans, "Like silk."

He strokes that wetness, increasing the friction until I go mad and begin to grind into his hand. He rubs my clit with his thumb.

I gasp, spread my legs wider. "Yes. That."

I'm on fire as he pushes fingers inside. I babble, saying words in a language I thought I'd forgotten long ago.

"Damn. I can't wait to feel all this softness around my cock."

"Yes. That's what I want. Please."

"After I taste you."

"Oh. Okay. Yes."

He kisses down my neck to my collarbone. I'm dripping

with desire and anticipation. He sucks my hardened nipple into his mouth, then his tongue does something that tugs at my core and makes me cry out.

He moves lower, kisses down my stomach. My thighs, open and vulnerable in the moonlight, tremble for him, for his touch.

He drops to his knees, teases my clit with his tongue.

Electric sparks shoot through me.

He sucks slow and deep. Hard and fast. Alternating. Devouring.

I whimper, threading hands through his silky hair.

His fingers slip inside as well, moving in and out.

Oh. God. His fingers gyrate inside and against me. I cry out. How is he doing that? How is he…?

That lovely wet tongue. Those bending, strumming fingers. My core tightens around him. I writhe and moan.

His tongue plays faster and faster. His fingers move quick and nimble, as if he's played this instrument a thousand times and knows the exact chords.

I come with an explosive release of pleasure, calling out a throaty, "God, don't stop! Don't stop."

39

SANDESH

Justice shakes and comes against my mouth with a sultry cry that has my cock so hard it's painful.

She writhes and convulses and shudders. I lick and taste the most sensitive part of her, hot and warm and salty in my grateful mouth. So good. So sweet.

When she's done, when she releases the stranglehold on my hair and the last throb and pulse dies against my tongue, with her body still sensitive and waiting, I rise.

I kiss her, long and deep. She moans at the taste of herself on my tongue, and it nearly breaks me.

With shaking fingers, I unbutton my slacks. Justice is there instantly, pulling them down and releasing my cock.

Grasping my shoulders, she jumps up and wraps her legs around me. I instinctively catch her ass as she lowers onto my cock. We moan in unison. I bury my mouth in her neck. "Justice."

She begins to ride me.

I'm gone, so deep into her, that it takes a moment to register the sound passing overhead. The hair on the back of my neck stands on end. My system goes on alert. I stop moving, and she makes a whimpering sound, beginning to move faster. I press her back against the tree, hold her there. "That sound."

"What?" She's breathless and her voice is fuzzy.

But I know that sound. "Do you have drones here?"

"What? No."

A concussive bang and flash of light ricochets through the trees, through my nerves, and I realize that somewhere on campus there's been an explosion.

We break apart. I trip out of the trees and onto the path, zipping up my fly.

Justice follows a moment later. Dress in place, eyes wide, she grabs my elbow. "Was that an explosion?"

"Yeah. Come on." I grab her hand and pull her toward the red glow in the distance where smoke rises into the sky.

The fire alarm sounds shrill and loud and is quickly joined by a computerized warning system telling everyone to seek shelter.

The walkway lights turn blue and begin to pulsate, and I'm trying to get her to move faster down the walkway toward the explosion, but she pulls against me, stopping me.

"This way. It's faster." Dropping my hand, she flicks off her heels and runs through the trees, dodging branches and leaping over roots.

I follow.

The hem of her dress held in one hand, Justice darts through the night as the well-trained soldier she is.

Adrenaline and a real fear for her and her family pounds in my chest like a boxer on a heavy bag. Still, I follow, learning the land by paying attention to her footfalls.

After a minute of full-out sprinting, her lean frame leaps over a hedge of shrubs and she lands on the main road, School Drive.

I'm right on her heels.

To our left is the mansion on the hill, which seems to have

every light on. In the distance, I spot the gatehouse at the main campus entrance. The same place I came through a few hours ago, but now it's on fire.

Stones and rubble are strewn across the entrance, blocking it. One guard is helping another one hobble away from the destruction, as a third yells into a two-way radio. A fourth is outside the gate, beyond the scattered stones, weapon drawn, scanning for approaching danger.

A thought occurs to me. I pick up my speed, catch up to Justice, bend to her ear. "Nix the warning system. It's too loud. If there are more drones, we won't be able to hear them."

Eyes wide and worried, she pulls to a stop, takes out her phone, and punches in a number. "Security. Turn off the alarm. We believe there could be more drones—"

Boom! An explosion in the distance lights up an area between two buildings.

We crouch down just as another blast, even further away, sends fire and debris shooting into the sky.

Sprinting over rubble, I get the attention of security personnel. "Can you light this place up? Turn on every light, floodlight, you have?"

I expect confrontation or dismissal but get neither.

With a nod, she speaks into a two-way, relaying the information. Being with Justice must be proof enough of my intentions or maybe the woman simply recognizes a good point when she hears it.

In seconds, lights began to go on all over the school, even lights inside classrooms and all along the walk. Despite everything, I'm impressed. They're seriously linked up here. The warning system goes silent.

I see it before I hear it, framed by the fires behind it. "There, there, there." I point at the sky, turn the guard by the shoulders, so she can see, but she shakes her head uncomprehendingly.

Justice springs up to us. "I see it."

Quick as a flash, she removes the guard's sidearm, aims, points, and fires repeatedly.

Pop. Pop. Pop.

The drone explodes in the air. Fiery fragments rain down and slam into the ground. Pieces scatter in all directions across the road leading up to the Mantua Home.

The guard looks over at her, skims Justice and her gown. "You hit a drone from the sky at night in a ballgown."

The guard and Justice stare at each other, because this is obviously something that a Parish Princess is not known for being able to do.

Not getting her point, Justice shrugs. "I'm keeping your gun." She turns to me. "We need to get organized. You're going to have to leave."

Nope. I don't see a bulldozer on her, and that's the only way she's getting me out of here.

40

JUSTICE

Balling my hands to keep from shoving Sandesh over the rubble, through the gate, and off the property, I repeat, "You need to leave. Go now. Get out of here."

Sandesh's entire demeanor changes from ex-soldier taking control to ex-soldier digging in his heels. "You want me to leave? Now? In the middle of this? No. Hell no."

"I have to find out what's going on. I need to... And the police. Sandesh, this is the last thing the IPT needs to be connected to."

He grabs my hand. "You're not thinking." He draws closer, whisper-close. "My truck is here. I signed in. There are cameras all over, video of us going into the woods, us running, and you shooting a drone. Think. We need to tone this down. Meaning, you can't run around with a gun right now. You're panicking. Think, Justice. Let the security here do its job."

He steps back and nods to the security guard watching us with interest.

Shit. He's right. External Security, unlike Internal, knows nothing about The Guild or my training. They protect the school and the campus, not the main house. I let out a breath.

The cops are coming. Probably the FBI. All the camera footage will be looked at. Some of it damning me. I look around.

Two other guards stare at us. I fucked up. Shot the drone from the sky. I can cover that. Tell the cops that my Special Forces boyfriend taught me to shoot.

I hand the gun back to the guard. "I'm sorry."

The woman takes the gun with a look that says she's not sure an apology is necessary. "No problem. You and your... friend can head back to the house. We got this, Ms. Parish."

I turn to Sandesh. Letting the adrenaline backlash do its job, I begin to shake. I put a hand to my head. Seeing me finally playing my part, Sandesh puts an arm around me as if to hold me up. I sag against him.

It's probably not enough to counter the scene the guards just witnessed. A vine of panic and anger is growing in my chest, sharp offshoots twisting and spreading out with angry red thorns that tug at me, telling me to go, act, do.

But Sandesh is right. The school, The Guild, has never faced this big a threat. A threat to all we've subtly and secretly accomplished.

I want at Walid. No doubt this is him. But not just him. I need to get home, see the security footage, and figure out which of my dumbass siblings has turned monster overnight.

The vines tighten. I tuck it all down for now. But I'm already plotting how to get my vindictive ass to Mexico. "Let's get back to the house. Check on my sisters."

∽

THOUGH THE CARE staff did a great job of getting the kids all into one room, things back at the main house are crazy. My sisters— girls rescued from war zones or who've seen violence firsthand —are at emotional extremes. The younger ones are cowering by the fire in the large family room, while the older ones in

Vampire Academy have grabbed the nearest objects and now stand watch, ready to fight.

The twins—Jules and Rome—hold fireplace tools. Those two are fierce. Especially Rome, who has a chip on his shoulder Atlas couldn't carry.

I'm glad Sandesh talked me off the edge earlier; getting me back here was the right call. I take control. "Okay, all. Deep breath." I send a warning look at the twins. "Put the irons down."

Jules does instantly, but Rome hesitates. His eyes dart to Sandesh. After a second of some internal debate, he complies. Kid is strung tight. Probably feels responsible as an older kid. Though the care staff are trying to calm them, they need family. Right now, I'm the only family here over eighteen.

Momma went down to meet with the police. Leland is busy handling Internal, shutting things down to keep off the authorities' radar while assessing the damage. Tony and Bridget went to the dorms to handle the situation there.

Who knows where the Troublemakers are?

Knowing them, they went to investigate, figuring that, since the girls in the main house were being trained for combat and groomed by The Guild, they could deal. It's unfair, but makes sense.

The dorm kids were sent by their families to an elite boarding school. They know nothing about covert ops and should be treated with kid gloves. Still, seeing my sisters huddled by the fire while the tougher of them stand guard, I'm overcome with anger.

Walid is going down.

The clink of fireplace tools shoved into the iron stand is followed by the sobs of five-year-old Bella. I make a move to go to her, but she launches herself past me to Sandesh. Her tiny, trembling arms latch on to his legs.

His eyes fill with a softness that melts my heart, and he hoists her up. "It's okay, Bella. You're safe."

She buries her face in his shoulder and he rubs her back, turning to the rest of the family. "If you all sit and listen, I'll tell you what's going on. Or, at least, what I know."

Damn. This man is perfect and knows the perfect thing to say.

Bella squirms out of his arms and pads, barefoot, across the room to join the others around the fire.

When everyone is absolutely still and quiet, Sandesh says, "First, I want you to know that you are safe."

My heart lurches toward him, drawn instinctively to his strength and kindness. Not only did he recognize that they need direction to get them settled, he also realizes that, more than anything, they need to be assured of their safety.

"The police have arrived. They are checking every inch of the grounds. Beyond that, the security at this school is top-notch and all the campus staff are on alert."

I raise a questioning eyebrow at him, because it's true, but I didn't tell him that.

He winks at me.

Yep, not a stupid man. "In addition, the school is on lockdown. New measures are being put in place to make sure this type of attack doesn't happen again."

"Who attacked us?" Rome asks, a set to his jaw that looks like he's ready to chew glass.

Right there with you, kid.

Sandesh spreads his hands wide. "We don't know that yet. We know someone flew a few personal drones over the school and dropped small explosive devices at the gym, tennis courts, and on the gatehouse, which was empty at the time. Falling debris injured one of the guards."

"If they'd wanted to hurt someone," Rome says, "they would've dropped the explosives somewhere with people, not the school gym or the tennis courts. All those are locked at night."

He's right, and I don't like it.

"Do you know what kind of ordnance they used?" Jules asks, pinning her lower lip beneath her teeth, then releasing. "Timed? Or did it go off when it hit?"

"It went off when it hit," I say.

We make eye contact. She whispers, "But how did they get past the cameras? There are only a few places—"

Her eyes widen. My gut twists. Because, yeah, she practically pointed out this was an inside job. Who else would know the hidden camera layout?

Jules and Rome exchange a look. Jules' face pales, then, realizing what she'd suggested in front of the kids, reddens. She doesn't try to overcorrect, either, with rambling or comforting explanations. She stays silent and lets the warm blood rush into her cheeks. Smart. Sometimes talking makes things worse. l

Sandesh comes over to me. I grab onto his arm, feeling the tension in his bicep. Somehow, the strength of him comforts me. I'll have to excise that reaction.

Leaning to my ear, Sandesh whispers, "I have an idea. A way to help with PR."

"I'm not sure all the PR in the world will be able to fix this."

He opens his mouth to expand when Martha comes into the room. "The police are looking for you, Ms. Parish. And you, Mr. Ross."

Great. Time to lie my ass off.

41

JUSTICE

My public relations office inside the Mantua Academy's administration building is a tiny square that should've held brooms and mops. It's an afterthought of a room at the very end of the guidance counselor's corridor. Right now, it seems two sizes too small. The office equivalent of *had too much turkey and pie at Thanksgiving and now have to wear my stretchy pants.*

Twenty-four hours after the attack, it's a hive of activity. The phone's been ringing off the hook with furious and concerned parents—people used to ordering others about. There've been numerous drop-bys from administrative staff, including my nosey siblings, who come and go with their hair seemingly on fire.

And the media attention... Forget it. I've been answering their calls since five a.m. It's now almost six p.m. Truly, I've felt less exposed during gynecological exams.

All this attention could go to my head. Or... straight to my trigger finger. A finger I'm currently using, along with all my other digits, to compose another school-wide email that gives away no information while reassuring everyone. Easy-peasy.

Sure.

When and why did Momma decide putting me in a situation where I'd have to be diplomatic and courteous to irate people was a good idea? Bet she's rethinking her decision now, because I'm floundering for words. The phone rings again. Not answering that.

This damn email. There's nothing I can say to these people.

For forty years, the school has practically dictated their reputation—an excellent but stuffy place to send your daughter. A place of diversity with scholarships for deserving children. A place that teaches the brilliant Parish children, women who become leaders and scholars and scientists and businesspeople.

Now, it's the target of intense and blistering scrutiny that I'm trying to mitigate. *Really* not a good thing when there's a covert operation that houses the world's most elite group of independent agents underfoot, and I'm so pissed I can barely see straight.

Another phone rings. My cell this time. I reach for it and knock over the three-page list of numbers, parents, and media I need to call back. Damn it. I pick up. "What?"

The person on the other end pauses. "Tell me that's not how you're answering the phone."

"This is my cell, Gracie. I can answer it any damn way I please. And, just so you know, I am being extremely courteous to every idiot reporter who calls me."

The landline on my desk rings as if to reprimand me for my lie. Glaring at it, I tuck my cell next to my ear, reach over, and unplug the cord. What Gracie doesn't know can't hurt her. "What do you want?"

"I want to know about this online story suggesting the school was attacked because of its charitable support of the IPT. What the heck is that about?"

I should get up and shut my door, but there is zero air in

here. I'm already at the very end of the hall. And most people have left for the day. I spin away from the door for some privacy.

"Look..." I stop, hearing the secretary walk in with another pile of messages. I pause, swivel back to her, and nod. She does not smile back.

Gracie waits, understanding without me explaining that someone is here. This is the way we grew up. Everyone knows the super-secret society drill.

"Thanks, Dariana," I say as the *swoosh* of papers hits my desk. "Have a good night."

Wordless, she leaves with the disgruntled scent of Tom Ford's Velvet Orchid trailing her. I don't take offense at her non-reply. It's been a long day for both of us, and her kids go here. She's worried and as dissatisfied as everyone else with the answers being given.

At least, we're making the right calls. Momma and the academy's principal decided to close the school early for summer recess. Finals will be given online, and we'll analyze and increase security during the off- summer months until this place is Fort Knox.

I wave away the perfume and lower my voice. "You read the article. What do you think it's about?"

"I think we're blaming our support of Sandesh and the IPT's work in order to distract from The Guild and their operations."

She's no idiot. "It was Sandesh's idea, just so you know."

"Sure. But you jumped on it. I thought you cared about this guy, or was that a trick to convince him to join The Guild?"

"Hey!"

"Please. We all know you don't do boyfriends, but you'll use a guy and his work to perpetuate Momma's global interests. He's your built-in scapegoat. Really, that's low."

This is by far the most frustrating call I've had today. "You really think that little of me?"

She remains silent, answering me with her non-answer.

My throat goes tight. "You're wrong, Gracie. To keep the kids safe, Sandesh told the FBI he had a history of confronting sex-slavers in Jordan. It was all his idea, and a good one. It doesn't hurt him or his operation, because—guess what? It's true. And if the FBI finds any link to Walid, this'll make the most sense."

"Sure, it's all about keeping the kids safe."

By *far*, the most annoying of my siblings. "Is there anything else, Gracie? Because I have to get back to my job."

She pauses for a long, breathy moment.

Looks like I'm not the only person annoyed.

"Have you decided to follow the warning this bombing has conveyed?"

I sit forward, elbows on knees, head cocked to the right, phone clutched in my sweaty hand. My right eye starts to twitch. "What message is that?"

"It's obvious, isn't it? This is Walid forcing us to keep our heads down and stay *in* and *at* our school."

Is it? It could be. Having the FBI and local law enforcement running around the school has made things difficult, limiting access to intel and the specialized equipment below-ground.

No one's going anywhere near The Guild until the authorities combing this place leave. For now, all necessary research will be done aboveground or at Gracie's club.

"Why would he want to scare us into circling the horses?"

"I think this first attack is meant to clear out the school, so Walid can launch the real offensive—reveal The Guild and take out those responsible for his brother's death."

Gracie has drawn some interesting conclusions about Walid's mindset. Or the traitor figured it out because of her connection to Walid.

The sound of an engine firing up and a car fasten-your-seat belt *beep, beep, beep* tells me Gracie is getting into her car.

"Hmm, good of you to provide Walid's motivation and his future plans. Do you have a date and time you think he'll be showing up?"

"Nice, J. I'm not setting you up. Just because I lob a common-sense grenade, make some obvious connections, you practically accuse me of being a traitor."

"Maybe I wouldn't accuse you of anything if you weren't living alone at the club, keeping your distance from the family, and constantly criticizing us. Not to mention, mysteriously providing insights into Walid's plans that are not *obvious*."

"What do I have to gain from any of this, Justice?"

"Hmm, I wonder. What would happen if The Guild ceased all operations? I guess you could run back to John and tell him The Guild is gone, reconnect with Tyler, and rekindle your old relationship."

Gracie lets out a long and weighty breath. "You know, I think I like this new suspicious Justice. You can learn the lesson I learned long ago."

"Which is?"

"Trust no one."

With that, she hangs up on me.

I stare at the phone, feeling under siege.

42

SANDESH

Hearing movement in the room, I bolt upright.
"Who's here?"
And where the hell am I?
"Sorry to wake you."
"Leland?" Oh, that's right. I spent the night in a guest room at the Mantua Home. I rub at the grit on my eyes. "Tell me you don't have a thing for blonds."

Leland laughs. "No. Definitely not my type. Look, I know you haven't gotten a lot of sleep, but I have a favor to ask."

I grab my cell from the nightstand. It's not even five a.m. Went to sleep around two hours ago. What's with this family and waking people up? Truthfully, I prefer the way Justice wakes me.

I hit the light. The room's still dim, but I can see Leland standing at the foot of this four-poster bed. The whole room looks as if it belongs in Victorian England. "What do you need?"

"What do you know of Justice's father, Cooper Ramsey?"

Her father? "He's a drug addict who left Justice to an abusive grandmother."

"The grandmother died in jail. Cooper was never charged with anything. But more important for this conversation, Mukta and I suspect he's working with the family traitor."

"What makes you think that?"

"I've been with Security all night going over camera footage. We didn't find much, but when we expanded the search to the campus perimeter for the week, we found Cooper taking pictures."

I swing my legs out of bed. This would be a big admission on a normal nine-to-five schedule, but at five a.m. and with Leland's hands tied by hosting the FBI, it's pretty obvious where this is leading. "Where does he live?"

∽

WEARING jogging gear donated by Leland, I run with steady ease down the wide blacktop of the Schuylkill biking trail. Hoodie's big enough to conceal and carry. Helpful.

The sneakers are a good fit, but not my style. Expensive, with too thick of a sole, so it feels like running on a loaf of bread.

As the trail angles up, the river drops down, and a series of five-story red-and-tan buildings comes into view.

I circle the apartment complex, doing recon. This isn't where I'd expect to find Cooper. It's expensive, pet-friendly, and has access to fitness trails and the river.

Easing off the trail and onto the grass in front of Building 7, I stop and stretch, waiting for my moment.

Don't have to wait long. A man with a dog goes inside, and I follow. He's kind enough to hold the door open for me. I thank him, dipping my head to pet his dog, mostly to avoid the security camera, but also because who could resist that friendly furry face?

As the man checks his mail, I slip into the elevator, quickly hitting the CLOSE DOOR button. Three floors up, I find Cooper's door, then knock.

No answer.

Before taking out the palm-sized pickpocketing kit in my shorts, I try the handle.

It twists open.

My shoulders tense. As quietly as possible, I swing open the door and enter.

The first thing that hits me is the smell. Of shit... and death. The next is a huge, slobbery, black-and-white Newfoundland.

I cut the dog off with a sweep of my body, guiding him so he's up against the wall and not causing trouble. I pet him, trying to calm the distressed sounds he's making. My hand comes away sticky with something too thick for slobber.

I bring it to my nose, sniff. I was right. Blood.

After confirming the dog is uninjured, I step into the main living area and scan with my Ruger.

Christ. It's rank in here, and dark. The blinds are drawn. Even still, there're lights on enough to see the man—dead, head wrapped in bubble wrap, strapped to a chair in the middle of the living room.

Gut in knots, heart pounding, I move past him and the kitchenette to make sure no one else is here. The throat-gagging stench seems to have become imbedded in the walls. I find the bedroom empty. The closet and bathroom—minus dog shit—also prove empty.

Back in the bedroom, I kick a leg under the bed for the box I'd spotted when looking to make sure no one was there.

It's a drone box. An *empty* drone box.

At my side, the dog whines. I pet him and head back out to the other room. It's no secret who the dead man I'm passing is. Judging by the long, black hair and distinctly Native American features—not to mention Justice's exact nose, visible even under the bubble wrap—the corpse strapped to the artist's chair is Cooper. And he's been tortured to death.

Chicken wire pierces his face and down the flesh of his naked body. His mouth, filled by a thick leather ball gag, is split in small red fissures at the creases. Blood has pooled beneath the chair. A dog-sized bloodstain saturates the beige carpet.

Shaking, nauseous, I walk into the kitchenette. Taking slow, deep, steadying breaths, I call Leland.

He answers on the first ring. "And?"

Not even a *Hello*. The man knows it's bad news.

"Found Cooper. He's dead. Someone tortured him."

Leland does not react.

I continue, "Also, there's a drone box here. I'm not sure how this is going to go down with the authorities. It'll tie Justice to the bombings in a way that won't be helpful."

Leland barely pauses to absorb the news. "Clean off any of your prints. I'll have someone there in twenty minutes to wipe the room."

"We need a rescue here, too."

"There's someone there?"

"A dog." A really nice dog. "Looks to be about two years old, male, and shaken up. I don't want to leave him here."

"I'll send someone to get him, but you have to get out of there."

I hang up. I'm not leaving the dog until someone arrives, but there's no need to argue the point with him.

Holstering my gun, then covering my hand with the sleeve of my hoodie, I go through cabinets. I quickly find what I'm looking for. Opening two cans, I slap them into the empty dog dish by the fridge, and as the dog is eating big, sloppy mouthfuls, I refill his water bowl.

While the dog eats, I fish bleach from under the sink and begin to go over any evidence I've left. As I do, I get a better feel for who Cooper Ramsey was. An artist, for one. There's an easel in one corner with a half-done picture of a Buddhist temple.

I recognize that temple. I've actually passed it on my way to the Mantua Academy campus. It's a beautiful and colorful structure. Question is, was Justice's father a Buddhist or just a fan of architecture?

And who would want to kill him? If not for the drone box and the torture, I'd say it was drug related. But drug deaths aren't long, complicated sessions used to get information. It's obvious from what happened here that someone wanted Cooper to tell them something. But what and why? And how does that tie into his supposed connection with the family traitor?

Circling the room, I let my thoughts circle, too. If I were looking for a go-between for myself and Walid, a person who could create distance between me and responsibility and also serve as a fall guy, Cooper wouldn't be a bad choice. And if Walid, as Dada told Justice, had gone on a sudden and extensive search to uncover information, he could've followed that connection, found Cooper, and ended up here. That explains the torture, but not the drone box.

Cooper wasn't exactly swimming in enough luxury to be buying drones for the fun of it. Other than the easel, the chair with him in it, a small, round kitchen table, and an abused, brown suede couch, there isn't any other furniture in this room.

There are a lot of decorations, though. Well, paintings. I've never seen a picture of Justice as a child, but the portraits that take up nearly every wall are of her, and the girl beside her, the one Justice has her arm slung across, is most likely her sister, Hope. There's a woman in the portraits, too. She resembles the blonde girl Justice has her arm around, so she's clearly their mother.

The portraits repeat again and again all over the walls, like the man had played one moment—one loop of thought—in his head for the last twenty-five years. Justice and Hope and their mother, over and over again, the same picture, but each version highlights something different, dissecting down to the smallest, clearest detail: a freckle, blue eyes, dark eyes, a smile, a wisp of hair, rosy cheeks.

Here and there, scrawled across Justice's arm or on her shirt, or as a tear coming down from her eye are words. *Anger is her drug of choice. Help her. There's still time.*

"This is sad as hell, Cooper," I tell the dead man, and the dog barks as if in agreement.

There's a dark shadow in every painting, too, just at the edge. As if the artist foreshadowed the dark days to come or asked himself over and over when it had all gone wrong.

43

JUSTICE

When I enter the house, I'm not surprised to find it bustling with family members who usually work or train belowground. Not a lot of places for them to go right now.

I maneuver around a few congregating in the hall and head to the library. Where's Sandesh gotten to?

I haven't seen or heard from him since yesterday. After his late-night interview with the FBI, Martha had found him a room somewhere. I'd been too tired to ask, and when I woke up at butt-crack-a.m. this morning, I didn't want to bother him. Of course, I was too busy today to text him, but he didn't text me either.

I turn into the library, looking for someone who might know where the big guy has been stashed—*if* he's still here and didn't head back home.

That thought sends a fit of disappointment flaring in my stomach. I shush that fit. I'm a grown woman, not a giggly, googly-eyed girl. Though, let's face it, if anyone deserves googly eyes, it's that fine man.

Three of my oldest sisters, Yamilia, Dalia, and Anna—who started and honed operations before there *were* operations—are at a reading table, sipping coffee. Wow, The Guild really *has* circled the wagons. We aren't usually graced with the appearance of so many of the Fantastic Five. Growing up, I trained with a few of them. Mostly Malia, who isn't here. I nod in their general direction and get some speculative looks in return.

Sheesh. Intimidating bunch.

Looking for my own comfort zone, I head for the table with Tony and Dada. They're huddled together at a small corner table near a black suit of armor.

Huh. They look so chummy. Co-conspirators? No. *Don't be paranoid.* Those two couldn't plan a lunch together.

I slip into the only available seat and Tony starts talking before I can ask about Sandesh.

"Justice, what do you think? It's time for us to consider my plan, right?" Tony gestures with his hands like a conductor uses a baton to convey the tone of his emotions, but, still, I can't figure out what he's saying.

"Huh?"

Dada shakes her head. "He wants us to fly to Mexico tonight. Ridiculous. We need to put up a united front right now, not disappear. Do you want to draw even more attention here?"

"*Attention*? Didn't you hear about the attack that has parents lined up outside, waiting to drag their kids outta here?" He walks his fingers across the table to demonstrating parents fleeing.

Dada *tsks*. "Your fear has made you reactionary."

"Not reactionary because I've seen the footage."

"You've seen the security footage?" This gets my attention. Right now, access to those videos is limited to those underground. And Leland completely sealed off the lower floors as a precaution while the Feds are here. "How?"

"I was in the control room when everything went down. After, I stayed and ran the tapes."

That's weird. He left Sunday dinner and went to the control room? "What's the footage show?"

Dada shifts, puts a hand on her side as if in pain. "According to him, the footage shows nothing."

"Exactly." Tony jumps forward. His weight slaps the table, sending it into Dada.

"Careful. Idiot." She shoves it back, protectively putting her hand over her stomach.

"Sorry, Dada." He frowns.

"What do you mean, *exactly*?" I prompt Tony.

"The drone avoided detection by our cameras. Which means Walid knew our layout. He's obviously watching us. There's no time to waste."

He's right. "I couldn't agree more."

Dada grimaces.

"You okay?" Tony asks.

I don't blame him. She looks... worn and tired. Why is her hand on her stomach? Could she—

"Justice?"

I jump a mile at Leland's voice, and laughter feathers around the room.

Leland stands at the entrance, beckoning me with a crook of one insistent finger. "Would you please accompany me to the next level?"

Silence. Every eye in the room turns to me.

Yeah, I have no idea why I'm being summoned to the "next level," aka the closed-off lower levels that not even the Fantastic Five are permitted to enter. This looks bad for me.

Tension ripples across the room.

I stand and walk across the silent room. Every eye seems pinned to me, speculating about what this could mean. Damn, this is so awkward. *Someone cough or say something.*

"Tragically," Tony says loudly and with a weepy tone, "we never saw her again."

The room erupts in laughter. Leland shakes his head. Tension broken.

And that's why Tony is my favorite sister.

44

SANDESH

The bright recessed lights of Mukta Parish's colorful lower-level office, along with a soft, rose-scented perfume, contradicts the fact that this place is the center of dark pain and anger and plotting.

This dual nature has also been the upbringing of the person I love, the person I can admit to loving in my mind, but not to her face. Even if Justice weren't sitting right next to me looking wary, I'd have a hard time telling her. Mostly because I'm not sure it's something she wants or needs to know.

She definitely doesn't need it right now. She's about to get hit with a new reality.

I stretch my hand out, covering hers. She lets me, and we both keep our attention on Mukta, seated at her desk, with her hands cupped upon it.

"Justice, we have some bad news to impart."

"If it's worse than 'your school was bombed by the man who killed your sister,' I don't want to hear it."

Behind Mukta, his usual ramrod straight posture on display, Leland clears his throat, an action that does nothing to ease the rasp in his voice. "We believe your father is involved with the traitor."

My hand goes tight around Justice's. I'm stunned. Is *this* the way they've decided to reveal to her that her father is, in fact, dead, murdered, and was tortured?

Justice pulls her hands out from under mine and puts it up in a *stop* gesture. "Cooper is drugged out and not capable of conspiring with anyone."

Mukta twists one bracelet around her wrist then another. "He's capable of following instructions, coming to see his daughter, and reporting back to his co-conspirator. He's capable of meeting with one of your siblings, following their orders, and getting in touch with Walid."

Justice clasps the locket around her neck. "You think Cooper helped whoever betrayed us?"

"Yes," Leland says. "We think he was a go-between, informing Walid and taking money for the job. We also believe he helped orchestrate the attack on the school."

"The attack? You think he worked with Walid?" She sounds as doubtful as I feel.

Mukta Parish shakes her head. "Not Walid. All signs suggest the attack was an inside job. Few would have the knowledge to avoid security. And though the traitor could have passed this information to him, I sincerely doubt Walid would target areas devoid of people."

"In fact," Leland says, "we believe the drone attack was the family member's plan to force us to cease operations."

"What proof do you have it's not Walid?" Justice asks. "Gracie thinks this is all strategic—keep us in the school, keep us busy, get rid of the kids, and then Walid can move forward with a second attack."

Mukta and Leland share a look. Mukta uncups her hands, lays them flat on the desk. "I believe our gentle Bridget is behind everything. There was written evidence in Cooper's apartment, communications between them. Not only that, she and Cooper were part of the same Buddhist temple, and she has implicated herself with prior statements, repeatedly advising her siblings to resist training."

My head is spinning. Bridget? My stomach turns. I can't imagine how Justice feels, but my shock is growing into rage. I don't understand why they're laying this on Justice right now. It seems cruel. Why not give her a chance to understand Cooper is dead first and grieve before breaking it all down?

A pained breath escaping her, Justice shakes her head. "Coop. Bridget and Coop? Are you sure it's her? Dada is sleeping with her informant. Tony is so angry. And Gracie practically gave me Walid's plan of action. She's also a tech genius. She could easily access computer info like my GPS and operate drones, *un*like Bridget."

Leland tugs at a button on his suit coat's sleeve. "According to the FBI, the drones were preprogrammed. Bridget could've hired someone for that. As for the GPS, Internal is analyzing some new material and information. We're hoping for an answer soon."

Justice shoots to her feet. "This isn't horseshoes, Leland. We find out *now*. We bring Bridget and Cooper in. We question them."

Enough. What is this game? I grab Justice's hand.

She looks down at me.

I meet her eyes, hoping she can see—*feel*—how much I want to protect her right now. "I'm sorry. I'm so sorry. Cooper is dead, murdered. I found him in his apartment. If he was the go-between for Bridget and Walid, there's a chance Walid found him and had his men torture him."

She doesn't so much sit as fall into her seat. "Torture?"

She stares at me, and I squeeze her hand tight, nodding.

Her eyes narrow. Finding the anger she once told me she

needed, she turns to Leland and Mukta. "You dragged Sandesh into this?"

I place a hand on her shaking knee, rub in circles, desperate to touch her, to ease her pain. A pain she wants so badly to block out that she's reaching for the one emotion she told me she uses to get through life. Cooper knew, too. *Anger is her drug of choice.* "I was asked to go, no dragging involved, and no danger to me. Leland had Cooper's place cleaned, and even made it look like Cooper had taken off for good, which keeps you from being tied to his death."

The tension around her eyes doesn't ease. In fact, it tightens. "*Cooper.* I almost believed him." Her lips trembles with rage or sorrow, I can't be sure. "And now he's taken another of my sisters." Her voice breaks on the last word. Justice bends forward, hands against her stomach, and growls, "I hate him."

Technically, it wasn't Cooper who'd started it all, but it's easier for her to blame him than Bridget. And, as someone who'd once held a lot against his own father, I know the turmoil that emotion can bring. I found my way through it, and I want to help her. It might not sit well with her, but she should know.

I get out of my chair, drop to a knee in front of her, then smooth her silky hair. "Justice. First, I want you to know your father's apartment was filled with paintings of you and Hope and your mother. You should also know, judging by his condition, Coop resisted interrogation. He loved—"

"Don't. Don't say it." Tears line her eyes… and then they fall. She swipes angrily at her wet cheeks. "He was an asshole. And Bridget. Bleeding heart. She brought Coop here. Probably hoped we'd have a relationship. Macro-view. Please. She's so much into peace that she won't even eat dairy from a cow. That has to screw with your head."

"Justice," I try to hold her, but she shakes her head. I drop my hands, aching for her. I want to give her a way, a way other than anger, to share and release her pain.

"Tucker." Leland has moved around the desk and is now using the office speaker phone to talk to someone in Internal. "Have you had a chance to go through the information found at Cooper's apartment?"

"Yes, sir. It's been sent to your and Dr. Parish's secure email."

Leland exchanges a glance with Mukta, who nods slightly and reaches for her computer. Leland asks, "Where is Bridget Sunya Parish?"

The clicking of a keyboard comes through the speaker, followed by a moment of silence, and then, "In her office."

"Have someone from Internal bring her to Mukta's lower office. Posthaste."

Leland clicks off, exhales a sigh of age and regret and sadness before bending over Mukta's shoulder to read what I'm sure are the documents sent in the email mentioned.

45

JUSTICE

My heart wails like a siren in my chest.
 Cooper.
 Dead.
Tortured.
Bridget... traitor.

I've never before understood that saying about people who weren't comfortable in their own skin. Now, emotions slice daggers across raw memories. Bridget teaching me Lao. Training together in the gym. In the firing range. Playing Mario Kart. Watching *Spy Kids* with tears of laughter streaming down our faces.

It hurts. I want to scratch, tear at my arms, my legs. I've always known what's right: my family. And what's wrong: those who went against my family. Family going against family... against me? I can't endure this helpless, aching pain.

Someone knocks on the door.

No one speaks.

No one moves.

No one breathes.

Time seems to stop, along with the place where my heart

should be beating. If I could put a knife to the tension, it would probably snap back and kill someone.

On impulse, I stand, grab Sandesh's hand, and tug him until we're flanking Momma's desk on the opposite side of Leland, whose face is blank. A united front.

Smoothing down her dress, Momma finally manages, "Enter."

Looking like a cross between a yogi and a math nerd with her lopsided bun and dark-framed reading glasses Bridget enters and keeps her eyes focused singularly on Momma.

My sister's composure sends a prickle of irritation along my skin. Her perfect pale skin is unflushed, but she has to know why she's been brought down here.

"You betrayed the family," I blurt, going for the jugular. "Forget me; that doesn't matter." Lie. It matters to me. "But conspiring with Cooper to take down operations? Why?"

For a long, long moment Bridget simply stares at Momma. Neither of them says anything, though their eyes remain locked.

I'd think this was a battle of wills, except I know Momma would never play that game.

After a minute of this shit, I'm itching to slap Bridget. I just accused the woman of betraying our family, of conspiring with Cooper and she's got nothing to say? "What the fuck, Bridge? Say something."

Bridget blinks, casts her eyes down. "I am ready for whatever punishment you see fit to give me."

My heart kicks hard in my chest. *She did it.* It *was* her.

"You admit this?" Momma leans a hand on her desk. Her eyes, always so clear, are cloudy and confused. "Tell me the truth, daughter. This is important. If you have any reason to cover for another, you must not. We need to be able to trust the others."

Bridget shakes her head "You don't have to worry. You've found the right person to blame."

My stomach rolls, hits a guardrail, then plunges over a ravine. It's all I can do not to puke or walk over and shake the shit out of her. I want to hurt her the way she's hurt me. But more than that, I want to know... "Why? Why did you do it?"

Bridget's eyes dart between me and Sandesh, Momma and Leland. A subtle flush rises up her neck into her cheeks. "I did it to keep you, the family, and everyone here safe."

"Bullshit." I jab an angry finger in her direction. "Safe? Telling Walid I was after him in Jordan, giving him step-by-step directions to track and find and kill me? How was that *ever* going to keep me safe?"

Her serene expression falters as she shakes her head. "That didn't happen. Yes, Walid was given information that warned him of your initial operation. He was told Jordan was a safe place for him and his brother to meet, but that was so your mission would end. I can promise you, contact with Walid stopped there."

"Liar. Explain how he tracked me into a Syrian desert."

Her brow furrows and her eyes widen at the information that has been kept in strictest confidence. She swallows, whispers, "I can't."

"And I'm supposed to believe that? From you, quite possibly the best liar I've ever met?"

She flinches, the red in her neck flushes over her cheeks.

"Let me ask you something," Leland says. His normally gruff voice is even deeper—sounds like he swallowed a razor blade. "We found a busted-up computer hidden in Cooper's truck. Our technicians were able to get the history off of it, and it showed Cooper reached out to Walid the night of Justice's mission. Are you saying you had no idea that happened?"

Bridget's hands flies to her mouth. Her eyes fill with tears.

"I..." The tears fall. "He wouldn't have known how to disguise his trail."

"He didn't," Leland says. "His timing was as shitty as his VPN. He sent an email warning Walid to leave Jordan at nearly the same time Justice was in his room. Which explains why Walid came back early from his dinner."

I'd wondered about him showing up. There hadn't been enough time for Security to hunt him down. I'd assumed it was coincidence. Now that I know Cooper's involvement, I realize there was another way I was being tracked. I reach up and tug off my locket. "Cooper gave me this necklace right before I left." I hold it up.

Sandesh exhales a sour curse.

Bridget's gaze focuses on the locket dangling from my hand. She says nothing.

Leland continues. "After Cooper warned Walid, *his* digital mercenaries tracked Cooper's IP. Within minutes, they'd hacked into his computer and discovered a GPS signal being sent from Jordan. Walid directed the men he had inside Jordan to follow the trail. It led them to Justice in Za'atari."

That not only explains how I was tracked; it wasn't my implanted GPS. It also explains Cooper's broken computer. Cooper must've realized he'd been hacked, panicked, and busted up the computer at some point. But not before they'd found me in Syria.

Absorbing all Leland has said, Bridget's straight shoulders begin to slump, her brow to furrow. She whispers, "Where is Cooper?"

With brisk surety, Momma answers, "Earlier today, he was found in his apartment where he'd been tortured then murdered."

Bridget's face pales. She staggers forward and falls into the seat before Momma's desk. She puts her head into her hands and, for a few moments, she sheds more tears for my father than I ever could. Then she raises her head, eyes swollen and red-ringed behind her glasses. "He must've thought he was helping to protect Justice."

"What?" She's lost her mind. "He did it to make money for drugs. That's what he does. It's what he's always done. You told him about The Guild, about what I do, and he took the first opportunity to make money off of me. *Again*."

Bridget inhales then exhales audibly for several breaths, her face blotchy red with emotion. "If what you say is true, then tell me why Cooper didn't tell the men torturing him where they could find his computer? The computer that could still be fixed and used to track you?"

I hate the yawning silence that opens up inside of me. I hate the lack of an answer. "He was too drugged up to remember!" I shout, balling my fists.

We stare at each other; she an almost unreadable mask, me a furious ball of hurt. I walk to where she's seated, stab a finger into her shoulder. "You deserve to lose your memory of this place. You deserve to no longer have any of this."

"I'm willing to accept my fate for what I've done, but I wonder, would you be?"

Is she seriously trying to turn this into some kind of lesson for *me*? "No, Bridget. I wouldn't. But I'd never do what you did. I'd never *choose* to betray you."

Bridget's gaze slides over to Sandesh.

For his part, he stands at military attention, silent as he watches my family falling apart.

Her look says what she doesn't: I *did* betray the family. If I hadn't, Sandesh wouldn't know about operations.

She returns her attention to me. "Everyone makes mistakes, but only a chosen few are forgiven and given a second chance. Cooper was brought here, so you could get to know him, spend time with him, and maybe let go of some of your anger. Cooper loved you, Justice."

Bullshit. "No. You don't get to talk to me about love or mistakes. What I did, what I revealed, came from being backed into a corner. Something that happened when I tried to rescue a girl. Someone who never would've been saved if not for The Guild. What you did almost got me killed, and you did it because you no longer believe in our work."

Bridget's chin lowers the slightest bit. It's the only sign in her straight-backed posture that lets me know I struck pay dirt. And I want pay dirt. She needs to feel something. All that equanimity shouldn't mean she can't be properly punished and hurt. Like she's hurt me.

"You're wrong," she says quietly. "I never stopped believing in The Guild. It was The Guild that stopped doing what it was designed to do. It was founded to rescue people, but ask yourself, Justice, were you rescued? You've spent a lifetime nurturing a rage that never brought you an ounce of relief. Now, you're an assassin trained to kill, a warped warrior, and is that what you want for our younger siblings?"

"Warped?" If she'd slapped my face, I wouldn't have been more surprised. "The laws are warped. The laws don't work. Or haven't you watched the news? Femicide is rampant. Misogyny is winning. And too many of us are sucking up the pain, Bridge."

Bridget breathes slow carefully, as if trying to hold back her own anger. But I see it there. Anger is my specialty, and I want more. "Is that what you want for *our* siblings? To accept their pain and be punching bags?"

Exhaling hotly, she answers, "In my way, I fight too. I look for opportunities to advance our cause, I inspire innovation and healing, and I do so without violence. My way works. Mostly."

Mostly? What a joke. "Bridget, the 'mostly' is what we're worried about. Girls like Cee and Juliette and Bella would've died without our intervention. They need us to fight for them, not hole up in a mansion and burn sage. Do you seriously think society is going to change because we asked *nicely*?"

A sad, small smile tugs at the corners of her mouth. "I guess we'll see. With the FBI here, it's not likely we'll resume clandestine operations. Let's see what happens when we put the full ingenuity and talent of The Guild into peaceful and lawful operations designed to rescue, change laws, and see laws enforced."

Fury races back. "You think what you did worked? You think dropping bombs on the school, gentle bombs because no one was killed, was the right thing to do?"

Under her glasses, her eyes fill with obvious confusion. She shakes her head. "You have my word that that wasn't me." She looks around at Momma and Leland. "You have to believe that I would never... It must've been Walid's men. You just informed me they were here."

I want to believe she's lying. I do. But I can tell she's not. Besides, why lie about this when she's admitted everything else? Cooper must've given Walid's men something, enough information that they were able to program the drones, but not enough that they'd been able to hurt anyone. Maybe, Gracie was right. Maybe, it was a message. A message I plan on ignoring.

I don't have to ask what Momma or Leland think of this new information. It's in their faces. Now that we know Bridget didn't operate the drones, we all know what has to be done. FBI or no FBI. Walid must die.

Bridget stands. "Please," she says, an edge of desperation in her voice, because she knows too. "let's consider another way. We could turn the information we have over to the police. We could..."

She trails off when no one bothers to even look in her direction. She's out. Done. And we won't be taking her advice on operations. After a moment, there's a knock at the door. We all know what that knock means. Internal Security is here.

Bridget's gaze sweeps over to Momma. Their gazes lock again. A tear traces a wet path down Momma's niqab. My heart breaks for her. I can't recall the last time I saw Momma cry. My throat grows tight with grief and fury. Momma exhales a long, low breath and says, "You will be kept under guard until we can make arrangements for your M-erasure."

Stiffening as she inhales deeply, Bridget turns and walks to the door. She doesn't look back when she whispers, "I'm sorry, Momma."

She opens the door. Eugie, a member of Mantua Home Internal Security, is there, ready to isolate Bridget and keep her out of the way. Until things are clear with the FBI, until we can M-erase Bridget, eradicating her memories of her own betrayal, she has to be our prisoner.

Bridget steps out and the door closes with a click as final as a knife in the back. Sandesh puts a hand on my shoulder. "You okay?"

I shrug him off. "Yeah."

He reaches out and with his thumb wipes moisture from my cheek. He shows it to me. "Are you sure?"

I swallow. The gaping pain of sorrow and despair overwhelms me, pinches my throat, squeezes my chest. Tears spring to my eyes, and I turn into him.

He grabs me, sweeps me up, holding me to his chest as the first sob breaks from my soul. He holds me until the last tear falls and there are no more sobs… no more strength, no more energy for rage.

46

SANDESH

A week after her sister admitted to betraying her, I'm standing in my bedroom in a tux, getting ready for Justice's thirtieth birthday bash. What we're about to do makes me extremely uncomfortable.

"Crap, this bowtie isn't cooperating."

"I think the problem is with your shaking hands. Need help?"

I glance at Victor sitting on my bed, digging into a bag of Lay's salt-and-vinegar chips. "Hell, no. Keep those greasy paws to yourself and don't eat on my bed."

Victor pops in a handful of chips. "I think you should calm down. It's a fiesta."

That's what he thinks. The party is incidental to the real goal of giving the FBI the slip. What was it Mukta said?

"This is what we do. Like a magician, we distract with one hand so no one looks at what we're doing with the other. In this case, the FBI will have their hands full with the guest list for Justice's birthday party, so they won't pay attention to your antics."

Our antics being Justice and I getting hot and heavy on the

dance floor, so when we leave, everyone will assume that we're leaving to fuck, instead of the truth that we're flying to Mexico so Justice can assassinate a human trafficker.

Sneaking off together will start a lot of press and rumors. Press and rumors Mukta and Leland are set to help fan the flames of, solidifying their efforts to use me and the IPT as cover. That's not something I can share with Victor. It's also not something I like, but it's what's needed to get Walid, and to keep Justice and her family safe.

I finally get the tie right and turn to Victor.

He shakes his head. "It's lopsided." Sprawled out across my gray comforter, he licks his fingers. "Are you ready for the information my informant dug up now?

I turn back to the mirror attached to the door of my bedroom closet. He's right. Dammit. I try again. "Yeah. What did you find out?"

"On Mukta, it's basically what you can read online. As a child, she was attacked with acid, then adopted by two aid workers, a wealthy lesbian couple. They trained Mukta in the art of business, but she's never stopped acquiring skills. She's got a shit-ton of degrees, two doctorates and not the honorary kind. It's my guess that she got interested in all that science when she was a kid. She had a couple of serious surgeries on her face, and that's where she met her right-hand man, Leland—in the hospital."

Bowtie as straight as I can make it, I give Victor my attention. "She met him in the hospital? Was he a sick kid?"

"No. Had a younger sister with leukemia who was at Children's Hospital of Philadelphia when Mukta was there having one of her surgeries."

"The sister?"

"She survived. Gotta love CHOP. Anyway, fast-forward a couple dozen years and the sister marries, gets pregnant, has un niño, and endures a pattern of domestic disturbances. For years, the police show up, but never take her husband in. Then, one day, out of the blue, the sister goes missing. The police suspect the husband, but they've no proof and they never locate a body. Not long after the wife goes missing, the husband abandons his home, takes the boy, and disappears."

Victor has my undivided attention. "Are you suggesting this guy killed Leland's sister and disappeared with the child? What happened to the man? What happened to the boy?"

Sitting up, Victor dusts crumbs from his shirt directly onto my bed.

"Dude."

"Sorry." He wipes the crumbs onto his palm, then deposits them in my wastepaper basket. "The disappeared father resurfaces six years later when he reports his eleven-year-old son missing. The kid ran away from home."

I swallow a growing dread. "Ran away or was killed like the mom?"

"Hold on, because this is where it gets interesting. Six months after the father shows back up, he's found dead by suicide. According to his suicide note, his conscience got the better of him, so he admits to abusing his son and killing his wife. The letter went so far as to direct the police where to find his wife's body."

"What happened to the kid?"

"He was adopted by the Parish family."

Chills ride down my body. "Tony is Leland's nephew?"

"Not that you'd know that by reading any of the adoption paperwork. Mukta's name is on all the official papers. Leland isn't mentioned, and as for any family related to Tony, it simply states none could be found."

I can't wrap my head around this. "Justice told me she was responsible for Tony's adoption. She said she found him in an alley."

Victor frowns, rolls the bag up, and puts it on my nightstand. "Do you think she lied?"

"Hell, no. She believed what she told me. They lied to her, probably the rest of the family, and maybe even Tony. But why?"

"I've got a guess."

I don't like the tone in his voice. "Go on."

"The records on the father's suicide suggest he'd been in a fight earlier that day. Apparently, there were bruises all over his body."

My blood runs cold. I know exactly what Victor is suggesting. It wasn't a suicide. And maybe the reason the family lied about Tony is because they didn't want to be associated with the death of the father. He could be right, but I'm not going to comment. Victor is my partner and tied to this enough; I don't want him drawn into this bullshit. "I guess we'll never know."

"Not so sure," Victor says, standing and dusting the crumbs off my bed and into his waiting hand. "I have to wonder how long it will take the FBI to start piecing some of this shit together. After the attack two weeks ago, they're still investigating the school and the family, right?"

I swallow to help my suddenly dry throat. "Yep."

He straightens, shoulders locked tight. "Does this have anything to do with why you were chased from Za'atari?"

I wait a moment before responding. "Do you really want in on this, man?"

He waits longer before answering, and my heart jumps into my throat. If he asks, I will tell him.

He shakes his head. "No. No, I don't. I honestly don't get why you do."

Hard to miss the splinter of annoyance in Victor's voice as he walks over and begins to fiddle with my tie. "Why're you going to this party?"

"Why wouldn't I?"

"Forget the fact that bombs were dropped on the place not too long ago or that students flooded out faster than water from a broken damn, you getting entangled with these people endangers the IPT mission, not to mention our press coverage."

Tie finally straight, he steps back.

Turning away, I slip on my dress shoes and bend to tie them, grateful to avoid his gaze because he's right. But, also, it's not that simple. "I'll keep that in mind."

Standing, I find his eyebrows drawn together in a scowl. A scowl he's directing at me. I take that as my cue to leave and head back to the living room, which is neat as a pin thanks to my current level of anxiety.

Victor follows me out. "It's not worth the money, man. Walk away. Learn whatever the fuck you need to learn, get back to letting go of the bad shit and making some good shit happen."

I pull my tuxedo jacket off its hanger in my coat closet because I'm ready to get the hell out of here and get this over with. "Look, Justice is the good shit, and her family—*most* of her family—are the good guys."

He crosses his arms, leans to one side. "Is this love or business?"

He deserves a serious answer. "It's both." And more. "Lo siento, amigo. I've got to go."

"Sure. Hurry along. Chase after that chick like a groupie tailing a tour bus, but you better hope that bus isn't lined with explosives, because this kind of stuff gets a guy killed."

∼

THE DOORMAN HOLDS OPEN the door as I exit my building. "Good evening, Mr. Ross. Your limo has arrived, sir."

"Thanks, Al." We share an awkward smile. Limos aren't

typically waiting to pick me up. In fact, I would've driven myself, but Mukta pointed out that, having my car hanging out on campus or the airport while I fly with Justice to Mexico, could be a bit eyebrow-raising.

Skirting the construction tape—they're always doing some construction here—I

introduce myself to the driver, who nods politely. I slip inside the car.

The driver walks around and gets in the front seat without shutting my door. A limo driver who trusts his passenger to shut his own door? Maybe he's new. I reach out and close the door. The driver pulls away.

It's nice in here, smells like mint and leather. Interior lights cast a faintly bluish glow on the sleek interior. There's a minibar and some snacks. Nice, but still not enough to lift my spirits. Victor comparing me to a groupie chasing a tour bus really got under my skin.

Honestly, it would be a hell of a lot better if I were being led around by my dick. At least I'd have single-mindedness on my side. Right now, every doubt in my mind is playing Russian roulette with my determination. Is the plan good enough? Will it work? Is there another way?

I roll my shoulders to loosen up. No good. It's not only nerves. It's also guilt. Victor said he didn't want to know, but that's not the same as giving him a choice on what's happening. After this mission—after Justice and her family and the school are safe—I'll have enough leverage to insist Mukta only involve the IPT in legal operations. Anything else will have to go through Victor, which means she'll have to bring him in on her operations. Something, I know she'll never do.

The limo turns a little too quickly, and I slide against my seatbelt in the long back seat. Where is this guy going? I press the button to lower the partition. "Driver, you missed the turn for 76. Has the venue been changed? I thought the affair was at the Parish home."

He doesn't answer right away, and my heart kicks in my chest. Finally, he says, "Sorry, sir, we have one other guest to pick up before we get there."

The partition goes back up. My palms start to itch. Mukta does things differently, so it might well be that we're picking someone else up, but given tonight's mission, I highly doubt it.

I'm on high-alert when the limo turns toward the Ben Franklin Bridge exit. There's no way Mukta would send a car that has to circle this far back in the wrong direction. I lean forward and press the partition button. There's an audible *click*, but it doesn't budge. He's locked it.

The driver speeds up. My gut churning, I take off my seatbelt and shift into the seat opposite of me, so that I'm seated under the partition. I knock. "Hey, buddy."

He ignores me, slowing the car for traffic. I shift back to my seat and grab the door handle. It's locked and so's the window. I pull out my cell phone. No signal. I should get a signal just fine, so it's likely jammed. Okay, if this guy *does* work for Mukta, his night is about to suck royally.

Leaning back, bracing myself with my arm, I kick out my leg and drive the heel of my shoe into the window... one, two, three times.

It splinters like a web.

Security glass. Barely cracked it with these rubber-soled, piece-of-shit shoes. My leg aches for my trouble—and me without a gun. I didn't bother, knowing I'd be searched at the Parish home. The last thing I wanted was the FBI to mark me as someone who goes to a birthday party armed. Damn it. Screwed myself over with that decision.

Leg aching, I keep kicking until the limo banks to the right and I fall onto the floor. I climb back into my seat as we veer off the exit and into a rundown area close to the docks that could double as a landfill—rusted metal fence, trash piled up alongside large, dented storage containers, a bulky, bolt-rusted crane with a precariously dangling claw.

The driver veers manically around the containers, as if he knows exactly where he's going. Lights hit us from behind. Another car here likely means this guy brought friends and this has been carefully planned out.

The limo jerks over a pothole and slams to a stop alongside a steel storage container. I can't see a difference from this container to the next, but stopping in this exact spot feels purposeful. Scrambling for a plan, I open the minifridge. It's empty.

The car behind us pulls up with a crunch of tires against gravel. Two men get out and stalk toward us with a ready-to-bust-heads set to their shoulders.

Chances they're friendly? Zero. Each man heads toward a different back door of the limo. Won't be easy to fend off two attacks, but it's even harder to coordinate two attacks. One of them will be first. I watch the men, noticing the one who looks quicker, more anxious. I ready myself at that side.

The driver releases the door locks with a *click* and both doors fling open, but not simultaneously. The faster man comes inside, leading with his gun.

Mistake.

I grab his wrist, pull, and lock his gun arm against my chest.

He tries to jerk free, but not before I get a shot off at the second guy, who jumps back and away. He's obviously the brains.

The guy whose arm I'm holding yanks again, but I secure my feet. Using the leverage, I jerk him forward while simultaneously slamming the back of my head into his face.

Crack. The guy's nose breaks like an egg and blood gushes out and across my hair.

Gusher Guy makes a whiny, distressed sound, and releases his gun. I grab the gun and let the guy go. He crumples onto the gravel.

Sliding out, I roll away from Gusher. When I get a good look at his face, my stomach rolls reflexively. His nose is bent to one side. The limo takes off.

Heart pounding, head pounding from Gusher's face, I scan for the second guy—the smart one—but I don't see him. The squeal of tires and the smell of burnt rubber alerts me to the limo changing directions, back at me. I don't even have time to run when I notice Gusher is up and charging at me.

I'm hyperaware of the amount of pressure I put on the trigger—next to nothing—the snap of the shot—loud—the recoil that rides up my arm—sharp and painful.

Gusher goes down, permanently. The limo, a few tons of pure black steel, bears down on me. In one seamless move, I raise the weapon and shoot at the tires. When they don't blow, I run.

My only escape is up, but none of these containers are climbable. I could climb the crane, but it's parked on the other side of this wall of containers, stacked end-to-end.

Scanning an option, I see a rusted orange ladder on the side of an orange crate. I sprint for it. The limo driver stops, honks his horn, revs his engine, then takes off after me.

In a running leap, I latch onto the ladder with my right hand. My body slams against steel. My arm jerks. My fingers bleed as the rusted metal slices them. Adding my other hand, I scramble up the ladder.

At the top, I pull myself onto the container, flip over, then take out my cell.

Below, the limo guns its engines again.

I look down. The limo is headed straight for—

I flatten out and hold on.

There's a crunch of steel, a slam that rocks my body, and a

vibration that shakes my skull. *Stupid fuck.* What good did that do?

Bringing my phone back up, I roll onto my back and see Bad Guy Number Two—the smart one, smarter than I gave him credit for—inside the cab of the crane. Before I can blink, he fires the Taser and lights me up.

47

JUSTICE

The thin spikes of my Louboutin pumps *tap, tap, tap* against the marble flooring of the front corridor. The sound echoes in the wide hall as I make my way to the gym.

With each step through the main corridor of the Mantua Home, the party energy increases, electric anticipation warmed by the promise of delicious food, rich conversation, bubbly drinks, with an anything-can-happen vibe.

Though it's early—barely eight—the house is a hive of activity. The serving staff, dressed in black-and-white uniforms, familiarize themselves with the home's layout by carrying trays of food into the gym, where, for now, all the action is. It's set up with lights and music like a high school dance to delight the kids. When all the guests arrive, the main celebration will be out back on the expertly manicured yard and lavish patio.

My younger sisters flit around here and there, many in flowing ball gowns, but some in shorter dresses. Three in tuxedos—well, Tony, Rome, and the youngest girl in Vampire Academy wear the tuxes.

Everyone has their marching orders: dance, mingle, strike

up conversations. Ask questions. Meet eyes. Shake hands. Be polite. Don't leave the party without permission. That's typical; Momma is big on courtesy to guests. No wallflowers here.

Music plays softly through the entire house, pumped from where the musicians play outside. It makes the gym seem even more *high school prom*. Momma let the Troublemakers pick the band, and I'm kind of surprised they like the acoustic stuff.

The overall effect as I enter is theatrical, bright and warm and full of opulent promise. Sort of perfect—if you're into that kind of thing. Tonight, I am. But only because of who I'm waiting for.

I'm tantalizingly aware of every movement of my blue silk gown sweeping my legs, plunging down my back, hugging my breasts and ass. Long slits up both sides make it easy for me to move. Never know when I might need to run or leave myself open for groping.

The latter I'm kind of hoping for. Speaking of Sandesh…

I peek out one of the long windows as guests arrive in sleek, black limos. It's like watching the Academy Awards as drivers escort ladies and gentlemen from the cars. People have gathered out front to chat, remark on the home, laugh, flirt, look hot and wealthy and successful for the hired photographers.

Many of the guests mill about in small groups before making their way through the house. Leland and Momma stand outside the large front doors at the top of the stone stairs, welcoming everyone. Leland looks sharp and handsome and confident in his tuxedo with the turquoise tie. Momma looks elegant in her silver-and-turquoise gown with matching niqab.

Bella wears a simple, unadorned yellow dress. She has a fistful of Momma's ten-thousand-dollar gown in her little hands and is clinging to it like a lifeline. Momma doesn't protest or try to have care staff take her; she merely directs her guests around the little girl as she greets them.

That's unusual.

"Looking good, J."

I turn from the window as Tony strides up to me. His dark hair is brushed back, hazel eyes playful and amused. He looks great in his tux.

"Right back at you." I run a hand along his tux. "Look out, ladies."

He grunts, flicks his chin toward the windows. "He here yet?"

We turn as one to the windows. "Nope."

We watch the parade of guests in silence and my eyes fall on Bella again.

"You see that?" I point to the child hiding behind Momma's dress. "She's not engaging with anyone, and Momma is just letting it happen." Momma has a thing for making sure each of her daughters interacts with the outside world in a forthright and open manner.

"Yeah. Whatever happened to her," Tony says, "it must've been something."

True. The fact that Bella gets special treatment means that her story prompts a great deal of sympathy from Momma more than any other she's ever heard. I wonder about that kid. Sometimes, new adoptees are quick to tell their stories, sometimes not. It's done in a therapy session, recorded, and then played for the family, but it's still a suck fest.

"I want to be there when Bella decides to tell her story."

"Maybe she never will."

I look at him; he can't be serious. "Of course she will. It's part of our culture. We might not share blood, but we can share each other's pain. Everyone tells their story."

"Not me. No one has ever asked me."

"But..." The argument dies in my throat. He's right. I know details of his story because we talked as kids, but he never formally shared his story with the family. "How come you got away with not sharing?"

An annoyed grimace crosses his face before he takes a step back. He shuffles his shoes against the wood floor, averting his eyes before gesturing out the window, around the room, and toward the front corridor. "You see them?"

He doesn't say *Feds*, but I know that's who he's referencing. Though most of the people in here are kids—both family and the children of guests—I spot the outsiders easily. Stiff. Capable looking. Dressed nice but not too nice. Muscular and thin, like they eat nothing but knowledge, and work out as a matter of survival. "It's to be expected. Lot of VIPs here tonight."

Set up that way to keep the Feds busy so Sandesh and I will be able to have plenty of eyes witnessing our grind fest. Though I know Sandesh is nervous, I'm not worried about it. If there's one thing I can do well with that man, it's let the sparks fly.

My insides flutter at the plan details. When I'm introduced to thank the guests, I'm to take the microphone, give a slurred speech, say something embarrassing about how hot Sandesh looks, then drag him out to the dance floor.

Yeehaw. I kind of like the idea of being the center of attention in that way, but since Sandy won't be here for a while, I'll have to entertain myself with my weird brother.

I grab his hand. "Okay, sis, let's show our siblings how it's done."

He rolls his eyes. "Whatever you say, J."

We exit through French doors held open by well-dressed servers, past a bartender bent over stacking crates, and the event coordinator aggressively speaking into a headset.

Outside, the air smells of the numerous flowers that now decorate the patio. Stone clicks under my heels as we descend the three-tiered stone patio, down the walkway, and out to the bunting where several enormous tents are set up, one for dancing.

"You should've asked for a pony, not this shit," Tony says.

I laugh as we hit the makeshift dance floor. "Shut up and keep up, old man."

Lights are strung along the inside of the tall, circus-high tent. The beat of the music thrums under our feet as we circle the dance floor. We're not the only people dancing. It's magical out here. There's nothing in the world like a Parish party.

Tony puts a hand at my waist and draws me closer. He's warm and comfortable and has a smile that goes from ear to ear. "J, remember when we'd play wedding when we were kids?"

I laugh. "Yeah, I remember." When Tony had first been adopted, I told him we were going to get married one day. I'd even forced him to practice the wedding. He'd been an extremely patient twelve-year-old. He'd never complained or tried to reason away my delusions. It'd been Gracie, sharp as nails, who'd clued me into the plain realities.

"You," I scold, pitching my voice like Gracie, "can't get married. You're related. Losers."

We laugh. Tony shakes his head. "But we ain't related." His gaze slides away. "Not like Jules and Rome. Or me and Leland."

"*What?*"

Laughing, he twirls me around, drawing me back a little too quickly so that I nearly bounce off of his chest. My balance isn't the only thing off. What is he saying about him and Leland? "Tony?"

He stares at me, not really seeing me, and says, "Manipulative fucks."

"What are you talking about?"

"Last year..." His voice trails off. His eyes widen as he looks over my head at something coming up behind us.

I spin, searching for what's putting that look on his face, and then I see her.

Gracie strolls across the dance floor in a deep-red gown. Her hair and body seem on fire as fast as she's moving.

My heart leaps, skips, and avoids the next beat.

As if it could leap, skip, and avoid the truth coming at us. Gracie on the dance floor? She hates dancing. Something is wrong.

Gooseflesh slides across my skin like someone has ghosted past my window, screaming into the night.

She's almost here. Tony sees it, too. We both tense.

"My turn," Gracie says when she's still two steps away and then swings herself at Tony.

I just manage to jump out of the way, but Tony's so shocked, he nearly bobbles her.

His arms come up even as they release me, and Gracie laughs as if it's a game we play. She turns her head away, but gives directions most definitely meant for me. "Don't panic. Go to Momma and Leland's office."

Already panicking, I thread my way through the growing crowd of dancers and take note of some of the agents along the perimeter moving, too. My heart picks up speed. My feet do, too. No one has to say it. I know.

Sandesh.

48

JUSTICE

Willing myself not to run, I step into Momma and Leland's shared office on the main level of the Mantua Home. More sedate than Momma's office underground, it's twice the size, has two desks, one for her and Leland, and two sitting areas, each containing a couch and four leather chairs.

My hands are slick with sweat. My heart's so high in my throat I can barely breathe. My gaze jumps around the room until I spot... Leland.

He's on the phone.

I cross to his desk.

He looks up at me and holds up one finger like this is any other day and I'm interrupting him.

No. Way. That phone is going out the window.

I reach for it.

Someone clears a throat behind me, and I turn, hoping to see Momma.

It's Bridget.

She wears a loose gold gown cinched at the waist by a belt of faux flowers like something a Greek goddess might wear.

Traitor. But, of course, they let her come to the party. Need everything to look normal for our guests and the FBI, even though it isn't normal. And, soon, *Bridget* won't be normal. She'll have her memory altered. She'll be M-erased. Good.

I push away from the desk and head to her. "What's going on?"

"Justice." Bridget uses her customary let's-get-calmed-down-and-seated-before-we-proceed voice.

The familiar tone, the normalness of it, hurts in a way I hadn't anticipated—a physical ache in the center of my chest to accompany my growing panic.

I shove it away—shove all the pain into a box. "Don't fuck with me right now, Bridget."

Leland puts a hand over the mouthpiece. "The limo we sent for Sandesh was found abandoned, the driver dead in the trunk."

The driver? Lewis? His poor family.

Straightening my shoulders, lifting my head while clenching my stomach, I ready for the next punch. "And Sandesh?"

Leland pauses as if listening on the phone.

Come on! I can barely fucking breathe right now.

"Leland."

He hangs up. "They took him."

I don't faint. Would never in a million years faint, but my legs, it turns out, can forget to keep me standing. I stumble back, plop right onto my ass in the chair in front of Leland's desk.

"It's Walid," I say, glaring at Bridget. "It has to be."

She shakes her head. "I know nothing. Maybe Dada. Her contact."

That makes sense and it's a lifeline I can cling to. "Leland, tell Dada to get her ass in here."

"I *am* here, abrasive one."

Dada, wearing a cream gown with black brocade and capped sleeves that show off her toned arms, strolls through the office's mahogany double doors.

I stand. Wet noodles have more strength than my legs, but I push past the chair.

The doors open and close again as Tony and Gracie enter. Tony has undone his bowtie so that it hangs around his neck like a loosened noose.

"No." Leland waves a hand at them. "We need to have actual family members out there, entertaining."

Tony spreads his hands in an are-you-serious gesture. "We got plenty out there. Ramla and her kids are here, bunch of showoffs." He comes up to me, puts an arm around my shoulder. "I'm sorry, kid."

Furious, I shrug him off. "Sorry is something you tell someone when they have no choice but to deal with something. I've got a choice, Tony. I'm going after him."

He stares at and into me for a whole three seconds before he nods. "I'm with you. Remember that. I'm always with you."

His support sends my right eye twitching and my lips trembling. I look away, toward Dada. She has both hands and her cell clasped protectively in front of her.

"You know things, Dada. You have a contact there. Find out where they fucking took Sandesh."

She holds up her cell. "I just texted him."

The doors swing open and closed again. This time, Momma enters, takes one look around the room and says, "I don't think they would hurt him."

It calms me down, even though we all know what she didn't add. *Yet.*

Eventually, they'll take him to Walid and the torture will begin.

The thought hollows my stomach. I have to get out of here and *do* something.

Dada's phone chirps.

I fist my hands at my sides to keep from sprinting over and grabbing it.

She looks down, clears her throat. "Sandesh is on his way to Mexico. My source..." She pauses, lowers her eyes. "Sean confirms this is so."

"I don't trust this guy," Gracie says, and despite the fact that she's much shorter than Dada, her voice and her tone command attention, even when standing next to Dada.

Dada stiffens and looks down at Gracie. "He has proven himself by getting us this information, and when he could have run—*should* have run—when another man was accused of being the spy, tortured, and killed in his place, he stayed to provide us insight. More importantly, you can trust him because we have his son."

She puts a hand on her belly.

Gracie gasps—literally gasps—then her mouth tightens and her eyes grow hard.

Shit. Dada's pregnant, and though I'd suspected it before, now that it's confirmed, I can see the swell of her belly.

Gracie looks sick to her stomach.

The room is silent.

After a moment, Tony says, "'Bout time you admitted it."

Bridget lets out a breath. "Strategically, considering The Guild's goals of secrecy, this is good news." Stunned, everyone turns to look at her. "Not the pregnancy. I mean, that's good, congrats and all, but I meant *Mexico* is good. Doable for our government. I saw some agents scurrying out of here, so they likely know Sandesh was taken. We'll find a way to pass on the information of where he is, and they'll go after him. They'll assume it's all related to his work with the IPT."

I see red—*literal* red—burst through my eyesight as if I'd been hit with a hammer. Why is she even in here? Old habits die hard, I guess. "We are *not* leaving Sandesh in the hands of that sick bastard while the government makes up its slow-assed mind whether or not to go in there."

"Justice is right," Leland says. "Even if the authorities do get him out, there will still be the issue of Walid and what he knows about us. We need to get him before that happens. Which means we have less, not more, time."

"Hold on," Gracie says. "Do we...

I lose her words, sinking instead into the cold dread suddenly lining my bones. I feel brittle and frozen and broken as my family calmly discusses the pros and cons of doing something that we need to already be doing.

Memories of Sandesh and me in that small room in Israel, of him holding me, his warmth against me and inside me, invade my mind, causing fear to rise like a knife to my chest. Fuck all this talk.

Wringing my hands, I stand and look around at my siblings. I need to cut through this bullshit. I need to lay myself on the line and draw *my* line.

I clear my throat to get their attention and look directly at Momma. "I love Sandesh."

A whisper of disbelief comes from each of my siblings, but I ignore them and keep my gaze on Momma. Mostly because I've never felt more vulnerable. "I'm going after him, Momma, but I'm not willing to make that choice for anyone but me."

Momma's eyes soften as she keeps my gaze, and I feel the warmth of being seen and loved and known.

She nods her acceptance of my declaration, my line in the sand, and I finally turn to the rest of the room. I don't ask, but they know it's been asked: *Who's with me?*

Gracie raises a hand and a devilish eyebrow. "I'm in. I like Sandesh, though obviously not as much as you."

"You know I'm in," Tony says.

"I will support in any way I can from here." Dada rubs a

hand along her stomach. "Sean can get you inside using the Tony's plan."

"Finally," Tony says. "If you all would've listened to me—"

"I can help," Bridget puts in. "I can—"

I hold up a hand, stop her from talking. "Not you, traitor."

"We'll have to revise Tony's plan," Leland says, saying he's in without actually saying it. "It never called for a rescue."

Momma touches her niqab and nods as her gaze scans the room. "But if I'm not mistaken, the original plan called for a second man. Justice, you'll have to choose someone from Internal, unless you have another idea."

I *do* have another idea. A man who will do anything for Sandesh, a man for whom this won't be *just* another mission, a man with the training to be part of the team and as many contacts as I have siblings.

Victor.

49

SANDESH

I wake up groggy, head aching, body trembling, and blind. Blinking repeatedly doesn't help. There's a moment of panic—how can I get out of here if I can't see. Slowly, my brain comes online and scolds me, *You're not blind; it's just really dark in here.*

Relief and terror battle for my attention. I take a deep breath, falling away from either emotion to concentrate on details. My pounding headache tells me that I've either hit my head or have been hit at some point. Every time I blink, which is often as my eyes won't accept my brain's analysis that it's really, really dark, dried blook pinches the skin of my forehead.

I shiver. Not just blindingly dark, but freezing, too. The thin material of my tuxedo shirt and pants aren't getting the job done. Shivers roll down my body uncontrollably and there's no way to get warm against the ice-cold stone floor. *Stone cold* suddenly makes perfect sense to me. I try to sit up. *Bam*! My head slams into the ceiling.

Motherfu...

That explains the blood on my forehead and the pounding

headache, which could've come from the fight in Philly. Although, I doubt it. My internal clock is telling me the fight happened days ago.

My attention skips from my aching head to the manacles on my wrists. I raise my hands and hear the *clink* of iron, feel the weight and pinch of chains. I move my feet and feel a similar heaviness, a cramping cold at my ankles and numb bare feet.

Looping my hands around my wrist chains, I pull. Sharp coils of pain twist into my bones and race up my arm. The wounds from whatever bits of raised metal line my manacles are so sharp and unexpected that nausea rises.

Bracing myself, I pull again and again until the clank of the manacles echoes in the room like the desperate wailing in my mind.

I stop.

Shivering all the way down to my ass, I fumble around with shaking hands along the gritty stone floor, ignoring the warm blood dripping into my palms. I find and trace the outline of a ring embedded deep into cement, too deep for me to pull out.

Using a hand so frigidly cold my knuckles feel arthritic, I brush my fingers along the chips and flakes of the stone ceiling. Cold. Rough. Pitted. A stone coffin. Or, if you happened to be a prisoner in France during the Middle Ages, an oubliette—a place of forgetting.

Forgotten will not be my fate. No. Walid has brought me here to torture me.

He thinks I organized the Jordan hit against his brother or, at least, played a big part. That means that the bone-rending pain I feel now is merely an appetizer.

He might even ask me a question or two, but mostly, he'll want to hurt me as badly and for as long as he can.

"You're quiet," a voice in the darkness rasps, and I shoot up again, slapping my head against stone with a *thud* that pierces my jaw and muffles my ears.

"Fuck!" I peer uselessly into the darkness. "Who the fuck's in here?"

"The one you sentenced here."

A Russian. I sentenced a Russian here? Great. I'm trapped in the dark with a nutjob. Here's hoping his hands are manacled, too.

"Sorry, buddy. You've got the wrong guy." Maybe the wrong century. How long could someone stay alive down here? Or am I speaking with a ghost?

The man shifts in the dark and metal scrapes against metal. Not a ghost. And chained, too.

"Liar. The woman you sent to kill my bosses caused this."

I can't help but laugh; it's that damn funny. Funny enough to overcome my pounding head, rough tongue, dried throat, frozen balls, and manacled hands. *That* damned funny.

"Like I said, wrong guy." Hell, wrong gender. Still, keeping him talking might get me answers, like where we are—unless this guy is a plant or some other kind of threat. Only one way to find out. "But we've got time, so tell me about it. How long have you been here?"

The Russian gives a humorless, dull, and pitiful laugh that quickly dissolves into tears, which then shatters into fits of coughing. Gunshot-loud, hacking coughs ricochet off the stone. This lunatic is close. Judging by the coughing, he's directly across from me.

I don't reach out, but if I did, I'm sure I could touch him. This space, I'm betting, isn't very large.

The man stops coughing and, for a few minutes, I can hear only his wheezing, wet, careful breaths in the pitch blackness. His ribs are likely broken.

I wait for him to settle down before asking softly enough to evoke a response, "What's your name? I'm Sandesh."

"Dmitri."

Dmitri. According to the preparation Justice and her team

gave me for our now-defunct mission, he's one of the guards for the sex-slavers Justice had called the Brothers Grim. Well, at least one of us deserves to be imprisoned and tortured here. "Where are we, Dmitri?"

"Mexico. The woman you sent..." He coughs for another minute before dropping back into his wheezing breaths and whispering, "She is the devil."

My woman's getting a reputation. I push thoughts of Justice away because worrying about her, about how she's dealing with all of this, is excruciating enough to make my aches and pains seem minor.

Through the dark, Dmitri issues a deep and pained moan coated with the phlegm lining his lungs. "I'm dying. It hurts."

"That's been going around."

"Sandesh?" He whispers my name, almost as if it's an entire question and then takes long, labored breaths to recover. "Will you... kill... him?"

"Who?" I shift my aching legs and the shackles on my ankles clink.

Dmitri stays silent for long moments before expelling, "The man who begs but never means it. Walid."

Great, I'm stuck in the dark with a poetic Russian. What are the chances? "Not sure I'm in a position to make that promise."

Dmitri coughs again. His coughs sound disturbingly like sobs. "They will bring you out. Strap you... to a chair. The first time... you still have strength. Act then. Don't do as I did." He falls into long moment of gasps. The wetness of those breaths puts pressure against my own ribs. "I thought to satisfy him and live by answering his questions as he asked. He begged me to answer so that he could stop." He laughs as if at another person, a dumber person who had done something naively amusing. His laughter erupts into coughs, then back into wheezing.

It's so dark that wheezing is the best way to tell the guy is still alive. "Walid tortured you? Himself?"

"Yes. Him. He likes it."

He must. It's been weeks since Jordan. Not good. "Describe the room. The instruments. Tell me as much as you can."

50

JUSTICE

Two hours after our plane touches down at a seedy, rundown, and secluded airstrip in Mexico, I stand inside the nearby hangar that houses the family jet, a Cadillac, and my team: Tony, Gracie, and Victor.

There's lots of shifting of feet and eyes. Gracie's landing on this dilapidated runway had been dicey, but our prospects of getting into the ranch are far worse. The mood inside this rickety metal structure that's so dented and rusted it looks like a toddler having a bad day could kick it down is tense. And awkward.

Dada's informant/boyfriend/baby-daddy Sean has come through on Tony's plan to get Victor and Tony onto Walid's estate. Problem is, the plan calls for them having to pose as mental-air-quotes-around-the-word *entertainers.*

Turns out, Walid gets off on pain—specifically inflicting pain, then watching pain inflicted by men having sex. He's some kind of torturer-voyeur. Guess I shouldn't have expected the morals' bar to be too high with this guy.

According to Juan, he has a routine. Torture captives. Down to business. Live sex show, anyone? That information was part of our research, but I'd never thought to use it against him. Honestly, I was so focused on getting both brothers at the same time, I didn't give it a passing thought.

Tony, however, did.

I can see why he was pissed that Momma had ignored his plan, but now that I know the details, I also know why she did. It's so unlike Tony's other mission ideas. It's elaborate with lots of moving pieces. Jordan was simple and likely would've worked if not for Amal.

"I don't get how strippers do this vulnerability thing," Tony says, looking wildly uncomfortable in his getup—and not for modesty's sake, the conceited idiot, but wearing a leather jock and sex toys toolbelt to a potential gunfight is scary as hell in theory and terrifying in practice.

"I feel so fucking exposed." His hands move around, trying to find some place to rest.

Not happening. Not with what he's wearing: a heavy gold chain around his neck and the leather jock that creates a *W* of his ass. The front sock part practically carries the imprint of his thingamajigger. Classy.

Not that I looked. *Okay*, I did, but it's unavoidable. Still, I have not said a word to him. Not one uncomfortable word.

Victor, currently rocking a black-leather G-string, looks completely comfortable. Although Sandesh has told me Victor had done a lot of undercover roles for the government, I'm still impressed at his calm. He didn't even hesitate when I told him the plan to rescue Sandesh. He was angry as hell, but, after ten minutes of cursing at me in Spanish, he took a deep breath and told me he was in.

"What are you complaining about?" Gracie asks. "I wish this guy preferred women. At least you're not being entombed inside a gaudy Mexican Cadillac."

Entombed. Not a good word choice.

"Mira, gringa," Victor objects, smoothing a hand over the

lime-green Cadillac. "Don't knock the car. That space is ingenious. Took me forty minutes to find the thing, and that was with instructions on where it was."

Gracie doesn't look impressed.

I wouldn't either if I had to ride stuffed into the secret compartment that makes up the car's back seat. "Stop complaining, Gracie," I tell her because I need her to calm the fuck down, "You're the only one small enough to fit. Sucks to be a shrimp."

"Easy for you to say," she bites. "You'll be stretched out on nearby hill."

"Yep, because I'm not a shrimp and I'm the best shot. But I do have to hike through the woods all by my lonesome tonight to get into position, which means I'll be dropped off a few hours before everyone else even arrives. So, count your blessings."

"Don't sweat it, Gracie." Tony swivels his hips. "You don't have the male sex-appeal part anyways."

Gracie rolls her eyes. "Trust me, you don't either."

"Oh, yes you do, amigo," Victor says, and winks. "Big time."

With a grin, Tony flips him the bird. Victor laughs. So far, Victor's proven a great addition to the team with all kinds of connections, a bone-deep loyalty to Sandesh, and no mercy when it comes to flirting with Tony.

Truth? Their casual banter is getting on my last nerve. "Does everyone know their part?"

A chorus of *yes*es and *stop asking*s answers me. I don't stop.

"Do you know what we do if the guards don't let our entertainers inside the gates?" Everyone turns to stare at me. "Yes, this isn't the first time I've asked. And, yes, I do understand that Dada has gone to a great deal of trouble to arrange this, but—"

"Look, chill out." Tony fingers the thick gold chain around his neck. "Walid is on a sex, drugs, and torture bender. His men are poorly trained. This is going to work out for us."

"There are four of us against dozens," Gracie says. "Don't get cocky."

Victor snorts. "He can't help himself."

I barely hear them. My mind is stuck on *sex, drugs, and torture bender*. My heart gallops in my chest. I need to get Sandesh out of there. I can't stomach the thought of Walid getting his groove on by torturing him and then moving on to some hardcore, live-sex-show shit.

"Tony." I swallow the panic. "Promise me you won't wait to take Walid out. The second you get—

"I know, J. I know." He pats the air with his hands. "I still think I should use something quicker." He waves down at the tools on his belt. "Look at this. Ball gag, whip—the tools on this belt would make taking Walid out a hell of a lot faster."

"It's too risky and invites retaliation by his guards," I say, for the tenth time. "Stick with the patch."

"You mention that before," Victor says. "What's the patch?"

Technically, I'm not supposed to tell him, but he's here and right now a part of my team. "It's a poison patch sewn within a reinforced, protective tag on Tony's thong. It works like a nicotine patch."

Victor's brows raise. He takes a step away from Tony. "It's absorbed through the skin?"

I nod.

"I could use one of those," Gracie says.

"We have exactly one patch. Besides, if you do your job right, you won't need anything but your gun."

Internally, I replay her role. I see her inside the secret compartment, imagine her climbing out, racing across the compound, making her way to the control room, and taking out the electric fence, so that I can make my way inside. While Tony and Victor handle Walid, Gracie and I will meet up and fight our way to the underground area where Sandesh is being kept.

Gracie says, "What if I get found? Shouldn't I have some kind of cover story?"

"Like what, Red?" Victor asks.

"Like maybe you wanted to try to add me to your show, broaden Walid's experiences?"

It's a great idea, except... Raising my hands, I look around the desolate plane hangar to emphasize my point. "We're shit out of eight-hundred-dollar bras, and there's no Agent Provocateur in sight."

Gracie's face heats. She bites her lip.

What's that about? I crook my fingers in an *out-with-it* gesture.

"Well, I don't think I'll need a costume." Before I can even process what that means, Gracie strips down to her skivvies, lacey and red and glittery as hell. That might be the sexiest underwear I've ever seen. *Seriously?* Rhinestones? Who wears that on the daily?

I can't help it—despite my nerves and churning gut, I burst into laughter. She's all business on top and party below. Tony sputters until he begins to cough.

Victor whistles long and loud. "Damn, Red, if I'd known you were hiding that, I would've been nicer to you."

"What's that supposed to mean?" Gracie thrusts out a lavishly tattooed hip.

Great. The last thing this mission needs is for these two to be at each other's throats.

I stab a finger into Victor's chest. Like stabbing chiseled concrete. "Knock it off."

"Joke." Victor holds up his hands. "Getting involved with one of the Parish clan is as smart as hiring your own hit man."

"That's a job I'd be willing to consider for you," Tony offers.

I roll my eyes like a fistful of dice. They come up snake eyes. "Enough! Let's get going."

51

SANDESH

I've been stripped of my shirt, have my hands handcuffed in front of me and my head forced down so that I'm looking at bricks and dirt as I'm marched down a damp, moldy corridor. One of the two guards on either side of me holds a Taser to my neck. Proof positive that Walid wants me alive.

"You're going to scream for your mommy," Taser Holder whispers in my ear, pressing the metal prongs deep into my skin.

I don't reply, but the two begin to take bets on how long it's going to take before Walid breaks me.

When that doesn't get a reaction, they try to trip me. I keep my legs through a miracle of willpower and awareness that somehow overrides how thirsty, weak, and dizzy I am.

The floors we pass are pitted red brick with the memory of dark bloodstains from the bleeding victims dragged down this hall. The stains increase as we near the torture chamber. Dmitri might not have a lot still going for him, but he does have a rock-solid memory—it's exactly as he described.

At the threshold to the chamber, the sour, defeated smell of shit, piss, and blood twists my gut. Apparently, Walid knows the most important thing about torture—fear.

I know that's not where this experience ends. Dmitri was very specific, but if I'm able to rally, I won't be sticking around long enough to experience Walid's talents. Even with my head forced down and my hands bound behind my back, I'm preparing for the fight ahead.

According to Dmitri, the room is large, with several torture stations, a stone bath, and a wall of spikes. He said the guards will secure my feet before they unbind my hands. I would rather have waited for that moment to attack, but Dmitri's account of the room and the element of surprise will force me to act long before I'm untied.

Just as Dmitri described, I see the edge of the stone bath, cracked and crumbling gray cement with blue spray paint markings. The moment I spy it, I plant my foot, twist the energy up and out. My foot slams into Taser Guard's ankle and there's an audible *crack*.

The man jerks, curses, and tumbles to the ground.

Even as he's falling, I'm spinning, ramming my lowered head into Guard Number Two. I drive him the way a football player drives a tackle dummy, but with greater success because this guy isn't expecting it.

I shove him as far as I dare before breaking away and rolling to the side. He stumbles back and his body slams into a wall of spikes, impaling him with a wild, horrified cry that quickly cuts off.

Damn. There's so much blood but he's still alive. He fell at an angle, with his body mostly on the ground, but his upper torso, shoulder, and neck are stabbed through with spikes. Blood runs in a crooked line down his chin. His lips are moving. Maybe in prayer. I look away.

According to Dmitri, Walid won't appear until the guards

secure the prisoner, strip off his pants with a sharp knife, and make the call.

He'll be expecting that call. I'm running out of time.

Back on my feet, I cross to the first guard, who rolls onto his side and raises his Taser.

I dodge, but one spike lands in my leg. The other misses me, rendering the Taser useless.

Reacting quickly, I land my knee and all my weight on his neck.

His eyes bulge, but he struggles to flip me off him by putting pressure on the ankle I broke. He can't even cry out at the pain, but it is there in his tearing eyes. Gurgling, he goes slack. Not dead, but out of the way.

I rip the Taser prong from my leg, fish the keys from his pocket, then undo my handcuffs. Sweating and breathing heavily, I cross the room—a well-used torture chamber with a dentist's chair, chains from the ceiling, spikes coming out of the wall, and several blowtorches.

Bending at the stone bath, I gag. The water smells foul. It'd probably been bathed in by miners a hundred years ago. I'm so damn thirsty, but I don't dare drink. Instead, I dip my head in and wash the blood from my eyes. Standing, I shake off the water and nearly fall over. So dizzy.

Black dots line my vision as I stumble over to the guard I left alive. He's passed out, so he can't follow. I drag him to a pipe and handcuff his sorry ass.

Sweating, heart pounding from the effort, I ready myself for the next leg of my journey. According to Dmitri, I'm at the bottom of a coal mine on a large compound. I need to get up and out of here, find Walid, and end this.

∼

The stone corridor is lit with caged lights spaced haphazardly along the ceiling, but their glow barely seems to stretch beyond their bars. It's dim and cold and the floor is uneven. To get through these tunnels is a struggle of will, but I have company—Dmitri, who I half-drag with me—and entertainment from the chatter on the two-way I boosted from the guard after hand-cuffing him to a wall.

An American with a Southern accent has spoken on it a couple of times. Alternating between English and Spanish, he seems more interested in sharing stories. Clown.

At least he's keeping me in the loop, and I have to admit, it helps to have that voice to focus on, as if somewhere, for someone, this is just another day at the office.

God, I'm nauseous. Hadn't realized how damn sick I am until I expended the little energy I had in that fight. Now my body is feverish and my steps sluggish and unbalanced with Dmitri's weight. To top it off, I've gotten lost in this medieval stone-and-shit tunnel twice.

I've only found my way this far thanks to Dmitri, who I had to backtrack to get. You think he'd be grateful that I stole keys from the guard and taken him out of the oubliette... but he's not.

"I can't walk," Dmitri says. "Leave me."

"Yeah, I know." Which is why, as weak as I am, I'm dragging this guy, naked and riddled with injuries, down the ice-cold stone corridor. Together, we sound like shuffling zombies. Good thing the guy weighs next to nothing and that no one else is down here. The two guards I took out seemed to be it.

"I'm dying. Let me die."

Not likely. If I could've gotten out of here on my own, I would've left the guy to die in peace. "Which way?"

Dmitri moans. He breaks into a fit of coughing, wheezes. "Down to get up."

Yeah. That's the crazy-ass directions that hadn't helped in the first place, along with all the talk of uneven stones.

I hoist him up as he almost trips. My arm muscles shake. "A little more specific."

Dmitri raises a trembling hand, as pale and bony as a corpse. "There."

Where? I search through the dimly lit corridor. It takes a second before I correctly judge where he pointed. A brick a little larger than the rest with a white streak down the center.

Dragging Dmitri forward, I use my shoulder to prop him against the wall, hitting the brick with my elbow.

The wall slides open. Hallelujah. Bright light erupts from the opening, and I have to blink at the blinding change. After a moment, I can see down the stairs. Stairs? Stairs leading down. Down to get up. Oh, shit.

I grab Dmitri and pull him back as I spot a camera bolted to the wall over the stairs. Did someone monitoring the camera, spot me? Helping Dmitri to slide down against the wall, I creep around the side, use the wall to support my gun hand, aim, and take out the camera.

I wait for an alarm or any kind of movement below.

Nothing.

My heart hammering in my chest, sweat slicking my body, I pick Dmitri back up—guy's practically unconscious—and hoist him into a fireman's carry. Leaving one hand free for my gun, I step down the first step.

Three things happen at once: an alarm sounds, Dmitri begins to convulse, and two armed guards appear at the bottom of the stairs.

52

JUSTICE

I reposition myself at the top of the tree-lined hill overlooking the barbed-wired-topped electric fenced-in compound of Rancho de Grim y Grimy. Leather-covered forearms against rough ground, my finger on the trigger, I'm stretched out along a natural depression and half hidden behind a shrub, watching the gate through the night vision scope on my rifle. I zero in on the man in charge of the gate, Walid's head of security

Of course, our recon had shown the compound's newest head of security—a broad-chested white guy who looks like he stepped straight out of Blackwater and into a more lucrative profession, but I still find myself repressing a gut instinct that tells me something about this guy is off.

He wears a baseball cap with *USA* lettering, dark sunglasses —at night—a .45 snugged in a chest holster over muscles so jacked they strain his T-shirt. He has that stay-ten-feet-from-my-person-at-all-times vibe.

Gotcha. I'll shoot from here.

Ten more minutes pass before the lime-green Cadillac drives down the road toward the front gate. My headset clicks.

Gracie. Again. "How much longer, Justice? I'm roasting."

"Please, you've been in there for two hours. People smuggled out of Mexico stay in that compartment for days."

"That's awful. You couldn't pay me..." She breaks off, then adds, "If my cyber skills weren't needed to rescue your boyfriend, nothing could get me into this Dante's Inferno. Nothing."

Yeah, it's a shit place to be, but telling her that will only make it worse. Anger is probably her best bet to keep from panic. "Just because you're as tall as a fifth grader doesn't mean you should whine like one. Chill. You're almost inside the compound."

My earpiece clicks again. Even the click sounds angry. I keep focus on the gate, but listen to Gracie vent, responding here and there mostly to encourage her—better anger than the fear it covers up.

When the car pulls to a stop before the guards, I silence Gracie with a play-by-play. "There're five men at the gate including the head of security, a big USA hat-wearing dude. He's leaning down to the car to talk to Tony and Victor. He's gesturing our boys out of the car."

Tony and Victor get out. Victor exits like he's at a show, doing a cute little pirouette that shows off his finely toned ass before throwing his head back with laughter.

USA shakes his head, motions them both to the side. They obviously have no weapons on them, and, at this point, are chilled to goose bumps—unlike Gracie, who must be holding her breath down there, sweating and miserable.

"They're checking the car."

With Tony and Victor away from the vehicle, huddled together like two men used to each other's intimate company, USA motions a couple guards to check the car.

My heart rate, elevated already, launches into top speed. While the vehicle is searched, Tony and Victor are held under armed guard—a man who looks maybe twenty, with a scruffy mustache that doesn't pass machismo. He's jittery and I keep one eye on him and the other on the car.

I hold my breath. Let it out. *Don't find her. Don't.* As one guard checks the front of the vehicle, the other gets into the back, crawling over the back seat. Holy shit. He's practically sitting on Gracie.

The guards inspecting the back of the car climbs out. I can't take any more of this. Yes? No? What?

With a nod, the car is cleared. Thank God. I wait for the front seat guard to get out so our boys can climb back in and drive into the compound, Trojan horse-style.

He doesn't. He backs the car up and drives it down the road a little way, parking it alongside the fence. Shit. They're not going to let them take the car inside.

"Justice, did the car reverse?"

"Fuck. Parked it outside the compound. You're like twenty feet from the front gate. You're east of the guard tower."

"Got it." She clicks off.

Does she have it? A golf cart is being driven down to the front gate. Looks like they expect Tony and Victor to ride in it up to the house.

Sure enough, they're motioned forward. I keep my finger poised on the trigger as USA decides to frisk them. Likelihood of him finding the patch? I judge it as next to zero.

Right again.

After the search, they're motioned into the golf cart. I'm holding every ounce of my breath. Sweat beads on my forehead. "Gracie. They're going in. They're—"

A nerve-rattling alarm cuts off my words and punches a hole right through the fabric of night and the thinnest of bad plans.

All hell, which had been biding its time waiting for the exact moment to royally fuck us, breaks loose.

Through my scope, I keep my focus on the scattered scene as USA reacts to the alarm. He's waving his arms, gesturing at his men, who are scrambling into action. As USA motions at them, Tony and Victor get out of the golf cart and get down on their knees.

The young guard with the gun trained on Tony and Victor begins to shout. Young, jittery, and panicked isn't good.

There's some kind of exchange between Jittery Guard and Tony. Jittery bends down and hoists Tony onto his feet and gets in his face. Have they identified Tony? What's fucking happening? Why the alarm? My finger itches to shoot, to get that guy away from my brother, but steeling my unease, I wait and see.

USA steps toward Tony and Jittery, casual-like, a smile on his face, as if there isn't an alarm sounding, as if he doesn't have a care in the world. Who is this guy? He says something to Jittery. Giving directions? Telling him to stand down? I have no idea.

Doesn't matter anyway, because Jittery isn't listening. He shoves Tony, then brings up his weapon. He's going to shoot Tony. Fuck. No time for wait and see, I take a breath, aim, and shoot.

Snap. The bullet strikes Jittery Guard's temple. His head jerks. Blood spatters. I swing my rifle left, aim and shoot another guard, who'd been turning toward my position.

Adrenaline floods my system and everything slows. I ride the hyperawareness, find USA scrambling away. I shoot. He zigs. I miss. Shoot again. He zags. Damn it. That's the most I've missed in two years.

I return my scope to Tony and Victor and let off a round of suppressing fire as they bolt. Meanwhile, USA, understanding now where the danger is coming from, has zigzagged his ass to the Cadillac, ducked behind it, and swung his gun in my direction.

His first shot misses by a mile. He needs a rifle.

I fire over the car, forcing USA to stay down while keeping clear of where Gracie hides. I don't need to take chances.

My heart is in my throat, the alarm pounding against my ears, my hope of getting Sandesh dwindling as USA opens the Cadillac's door.

Damn tinted windows. I shoot again, which is useless because I can no longer see USA.

I switch targets as a black Land Rover with dark windows tears out of the gate. It races up the hill, over brush and stones toward me. I keep firing at it. Doesn't take long to realize it's bullet-proof.

Shit.

Someone in the car fires back at me.

I'm definitely *not* bulletproof.

The dirt in front of me bursts up.

Too close for comfort.

I duck.

The shots stop. The car doesn't.

Fuck this.

Surveying my escape route, I reach out to my sister. "Gracie?"

Her voice comes through the headset, clear but soft. "Go. I've got USA Ballcap."

Don't need more encouragement than that. Unhooking my NVGs from my belt, I put them on and crab-crawl backward until I can run at a crouch.

53

JUSTICE

Hidden among trees and darkness, I adjust my night-vision goggles and watch my pursuers.

The Land Rover stops at the edge of the woods. A group of men get out.

The stock of my rifle pinned to my side, barrel aimed safely away, I run through the trees. My mind sifts through a mental catalogue of satellite images. At the bottom of this hill, the ground becomes even and flat, a straight and open shot to the barn.

Movement behind. Shit. Men dispersing into the woods.

I run faster, but I don't know where to go. If I run toward the barn, breaking from the cover of trees, someone will spot me. If I keep going, I'll overshoot my entry point. Twisting left and right to look for an option, I nearly crash into a giant log blocking my way. As it is, I toe into a leap and catch the tip of my boot on a broken limb at the top. I pitch forward and slam into dirt with a muffled *umpf*. Way too much noise.

Someone shouts in the woods.

Rolling to my feet, I focus my hearing, seeking out identifying sounds, determining location, distance, and intent.

They're close. My head buzzes. My heart rate doubles. My ears thrum.

Digging my way quickly under the fallen log, I make barely enough space to hide. If they have NVGs, I'm dead.

Controlling my breathing, I wait. Almost immediately, I hear footsteps. They're so close I can't believe they didn't see me hide here. Maybe they did. I don't move an inch.

I hold my breath as someone climbs over the log. His dirty boots land centimeters from my elbow and my whole body grows cold and focused, ready for the fight. He moves away.

Relief puddles my insides. I wait as long as I can before my need to help Gracie and get to Sandesh overwhelms my fear of being shot.

As silently as possible, I roll out and backtrack. Their voices get far enough way that I feel comfortable running.

I'm heading around the other side of the woods when I see it—the Land Rover with all four doors open, lights on, car idling and no one home.

Is this a setup? It could be.

Stalking out cautiously, I make my way to the vehicle.

No one stops me, no one jumps out and threatens me, because no one is here.

I crouch run to the front of the car, slip into the Land Rover. Seat warmer. Nice.

Switching off the lights, I head down the hill and straight for the stables. Now that I have a sec, I click my mic. "Gracie?"

There's a long pause. A pause long enough that I imagine my sister climbing out of a leather seat and being shot by a huge idiot wearing a USA baseball hat. My throat dries and my heart freezes, then my mic clicks.

"In mineshaft. Fence down. You close?"

Gracie. Alive, even though her voice is garbled. And she's gotten inside and turned off the electric fence. Whoa. Take that,

USA Ballcap. You're no match for a half-naked redhead with mad cyber skills.

"On my way."

Static. "ETA?"

"Ten. Copy."

The crackle of a mic. "Can't wait."

Fuck. "I'll catch up."

"Roger."

Clicking off, I slide my body down while steering over bumpy ground. I inch the vehicle closer to the gate, grateful this thing's bullet-proof. If someone shoots, it means I'm already made, so the best option will be to drive straight through the fence. It's bold, but I'm not exactly in stealth mode right now anyway.

I slow the Land Rover to a roll as I near the fence. None of the lights on the fence are on and no one is shooting at me. Heart tripping hard in my chest, my hands shaking, I begin to believe this might work. I might be able to sneak inside.

Stopping, I get out and pocket the key. It's so quiet. No guards and the alarm has even stopped. It's quiet enough that if the electric fence were humming, I'd hear it. Not that I don't trust Gracie, but I chuck the bottle of Benadryl I found on the passenger seat. It hits and bounces off, rattling to the ground.

Hating the idea that the fence could flick back on at any moment and I could be on top, legs straddling either side, when the juice comes back on, I sling my rifle onto my back.

"J. Over here."

Flicking up my NVGs, I look through the fence. Tony.

He's at the end of the stable, dressed in a guard's uniform.

Tony. Brilliant, wonderful Tony. He's taken out a guard, stolen a uniform, and is now ready to get this thing done and get out of here.

He waves. "Hurry up." He steps back into hiding.

I take a running leap, hit the fence with a *clang*, and

scramble over the barbed wire. Landing like I've been training for this my whole life—I have—I sprint to where I'd seen him.

Around the stable, nose prickling at the smell of manure, I spot him. Relief surging through me, I reach for his hand.

He reaches for mine.

I skid to a halt.

Walid.

He's standing behind Tony with a group of armed men.

"Get down!" I shout. Quick as my boiling hatred, I bring up my sidearm.

Tony steps up, intercepts my hand, pulls me forward, twists my wrist into a lock.

I cry out, drop the Sig as much from shock as pain.

He catches my gun and releases me. He looks me dead in the eyes and says, "You need to come with us."

It takes me a minute.

It takes me a lifetime.

It takes my breath away.

"*You?*"

54

SANDESH

The men at the bottom of the stairs freeze. They're looking from light into darkness. This fact alone saves my life.

I roll Dmitri off my shoulders, drop, and shoot. I'm not surprised I miss because my hands tremble and the light is blinding.

One of the men, the better trained, belly-crawls to safety. The other stays in the open, reaches for his gun. He makes an excellent target, even to my dwindling abilities.

The shot hits him in the chest, and he falls dead to the ground. The alarm thrums against the walls like an accusing, stone heartbeat.

On the step behind me, Dmitri stops convulsing. I reach over to confirm what I already suspect, but, surprise, Dmitri still has a pulse.

Grabbing him under his armpits, I drag him back around a corner and sit him against the wall. "Dmitri, Dmitri." I lightly slap his face. "Is there another way out?"

I listen to the static of my two-way to see if the guard below had called for backup. Lots of noise. People checking in, but most of it has nothing to do with me.

Turns out, the real problem is at the gate. The ranch is under attack. Two guards have been shot three from a distant hill. Hell of a shot by the sound of it.

Warmth rolls into my chest. *Justice.* My mother taught me that a man shouldn't keep his woman waiting, so I better get moving.

I pat Dmitri on his shoulder. The Russian is as good as dead, even if he were to get the best and most immediate medical attention. "Rest," I tell him. And as the child long ago once told me, I add, "There is more."

Dmitri's eyes flash open, clear, and he focuses on me. "Kill. Walid."

His eyes drop to half-lidded, and freeze. The once-real human, the broken and tortured body, become nothing more than an empty reminder of too much pain and anger.

I close his lifeless eyes.

The two-way squawks to life beside me, and the guy with the Southern accent says in a voice a hell of a lot less cheerful, "I'm handling that mess in the mines."

Shit. He's coming for me. Ready or not.

Ready.

∾

CROUCHED behind Dmitri's body by the only exit, the one that leads down and then up, I'm debating if the sudden silence from the alarm is a good or bad thing.

Actually, I'm sure it's bad. It likely means the guards have organized. They definitely changed frequency on their two-way, leaving me no more insight. I have no idea how many men are in the camp and how many of those they're sparing to send down here.

I have two semiautomatics, full clips, taken from the torture guards, and a good ambush position. I'll wait for them to come through that damn door before shooting. At least, that's the plan.

Too bad my fight-or-flight reflex sings so loudly it's getting harder and harder to stay put. Waiting is *not* fun right now. It feels the opposite of proactive, but it's not the opposite of smart. If I try to go down those steps, the steps that lead to some kind of elevator—I heard the thing creaking to a stop a minute time ago—I'll be killed.

Forcing myself not to respond to the nerves that are bullying me to *fight- fight-fight*, I let out a calming breath, empty my mind, then aim my weapon.

The stone wall swings open with a *whoosh*.

Wait for a visual. Justice is here; it could be her. It might. Wait.

It isn't.

A huge guy with a baseball hat steps out of the opening, weapon down. I almost press the trigger but stop when a woman's voice speaks up from behind him. "Don't shoot."

I know that voice. The big dude turns to the side as if to push someone back, but that person shoves him in the ribs, then steps in front of him.

"Gracie?" What the hell is she wearing? "You're rescuing me in your underwear?"

Gracie shrugs. "All the cool kids are."

She eyes me—shirtless, pants ripped. Guess I'm not exactly styling.

Gracie elbows USA in the ribs again and says to me, "Don't shoot this idiot. He's with me."

I lower my weapon and climb out from behind Dmitri's dead body. "What's going on?"

Gracie jerks a thumb at the big guy. "This is USA Ballcap." She gazes up at him. "I don't trust him."

The big guy grins down at the feisty redhead and sparks fly.

Temperatures rise. Global warming increases. He reaches a hand toward me. "I'm better known as Agent Leif McAllister of the FBI. You can call me Dusty."

The FBI working in Mexico? And he has a Southern accent. Sure. Why not? It's not like this day could get any weirder.

Gracie inches forward. "Sorry, Sandesh, there's really no time for a debrief."

Her cheeks are flushed. Excitement? Nerves? Something else? She says, "This guy says he knows Tony. Like I said, I don't trust him, but he's gotten me safely this far. He also says he can get us out of here so we can reconnect with the rest of our crew."

"I can get you out if you follow my rules," Dusty says.

Gracie stops, bites her lip as if remembering an important detail. "I'll follow your rules up until we kill Walid."

I can't get my head around any of this. I tell them, "Kill whoever you want. I'm only interested in finding Justice."

Dusty laughs. "You and half the world's population."

55

JUSTICE

The yellow lights perched along the outside of the barn flick on, casting shadows across Tony. His eyes seem a thousand years old. "I can explain, J."

He can *explain*? Explain betraying The Guild? Betraying me? Betraying the entire family? Letting Bridget take all the blame?

No. My confused brain rejects the idea, but I'm struggling because his eyes, my brother's eyes, my friend's eyes, stay on me, stay locked on me, and they're saying, *Trust me. This isn't what you think.*

Disbelief and panic clasp hands around my neck, trapping my heart in my throat. I've got no reasoning left so I let my training kick in. *Assess the situation. Assess options.*

Four armed men stand behind Tony. They have guns trained on me. My weapon is on the ground, unreachable. Only one option is likely to keep me alive.

I hold up my hands. "What do you want me to do?"

Tony lets out a breath and says so softly that his voice floats to my ears like the airborne seed of a dandelion, "I have to search you."

He keeps his hands spread out as he reaches forward.

A chill runs down my body, and every instinct in me warns me not to let him touch me, but I stay put.

I grind my teeth as he searches me. I can't utter a word, but the thought *betrayer, betrayer* echoes in my head over and over.

His face comes so close to mine I can see the regret in his eyes when he feels along my arms, my back, my butt. He takes the knife strapped to the outside of my leg, takes the rifle hanging at my back, but he leaves the knife strapped on my calf under my pant leg.

What's going on? He obviously felt it. Hell, he gave me that knife when we'd been getting ready, watched me hide it there.

Done, he stands up. His eyes focus so intently on me that I can almost hear them telling me something. *Trust me.*

Can I? Dare I? What's going on? I swallow.

Tony steps back. "She's clean."

He hands the weapons he took from me to the closest guard. It's then that I realize Tony isn't armed.

What. The. Hell?

As if given leave to move, Walid and the two big guards flanking him step forward. Walid smiles at me with beautiful, perfectly straight teeth. Like he'd taken the money from selling broken and used women and had gone straight to the most expensive orthodontist in town. I want more than anything to tear that smile out, one tooth at a time.

One of the two men flanking Walid says, "I think I should search her. I don't trust him."

Walid considers this and then nods. "Search her."

The guard moves toward me. I ready to make a stand, but Tony puts a hand to the guard's chest, stopping him. He says, "No one, and I mean no one, is going to touch my sister."

The guard glares at him. "I'm going to search her."

Tony keeps his arm against the guard's chest and says,

"Walid, if you want what I have to give you, if you want your brother's murderer, you will stay the fuck away from my sister."

Walid licks his lips. Other than that, he stays utterly composed. A man who's faced a thousand tense situations, a thousand desperate moments, and survived them all.

He waves his hand to indicate his guard should withdraw.

Anger flashes across the guard's face as he steps back.

"You see," Walid says, "nothing means as much to me as getting my hands on my brother's true killer, Mukta Parish."

56

JUSTICE

The heavy smell of shell casings coats the air as I'm marched through Walid's compound surrounded by four armed men. Walid and Tony, like long-lost friends, lead this pack as we walk past the stables toward the house in the distance.

My hands are raised, my jaw so tight I can practically hear my molars grinding.

Tony.

Tony who knew what it was like to be used; Tony whom I love, who I begged Momma to adopt, has conspired with Walid against me, against our family, and against Sandesh—who wants nothing more than to help people.

It's a good thing armed guards surround me. If not, I'd jump on Tony's back and pound his face into the piles of horse dung saturating my nostrils. Then pounce on Walid.

Oblivious to my rage—or ignoring it—Tony walks side-by-side with Walid like a confidant. A brother.

We pass onto the porch of the main house, an expensive villa with a dry fountain and a thousand ruined lives paying for every spectacular piece of architecture, each handcrafted item of furniture, with enough luxury to satisfy a tycoon.

We go through a set of arches, down a redbrick-lined corridor, then into an expansive office, and all the while I'm plotting how to get loose and kill Walid.

The brightly lit room we enter has a Tuscan ranch feel with terra-cotta tile flooring, exposed beams, leather couches, and heavy, parchment-colored drapes.

One of the guards—he seems in charge—orders two of the others to go help someone named Dusty.

They turn and head out, and the other two stern-faced guards left accompany me, Tony, and Walid into the room.

Completely at ease, Walid sits on one of the two red-leather couches.

A little awkwardly, Tony sits beside him.

Sure, let's all get comfy. *Fuckers.*

I stand, surveying the room, the layout and possible escape routes.

Walid's two personal guards position themselves to keep me in line. The first one, the in-charge man, who has a thick forehead and matching neck, stands opposite of me, directly behind Walid and Tony on the couch.

The second man, sporting cold, steel-blue eyes, stands behind the other unoccupied couch with his gun raised in my direction. His eyes say he won't hesitate to shoot, and he's far enough back that he'd be able to shoot me long before I could make it to him.

Plan B? Create time to make a plan B.

"So, Tone," I say. "You're friends with human traffickers now?"

He cringes, looks away. "Not so much friends as enemies with a common interest."

Something in my spine snaps to attention. My hands fist at

my sides. My bones fuse into one giant club of anger. "Which is?"

Tony meets my eyes again and, this time, there is no regret. Only rage. "Stopping Mukta Parish so that she never warps another child's mind. Never takes another kid from the streets and turns them into a killer, into someone who can never be good enough. Someone allowed only two emotions—anger or shame. Someone forced to hate his own gender."

My heart lurches, splits, and breaks in half. Unbelievable, stunning vibrations of pain shoot through me. I double over.

Walid laughs. "Women. They are the most devious of sexes. If not controlled, they will poison the world. With complaints. With excuses. With the vagaries of being female."

Despite my devastation, I rally the muscles in my spine and torso, order them to straighten. Fuck Walid. Fuck Tony. Anger boils in my cells, but I push it down. I need to stay calm, find an opportunity to break out of here, and save Sandesh.

Locking eyes with Tony, I see his flicker once, twice toward the couch nearest me and directly across from him and Walid. Fucker wants me to sit. He's obviously trying to help. *Oh, sure, Tone, why not? You'll turn on Momma, but you'll help me. You shit.*

Pushing aside the feelings I can't afford, legs like steel, unbending and tense, I walk to the couch. Steel-Blue Eyes keeps his icy gaze and his gun on me as I move. I more fall than sit, and there's a sharp *crack* as my weight hits the seat.

Once I'm seated, I don't really need Tony's help to understand why he put me here. I see a fraction of Victor's reflection in a sliver of glass behind one of the heavy drapes. If it weren't for where I'm sitting, I wouldn't be able to see him.

I keep my eyes focused on Walid, trying not to reveal my growing confusion. Tony knows Victor is there, he must. Why else would he direct me to sit here? What's going on?

Maybe I can find out if I can keep him talking. "This has been about Momma? You couldn't have, oh, I don't know, told us how you felt? Brought it up over an awkward Thanksgiving dinner like a normal person?"

Tony laughs. It sounds sarcastic and hurt and laced with hundreds of emotions and thoughts I can only guess at. "You mean like write a letter? A letter that told everyone in my family of female fanatics exactly how I felt?"

Female fanatics? Has he felt this way all along? Is that why he betrayed us? Or is he trying to appeal to Walid? Or are both things true?

Obviously, his betrayal is real. If it weren't, if he hadn't been able to supply some proof, Tony would never have been able to get to Walid and convince him to trust him. And he's not lying about the letter. He *did* write a letter to Momma, the one with the plan for dealing with the Brothers Grim. Other than the plan part, I never saw it, so I have no idea if it stated what he says it did. But that's not important. I have all the information I need because of what's being left out—Tony isn't telling Walid this plan to break in here today was his. Only that he hates The Guild and Momma. He's not telling him about Victor. He's walking a fine line.

The Guild taught me as a child that some of the best lies are those rooted in truth. Tony betrayed me and the family, he supplied proof of that to Walid, allowing us all to be in this room, close enough to kill Walid, but now he's trying to make up for what he did?

If that's the case, what does Tony want from me? Why direct me here?

In the glass, I see a glint of the gun Victor has raised. Is he waiting for some kind of signal? Or maybe just the right moment? Hmmm. Tony sits so close to Walid, he's capable of delivering the poison if he's offered the right opportunity, the right distraction.

I get it—or think I do. Like a pickpocket, Tony's asking me for that help, asking me to be that distraction.

If there's one thing I'm good at, it's pressing buttons. "Tone, you don't think The Guild did the right thing killing that slime, Aamir?"

"You bitches," Walid says. His outrage and disbelief make his words drop low and heavy. "You are trying to overturn the natural order of things. Women are to be bedded and fed and kept out of the way."

"Come on, now." Tony drapes an arm behind Walid's shoulders, simultaneously squeezing his thigh. Distraction on top of distraction, but I'm paying attention and see Tony's thumb brushes against Walid's neck. "She's playing you."

Walid knocks his hands off his knee. Too late, and not even the area he needed to worry about. The poison will take some time to work. I was told between eight and twelve minutes to kill, but I never asked how long until Walid would show a reaction. And I never wondered, never thought I'd be in a position where it would matter, how long it would take the guards to notice those reactions aren't natural. Once they notice, how long until they figure out who did it?

I can't wait to find out. I meet Tony's eyes. Almost imperceptibly, he nods. *Not for nothing*, as Tony would say.

I cross my legs, ranch-hand style, right foot on left knee. My pant leg rises up, making it easier for me to get the knife. As casually as if I'm telling him the weather, I say, "The natural order seemed pretty clear to me when I shoved that little piece of metal into your brother's heart and he pissed all over himself."

The room goes rage quiet. Walid's face turns a furious shade of crimson. "You will piss blood when I dig my knife into your gut."

He tries to stand. Tony grabs him by the shirt. "Knock it off."

Thick Neck Guard puts his gun to Tony's head. Tony goes still. By the look on his face, he finally registers the shit he's gotten us into. Hmmm, it only took a gun to his head.

Walid, stands up, reaches into his pocket, pulls out a knife, and flicks it open. He stalks toward me. "Your brother can cry over your corpse as I did my brother's."

"Come on then, Wally," I taunt through a bone-dry mouth. *Please, Victor, understand the signal.* "Let's go!"

57

SANDESH

The rickety mineshaft elevator rocks to a stop at the top with a *pop* that spits out coal dust and congealed mechanical oil. Even the throatful of water I chugged from Dusty's flask doesn't keep me from coughing.

I cover my mouth and blink to clear my eyes. There's a short tunnel leading out. It's lit by a single caged lightbulb that illuminates four men at the mouth of the mineshaft with weapons drawn.

Dusty uses his Glock 22 to motion me and Gracie out of the metal box and to the side of the wood-beam-supported tunnel. It's not difficult to play the weary prisoner, shuffling forward, keeping my head down. I've had practice of late. Plus, I'm weary as hell.

Gracie does the opposite. She struts out like she doesn't give a damn, though I strongly suspect that's an act.

The waiting guards keep their weapons drawn. For the most part, their gazes follow Gracie, not me. Not surprising. What really surprises me is how much attention they're giving Dusty.

Whoever he is, Dusty has the respect of the men who work

here. He strolls out with an almost good-natured casualness, as if he goes down into mineshafts and takes prisoners out every day.

The hair on the back of my neck is standing on end. I don't trust this guy, don't trust this plan, but it's the quickest shot at getting to Justice, so I'm taking the chance.

Speaking in Spanish to the men, Dusty asks them what's going on in the camp. I'm fluent in Spanish, so my heart freezes when they tell him the other woman has been captured because her brother lured her into a trap.

Beside me, Gracie makes a small, pained sound.

My hands clench into fists. Fucking traitor. If one hair on Justice's head is touched, I'll kill Tony.

Dusty doesn't miss a beat. With a flow of Spanish almost too quick for me, he tells the men that he has a confession. He says, "I sort of feel bad about it, but facts are facts. I'm still working for the FBI. Things here are going to go bad quickly."

The man has balls. Telling a group of guards with guns trained in your direction that you've basically lied, infiltrated their ranks, and tricked them isn't how I would've played it.

Dusty continues, nodding in my direction and emphasizing that the kidnapping of an American is a serious crime. He's a fast talker and appeals to their sense of self-preservation.

"I like you all, and don't want to get you in trouble, so I'm giving you a chance to get out of here before the rest of my people show up with the helicopters."

Dude is a good liar; I almost believe him.

The guards begin to talk among themselves, but Dusty doesn't let up. "Of course, you'll have to leave those weapons," he says, as if it's a no-brainer. "I can't help you if you're caught with them. If you're caught without guns, though, I can get them to let you go. No questions asked."

An absolutely stellar liar.

The men begin to argue and the hair on my arms begins to

follow the hair on my neck. They don't want to leave the weapons. They're not sure they should trust Dusty.

At this, Dusty turns his gun on them. "Don't be stupid. Walid's going down. There's nothing for you here. Leave the guns and go."

I'm pretty sure the air in the tunnel has gotten a lot more congested, what with the size of Dusty's balls taking up so much space.

The men freeze and I ready myself to act as the long, tense moment continues to play out.

"This isn't a game of cards where I take all your money, then give it back." He grins at them and I get the distinct impression that example was a real event. "Go on now. Get going."

Slowly, the men place their guns down on the packed dirt and back out of the tunnel.

Dusty turns to me and Gracie. "Let's give 'em a little while to spread the word before we head out. No need to escalate."

I grab a semi-automatic rifle from the pile. "I'm not waiting."

The shreds of my tuxedo pants flapping around my ankles —flimsy things weren't built to take any kind of real movement —I step out into the night.

58

JUSTICE

"Come on, Wally. Let's go!"
Everything seems to happen in one horrifying time-lapse instant.
I reach for my knife.
Victor breaks from the curtain.
The thick-necked guard behind Tony turns toward him.
Victor shoots.
With a slap as loud as the bullets that kills him, the guard slams against the terra-cotta tiles.
Jerking his weapon from me, Cold Eyes shoots Victor. One, two, three times in his naked torso. Victor falls against the curtains, grasping at the velvet gold panels. They slip through his hands, as he slides down to the floor, leaving behind a bloody mess.
Even as I'm see this happening, I'm throwing my knife, strong and true at Walid.
With a greater sense of self-preservation than I give him credit for, the man I have hated nearly all my life drops down, slamming his knee against the marble coffee-table with a crack that saves his miserable life.

"Don't move," Cold Eyes orders, his gun back on me.

I don't move. The room goes still.

Slowly, achingly slow, Walid stands. With a vengeful, twisted smile on his face, he hobbles toward me.

That sick smile tells me all I need to know. I'm going to die in pain.

Now would be a *really* good time for that poison to kick in.

Sensing a gun at my back, I brace my feet and spread my hands wide, as if offering Walid a target. Actually, I'm distracting him. Pickpocket style.

Walid's eyebrows raise in shock as he stops and grunts. The knife in his hands drops. He reaches up, fumbling fingers clasp his shoulder and my knife jutting out like an insult.

Cold Eyes realizes Tony stabbed his boss at the exact same time Tony is vaulting over the back of the couch. The gunshots ring out.

Tony drops behind the couch and out of sight.

Walid curses, a bloody rumble like mountains crumbling to stone, then crashes to the floor, vomits, and begins to convulse.

Cold Eyes jerks his weapon at me as Walid's other guards burst through the doorway.

Adrenaline brings my impending death into slow and detailed focus.

Bam! Bam! Bam! One of the people in the doorway shoots.

Cold Eyes jerks with each shot and falls.

My brain does not compute.

I look again at the doorway. My heart leaps. Not guards. My man, Sandesh, has busted in with Gracie and... USA Ballcap?

Striding in, Sandesh shoots at Cold Eyes until he's dead, dead, dead, then he turns his weapon on...

Tony? Relief surges through me when I see my brother uninjured, then my stomach plunges. Tony has a weapon in his hands. He must've grabbed the gun from the guard Victor shot.

Tony and Sandesh have some serious weapons pointed at each other.

Guttural choking noises issue from Walid, whose nervous system is closing up shop as he convulses on the floor, a knife stuck deep in his neck.

Before my brain can assemble all the pieces and put words to them, Gracie struts past USA Ballcap.

"Stand down, big guy," she says to him.

Now that she points it out, I notice USA has his gun on Sandesh.

"But..." USA starts, then trails off at the look on Gracie's face.

Keeping her own weapon trained on Tony, Gracie shakes her head. "Go keep an eye on the door. This is between family."

My brain is definitely not working right, because USA just nods and says, "Yes, ma'am," before moving to the door, standing halfway in and out of the room.

Gracie motions with her gun. "Drop it, traitor."

Swallowing, Tony puts his weapon on the floor, takes three steps back, then holds up his hands.

I'm still staring at her in disbelief when I feel Sandesh's hand running over my body.

"You okay?"

I look at him. He's beat to hell. "You clearly haven't looked in a mirror lately."

"Justice..." He leans closer, worry lines his swollen and bruised face. He has bruises over his ribs, his pants are torn, his lips cracked and dry.

A knot rises into my throat. "He hurt you?"

Shaking his head, Sandesh rubs his nose across my cheek. "Justice, please. Are you okay?"

Warmth crawls across my skin and down into my muscles. *Am* I okay? "Yes. But... Shit. Victor."

I point toward the bloodied curtains.

"Victor? Victor is here?" Sandesh starts forward.

I stop him. "Give me the rifle."

59

SANDESH

I hand Justice my weapon without hesitation, trying desperately to piece together how Victor has gotten here as I rush across the room.

Taking over for Gracie, Justice points the rifle at her brother's chest. "Move back farther so Sandesh can help Victor."

Once clear of the couch, I see Victor, dressed more scantily than even Gracie, curtains covering part of his bloody torso.

"Fuck, Victor." I drop to my knees, then begin to make a tourniquet from the curtains with shaking hands and my heart in my throat. This is not right. This can't be happening.

Still conscious, Victor grips his gun in his hands. His eyes widen. "Got shot, Sandman."

I nod, letting him know I see it, that it's true.

Gracie shoves in next to me, handing me a bottle from the rolling bar.

We don't speak. I pour the contents over my hands, wash them like a raccoon in a stream, then douse the vodka onto Victor. He hisses.

"Don't move, Tony."

Hearing her voice, I look over to see Justice has stepped closer to and is threatening her brother.

Tony puts his hands up higher.

I get back to work. I've managed to rip some of the curtains, but they're well-made, and with my condition right now, it's not quick enough. I turn to Gracie. "Get Walid's knife and cut strips from the curtains. Let's stop the bleeding."

She rushes over, grabs the knife, and is back in an instant, cutting strips. She's good, making quick, tidy bandages and handing them to me.

We get the big bleeder in his shoulder tied off, and I can see the wounds better. Relief loosens my muscles so they're warm jelly. I pat Victor's shoulder. "It's actually not so bad."

Victor grimaces, makes a fuck-you face.

"Where's he shot?" Justice asks, having come around the couch. "I can't see anything but blood."

Gracie answers, "Arm, skimmed, superficial. Shoulder. That's the worst one. There's going to be some muscle damage, but it won't kill him. The last one in his hip is barely bleeding. He'll make the plane ride back."

"Hip bone," Victor moans. "Oh. I need that thing." His head lolls back and forth against the tile. "I really need it."

I pat him on the shoulder. "You're going to live. And fuck. And samba."

"Samba?" Victor says, raising an eyebrow. "Racist much?"

He closes his eyes and passes out.

Gracie and I continue to work to make him comfortable and stop the bleeding.

From his place in the doorway, Dusty says, "Looks like the grounds are clearing out, which means we need to get moving. I'm going to go look for a vehicle."

He leaves, and Gracie stands up, staring at the doorway where he'd stood. "I don't trust him. I should go with him."

Justice reaches into her pocket and tosses a key at Gracie. "Land Rover. Behind the stables."

She catches the key but shakes her head. "It's not big enough."

"It is," Justice says, keeping her weapon on Tony. "He's not going with us."

Nodding, avoiding any eye contact with her brother, Gracie leaves the room.

When she's gone, Tony's head falls forward. He lets out a breath. "I'm so sorry, J."

I'm pretty sure *sorry* isn't what Justice is looking for.

60

JUSTICE

"*Sorry?*" I repeat Tony's apology with disdain. *Sure, no problem, consider it forgotten.* "I don't give a shit how sorry you are. You didn't spill a drink on my shirt, you *betrayed* our family, The Guild, me, and Momma. You betrayed the woman who rescued you from the gutter."

"No." He shakes his head and lifts his eyes to mine for the first time. "She took me from the streets and made me kill people. That's not saving me."

"So, you decided to join forces with a human trafficker to teach her a lesson?"

"No. No, J. I wanted to keep you safe. Take out these fucks in a way that was smart and controlled. You weren't listening. And you kept fucking up." He closes his eyes, opens them. "Momma... I told her you were too emotionally involved to execute the operation. She ignored my letter, ignored the truth staring her in the face—that you wouldn't walk away when you needed to."

That letter sounds like a fucking manifesto. "Thanks to you, we'll never know how it would've worked out if I'd had my team behind me."

"Bullshit. We know. Amal proved it. If you'd left her, left that room, both brothers would be dead now."

"I couldn't fucking leave her, you ass."

"You could. Should have. You could've gotten her later, after the brothers were taken out. Just like Cee. Don't you get it? You were too close to this. That's why I had to take it on myself to stop your reckless ass. It seemed so simple—get them to Jordan so you can't touch 'em, and force the family to my plan, the safer plan, the makes-sense plan. Our team goes into Mexico while the A-team gets Aamir. Understand?"

I do and I don't like it. This was always *my* mission. *My* duty. "You warned the Brothers Grim about the threat, sent them to Jordan to keep my plan from moving forward so we'd do yours instead?"

He nods. "I complained to Bridge. She thought my plan was less risky, too. She came up with the idea of warning the Brothers. We came up with the plan on how to warn them together."

My stomach rolls. In all my calculations, I'd never suspected it could've been the two of them. Never. "When that didn't work, you sent the drones so Momma would become afraid, feel boxed in, and let you move forward with your plan?"

Again, he nods and adds, "Not Bridget. I went behind her back."

Backstabber. He also let her take the fall.

"And when that didn't work, when Momma planned to let me go to Mexico with Sandesh as my backup, you gave Walid to Sandesh."

His shoulders tense as his gaze darts to Sandesh. He shakes his head. "I heard about it after. Dusty—the guy with the USA hat—even tried to stop that from happening."

Dusty, a.k.a. USA Ballcap. "How the hell did you develop a bromance with that guy?"

Tony crosses his arms. "He's legit FBI. Met him by accident at a bar. Believe that?"

He's talking so fast his South Philly has taken over.

"No, I don't believe it." You don't *accidentally* run into an FBI agent at a bar who wants to help you do covert ops. I'll look into that later. "So, you join forces with some FBI guy. What? You had money, and he had skills?"

"Basically. He was sick of human traffickers getting ignored for drugs. Took what the government calls a hiatus. Came to work for me. He got in here as the new head of security. Helped keep everything running smoothly, so we'd be better able to implement my plan."

I snort, a sound that tightropes between anger and disgust. "Maybe my plan would've worked, if you'd been behind half as much as your own plan."

His dark eyebrows crash together. "It would've worked until that shit at the massage parlor. After that, Aamir, the smart one, stepped in. He figured Walid had a leak here. It got dicey. Dada's informant was almost found out. Still, with Dusty's help, I had it covered. Know how hard that was? How much I had to work? I covered for your mistake and saved that Sean guy for Dada. *I* did that."

"Oh. Well. Bravo. Way to go. Would you like your silver star pinned to your chest now or would you like to wait for the ceremony?"

"Smartass," Tony says, and he says it like it's a compliment. Like it's love. "It should've ended with them going to Jordan. Only an unfeeling, uncaring lunatic would send her daughter to Jordan without backup, knowing the brothers were suspicious."

He spits the last. Literal spit flies from his lips. He's furious and not just at Momma. At himself, at his inability to see what she'd do. "I hate her."

"Watch it, Tony. I might still shoot you." My hands tighten on the rifle.

He begins to laugh. "I wish you would. That'd make it easier."

Cold runs down my body; he's serious.

He lets out a long gust of air, sucks in an even longer breath, then leans a hand on the back of the couch. "She was gonna let you get yourself killed, like you didn't matter. Well, fuck, you matter to me."

He turns away. Tears are falling down his face. He's shaking. Sad. Broken?

My anger is giving way to pain, grief, and confusion. I love him. He's my brother.

No. Stay angry. Stay sharp. "If I matter so much, why bring in Cooper? You and Bridget conspired with him, told him what I do. That bit of brilliance almost got me killed, gave Cooper, a man you knew was an addict, a way to make money off me and betray me."

"Damn, Coop." He seems confused now, unsteady. "I don't know why he would tell Walid you were in his room. It makes no sense."

Actually, it makes sense if he didn't know I was in the room and thought he could stop the murder. I'd left the necklace in my room at the hotel. Cooper could've thought I was still in my room. He could've thought warning Walid would've kept me from my job.

I don't say this. Can't.

"You have to see though that when it came down to it, he died to protect you. He was trying, J. Been sober for years."

"No, he was high as hell every time I saw him."

His gaze drifts away. His hands shake against the couch. He fists them. "Nah. Think I'd have let him within a hundred feet of you if he was still using? No f'in way." Tony's eyes slide over to Sandesh, then back to me. He sighs like he has nothing else to lose. "I love you, J. Loved you from the moment you rescued me."

Something in my chest cracks open and pain floods in. I try to hold it back, try to make it stop, try to damn it back up. "Liar! You love me? Like the way Cooper loved me? He left me to be tortured in that basement. He left Hope to die."

"No. Hell, no. Didn't you ever wonder how Mukta found youse? Some rich woman in the Northeast found two girls in Virginia?"

"The Guild."

Tony leans heavily on the couch. He's really trembling now, like a sudden fever has overcome him. Adrenaline backlash? "Come on, you know better. The Guild isn't all-powerful. Cooper went to her after being forced to leave you with his mother-in-law."

"*Forced*?"

"Court gave her custody. Man didn't have a chance. A brown-skinned drug addict versus a middle-class white woman who's also your grandmother. No contest."

What? My father had been forced to *leave* me? To give me to that crazy woman who sold me and Hope to Walid? No. There are laws— Fuck. It doesn't matter. It doesn't change things. "He could've taken us. He could've run to the reservation. He knew what she was."

Tony shakes his weary head. "Did what he could. Drugged as he was, found his way to Momma, a woman he knew adopted kids. Told her and Leland about youse."

"*Cooper*? Cooper was the one who told Momma about me and Hope?"

Tony nods. His eyes tell a thousand things, a thousand secrets I'd never have guessed. The Guild, the Fab Five, busting into the basement that night, it seemed... I never questioned how they knew, how they found me. I had too much guilt that they'd gotten there too late for Hope.

I've had it all wrong this whole time.

Tony shudders, coughs. "Cooper told me that he hung

outside Momma's office for three days, begging her and Leland to help. They finally listened. A day too late for Hope. But not for you. My Justice. My best friend." He taps his chest. "This tattoo, 'All for one,' is for you. *You're* the one. You with the good heart. You really want to save people. Not Momma. Never her."

I have to force my throat to swallow past the root of growing panic. "She rescued us. She rescued you from that alley."

"No, *you* did. They set it up. They took even that from me, but you didn't know it. You did what they knew you would."

"What? Who set it up? Took what from you?"

My throat is going into lockdown. Alarms sound in my head; doors close in my heart; prisons spring to life in my soul. I lower my gun, tasting the salt of tears on my lips. "Tone, why are you shaking?"

His glazed eyes roam up to me. He blinks, jerks his head. "Oh. The patch." He waves a hand. "Smeared it. Got no reason to live now anyhows."

Tony falls over.

I hear my own screaming even as I'm running to him, dropping to him, grabbing him. "What did you do?" I shake him by his shoulders. "What did you do? You stupid idiot!"

Sandesh is there, reaching across Tony. He pulls my hands away. "Careful. Don't touch."

It hurts so badly, I can't breathe.

"He's got your back." Tony tucks his hands into his armpits. He gasps for breath.

I want to move him, make him comfortable because he landed oddly, his right leg bent back, caught under his ass.

He begins to convulse, his teeth chattering.

How do I fix this? How do I stop it?

Tony is staring at me. "I did good, too? Right, J? Not all bad." His hazel eyes, the haunted eyes that once looked out from the face of a starving twelve-year-old boy, pin me. Beg me.

My heart breaks into a thousand irreparable pieces. It will

never be whole again. "Yeah, Tone." I speak over my sobs. "You did a lot of good. You were my best friend. I love you. I will always love you."

He closes his eyes. "Don't cry, J."

A smile crosses his lips. A smile that twitches at the edges, then... goes flat.

61

SANDESH

During the last month, the energy in my apartment has changed, and not subtly either. I can't think of the perfect word for it—this shift in atmosphere since Justice has been staying here.

There's probably a French word for the buzz of warmth, the charged peace, the surge of contentment, the electric joy of waking up every morning beside the person I love, but I don't know it.

All I can call it is... *blessed.*

That fits but doesn't cover the thrill of falling asleep with her in my arms, knowing she's safe. Or the jolt of awareness I feel upon waking, like right now, with her warm and asleep beside me.

Or the way my heart lifts every morning when she rolls over and kisses me then makes love to me and I fall back to sleep in a satiated heap.

Or the pleasant way it hurts when she disentangles herself from me and the sheets, then leaves the bed in the morning.

Or the way my heart jumps, *hip-hip-hooray*s in my chest

when she returns, carrying a cup of coffee as hot and dark as her eyes.

Blessed doesn't cover it, which is why I'm so worried about her. Most specifically, her refusing to go home. Justice cutting herself off from her family is... unlike her.

With a groan, she rolls over, sees me staring at her, smiles, then kisses me lightly. "This is a first, you waking before me."

The plans I have for a romantic morning got me up an hour ago with nerves, which is probably why I should keep my worries and thoughts about her family to myself, and yet... "I think you should go visit your family."

She frowns, shakes her head. "I told you, I can't face that house knowing Tony won't be there."

"You sure it's not because you're angry at your mother?"

She closes her eyes, asking for patience or maybe for me not to see her so clearly. When she opens them again, it's with a sad smile. "I'll go make you some coffee."

My body floods with worry and warmth. I love this woman. "Okay."

She rolls out of bed and I watch her go. Something I learned from nearly the first moment I met her is that I can't push Justice. All I can do is continue to give her the time she needs and the understanding, and, most importantly, show her that I'm not going anywhere. Which is exactly what I'm going to do the moment she can no longer see into this room.

I jump up and make the bed in record time, military tight, then get the box stashed under it. Inside, there're rose petals, a hand-drawn sign that reads *Home Sweet Home*, and a black bow tie. Can't say I'm not classy. Is it enough? Should I have...

I don't know. I've thought of this in a thousand different ways, but, in the end, I decided to make it simple by offering to share myself and my life with her.

Committing to the plan, *again*, I sprinkle rose petals across the bed, hang the sign across the headboard, put on the tie, then lay my naked self strategically across the bed. Just in time because I hear her making her way back to me.

Shit. Almost forgot. I sit up, reach into my nightstand, pull out the hand-carved wooden box, then settle back into position.

Justice walks in, fingers looped around the handles of two coffee cups, the other hand holding an iPad. She's staring at the tablet. "Cats can pretty much escape anything."

Cats? "What are you looking at?"

"This video..." She shakes her head, laughs. "It's—" She looks up, a beautiful, seductive grin spreading across her face. "That's the hottest thing I've seen in my entire life."

Good. It's already working. I'm naked and actually sweating, because doubt keeps hammering at me. Should I have gone for an expensive ring?

No. Dada assured me that Justice would want nothing she'd have to take off for missions. And nothing too expensive; to Justice, who grew up with a show of wealth designed to hide what lies beneath, it would mean less. Dada gave me the idea I went with, and I'm trusting it all now as I open the box revealing two smooth garnets and a series of light and dark leather cords.

A smile on her face, Justice comes closer, placing the coffee cups and iPad on the nightstand. She peers into the box. "Arts and crafts? Kinky. I can definitely use the leather cords."

I try to bite back my eager smile. Try... and fail.

I clear my throat. "These stones are from Syria. From a jeweler I met in Za'atari. They represent hope and strength and perseverance, and they're red because Choctaw brides traditionally wear red."

I pause, trying to judge how she's taking this.

She pumps her eyebrows at me.

Good sign. I swallow and press on. "And the leather, light and dark, for good times and bad, for us to braid together, to braid the gems into. I wanted something that represented us, symbolized us. Something you could wear on your wrist. Something..." *God, stop babbling.* "That's if..." *Don't be a fucking coward.* "Justice, will you marry me?"

For a moment, she's stock still, but then she launches herself onto the bed, sending the flower petals, the box, and me bouncing.

Moving the box gently onto the nightstand, she straddles me. Heat shoots through my body. I almost forget that she still hasn't answered me.

"Yes," she whispers against my lips. "Yes."

Her tongue slips into my mouth.

We're both breathless by the time she pulls back and stares at me with eyes like a cool, starless night, so endless not even the gods could imagine the edges.

She says, "I want to meet your mother."

Not exactly where I thought this was going. "Okay. It's just—"

She puts a finger against my lips. "Enough with the delays. I get it. But you've definitely met my family, and I've even met your grumpy dad—"

"Most awkward lunch ever."

She laughs then stops herself. "I'm serious. I want to meet her."

What can I say? She knows that I don't even address Mom as *Mom* anymore because it upsets her so much. She remembers me mostly as a boy, not a man. "Okay."

"Okay?"

I nod. "For you, Justice, anything."

"I love you, Sandesh."

"I love you, Justice."

She grins as she squirms on top of me. "Oh, I can feel that."

"Cocky," I say, rolling on top of her.

She cries out and I maneuver myself so she's under me and I'm pressed hard against her entrance.

"Pun intended."

She laughs, lifts her lips, then kisses me until my head spins and my body rages.

I push inside her.

Fucking blessed.

∽

BY MY STANDARDS, it's still early morning, but Justice insisted. My hand tightens around hers as we walk up the stone stairs to the private nursing home where Mom lives. My heart picks up its pace. I want the two women I love most in this world to meet, but I can't be sure Justice will get to meet Mom. Mom might be someone else today. Scratch that. She might be *somewhere* else today.

"Don't do that, Sandesh."

I look over at Justice. Clothes casual, black jeans and a button-down top, hair pulled into a long ponytail, but her eyes are dead serious. "Do what?"

"Worry."

How can I not? "Don't expect much. I can never be sure how she'll be with a stranger. Sometimes, it can be hurtful, like not being able to call her Mom anymore, but she's... she's a good person."

Justice squeezes my hand. "I know enough of you, the man she raised, to know that, however she appears now, she is a good person. She provided the shoulder you rested on, the heart that comforted yours, the soul that taught you to love. This disease might keep her from us, but it can't diminish who she is in my eyes. Ever."

A sudden, weighty presence lodges in my throat, making it hard to swallow.

We push through the front doors and enter the brightly lit

corridor. Doesn't matter what time of year it is, this place always smells of pinecones and cinnamon.

After checking in with Security, we stroll down the hall. Justice points to amateur paintings lining it. "They're rather elegant. Are these done by the people living here?"

Funny, I stopped seeing the paintings long ago. This hall has become a place filled with worry and sometimes dread. "Yeah. I brought Mom here after I met the head of the community, a kind woman who knew I was concerned about Mom's quality of life. On the day I met her, she said to me, 'Talent, joy, love of life, and creativity don't have an expiration date. That's a limit placed by smaller minds.'"

Justice frowns. "Sometimes pain makes you feel that way, too—limited."

Bringing her hand to my lips, I kiss her knuckles. She means her own pain over Tony's death, over her father's death. "But you, like your eyes, are limitless."

She smiles at me, then nods. The further we get from the shock of it, the more she's able to talk about what happened.

I like that she trusts me with her memories of her brother, as well as her regrets, but I'm still worried about her cutting herself off from the rest of the family.

At least, she asks questions now, because she doesn't remember a lot about our escape from Mexico. Shock and grief can do that to a person. I have to admit, for a long time, everything felt unreal to me, too, especially the memories of how Tony died.

The escape from the compound was rushed and damned awful. Justice was rocking, sobbing over Tony's body, when Gracie returned.

Gracie had taken in the scene and had totally lost it. Her screams...

It'd been all Dusty and I could do to organize them and carry out Victor, who'd passed out. Dusty had turned out to be a good man. He stayed behind to take care of Tony's body. To this day, we have no idea what happened to Tony's body or to Dusty, who went underground.

"Sandy!" My mother's voice whoops through the hallway, startling me from my thoughts.

Justice pulls her hand away, and I feel the loss, though I get why she did it. Best not to confuse Mom with our relationship until we get a sense of how she's going to react.

I grin wide as my mom shuffles down the hall with a fist full of balloons bobbing above her head. In one hand she clutches the string, in her other, she holds a stuffed teddy bear. My heart is as light as air. I bend and greet her with a gentle hug. "You look great, Lina."

She kisses my cheek in turn. "Did you see my balloons?"

"I did." I step to the side. "Did you see my friend?"

Mom lets out a delighted squeal and tosses up her hands. The balloons fly into the air.

Justice grabs the string, bringing the balloons down with a flourish.

Mom claps her hands as Justice hands the balloons back to her. Yanking the strings away, Mom says, "The balloons are mine."

Justice nods her understanding and Mom's face becomes sly, almost predatory.

"So is that young man. You better treat him right."

I move to intercept the awkward moment and guide the conversation, but Justice cuts me off.

"I will, Lina. Promise."

Mom smiles wide. "He's very handsome, isn't he?"

Smiling back, Justice gently kisses her cheek. "Yes, he is."

And my mother, the woman who has been lost to me off and on for five years, flushes. Her eyes grow slightly more aware. "What's your name, dear?"

"Justice Ramona Parish."

She nods. "Justice Ramona Parish." She repeats it as if chewing on it, tasting it, savoring it. "See, Sandesh?" she says. "I always told you there was justice in the world."

My eyebrows must shoot up to my forehead. I can't help but laugh—hard. She has. Repeatedly.

Reaching out, Justice hugs my mom, laughing softly. Mom laughs along with her, and the two of them...

I have to tell my heart to settle, and then tell it twice more. It doesn't work. There's too much fullness in my chest to feel anything but joy.

How did this happen? How did a gun-wielding assassin, a smart-ass vigilante with a nose for trouble and a yearning for intrigue, capture my heart so completely?

Maybe that's just the way blessings work.

Mysteriously.

62

JUSTICE

I love my sister Dada, honestly, I do, but I could cheerfully strangle her right now. Why didn't she take into account my lack of crafting abilities when she suggested this bracelet-braiding idea to Sandesh?

I'm sweating as I re-tie the complicated knot meant to hold the gem in place in the center of Sandesh's marriage band. Gah, I've watched this YouTube video three times on knot-tying, but it's no use. Tony was the sailor, not me.

My throat works at the thought of my brother. I miss him so much it causes a physical ache. I send him my love, wherever he is in the cosmos, and focus my grieving mind back on the task.

"Fuck," I breathe as the red gem skitters from my knot and across Sandesh's high-top table. It spins across the glass surface, refracting the sunshine from the large balcony door.

Sandesh grabs the gem before it falls off. Unsuccessfully covering his smile, he asks, "Are you sure you don't want me to do that part for you?"

For a moment, I simply stare at him. *Yum.* He's so handsome. I shake my head. "Nope. I want you to see *me* when you look down at this damn thing. Me in all my fucked-up, can't-craft glory."

He hands me the gem with a, "Then it will always be beautiful to me."

Awww. My shoulders relax. I take the gem and try again to tie a knot around it. I weave the first bit of the knot then insert the gem and... the instrumentals on Green Day's "Espionage" blare from my hoodie pocket. Gah.

I fish out my cell and answer. "Hey, Momma."

"Daughter."

Hearing Momma's voice on the phone has grown commonplace for me. She calls all the time and basically says the same thing every time she calls.

"You need to come home."

"*Need*? Not sure I do."

"Please, Justice."

Please?

"There is a growing unrest here since Tony's disappearance."

I flinch at the word *disappearance*. Momma chose to present Tony's death to the FBI and media as a son leaving for parts unknown to find himself. It's been widely reported that he's in the Himalayas, climbing with Sherpas, in Peru doing ayahuasca, in India, in Bali, in Cambodia... I can't help but wonder how many of these rumors Momma started herself.

Without answering, I cover the phone and tell Sandesh, "Right back."

He looks up with concern, but nods without commenting.

That man, right there, is the best.

I open the slider and stroll out onto his balcony, walking to the edge. In the distance, the Schuylkill River looks muddy, churned up from a storm last night that raged for hours. The banks are swollen. I'm about as clear in what I'm doing as that water. I once told Sandesh that I'd never leave The Guild, but it turns out, leaving was as easy as having my heart broken. As easy as the dreadful realization that all that anger, all that hate I'd indulged in for years helped cost the life of one of the people I loved most in this world.

"He's dead, Momma. Everyone in our family knows that, so what's the unrest about?"

There's a long pause. She doesn't like me using the D word even though we're on a secure line.

"The units are divided on whether Bridget should be M-erased. Her part in Tony's plan was less involved than his, less aggressive, in that she only took part in warning Walid to alter your mission and didn't send the drones. The older groups, the Fantastic Five and the A-Team, want her punished. They believe it will thwart cohesion if she is not. The younger groups, starting with the Troublemakers Guild and Vampire Academy, want her spared. They believe that, fundamentally, she was acting by the group's rule."

"Which rule?"

"The rule that states that no member of The Guild will willfully allow another member to put themselves in unacceptable danger or risk if there is an alternative."

My right eye begins to twitch. "That's the rule that Tony stated in his letter."

"It is."

Momma. Getting information from her is like pulling teeth. "Has that letter somehow gotten out?"

"It has. Not just the plan your brother outlined, but his plea for us to change the way The Guild operates."

Tony, you sure could've done things differently. Then again, after reading his letter, I understand why he felt he had no choice. Because of our family's culture, because of my steadfast and unwavering adherence to it, he'd decided that the only way to get things to change was through Momma.

The truth is, he was right. The Guild changes only from the top down.

"And you want me to convince the younglings that things have improved and we should all go back to being happy little spies?"

"Justice, there's no one else. Bridget obviously has no right to say anything. Dada is consumed with her pregnancy and her new husband."

Husband. I still can't believe that Dada got married while in Mexico. Talk about keeping a secret, but now that her baby-daddy has taken up residence at the Mantua Home, she's more than happy to shout it from the rooftops. Good for her.

"Gracie is her usual distant self and the older teams don't have the same relationship with the younger teams that your unit does—did."

A crow lands on the balcony railing for a beat of time before noticing me and flying away. "Well, maybe that needs to change. Let the Fantastic Five or the A-Team step up."

"I'm working on it, but you know those older units. They've made their marks internationally, have decade-long covers, and have always considered themselves the elite squads. Change doesn't happen overnight."

Annoying. And correct. "And what if I agree with the younger kids? What if I think Bridget shouldn't be M-erased?"

As soon as I ask, I realize it's true. This last month has been exhausting. Where do I put the anger when there's no one left to hate?

Turns out, I put it on me. If I've berated myself once for not giving Cooper a second chance, I've done it a thousand times.

"As much as I love our dear Bridget, as much as I understand her drive to heal the world using what healed her from her addiction as a child"—I cringe at the mention of Bridget's preteen addiction—"as much as I tried to appease her gentle requests with outreach programs and lobbying globally, I believe not punishing her would be a mistake. How else do we control the others if not through that fear?"

"Maybe we don't. Maybe, instead of fear and manipulation, instead of lies and obfuscation, we try giving them a voice, teaching them to be trustworthy by respecting them."

"With so many people, so many personalities, so many issues, I find that unrealistic."

Of course she does. "Momma, maybe things would've been different if you'd chosen to listen to Bridget, to present Tony's plan to the family, or, at least, his fears."

There is a long silence on Momma's end and then Leland, who's always lurking on these calls, speaks up. "Justice, Leland here. This isn't only about keeping the younger units in line for unity's sake. There's a broader, more dangerous issue."

Leland is as opaque as Momma. "Meaning what? Dumb it down for me."

Inside, Sandesh's cell rings. He picks up, walks over, then shuts the slider while mouthing, *It's Victor. Still okay for tonight?*

I give him a thumbs-up for our dinner with Victor, then return my attention to Leland.

Leland says, "Tony's interaction with the Fed, Dusty, in Mexico has us worried that the FBI has been on to us since further back than the drone attack."

Shit. My heart picks up its pace. "You got intel on that?"

"Our intel tells us Dusty took a hiatus from the job and disappeared, but we're also informed there are files open on our family activities."

"And you're worried the younger, less-elite generations"— yeah, that comment from Momma annoyed me—"are going to do something or give something away that could bring down your whole house of cards?"

Momma grunts her disapproval before saying, "Our operations are a sophisticated outreach for global balance, countering multiple unfair and brutal realities for women. We aren't seeking power for power's sake."

That answer is as unsatisfying as it is frustrating. Mostly because I agree with her, but also because I need for things to change in the family, and she seems hell-bent on keeping things the same. Time to try a power move. Maybe things can change from the middle on up. "Look, I'll come back and I'll train with VA, but I need some things in return."

"We're listening," Leland says, and there's genuine relief in his voice. Must be worse there than I thought.

"First, I want the rules changed on missions. Anyone involved in the operation—not just you and Leland—can call off a mission with sufficient cause."

"Agreed," Momma says, and I'm thrown off enough that I hesitate for a moment.

Regaining my bearings, I say, "Second, I wasn't joking when I said I agreed with the younger group. Bridget needs to be spared. Not only because there is that rule, but also because the younger class needs a win. If you give them that, let them know that their opinions are valued and respected, and that things are shifting, I can get them to toe the line."

Fingers crossed.

"We can do that," Leland says with a growing agitation in his voice. "Anything else?"

"Cee. I want her brought in."

"Justice." Momma objects with a speed that has the hair on my arms rising. "She is a difficult case. Not only because of her anger issues, but because she comes with more baggage than you know. Adopting her could draw eyes here."

If there's a target on her back that's all the more reason to keep her safe. "I need you to do that, Momma. She's my save." The reason I fucked up the mission. "I need her."

There's another long pause. "I'll see what I can do, but I can't promise anything."

Leland jumps in. "When will you return?"

I'm tempted to say, "I'll see what I can do, but I can't promise anything," but I've gotten some major concessions and I know I've pushed them as far as I can, so I say, "Tomorrow," then hang up.

63

JUSTICE

"You got this," Sandesh whispers as we stand before the doors of the Mantua Home with the sound of a kiddie soccer game not too far away.

I squeeze his hand as the tears come. I let them fall.

For a moment, I can't go up the steps to the house, can't go in.

Then, with a swipe at my eyes, I finally push the doors open and step inside.

It's like I never left. Same gym sounds floating into the foyer. Same smell of fresh flowers on the same marble table by the same split, winding staircase, and yet, everything has changed.

"Woot! Justice!" Someone calls from the gym.

I turn to see Jules smiling at me. She's in a fighting stance with Malia, one of the Fantastic Five.

I wave and tell them, "I'll be back in a sec."

Malia nods and quickly brings Jules' attention back to what seems to be a demonstration of fighting techniques for Lost in Translation, who are seated around the edges of a fighting mat.

My heart lifts, even as a pang of pain lances my heart. I missed them, my family. "See?" I tell Sandesh. "Fantastic Five is training. That means things are changing. Proof positive that I can get one more concession from Momma."

He snorts in disbelief.

"You'll have to back me up," I tell my somewhat doubtful fiancé as we stroll hand-in-hand through the Mantua Home's wide, sunlit corridors. "It's a wedding present."

"China is a wedding present. A toaster oven is a wedding present. Hell, a *wedding* is a wedding present. You're asking for Mukta to allow Bridget to go to Jordan with the IPT. That could lead to a deeper investigation of your family ties to that mission in Syria."

I smile, keeping pace with him, and tease, "Yeah, you people at the IPT are trouble."

"I'm serious, Justice. The Feds are already suspicious."

Understatement, but they're the suspicious sort, and, sadly, not stupid. Which is why Leland wants the family to stay away from Jordan and Syria until things quiet down.

"But she asked me, Sandesh. She called and asked if she could work with the IPT there. She said she doesn't want to be here as a constant reminder of the no-consequences-for-bad-actions thing."

He falls silent because we both know that's an unfair statement. Bridget has been isolated from the family, ostracized, and stripped of her privileges teaching at the school and the house, and she's lost all security clearance below ground. Plus, her heart is as broken over Tony as mine.

"I don't need dishes or a toaster oven. I don't even need a wedding. I need to fix what I can in my family, so doing this for Bridget makes sense."

I don't say what I know he understands—that I will never be able to fix what went wrong between me and Tony, and that makes me more determined to fix the relationships I can.

He starts to say something. Maybe he wants to reassure me again that I don't have to accept Momma's request to help the family, that my mistakes don't make me solely responsible for our issues, that I deserve some time off, but he doesn't say any of that. He simply nods.

And that, right there—him accepting my choice to do this—is another reason to love him. Every day adds one more reason.

Spotting a sibling-relationship-building opportunity, I drag Sandesh to a stop before the wide, arched doorway leading into the library. Inside the brightly lit room, Rome sits at one of the long tables in front of a computer, typing like a lunatic. He's another cyber geek in the making. Maybe feeling my eyes on him, he glances up. Such a cute kid.

I smile at him. "You available to train tomorrow around noon?"

He turns left and right in a *Who me?* kind of way.

"No one else in the library, kid."

Registering this, his lips twitch into an uncertain smile. He gives me a tight nod.

Yeah. Can't blame him.

I turn away, meet Sandesh's alert blue eyes.

He rests his nose against my cheek. "He'll come around."

He's right because I'll continue to reach out to Rome to make sure he's okay. I'll find a way to talk to him, so that he knows—no, so that he *feels*, he belongs here. I'll do that for Tony, who never felt that he did.

When I got back from Mexico, I finally read Tony's letter. In it, he spoke of his pain at never feeling good enough. He spoke of not thinking he deserved to be in The Guild.

I never knew. Also, I never asked. That's something I intend to change with Rome and with all my siblings, including Bella.

As we walk, Sandesh squeezes my hand. "You okay?"

The easy thing to say would be *yeah*, but it isn't the real thing to say. Swallowing regret and sorrow and the ache of missing Tony, I say, "No. But I feel better being here, knowing I can change things. Promise you'll back me up with Momma.'

"Yeah. But if your mother says no—"

I shake my head and continue down the hall. "She won't. Trust me. I can convince anyone of anything. I am a kick-ass public relations specialist, remember?"

Sandesh bites his lip and nods at me like he wants to say something else.

He doesn't say a word. Smart man.

We pass the intersecting hallway and someone steps out from the elevator and calls out, "I see it worked."

I startle. Even with a baby bump, my gorgeous sister is stealthy. "What worked?"

Dada points at my wrist, at the braided band of light and dark leather with the garnet woven within it. "The proposal. You said yes?"

Sandesh nods. Looking like he's won the blue ribbon, he holds up his bracelet. "She did."

Dada moves closer and examines it, then her critical gaze looks to me. "I can show you how to fix this."

Face heating, I glare at her.

Sandesh pulls his hand away. "No, it's perfect. Thanks."

Aww. Love for him, sharp and steady, fires another neuron and etches another cherished memory.

Dada looks like she wants to argue the fact, but I interrupt with, "Just saw your baby-daddy out front, surrounded by munchkins playing soccer. You might want to rescue him."

With that distraction firmly tossed, I lead Sandesh the rest of the way down the hall to the open doorway on our left.

Holding his warm hand loosely in my own, I slip into the drawing room.

The *drawing* room.

Momma's idea of a joke. It's *literally* a room for drawing—

more accurately, painting—not the traditional drawing room for greeting guests. Hardy, har, har.

The room contains easels, stools, blue-and-red cabinets splotched with every shade of paint, along with shelves lined with art supplies. The astringent smell of paint cleaner and the dull smell of paint envelop us. I rub my hand back and forth against my nose. Ew. Artists might have acute sight, but their olfactory senses have to be diminished.

Two artists sit on stools, painting at easels. I wasn't expecting this. I'd thought only Momma would be here. The kid is all skin and bones and stiff shoulders. Someone from the school? Maybe. But whatever Momma sees in this frail girl makes her special indeed.

Momma has taken off her niqab, revealing her scars. Mostly she doesn't, not even with her daughters. She only shows her scars to girls so broken that they find comfort with people as wounded as themselves. Just one more way Momma makes herself vulnerable to strengthen others.

That's Momma. The woman who rescued me. She isn't perfect, but she does want to do good in the world, and I'm going to be making sure that includes Bridget. "Momma, Sandesh and I are here to speak with you."

I expect Momma to put on her niqab before turning around.

She doesn't. She turns from where she paints a colorful landscape dotted with wildflowers.

The slight spasm of Sandesh's hand is all he gives at the sight of Momma's horrible scars.

The vibrant beauty Momma paints only seems to highlight the peaks and valleys of her damaged skin.

"Come in, Justice. Sandesh."

Technically, we are inside, but Momma means for us to stop lurking in the doorway.

I let go of Sandesh's hand, walk over, then kiss her cheek.

Momma grasps my hand and looks at the band woven with the garnet on my wrist. Her eyes travel to Sandesh's wrist and the matching band there. "I see it worked."

He winks at her. *He* winked *at Momma?* Conspirators. How many of my family were in on this whole get-Justice-to-marry-Sandesh thing?

"Thanks for the advice," he says. "Short and sweet."

Hmmm. Guy had had a freakin' army on his side.

"Nice to see you approve of the whole wedding thing because I'm here about a wedding present."

Momma raises one damaged eyebrow where the eyebrow should've been. "Okay. But first—"

"Nope. No. I need—"

Momma puts up a hand, silences me. "If it is in my power to give, it will be yours."

Oh man, she's going to regret that.

I grin at Sandesh as if to say, *Told you.*

He shakes his head in disbelief.

"I interrupted," Momma says, "because you are being rude. You have not said hello to your newest sister. I believe you have met."

Huh? I take a closer look at the other artist and suck in a breath. It's *Cee.* Cee, who I saved. Cee who, in turn, saved me. Not only from that drunk man the night we first met, but by giving me someone like me, someone to truly save. After Tony, I needed that.

Cee pushes her stool back with a scrape and stands. Same bony body. Same half-challenging, half-wary-tiger, red-brown eyes.

I lick lips gone dry, move toward her, then pause. I've got to take this easy. She's been through a lot.

In many ways, Cee *isn't* like Hope. Not physically. Hope had lighter skin, blonde hair, and blue eyes. Cee is Latina, with dark eyes, hair, and skin. And yet, she reminds me of Hope. In the tension of her shoulders. In the take-me-on-and-you'll-get-more-than-you-bargained-for gleam in her fierce eyes.

That's how Hope had protected me, by standing in front of me when Aamir came for me.

I hold out my hand. "It's so good to see you, Cee."

Cee's fire-burned brown eyes look at my outstretched hand. She shakes her head. "I know it was you."

I drop my hand. My gut turns. I look over at Sandesh, who moves a step closer, as if to say he has my back.

In a flash, Cee darts forward and tucks her arms around my waist. She holds me tight, breathing into my neck. "You were the one. You didn't give up on me."

Oh.

A moment of warm surprise, then, with my throat growing tight, I wrap my arms around the teen's thin body. We stand that way for a long time, holding onto each other.

From behind, Sandesh places his warm, strong hand on my shoulder. And something in my heart, a very small piece, but one I desperately missed and needed, repairs itself. I feel a spark of something that has been missing in my life for a long time: Hope.

EPILOGUE

Momma

I have held meetings like this one—a daughter of mine seated before me in my underground office, Leland standing by my side—for four decades, but none has ever felt this jarring.

I have done things I'm not proud of, but always, I believe, I've made my decisions based on the greater good. Now, I'm not so sure. The wheels of our family, of our family's clandestine operations, our global outreach, have grown too complex over the years. I fear that I have lost control.

With my heart both hopeful and full of pain, I ask my sixth adopted daughter, a rare intellect I had the distinct honor to rescue and raise and watch blossom, "Are you sure, Zuri? There is no way the patch could kill two men?"

Her spine as erect as her honor and her courage, my beautiful gem, a scientist and a woman as creative as she is intelligent, repeats the answer that has my heart aching.

"Yes, Momma." Her lovely Kenyan accent adds a lilt of softness to her every word. "I'm sure. The patch was designed to be effective against only one. In addition, there is no physical way to spill such a thing. The edges of the patch contain an unparalleled adhesion. The poison remains in the center and it is activated through absorption. A unique—"

I wave my hand to stop her from finishing. If I let her go on, she would launch into complex and technical details that have no bearing on this conversation. As much as the scientist in me will later want those details, for now, I need to digest what she's told me.

Beside me, Leland, who, up until now, has remained silent, asks, "The thefts from your lab, the ones that brought you here today—what was taken exactly?"

Zuri's eyes dart to me. We are very strict about our experimental initiatives. Even Leland does not have full access to all of our endeavors in that area.

I nod at her to answer his question. He has as much right to this information as anyone.

With a raised brow that shows her surprise, she says, "There were two experimental compounds taken. The first has only recently shown great success—a vial of chemicals that can temporarily cause memory loss. The second was our more tested and available Stasis, which produces a state close to death for anywhere between one to two hours."

Leland draws in a sharp and pained breath.

I can feel his hurt, the deep pain of Tony's betrayal, his ruse, and the equal loss of letting down his long-dead sister, Naomi.

"Thank you, daughter," I say. "I know I don't have to advise you to speak to no one—"

She rises from her seat as stately as a queen and blinks down at me for several breaths, before saying, "I would never."

It comes out as *nevah* and the sound of her anger is

tempered by that soft accent. All the children love to hear Zuri speak. She is the one most often requested by the littles to read at story time.

I exhale a ball of distress and grief and try to repair the indignation I see on her face. "I know you would not. You hold more family secrets than anyone in this home, including me."

She smiles sadly at that because we both know why that is true. She says, "What are you going to do?"

"Ah, but that is one secret I will have to keep."

She smirks. "Meaning, you have no idea."

I nod in her direction. Smart can sometimes be annoying.

Reading the tension between Leland and I, and no doubt seeing exactly what is now needed, she says, "You know where my lab is if you need me."

The moment she is out the door, I turn to Leland. "This is not your fault."

Hands fisted at his side, head shaking, he says, "I thought to give him an equal chance here by *not* claiming him. I thought..."

"The fact that we never told him of his relation to you isn't what caused Tony's distress. Or what caused him to leave. Or what caused him to choose to fake his own death."

No, that reason lies in his own mind—his own feeling of not belonging.

I pick up Tony's handwritten letter and the two pages we shared with no one. An easy thing to do when we only typed out a portion of the letter to share with the children.

I read, "*I watched her being beat by him. I hid and watched so many times. If only I'd followed through on my instinct, I could've done something to him while he slept. I could've begged Mom to run. I could've... But I didn't. And then it was too late.*

"*There was nothing I could do to help her the night he finally went too far. I tried. I fought him, but he was too strong. I will carry the burden of my mom's murder, the burden of my failure, the pain of having failed her, for the rest of my life.*

"That's why I promised myself when I came here, when I met my new family, I would never let that happen again. I would never stand by and watch another person I loved be hurt if I could stop it.

"How could I do otherwise? After coming to this home and learning our secret, learning what all my sisters had suffered, how can I not act? I won't. I won't hide while another woman I love is destroyed, not when it's in my power to stop it. Please listen to me. Justice is as close to this mission as a person can get. She is headed on a path of destruction. I know it's not my place to say, to object to a mission years in the planning, a mission that's undergone layers of scrutiny, but I'm doing it anyway.

"You have to know that, since the moment I stepped inside the Mantua Home, since the day I arrived and was welcomed by this wonderful family and my sometimes-crazy sisters, I have only felt regret and fear. Regret that I was never good enough. That I couldn't rescue my mom. That I couldn't fit in, that I couldn't find a way to belong. Fear that my sisters might find out what I let happen. Not for one day did I ever feel worthy of The Guild."

I stop reading and look at Leland. We share a glance that wordlessly conveys what we feel. There are decisions piled on decisions and none were easy.

I see his doubt even before he asks, "I know it's complicated, but would he have felt he belonged more if he'd known he was my nephew from the beginning?

I know Leland is in pain. I know he's floundering to find his way through this emotionally, but I have no tolerance for this indulgence. "We made the decision based on our family dynamics. Based on complex, myriad personalities. We made it based on psychological recommendations, based on continued family cohesion. We gave Tony the same thing that all the children here shared: they were rescues. If he was seen differently..." I shake my head, remembering the difficulties of that time, the fights between the Fantastic Five and the A-Team, the animosity they caried toward the Spice Girls. It would've been worse if they'd known the truth about Tony

"You did it to protect our family," Leland says. "But you also did it to protect me."

He's right, of course. Questions would have inevitably arisen if Tony's relationship to Leland was known, questions that could've led back to a dark time and a dark decision.

"It is what it is, Leland. Decisions made that seemed right, that seemed to balance so many issues. My only regret is not finding a way to let Tony share his story. If I had done that, found that way, would he have felt more accepted?"

Leland rolls his head and sighs at the ceiling. "If I had a dollar for every regret I have…"

With a mild laugh, I say, "You surely do."

He smiles, sits on the edge of my desk and lifts a hand to my scarred face. He places it gently against my cheek. There was a time when I wouldn't let him touch me so, but that time has long passed.

I lean into his hand. He whispers, "You know they'll figure it out."

I lift my head from his hand, a moment's comfort is all I ever need, all I can afford. "Of course they will. They're a house full of spies."

"Should we tell them?"

My voices rises before I can stop myself. "Absolutely not."

He shakes his head. "Mukta, it will be another mark against you, another way your children will see you as manipulating them and their lives."

"Perhaps, but I don't care. For me, it comes back to fairness."

"Fairness?"

"I have been unfair to Tony. I see that now. I ache for him.

And so, I have to ask myself, isn't it only fair to give him a head start on his sisters?"

Leland's eyebrows raise. "After you let Bridget keep her memory, head off to another country and do charity work, when they find out their brother is still alive, no one is going to just let Tony get away. This is going to get ugly."

I shrug. "We'll cross that bridge when we come to it."

DIANA MUÑOZ STEWART

Diana Muñoz Stewart is a bestselling author who writes romantic suspense with a focus on diverse characters, action, adventure, family, and love. Her work has been praised as high-octane, edgy, sexy, and fast-paced.

Diana's work has been a BookPage Top 15 Romance, a Night Owl Top Pick, an Amazon Book of the Month, an Amazon Editor's pick, a Pages From The Heart Winner, a Book Page Top Pick, Golden Heart® Finalist, Daphne du Maurier Finalist, A Gateway to the Best Winner, and has reached #1 category bestseller on Amazon multiple times.

Diana lives in an often chaotic and always welcoming home that—depending on the day—can hold husband, kids, extended family, friends, and a canine or two. A believer in the power of words to heal and connect, Diana has written multiple spotlight pieces on the strong, diverse women changing the world. Sign up for her newsletter to receive the latest information on her new releases: https://dianamunozstewart.com/newsletter/

ACKNOWLEDGMENTS

As always, a huge thank you to my wonderful family for their support and encouragement as I've reworked this novel.

This book would not have taken the shape and polished finish it has without the hard work and skilled eyes of my editor Mackenzie Walton at www.mackenziewalton.com. I owe her a debt of gratitude for all of her incredible insights. I'm also deeply indebted and appreciative of the remarkable Judi Fennell at www.formatting4u.com for her incredible copyediting skills, attention to detail, and unwavering support of my work.

All the credit for the artwork on the gorgeous cover for Hidden Justice goes to the talented and skilled digital artist Elizabeth Mackey at www.elizabethmackeygraphics.com. She's a joy to work with and a real treasure. Thanks a million times for all you do, Elizabeth.

For helping me get through my everyday grind, all my endless gratitude goes to my assistant, Michelle Burleson. Thanks, Michelle, for allowing me to be focused on writing while you do the hard work of promoting and organizing my business and social media.

Finally, a huge and undying thank you to all of the readers who have taken a chance on the Spy Makers Guild and my other series. You all are rockstars!

SPY MAKERS GUILD SAMPLE BOOKS

You can read the first few chapters of Gracie and Dusty's story in RECKLESS GRACE here: https://bookhip.com/NPTGCBT

You can read the first few chapters of Dada and Sean's story in the Spy Maker's Guild Novella, FIGHTING FATE here: https://BookHip.com/NPTGCBT